ROMEO
AND/OR
JULIET

D0032029

ROMEO
AND/OR
JULIET

a chooseable-path adventure

BY RYAN NORTH
AND WILLIAM SHAKESPEARE
AND YOU BECAUSE YOU DECIDE WHAT HAPPENS NEXT
NOT TO MENTION ALL THE ARTISTS WHO MADE SOME GREAT ILLUSTRATIONS
SO REALLY THERE'S A LOT OF CREDIT TO GO AROUND HERE
AND THAT DOESN'T EVEN MENTION THE EDITORS, DESIGNERS, AND TYPESETTERS
ALL OF WHOM DO IMPORTANT WORK THAT GOES UNACKNOWLEDGED ALL TOO OFTEN

RIVERHEAD BOOKS
NEW YORK
2016

RIVERHEAD BOOKS
An imprint of Penguin Random House LLC
375 Hudson Street
New York, New York 10014

Copyright © 2016 by Ryan North

Also, way to go on reading all this small print! Lots of readers just skip over it (they think it's "boring"), but it's nice to see that you, for one, are getting your money's worth out of this book by reading every single word it contains. In thanks, here are some special words just for you that won't appear anywhere else in this book: *callipygian*, *saudade*, and *mamihlapinatapei*. Look at those words! Those are some quality words, and everyone else who picked up this book is missing out.

ISBN 9781101983300

Printed in the United States of America

1   3   5   7   9   10   8   6   4   2

Book design by Sabrina Bowers

This is a work of fiction. Actually, it's a book *containing* a work of fiction, but you get the idea. Incidentally, did someone file this book in the "Choose One's Own *Nonfiction* Adventure" section? Bad news on that front, friend: names, characters, places, and incidents in this work either are the product of the author's imagination or are used fictitiously, and any resemblance to actual persons, living or dead, businesses, companies, events, or locales is entirely coincidental!

*For Mom
and/or Dad*

"A man can die but once."
William Shakespeare, *Henry IV*

"Devine, si tu peux, et choisis, si tu l'oses."
Pierre Corneille, *Hérachlius*

ROMEO
AND/OR
JULIET

1 As we now know, William Shakespeare (1564 AD–whenever he died) was well known for borrowing from existing literature when writing his plays. Our previous publication, *To Be or Not To Be: That Is The Adventure*, firmly established that the award-winning play *Hamlet* (I know, turns out there are awards for plays) was lifted wholesale from that recently rediscovered text. We suggested, then, that *To Be or Not To Be* was both the earliest example of the "book as game" genre, as well as the first instance ever in the then-newish English language that was kicking around of an adventure being chosen by YOU, the reader.

We were wrong.

THIS book, which you are now about to enjoy, really IS that earliest example of nonlinear second-person narratives that are more fun than they sound. We did some more research. It's true this time.

When Shakespeare sat down to write *Romeo and Juliet*, he had a choice: he could make up his own story, or he could flip through this book, *Romeo and/or Juliet*, and just stone-cold copy down what he read. As we now know, he chose the latter. This book he plagiarized from was lost until recently, when I found it again. It was just over there. Someone had put a coat over it, which I think is why we didn't notice it earlier.

Romeo and/or Juliet is presented here with the original text, unaltered from when Shakespeare stole it. All we've added are some rad illustrations, and we also put adorable little hearts next to the choices Shakespeare made when plagiarizing this book. That way if you follow that path when you make a choice, you'll get the same play that Shakespeare ended up with! However, that is not the only story in this book, and honestly, a lot of the others are way better. Feel free to explore your other options, as there are over 46,012,475,909,287,476 distinct adventures contained within this book! Though, to be fair, after the first quintillion a lot of them are probably going to seem pretty familiar.

Now, prepare yourself for what's called "the greatest love story ever told" for some reason. Gingerly place your emotions into the front car of the roller coaster. Strap them in tight. Kiss them on the forehead and tell them you love them and that you'll see them soon. Too late: this emotional roller coaster JUST GOT STARTED. Whoah. This is going to be INSANE.

O Romeo and/or Juliet, Romeo and/or Juliet! Wherefore art thou Romeo and/or Juliet?

RYAN NORTH
NOTED SHAKESPEARE SCHOLAR/ENTHUSIAST

So, intelligent and well-informed reader of interactive fiction: what would you like to do now?

 Get the book spoiled for you right off the bat: *turn to 3.*

Play without spoilers: *turn to 36.*

Learn more about the author: *turn to 22.*

2 Okay, so the only way you could be reading these words right now is if you (SOMEHOW?) ignored all the very clear instructions to make a choice, and instead (again: SOMEHOW??) thought you were reading a regular boring book in which you can just sit back and enjoy the ride and never ever get to make any choices.

THIS IS NOT SUCH A BOOK.

You agree to start making choices and say that your first one is to go back to the previous option and, you know, read harder this time. You promise that you're going to read really hard until you understand how a choice works. You swear it.

I BELIEVE IN YOU. Alright, go do that! I don't want to see you wandering back here again!!

Try again, chuckles: *turn to 1.*

3 Haha, right! No need to experience this story as it unfolds: I'll just STRAIGHT-UP TELL YOU HOW IT ENDS. That's way more fun and definitely how stories are meant to be experienced!

Here's your spoiler, written all fancy-like so at least you have to work for it:

Two households, both alike in dignity,
In fair Verona, where we lay our scene,
From ancient grudge break to new mutiny,
Where civil blood makes civil hands unclean.
From forth the fatal loins of these two foes

A pair of star-cross'd lovers take their life;
Whole misadventured piteous overthrows
Do with their death bury their parents' strife.
The fearful passage of their death-mark'd love,
And the continuance of their parents' rage,
Which, but their children's end, nought could remove,
Is now the 392-pages' traffic of our bookly stage;
The which if you with patient eyes attend,
What here shall miss, our toil shall strive to mend.

You're just lucky that this book has like a bunch of different stories in it, so you can't really have the whole thing ruined for you even if you want to (WHICH YOU SHOULD NOT, BY THE WAY). So I guess that's check AND mate, narratively disinclined reader. Looks like you still have to read this whole book after all! All you really learned is that Romeo and Juliet die in one of the endings, which, come on, was definitely gonna happen anyway. They ARE star-cross'd lovers, after all.

Hey! Let's find out if you can make it happen!

 Choose your character: *turn to 36.*

4 You are Juliet! Right now you're sitting in your bedroom chatting with your nurse and only friend, Mrs. Angelica Nurse. YES, her last name is "Nurse" and she works as a nurse. Don't judge, Juliet. It's not like you haven't capuleted a few times before.

We've all seen it.

ANYWAY. Your nurse, "A. Nurse," leaves you because it's 9 a.m. and she has things to do, among them getting this house ready for the crazy party your parents are throwing tonight. Yes, a crazy party on a Sunday! Who throws a party on a Sunday night? The rich who don't have to work, that's who! This includes your parents, and, assuming they die without producing any male heirs, eventually you as well!

You have things to do too, Juliet. You tear through some quick stomach crunches (three reps of ten) and some pec blasts (four reps of eight), and you're ready to start your day. So! You're well muscled and your family's rich. What's for breakfast?

Haha, just kidding. Your parents have already planned out your whole day for you weeks in advance. When you get downstairs, Mom and breakfast are already waiting for you. She puts your protein shake on the counter, tells you to drink it up, and leaves.

"Yes Mom," you say automatically.

Drink the protein shake: *turn to 5.*

5 You reach for the protein shake and bring it to your lips. And because I'm sure you want to know what you're drinking, let me give you the recipe!

JULIET'S PRO-POWER MIRACLE SHAKE

Ingredients:

> one pound of protein *(animal flesh, basically; you get yours on standing order from the Merchant of Breakfast downtown)*
> milk

Instructions:

1. Add meat to giant glass.
2. Pour in milk until mixture is of desired milkiness.
3. Shake vigorously.
4. Enjoy!

It's about as good as it sounds. And it sounds great!!

You chug down breakfast quickly and efficiently, wiping your mouth with the back of a well-muscled arm, and you're off to start your day! Time to grab this day by the horns and wrestle it into submission!!

Only, at this point your mom sticks her head in and says, "Juliet, would you be a dear and clean your room?"

"Yes Mom," you say automatically.

Go clean your room: *turn to 6.*

6 You go upstairs and clean your room, Juliet, just as you were told. When you're done you shout downstairs to your mom.

"I'm done cleaning, Mom!" you shout.

"Good girl!" she replies. "Please sit there and do your lute homework until I call for you."

"Yes Mom," you say automatically.

You spend several hours practicing on your lute. Yesterday your mom said that if you get good enough at it she'll allow you to perform at one of their parties. You don't even like the lute that much, but the idea did get you a little excited. Of course, in her next breath she said you were nowhere near good enough at lute yet and doubled the number of pieces you have to learn by the end of the week.

After a while you hear your mother calling up to you. "That's enough, Juliet!" she shouts, probably tired of hearing the first few bars of "Minor-Key Study Piece for Intermediate Lute Students #52" over and over again. "You've got two hours of personal time now, but don't leave the castle!"

"Yes Mom!" you say, super excited. Any free time you get is the best time of your day! And that's not saying much, actually!

But enough about that sad stuff: it's time to have some FRIGGIN' FUN.

Go have fun: *turn to 7.*

7 So, the thing is, you're not allowed out of the house, and everyone's busy with prepping for the party. Even your nurse can't talk to you right now.

You flex your way downstairs to the servants' kitchen and ask if there's anything you can do to help out, and while you DO help them open up a few tricky jars, it only takes half an hour at most to go through every tricky jar you can find. Soon all the jars are opened and you're surreptitiously screwing on a few lids super tight so at least you'll have something to do tomorrow morning.

It's pretty boring, Juliet! I should've told you this sooner, but your life is pretty boring these days. All days, really. The sad fact is, it's boring to live in a castle with your parents where nothing interesting happens and you got big into muscles because then at least you'd have something to do while standing around bored for hours (that something is building muscles).

So that's what you do (you go work out so that you might maintain your existing muscles and maybe get better ones too), and before you know it your free time is almost over and it's time to go back into your room.

Finish your workout: *turn to 8.*

8 You gingerly put down the weights you were blasting and wipe down your workout equipment. Then you change out of your wet and sweaty and gross and stinky and entirely unsexy "Juliet workout tights" and into your much less sweaty and at least slightly sexier "Juliet hanging-around-the-castle tights" with your favorite red dress on top.

You're just pulling it on when you hear Angelica calling for you. "In a minute!" you reply, but a few seconds later you can hear your mom and Angelica outside your door. Your mom is asking where you are, and Angelica is saying that she already called for you.

"I called for her already! I swear I did! I swear on my virginity at age twelve!" she says, which is kinda weird and a little bit pervy.

"That was kinda weird and a little bit pervy," you mutter to yourself, making the final adjustments to your dress. You leave your bedroom and greet your mother and nurse waiting outside your door.

"Guys, calm down, I'm here," you say. "What do you want?"

Your mom sends your nurse away. "Juliet and I must talk privately," she says.

"Okay," Angelica says, leaving.

"Wait, I just remembered, actually you're allowed to hear our secrets," your mom says.

"Okay," Angelica says, returning.

"Wait, before we start," your mom says, "POP QUIZ: how old is my only child?"

You'd like to say she's testing your nurse, but you're not entirely convinced your mom actually knows.

 Let Angelica answer: *turn to 9.*

Answer for her so that—wait, nevermind, Angelica's answering already. That's what you get for never speaking up, Juliet. GUESS WE'RE GONNA LET ANGELICA ANSWER AFTER ALL. *Turn to 9.*

9

Angelica says your 17th birthday will be this July 31 (hey, that's only a few weeks away! EXCITING) and she knows it down to the hour because her own child, Susan, was born that very same day.

SPOILER ALERT: Angelica tends to go on a bit, so I'm gonna cut this down to just the highlights because nobody's getting paid by the word here. Brevity is the soul of wit! That's a saying you can attribute to ME, the author of this crazy branching novel. Make sure nobody else steals it.

So! Here are the Angelica highlights:

- you were born July 31, and she knows because her own baby was born the same day
- that baby is named Susan (nice name)
- that baby is dead now (WHOAH, DANG YO)
- there was an earthquake on your birthday 14 years ago (irrelevant information, feel free to forget this right . . . now)
- you stopped breast-feeding on that very day (okay, that's fine)
- she put wormwood on her nipple to wean you (okay, whatever, let's move on)

- this made you mad at her breast and you and the breast had a falling-out (how are we still talking about this?)
- the day before the combination earthquake/weaning, you fell while walking and bruised your face and Angelica's husband picked you up to comfort you
- her husband is dead now too (OH WELL)
- her husband asked you if you fell forward on your face, and then asked if when you grew up you'd "fall backwards" instead
- what the heck?! That's a sex euphemism!
- her late husband made sex jokes to a three-year-old child
- may I just reiterate, what the heck?!
- SERIOUSLY!
- seriously
- anyway, three-year-old you said "Yes!" to this question that you could not possibly understand and it was SO HILARIOUS that here we are talking about it OVER A DECADE LATER

At this point your mom (TOTALLY of her own volition and not because I'm getting tired of this myself) asks Angelica to be quiet, which she eventually does, but not before adding:

- the bruise on your head was as big as a rooster's testicle

WOW. You want to end this here, Juliet?

 Ask them what they want to talk to you about: *turn to 10.*

Wait, hold on, I don't really have the context for the rooster's-testicle thing. How big are we talking about here? *Turn to 418.*

10 Your mom says she wants you to get married and have kids right away. You know, like she did when she was twelve! She says you're overdue, Juliet!

MOMS, am I right??

Anyway, she's organized this party tonight so that you can meet your future husband, to whom you are, as of a few hours ago, already promised. She's set it all up, wheels are already in motion, so you'll definitely be marrying the dude you meet tonight. Also, she says, it's a masked ball, so everyone will be hiding their faces!

You note to yourself that this is a terrible-themed party to have if you actually want to judge how attractive people are, so this dude she wants you to marry must be an uggo.

"Juliet," your mom says, "don't you think this surprise mandatory arranged marriage is the most wonderful news??"

Alright, this is getting serious. If you keep doing everything your mother asks of you, you're going to end up married to a stranger, and not just any stranger, but one who thinks the best way to meet women is to get their moms to promise women to him sight unseen. You wanna get out of here, see the world, maybe start making some decisions for yourself?

Or do you want to say "Yes Mom" automatically?

Run past them, tear out of the house, never look back: *turn to 25.*

 Say "Yes Mom" automatically: *turn to 11.*

11 "Yes Mom," you say automatically.

Your mother smiles and keeps talking. She says that here in Verona all the ladies get married at your age. (What? That's not true and has never been true—just because she got married at that age doesn't mean YOU have to be a teen mom too.) She says the guy she wants you to marry, Tom Paris, is big into you based on what scant information he's been told—mainly that you're female AND fertile. Angelica volunteers that he's the greatest man in the whole world and that his body is as perfect as a wax sculpture.

You can't think of a single wax sculpture you'd ever want to spend the rest of your life with.

Your mom asks you if you can love this Paris guy you've never met or even heard of before just now, and it would be really convenient for her if you could because, as she said, this whole thing is a setup to get you married off really quickly!

What do you want to do, Juliet?

Again: run past them, tear out of the house, never look back: *turn to 25.*

 Say "Yes Mom" automatically: *turn to 12.*

12 Alright? You stay exactly where you are and say "Yes Mom" when your mother expects it.

Your mother goes on to tell you to check out Paris's rockin' bod and his rockin' eyes in particular. She says he's a book of pure love that only needs a cover (that's you, Jules). She says it's not right that someone so beautiful as yourself should hide from someone so bangin' as him.

"Also, if you marry him you'll gain access to his wealth," she says.

"And you'll lose nothing by having sex with him either, because sex in the context of a monogamous marriage is cool and fun."

"In fact, you'll gain from having sex with him!" your nurse adds. "Because you'll get pregnant. And then you'll be bigger!" Yes, factually that is how pregnancy works!

"Yes or no?" your mom says, concluding, "Can you promise me that you'll fall in love with this dude you've never met? I cannot stress this enough: Tom Paris's bod is rockin'."

 Say "Yes Mom": *turn to 13.*

For once in your life, say "NO Mom": *turn to 44.*

13 Aw man! Seriously? Juliet, I was hoping you'd want to go on a fun and exciting adventure, not agree with everything your parents say and get married to a stranger in the first few pages, THE END. But I GUESS there's some adventure to be had in marrying a rich dude that your mom likes, so, um, here we go?

You behave exactly as your parents want, and you tell everyone that you'll do your level best to love this Paris guy. And as soon as you do, a servant enters and reminds your mom that it's 8 p.m. and the party has started, the guests are here, the staff are cursing the nurse, and everything is entirely out of control.

Better get on that, everyone!

Your mom slips on her mask and tells you that she expects you downstairs and partying momentarily. And listen, I'm not exactly what you'd call "wow so impressed" with how you've been playing Juliet so far, so why don't you be Romeo for a while? He's the other person whose name is on the cover. He's on his way to your house right now with his friends Mercutio and Benvolio, so this'll be fun! You'll get to crash your own party!

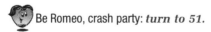 Be Romeo, crash party: *turn to 51.*

14 Benvolio shakes your hand repeatedly. "Good morning, good morning," he says. You ask him if it really is morning, and he confirms that it is, and you figure that's enough small talk! Time to talk about the important things: your feelings.

"Let me level with you, Ben," you say. "Here's my whole deal: I love someone but she doesn't like me back."

Benvolio agrees that yeah that sounds bad, and that love can be rough sometimes.

"What's rough is that love is supposed to be blind, but it can still see its way into making ME do whatever it wants!" you say, personifying your emotions as an imagined third party whose tyranny allows you to preemptively absolve yourself of responsibility for your own actions.

That's right. Don't think I didn't notice.

You're about to talk about love some more when you realize it's breakfast o'clock and you haven't eaten since it was dinner o'clock! That was yesterday!

 Redirect the conversation towards breakfast: *turn to 28.*

Forget breakfast! Talk about love some more. *Turn to 20.*

15 Oh. Okay. Well you're in luck, because Will submitted a bio too:

> William "Will" Shakespeare is a writer (and sometimes actor!) who enjoys the unique challenges of both plays and sonnets. Stage credits include a production of *Sejanus His Fall* and, more recently, "Kno'well" in *Every Man in His Humor*. Will is a founding member of the Lord Chamberlain's Men, a boys-only acting troupe and theater construction partnership. When not on, around, or behind a London stage, Will can probably be found in Stratford-upon-Avon, home of his second-best bed and first-best wife, Anne (love you, sweetie!). He hopes that one day his writing will be recognized as "not of an age, but for all time."

There! Nothing left now but to:

Choose your character: *turn to 36.*

16 "We could stab all the Capulets!" you say.

"Yeah, I mean, probably," Benvolio says. "But I'd love to end this without bloodshed. The problem with 'an eye for an eye' is that it leaves everybody blind," he says.

"Not if you were born with two eyes," you say, gesturing to your eyes with your fork, "which I was. But if you don't want to kill them all, that works too," you say. "I'm a lover, not a fighter. What if I just married all the Capulets instead?"

Benvolio does not think this plan is very good and raises several objections, including the fact that a bunch of the Capulets are already married. You're about to pull out some documentation showing how this is actually a viable endeavor if only you could get some laws supporting non-monogamous relationships passed, but then your food arrives!

Let us eat a breakfast: *turn to 32.*

17 "Hey Ben, where'd you get that vest? And in an unrelated matter, where'd you get that blood on your face?" you say.

"Both at the same place," Benvolio replies. "I'll tell you all about it. Over breakfast?"

"IT'S LIKE YOU READ MY MIND," you say. And if we're being accurate, it's more fair to say it's like he read your mind and chose options you'd already tacitly rejected—but yeah: crazy coincidence!

Go have breakfast: *turn to 38.*

18 You hold out your hand in front of you and begin to describe Rosaline to your cousin. Here's what you say:

> She'll not be hit
> With Cupid's arrow. She hath Dian's wit.
> And, in strong proof of chastity well armed
> From love's weak childish bow, she lives uncharmed.
> She will not stay the siege of loving terms,
> Nor bide th' encounter of assailing eyes,
> Nor ope her lap to saint-seducing gold.
> Oh, she is rich in beauty, only poor
> That when she dies, with beauty dies her store.

Benvolio seems to catch on to what's going on. He holds out a hand in front of himself and asks, "Then she hath sworn that she will still live chaste?"

You're now both standing with your arms held out in front of you. You reply,

> She hath, and in that sparing makes huge waste,
> For beauty, starved with her severity,
> Cuts beauty off from all posterity.

She is too fair, too wise, wisely too fair,
To merit bliss by making me despair.
She hath forsworn to love, and in that vow
Do I live dead that live to tell it now.

Benvolio lowers his hand.
"Man, forget about her," he says.

 Say it's impossible to forget about Rosaline: *turn to 52.*

Actually try to forget about Rosaline: *turn to 39.*

19

You and Benvolio start walking as you talk. Benvolio tells you that you need to own your feelings, saying that if you want someone and you can't have her, that's not HER problem: that's YOUR thing, and you need to fix it. You make your way by unspoken agreement downtown, and as there's not much shade here in fair Verona, you find a nice alleyway where you can sit down and chat.

Benvolio gives you some very reasonable advice to get over Rosaline (avoid being in the same places as her, do nice things for yourself, join a club to meet new people) and during all this you're nodding and saying things like "I see" and "Mmmhmm" and "Interesting, interesting," and both Benvolio and I think you're making great progress until you suddenly stop in your tracks and say, "Whatever, man, I can't ever forget her and that's that.

"As everyone who has ever been a teenager and in love knows," you continue, "that one, singular love lasts the rest of your life and torments you always. Adults literally never get over whatever one person they first liked when they were a teen. That's just how life is. That's just what the emotional life of grown men and women looks like."

Benvolio sighs, deeply frustrated.

"Come on, Romeo, listen to me," he says. "You just need to meet someone new and you'll forget about her, I PROMISE. It's like when you get a NEW eye infection, and then that cures whatever old infections were making your eyes all crusty and gross!"

This line of argument isn't really working for you and is also meganasty, so you're looking for an out. Conveniently, you notice a man uncertainly peering into your alleyway. Trying to sound as friendly as you can, you ask if he'd like to join you in the shade.

The man studies you both for a moment and, deciding that you're probably not going to murderize him, comes closer and sits down beside you. "Hi," he says. "I'm Peter."

You and Benvolio introduce yourselves.

"Hey," Peter says, "can you read? I've got this piece of paper here and I need to know what it says on it."

 Tell him you can read: *turn to 50.*

Tell him you are illiterate: *turn to 37.*

20

"So, as I was saying," you say, trying to get thoughts of breakfast out of your head, images of orange juice with just the right amount of pulp and eggs that are perfect, better than perfect, they're the eggs you'd eat in your dreams if only you dreamed bigger, impossibly bigger, and the bacon is so tasty that you roll your eyes like it's a joke, because it's ridiculous, nothing should taste this good, and when you swallow you're certain anything this tasty has to have some supernaturally terrible hidden price attached to it, like with every bite you exchanged a few days of your life, but it doesn't matter, you'll pay it, you'll pay it and you'll say thank you and you'll be back in a few weeks, digging deep in your pockets just to have it again, "love sure is an emotion that I experience deeply! Do you . . . also like love?" you ask.

"I think it's okay," Benvolio says. Then Benvolio points towards some blood on his face that you hadn't noticed before, obviously trying to draw your attention to it. Guess what? You're still too into talking about love AND thinking about breakfast right now to really pay any attention to it!

Continue talking about love: *turn to 48.*

Okay, I'm sorry, but I could really go for some breakfast. Can we go someplace where I can eat some eggs and continue this conversation? *Turn to 38.*

21

It's not a very big garbage can, and it's way too small to fit you inside. You've got one foot on top of the garbage that's already in it and you're gingerly placing an orange peel on your head when Benvolio catches up with you.

"Romeo!" he says. "You're so crazy! Hah hah hah! Are you trying to hide in that garbage can?"

"Ay me!" you say, wanting to say something else instead of "Ay" but this is a family book so you can't use words like—OH NICE TRY, YOU ALMOST GOT ME THERE BUT I'M NOT SAYING IT!

IF YOU SAY WORDS LIKE THAT THEN BABIES AND SENIORS ALIKE SCOWL AT YOU, YOU SHOULD KNOW THAT!

Talk to Benvolio: *turn to 14.*

22 Ryan submitted a bio to go along with this book, so you're in luck!

Ryan North is a *New York Times*–bestselling writer and cartoonist. He's written comics like *Dinosaur Comics*, *The Unbeatable Squirrel Girl*, *Adventure Time*, and *The Midas Flesh*, which is a story about a man where everything he touches turns to gold but then he accidentally kills the entire planet before he suffocates because the air touching his lungs turns to gold too. And that's just in the first issue! As an editor, he's coedited the *Machine of Death* anthology and its follow-up, *This Is How You Die*. He has other interests beyond stories about death, honest. He lives in Toronto with his wife, Jenn, and their dog, Noam Chompsky.

No, I wanted to learn about the OTHER author! *Turn to 15.*

Actually, now I want to learn about the artists: *turn to 475.*

23 "Do the Capulets even have any daughters your age?" Benvolio says, digging into the food piled in front of him.

"I don't know, probably," you say while chewing. "I'm going to marry Rosaline first, though. Just as soon as she realizes she wants some Vitamin R."

"Vitamin Rosaline?" asks Benvolio.

"No no, Vitamin Romeo," you say.

"What's a vitamin?" asks Benvolio.

"Listen," you say, pushing your breakfast to the side so you can have some real talk. "If we're gonna end this without bloodshed, we need a plan. A real plan."

"To do what?" Benvolio says. In response, you slide your breakfast back in front of you and cut off a bite of your food and put it in your mouth, all while maintaining unbroken eye contact with Benvolio.

"You and me are going to end our parents' strife," you say through a dramatic mouthful of egg.

"How?" Benvolio says.

22-23

"Easy," you say. "We spy on them! One of us tags my parents, the other takes the Capulets. Once we know their secret hopes, dreams, desires, fears, and weaknesses—once we know them better than they know themselves—we use our knowledge to manipulate both people and events to achieve our goals. We'll guide them towards peace without them even knowing we're there!"

"Ah, I get it!" says Benvolio. "So the Capulets and Montagues will think they're making their OWN decisions, but we'll actually be the ones in charge of what they decide. We'll be like gods! Or like people playing one of those Choose Your Own Ad—"

"Yes," you say, interrupting, "yes, we'll be like either of one of those two things. Are you in?"

"Absolutely," Benvolio says.

You signal for the bill. When it arrives it turns out that mascot is back again, printed at the top. Now he's frying an egg and saying, "All that glitters is our golden eggs special: two served as you like them with coffee or juice and your choice of home fries or toast, every day before eleven a.m.!"

"Huh," you say.

"So do you want to shadow your own parents or the Capulets?" Benvolio asks as you make your way outside the restaurant.

"I clearly know my own parents best," you say, "but on the other hand, familiarity might blind me to certain things that an outside observer would see. It's a tricky problem; however, I think we can both agree on what the extremely obvious right choice here is."

"I'll follow my parents. You take the Capulets." *Turn to 54.*

"I'll follow the Capulets. You take my parents." *Turn to 30.*

24 Friar Lawrence is a friend of yours, and that makes you happy, because all the coolest teens are friends with friars. You soon arrive at Friar Headquarters, where he lives.

"Friar, it's me!" you say, knocking on the door even as you open it to let yourself in. "Anybody home?"

"Romeo, is that you?" comes a creaky voice from the back. "Good lord, what time is it?"

"Um—probably around ten?" you say, closing the door behind you. "Were you sleeping?"

Friar Lawrence stumbles out of the back room. He was definitely sleeping. Dude's a mess. He grabs hold of your arms, his wild eyes staring intently into yours. His breath is AWFUL.

"Ten a.m.?" Friar Lawrence says. "TEN A.M.?!"

"Ten a.m.," you confirm.

Friar Lawrence's wild face instantly changes into a smile. "Then my experiment was a complete success!"

"What? What experiment?" you say.

"The experiment of being dead for forty-two hours, of course!" he says. "It worked, Romeo! It worked!"

"You spent forty-two hours . . . dead?" you ask.

Friar Lawrence waves his hands around his face, like he's trying to get rid of a fly. "No, no, obviously I wasn't dead. But I faked it! I took a swig of this serum and it induced deathlike symptoms for precisely forty-two hours! Now I don't have to do jury duty!"

"Friar," you say, "are you telling me you faked your own death . . . to get out of jury duty?"

"My mother also wanted me to water her plants while she was traveling," he says. "Don't worry about it. Now that I can fake my own death whenever I want, all my problems are over!"

"I'm actually hoping you can help me with one of mine," you say.

"Oh?" the Friar says suspiciously, uncapping a vial of liquid and holding it near his mouth.

"It's no big deal," you say. "I'm just tired of feeling sad and want to forget about a woman."

"Oh!" the Friar says, relieved. He screws the cap back on the vial and drops it into his pocket. "That's easy." Turning around, he rummages through a giant pile of herbs and potions. He finds a red one and thrusts it into your hands.

"Here," he says. "Two sips of this and you'll forget about whoever you love for forty-two hours. Done!"

"What's the catch?" you ask.

"Oh, when it wears off, two days of longing will come flooding back to you all at once. It's pretty soul-destroying."

"Neat," you say. "But is that all you've got?"

"It is unless you want to fake your own death!" he says. "Which, as I've said, is really easy now."

"INTERESTING," you say.

Decide to forget about Rosaline for 42 hours: *turn to 49.*

Decide to fake your death for 42 hours instead: *turn to 35.*

25 You push your way past your mom and your nurse and run out of the castle. No WAY are you staying in that crazy house. You're sorry your mom got married too young and that damaged her, but that doesn't mean you're going to stand around and let her do the same thing to you. Sorry, Mom. Sorry, Angelica. But right now you're running away from home, LITERALLY.

You've made it a few minutes from your house when you realize all you've got on you is the dress you're wearing, so you do something you're not accustomed to doing: you make a decision. And that decision is to run back to the house, jog in through the back entrance, and pack a bag with clothes, money, jewelry to pawn, a map of Verona, some free weights, and some snacks. Then you run away from home again.

Once you're clear of your parents' estate, you stop to rest for a bit. You pull out your map and examine it. There's one place in particular you always wanted to see but your parents never gave you permission to visit: the Romeo District. It's got that name because all the guys there hit on the ladies!

Let's go see if it lives up to its reputation!!

Go to the Romeo District: *turn to 46.*

You know what, nevermind, return home again: *turn to 33.*

26 "I appreciate how you tried to break up this fight," you say, "but I'm a lover, not a fighter. Let's play to my strengths. What if I just married all the Capulets instead? Then they'd be in our family and we wouldn't be able to feud anymore, and then the Capulet line would become extinct, assuming I required that all my spouses, male or female, took my last name. Also, we'll need to repeal bigamy laws but I've done some research on this"—here you begin to pull out a stack of papers from beneath your shirt, placing them on the table between you—"and I think that with a few years of concerted lobbying, real progress can be made."

Benvolio flips through the papers. "I can see you've actually put quite a bit of thought into this," he says, impressed, "and I respect that you're looking at the long game, but I think this is one problem that won't be solved by you marrying everyone."

"Weird," you say, taking the papers and stuffing them back down your shirt. Just then, your food arrives!

Finally, it's breakfast! Eat a tasty meal! *Turn to 32.*

27 You are Romeo!

You've been wandering around town since dawn. You were up early and sad because you are SO IN LOVE with Rosaline! She's perfect, you tell yourself. She's a real grown-up lady, beautiful, with legs that won't quit, and with arms that won't quit, and with the rest of her that's unwilling or unable to quit as well. But she's more than just a collection of limbs, isn't she? She's a full-fledged AWESOME WOMAN, and she's clever and funny and interesting and you're certain two people have never been better suited for one another!

The only problem is that she doesn't return your affection. Like, at all.

Dude, you're not even at the "Oh, Romeo, I like you as a friend" level. You're at the "It's 'Romeo,' right?" level, the "Listen, Romeo, I've um—taken a vow of chastity" level, the "Hey I just remembered this vow lasts my entire life, so, um, sorry" level.

You can't figure out why she wouldn't bend the rules even a little for you. You're a 15-year-old boy who confessed your love to a woman in her thirties within five minutes of meeting her! What's not to like?

All this walking hasn't helped you make any progress on this problem, and you're stuck on what you're calling "Stage One": trying to figure out the precise series of sounds to make, emotions to emulate, and actions to undertake in order to make Rosaline fall in love with you. BECAUSE THAT'S HOW ROMANCE WORKS.

You're pondering this problem when you spot three people in conversation up ahead. They look like your parents, Charles and Rosemary, talking with your best friend/cousin, Benvolio! Benvolio's great, and right now he's wearing this super-cool vest. It's got like—badges on it? And tassels? I know that sounds terrible but it's really working for him.

I'm still checking out that vest when your parents and Benvolio notice you standing there: your mom and dad abruptly leave while Benvolio turns and jogs towards you. "Good morning, cousin!" he shouts, waving. You pretend not to notice because you're sad and want to be left alone, and also because while Benvolio's a good friend, he kinda takes everything literally, which makes him not the best person to talk about feelings with.

Actually, you saw Benvolio earlier today, only you didn't want to talk to him just then because you were walking around crying over your feelings (Oh, Romeo. Wherefore art thou such a wimp, Romeo?), so you jumped into the woods and then hid while crying until he went away because that's how you solve your problems. But there are no woods here! There's only a garbage can. What do you want to do?

 Talk to Benvolio: *turn to 14.*

Hide in the garbage can: *turn to 21.*

28

"Breakfast!" you say. "Dude, let's eat some. Where shall we dine?"

You're about to give Benvolio a chance to respond when you realize he has blood on his face! It's been there this whole time and you're just noticing now, you jerk! Although honestly part of the fault is mine, since I'm in charge of scene description here and I didn't notice either. I was too distracted by his cool vest! SPEAKING OF WHICH, I've had some time to check out that vest some more and I'm pretty sure there are some sequins sewn into it. It's so great. Can you ask him where he got it?

Ask him about the vest: *turn to 17.*

Ask him about his face . . . OVER BREAKFAST: *turn to 38.*

Ignore the vest, ignore the face: my name is Romeo and I am here to talk about love: *turn to 48.*

29

"She refuses to fall in love with me. She's smart, and as clever as Diana! As you know, Diana is the Roman goddess of the hunt, and also the goddess of the moon and birthing. She can also talk to and control animals."

"Like Aquaman, but for land!" Benvolio says, and here he's intending to refer to the Greek sea god Poseidon but has clearly forgotten his name and is trying to bluff his way through that mistake. "Aquaman"? Really, Benvolio?

"Exactly. But she's shielded from Cupid's arrow by her +2 shield of chastity. She won't listen to my words of love!" you say.

"That's her choice," Benvolio says.

"She won't let me look at her with my eyes of love!" you say.

"Again, it's really her choice to do that or not," Benvolio says.

"She won't even open her lap to receive my golden gift of love!!" you say.

"I don't think you can fault her for this," Benvolio says, "as consent is the center of any defensible system of sexual ethics."

You look at him angrily. He's not getting what you're saying, so you decide to take a different tack. "She's rich in beauty, Ben," you say, "but ACTUALLY she's really poor, because when she dies her beauty dies with her, on account of how she's so into celibacy! And that SUCKS, because she's so hot that those children would be super hot too!"

Benvolio stares at you, one eyebrow raised.

"You know, EVENTUALLY," you say.

Benvolio lowers his eyebrow.

"Anyway," you say, "she's sworn off love and in so doing has killed me. Metaphorically. I'm only alive now so that I can tell you about it."

"Man," says Benvolio, "forget about her."

Say it's impossible to forget about Rosaline: *turn to 52.*

Actually try to forget about Rosaline: *turn to 39.*

30 You sneak your way over to Capulet Castle, noticing on the way over how all the servants are running around with decorations, flowers, and streamers. You can't tell if they're cleaning up after a party or preparing for the next one, but you smile: the hustle and bustle this generates will make your infiltration easier. Plus, even the security guards are helping out with the work, so sneaking in here is actually super easy.

Once inside the castle grounds, you look around. You haven't really thought of the best way to approach this, but you know you need to get inside and close to the Capulets. A few ideas suggest themselves, but two of them stand out as being really terrific:

Disguise yourself as a maid: *turn to 42.*

Disguise yourself as an innocuous wall; nobody ever suspects walls: *turn to 55.*

31 The amazing thing about breathing is that it's so instinctual! It's very hard—very near impossible—to suffocate yourself by simply deciding to die. Even if you have the willpower to hold your breath until you pass out, the second you do your body will begin breathing for you, saving your life. Your body wants to live, Romeo.

However, your body didn't count on your trying to breathe, talk, and eat breakfast at the same time, AND on your being so terrible at it. You choke on your breakfast, it blocks your windpipe, and two minutes later you are dead. If only someone had previously invented some sort of eponymous maneuver, perhaps involving a series of abdominal thrusts, that could've saved your life! But they didn't and you're dead, the end!

At your funeral no smokin'-hot babes show up (including Rosaline), which disappoints you because you are now a ghost and you hoped a lot of hotties would come to your funeral. NO DICE, friend. But the good news is there are still ghost babes around! They're just hanging out in the church. You hit on them instead. You say, "Hey baby, ever sex a dude during his own funeral?"

They all think that's pretty inappropriate for a bunch of reasons actually.

Sorry, Romeo. You do not make a sex during your own funeral in this ending. And I know, I know: what's the point of reading this book—ANY book—if funeral sex doesn't happen in it even when it totally could?

You throw this book away in bitter, horny disappointment.

THE END

32 Jessica appears at the table with your breakfast orders. You thank her and soon you have begun the mechanical and chemical process of eating, which is required to sustain human life. Without it you'd be forced to rely on your fat and muscle reserves, and those would be depleted in only a few weeks at the most! The first step in eating is to carefully push the prepared egg dish in front of you into your stomach via your face. You decide to do this in tiny stages, one forkful at a time.

That accomplished, you use the teeth protruding into the flesh of your mouth from your skull to slice and grind the food into smaller pieces.

This aids in digestion.

Learn more about eating: *turn to 40.*

Continue talking: *turn to 23.*

33 Okay, so, Jules: you're making a lot of very big decisions very quickly here. In the space of only two moves you have decided to take command of your life and run away from home, and then instantly decided to reverse that so that now instead of running away from home you are literally running back towards home. Maybe you want to consider your choices a bit more carefully in the future? Because later on you may well end up with a "Stab this dude" option and there's not gonna be an "Aw frig, someone's coming, unstab this dude fast!!" option then.

Alright!

You run back to your house, taking the long way this time so at least you can have a slightly longer taste of freedom, and when you get there you see the party has already started. You slip in through the back and join the party.

Join the party. *turn to 58.*

34 "Anyway, let's NOT go to the party!" you say. "We weren't invited, and plus I'll just get even more obsessed with Rosaline. Instead, let's go get some breakfast, yeah? It's breakfast season, and I'm colluding for some fooding!" you say.

"'Colluding for some fooding'?" Benvolio asks.

"I'm heating for some meating," you say. "Like, food meat, not 'meet someone' meat."

"What?" says Benvolio.

"NEVERMIND," you say, grabbing your friend's arm and dragging him down the road to your favorite restaurant: the Merchant of Breakfast.

Arrive at the restaurant: *turn to 45.*

35 You take the bottle of Fake Death Juice, thank the Friar, and return home. You sit down on your bed. You get up and tidy up your room a bit, for when people find you. You sit down on your bed again. You realize you never asked the Friar how much to take, but probably it's the whole bottle, right? That's how medicine works, right?

You chug the contents of the bottle.

"Here's to my love!" you say, then wipe your mouth with the back of your hand. As you lie down, you already start to feel dizzy. "Dang, Friar, your drugs are quick," you mutter. You hold one hand up in front of you. "And thus, with a chug, I 'die.'"

The last thing you're aware of as you lose consciousness is your own hand slapping you in the face.

Time passes: *turn to 59.*

36 You have just been born! Congratulations, good work on that thing! Now SURPRISE, babies are boring, so we're going to jump ahead in time to a point where you're a COOL TEEN and you've already lived a reasonable chunk of your life. I can promise you that most of what we're going to see now will be FLABBERGASTINGLY INTERESTING. Teens do all sorts of interesting things! They make friends, they shed tears, they totally make out, AND OTHER THINGS TOO, PROBABLY. I think we all can agree that high school rules and is definitely the most important part of your life. So let's join this awesome stuff already in progress!

Where you are is Verona, in Italy. When you are is Sunday, July 21, 1585, 8:18 a.m. Who you are . . . well, that's entirely up to you.

Are you:

ROMEO? He's a 15-year-old teen who loves love, loves being in love, and loves being in love with love! Big into love, this guy. He's deeply, sincerely in love with Rosaline, who is smart and pretty and SO PERFECT OMG. It's weird we haven't mentioned her in the title though? Anyway, Romeo's interests include thinking about women and also not being called up to the front of the class while thinking about women. Last year he moved out of his parents' house and into a tinier house that his parents also own.

Romeo's got a +1 perk to composition and elocution (that's, like, talking), but a −1 weakness against moderation and foresight. If you think you'll need to recite poetry in this adventure, he's a good choice. He's allied with TEAM MONTAGUE.

JULIET? She's a 16-year-old teen who is a dainty flower, as fragile as a spider's web in the morning dew. Naw, I'm just having a little fun, like when you call a short guy "Tallo" or "Doctor Heightsworth." Juliet's actually SUPER RIPPED, and her top six interests are: muscles, boys, getting muscles, getting boys, kissing boys, and kissing her own muscles. Look, you can play as a boy who wants to meet a girl or as a girl who wants to meet a boy! Each has what the other wants, and you can control either of them. Hey, this book is gonna be EASY.

The downside to Juliet is, her parents micromanage her life and tell her what to do all the time, which leaves very little time for chatting up boys. She never gets to decide anything for herself, she barely leaves the house, and her nurse is her only real friend. It's a little sad when you think about it. She tries not to.

Juliet has a +2 perk to muscles (OBVIOUSLY) but a −2 weakness against the mad hotties. She's an excellent choice if you want to solve your problems with muscles, and why wouldn't you? She's on TEAM CAPULET.

 Play as Romeo: *turn to 27.*

Play as Juliet: *turn to 4.*

TIRED OF READING THIS STORY ALREADY? Haha wow that didn't take long. There's a bunch of nice pictures on the cover you can look at while you wait for everyone else to finish reading this book. *Turn to the cover; the end.*

37
"I cannot read," you say, lying to an almost complete stranger for your own amusement. "I am illiterate. I am, in fact, aliterate, which is to say I have not even conceived of literacy before. I am so far from reading that I actually stand outside the literate/illiterate dichotomy."

"I thought 'aliterate' meant that you could read, but that you choose not to," Benvolio says.

"Well it also means that I can't read AND I choose not to do so," you reply. "Which I guess would be an easy choice to make, given those circumstances. Anyway," you say, turning back to the guy who asked you the question, "what is it you wanted me to read?"

He's long gone. Oh well! Your stomach grumbles and you grab

Benvolio's head. "Dude, let's get some breakfast," you say. "I was going to mention it earlier but then I decided not to for some reason."

"Okay," Ben says.

The two of you make your way to your favorite restaurant: the Merchant of Breakfast!

Arrive at the restaurant: *turn to 45.*

38

You take Benvolio's hand and tell him you're going to this amazing little brunch place you know. Everyone loves brunch, OBVIOUSLY, but you super-love brunch. You are so big into brunch that your middle name should be "Brunch," but you've spent several weeks trying to convince your friends that it's "Doctor Lovesworth" so it's too late for that now.

"The quality of the eggs Benedict there is off the hook," you say to Benvolio as you lead him down the road. "They have twice-fried bacon that's insane. I'm going to ask you about your face over breakfast."

"Okay," says Benvolio, a little hesitant. He pauses. "I got into a fight at the—"

"Shh," you say, pressing your index finger against his lips. You look up the road, still shushing him. "We're almost there."

You soon arrive at your destination: an adorable restaurant situated beneath a carved wooden sign reading THE MERCHANT OF BREAKFAST. Beneath it is a freshly painted illustration of what seems to be their new mascot: a smiling giant anthropomorphic egg happily frying up a regular egg. He's got a voice balloon. "I know not why I am so tasty!" he says.

That's new.

You take your seats and a waiter comes by, introduces herself as Jessica, and gives you menus. She's got a red-and-white-checkered handkerchief in her belt: everything's so homey and fun here! Looking at the menu you see an image of that egg-frying-an-egg mascot again, only now he's saying, "If you fry us, do we not become extremely tasty?"

"Here's a round of water. Can I get y'all some coffee to start?" Jessica asks.

"Coffee please, two milks, two sugars," says Benvolio. "And the Pound o' Flesh looks good. Yes. I will have that. Bacon, please."

"Certainly," Jessica says, and turns. "And for you?"

You glance at the menu. All the dishes have cute names now. You're trying to decide between the "Eggs That Many Men Desire" (scrambled, apparently), the "The Devil Can Cite Spinach and Ham for His Purpose" (spinach and ham quiche), and the "Love Is Blind, If by 'Blind' You Mean Delicious and by 'Love' You Mean This French Toast."

After a few moments of careful consideration you do manage to choose your own breakfast, let Jessica know your choice, and get some juice to go with it. "I'll be back with that in the twinkling of an eye, sweetheart," she says, and she's gone. You and Benvolio look at each other.

"So hey, what's up with your face?" you finally say.

"I was at the beach—you know the one by the lake?" You nod. It's the best beach. "Well, I showed up and dudes were biting their thumbs at each other," Benvolio says. "I didn't know if the law was on their side or not."

He takes a sip of his water. "Frankly," he says, "I'm not even sure why we HAVE laws about where and when citizens are permitted to bite thumbs. Seems kinda dumb."

"Welcome to Verona," you say.

"Yeah, well, I broke it up but it still got a little bloody. Tybalt Capulet punched me in the nose, so I punched him back on his shoulder and then stole his vest. That's justice," Benvolio says.

You nod. "Beach justice," you whisper, eyes wide.

Benvolio looks around the room to see if anyone else is listening in. "Our family and the Capulets keep fighting, cuz. I dunno. There's got to be a way to end this."

"I know just the thing!" you say.

Suggest killing all the Capulets: *turn to 16.*

Suggest marrying all the Capulets: *turn to 26.*

39
"Huh," you say. "Okay, well, I mean—I could try."

"Oh," Benvolio says, a little surprised. "Okay, well—good! Perfect, actually!"

You shake Benvolio's hand and leave. There's only one man who can help you now.

Go to Friar Lawrence's house: *turn to 24.*

40
While you chew, you mentally review what you know about eating. You think of the many substances you require (air, water, food) and reflect that if you cannot access them for even a second then a timer starts, and when that timer ends, you will die. Of air and water and food you like food the most, since that's the one with the longest timer. You can live weeks without food. Weeks! At the most you'll only last three days without water, Romeo, and you'd be lucky to last three MINUTES without air.

Breathing, drinking, eating: they're really just ways to postpone death for a little longer. Each breath buys you a few more seconds. Each drink, a handful of days. This meal will keep you alive for at least another 24 hours, assuming you don't fail to drink or breathe in that time. But mess that last one up and it's just about instant death, huh Romeo?

As you reflect on that, you suddenly become aware of your breathing, and shortly afterwards you're also suddenly aware of how you're now breathing manually. In, out. How long does a breath normally take? Why is this so hard? Anyway, don't worry, Romeo: there's probably lots of oxygen in the room. I mean, it's invisible, so it's not like you can say for sure. But the odds that this breath will be your last because all the air randomly moved somewhere else are pretty small. Right?

Anyway, Benvolio is asking you something about the Capulets! You should probably use your manual breath control to handle your respiration needs while ALSO expelling air such that your vocal cords vibrate in a controlled way. If you can pull it off, you'll be able to talk without dying!

Talk without dying: *turn to 23.*

Choke and suffocate: *turn to 31.*

41 Benvolio chooses rock. You wrap your palm around his fist.

"Paper wraps rock," you say. "I win, so you have to go marry Juliet. Sorry, dude."

Benvolio stares at his fist. "Wow," he sighs. "Rock's never let me down before. Okay, that was a good practice round. For real this time!"

You sigh. Classic Benvolio.

"FINE," you say. "But this is the last time."

You hold out your hand. Three . . . two . . . one . . .

Choose rock: *turn to 79.*

Choose paper: *turn to 60.*

Choose scissors: *turn to 67.*

42 You make sure nobody is around, then sneak into the castle, looking for the maid clothes depository. There's gotta be one, right? You know, a big unguarded room where they keep all the maid clothes??

Turns out, yes, a castle this size does require such a room! You enter the maid clothes depository and exit a few moments later disguised as Maid Romeo. To be honest you kinda thought there'd be clothes for men in there, but you now realize you were thinking of a butler clothes depository. Anyway, it doesn't matter! Your maid outfit is AMAZING. A black dress with white ruffle details covers your waist and stops well above your knees, with sheer black stockings taking up the slack. White frills encircle your shoulders, and a lacy white apron runs down your front. A black maid's cap, a feather duster, and a tiny black bow at the top of your apron complete the ensemble.

You smooth down your apron, brush off your cuffs, and get to work.

Clean Mr. and Mrs. Capulet's room, maybe they'll be there: *turn to 89.*

Clean some other room: *turn to 56.*

43 Alleypal's ball isn't until tonight, so you burn up the rest of the afternoon quietly reading, which you do because as a cool teen you just LOVE reading, and not because as the author of books I'm desperately trying to make reading seem super cool, WHICH IT IS ANYWAY.

You invite your friend Mercutio over to read and, eventually, party at Alleypal's shindig with you. He says he's not interested, but then you send a messenger to tell him you've got snacks, and he arrives shortly afterwards, drenched in sweat. He ran the whole way: now, there's a dude who loves a free meal! Besides food, he's also fond of puns.

I LIKE HIM ALREADY.

Alright, now it's 10 p.m.! Time to put down your nerd manuals and go party!

Go to the ball: *turn to 51.*

44 Oh, so now you want to start living your life on your own terms? Better late than never, I guess!

"Um, no, no, I'm not going to promise to fall in love with someone I've never met, MOM," you say. "If you think he's so rockin', you marry him."

Just then, a servant enters and reminds your mom that it's late and the party has already started, the guests are here, the staff are cursing the nurse, and everything is entirely out of control.

"We'll talk about this later," your mom says. As you all make your way down to the party, which is already in progress, your mom takes your hand and squeezes it hard enough to hurt. She smiles at the guests like she doesn't have a care in the world.

"You will check out Paris's pecs, young lady," she hisses at you through a smile, "and you will like them."

You squeeze her hand back, hard enough to hurt more.

"I'll do what I please, Mom," you say, smiling just as pleasantly as you can.

Join the party: *turn to 58.*

45 You soon arrive at your destination: an adorable restaurant situated beneath a carved wooden sign reading, THE MERCHANT OF BREAKFAST. Beneath it is a freshly painted illustration of what seems to be their new mascot: a smiling giant egg happily frying up a regular egg. He's got a voice balloon. "I know not why I am so tasty!" he says.

That's new.

You're shown to your table, and a waiter comes by and introduces herself as Jessica as she passes you menus. They're smaller than what you were expecting.

"Our regular breakfast hours are almost over," she says, "so you can only order from the smaller post-breakfast menu now. Sorry."

Looking at the menu you see an image of their mascot giving a thumbs-up and saying, "He is well paid that is well satisfied . . . at breakfast, which we serve with a smile all day long!" You glance down at your options. They are as follows:

- coffee (as you like it)
- two eggs (cooked) on a plate

"This place is way better at the start of the day," you tell Benvolio.

You both order the eggs and start chatting while you wait for your food to arrive. Benvolio mentions how he got into a fight with the Capulets earlier, and how frustrating it is for two families to hate each other so much that anyone even tangentially connected to them never knows when they're going to end up in a street brawl.

"It's a hard thing to plan your day around," he says. "I got things to do, you know? And then I end up biting thumbs or getting thumbs bitten at me and boom, I'm late for my doctor's appointment and need to wait another three weeks before I can see him. And yeah, maybe I stole a cool vest off of one of the people I beat up, but that's not enough, you know?"

"It's lucky it fit you at least," you say. He nods.

"Our family and the Capulets keep fighting," he says. "I dunno. There's got to be a way to end this."

"I know just the thing!" you say.

Suggest killing all the Capulets: *turn to 16.*

Suggest marrying all the Capulets: *turn to 26.*

46 You make your way down to the Romeo District. Your parents aren't going to marry you off, but that doesn't mean you can't find a dude on your own terms, right? Nothing serious though. You're 16; there'll be plenty of time to get serious when you're way older and way less nubile!

You find yourself a promising-looking place called All Too Precious Brew and sit yourself down at the bar. In front of you is a tiny little book with "BEER MENU, FEATURING THE WINTER'S ALE" printed on the front. Hey, Juliet! It's like one of those An Adventure Might Happen Depending on Your Choices books, except instead of choosing to go on an imaginary adventure that didn't actually happen, you get to choose a beer in real life and then you get to drink that beer!

You open up the book and peruse your choices. There are a few that look interesting:

- *Stout and Bitter*
- *Pale and Singl-Ale*
- *ImTEARial Stout*
- *Barley Whine*

Hey, all the drinks here are sexual-frustration themed! You figure there must be a lot of horny dudes down here in the Romeo District. Either that or the brewers need to get out more. Maybe both?

Probably both?

Anyway, you choose which beer you want, AND THEN, you choose to order it. Your adventure in beer is well under way!

A few seconds later, the bartender delivers your beer. You hold it above your head in a toast. "I drink to the general joy of the whole bar," you say, and then you take a swig.

As you lower your beer from your lips you notice that the two seats next to you now have men in them. Hah! Classic Romeo District!

Examine dudes: *turn to 57.*

Ignore dudes: *turn to 75.*

47 Another couple of days go by.

Time passes: *turn to 62.*

48 You look away from Benvolio's face, pretending not to notice the blood on it. "Hey, I know what'd be fun!" you say. "Let's talk about love some more!"

"Before we do that," Benvolio insists, "I just wanted you to know I got into a fight. Tried to keep the peace, but dudes were biting their thumbs at each other like crazy."

"Dang, sounds off the hook," you say. "Not unlike, I hasten to add, the emotion of love."

"It was," he says. "I never saw so many thumbs get bit. Must've been at least four or five, easy."

You consider asking him more about the thumbs but then suddenly decide you would still really rather talk about love some more! Geez, Romeo. You are as constant as the northern star, which is to suggest sarcastically that you are not constant at all, but rather boiling with random and unpredictable fiery energies held just beneath your surface. The only way you'd appear constant is if you were viewed from far away on a planet whose northern axis extended almost directly through you!

Okay, listen. From now on I'm gonna try out metaphors like this somewhere else before writing them down here live. Anyway, Benvolio is still expounding vis-à-vis thumbs, and you decide to interrupt him.

"Let me stop you right there," you say. "This fight you were involved in had a lot to do with hatred, but it actually has more to do with love, which is what I would prefer to talk about and the subject upon which I will expound now."

"Okay," sighs Benvolio.

You clear your throat and hold up one hand in front of you. "O brawling love, O loving hate, O anything of nothing first created!" you say.

Benvolio looks at you. "You mean, like, love that comes from nothing?"

"O heavy lightness, serious vanity, misshapen chaos of well-seeming forms!" you reply, still holding your hand out in front of you. It's practically in Benvolio's face, Romeo.

Benvolio looks at you again, then steps to the side to avoid having your hand so close to his face. "So, like, beautiful things muddled together into an ugly mess?" he says. He pauses for a second, confused. "You, um, still talking about love?"

"Feather of lead, bright smoke, cold fire, sick health, still-waking sleep, that is not what it is!" you say. "This love feel I, that feel no love in this."

Benvolio takes a second to parse what you're saying, then seems to figure it out. "You feel love, even though nobody loves you back. Got it," he says, and then he starts to cry.

I'm serious, he's crying! Geez, Benvolio! It's not that bad.

"I'm crying because of how sad you are," Benvolio says.

"Oh," you say. "Hah hah. Wow. Um, that's weird. Wow wow wow."

Benvolio cries some more.

"Listen," you say, attempting to comfort him, "this is what love does! But now your crying at my sadness is making me even sadder, so if you don't stop, then I'll cry and then you'll cry more and we'll have an infinite feedback loop of sorrow."

Benvolio sniffles and wipes his nose on his sleeve. I guess he's comforted! Mission accomplished!

"Anyway, bye," you say, walking away, but Benvolio follows you like a lost puppy.

"Romeo," he says. "Please, I don't understand. Do you love someone, and if so, who is she?"

"A woman," you reply.

"Yes," he says, "I figured as much. But what's she like? What makes her so special that she could capture your heart so completely? Please. Tell me all about her."

You picture Rosaline in your mind, this wonderful woman, this fully formed person with whom you've forged one of the deepest connections it's possible for one human being to create with another.

"She's super hot," you volunteer.

Tell Benvolio about Rosaline: *turn to 29.*

Tell Benvolio about Rosaline in the classiest language you can muster: *turn to 18.*

49 You take the bottle of forgetting juice from the Friar, thank him, and go home. You sit down on your bed.

"Here's to my love," you say, holding up the bottle in front of you. You take two careful sips.

You're not sure it's working. You still remember . . .

. . . something? You were drinking to forget something, right? Whatever it was, it couldn't have been that important, since you've already forgotten it.

Something inside you screams that what you're doing is insanely dangerous. You put the bottle aside. "Either this potion worked, or it didn't, but either way I got no business drinking any more of it!" you say.

You go out that night to hang out with Benvolio, and he asks you how it's going with the whole Rosaline situation. You've never heard the name before in your life.

"Who?" you ask.

"NO WAY," he says. "You actually forgot about her?"

"Apparently?" you say.

And while you cannot remember what you've forgotten, you do remember how you managed to forget it. You start taking a measured dose every 41 hours to keep remembrance at bay. You end up with a standing order of the liquid with the Friar and keep this up for almost half a decade. In that time you meet someone new, marry her, and have two wonderful children, a boy and a girl.

And then, one day, you slip. You forget to take your medicine, just once. You're out playing with your kids in a park when it happens: all of a sudden, you remember Rosaline. She comes rushing back to you. You remember her beauty. Her scent. What she meant to you. How you yearned for her with your entire soul and how you KNEW with every fiber of your being that you were meant to be together.

You fall to your knees.

"Oh dear God in heaven," you say, "I can't believe I was EVER such an obsessive kid. Geez. How embarrassing!"

Your kids run into your outstretched arms, and you pick them up, place them on your shoulders, and return to your wife to live happily ever after.

THE END

50

"I can read my own fortune in my misery!" you say, which I guess technically lines up with "Tell him you can read."

Peter looks at you, confused. "Okay, that's cool," he says, "but can you read, like, words? Words written on a thing?" He holds up the piece of paper he's been clutching in his hands. "If I showed you this thing, could you read the thing?"

"I can if I understand the language it's written in, including its grammar and alphabet!" you say, snatching the paper out of his hands. It looks like a list of names.

"This looks like a list of names," you observe keenly as you begin to examine it closely. I've taken the liberty of annotating it so you can be clear on who all these people are, because I am NICE and also a GOOD AUTHOR. They include:

- Seigneur Martino and his wife and daughters **(Okay, cards on the table: I have no idea who these people are.)**
- County Anselme and his beauteous sisters **(Again, no idea, but they sound real beauteous.)**
- The lady widow of Vitruvio **(Vitruvio, you old dog! Left behind enough male widows that the lady needed an identifying adjective, did you? Hah hah hah! Classic Vitruvio!)**
- Seigneur Placentio and his lovely nieces **(I'm sorry but I don't know who these people are either; also: I MAY have been bluffing about knowing Vitruvio earlier.)**
- Mercutio and his brother Valentine **(Mercutio! I actually know this guy! You know him too, Romeo. He's your other best friend, besides Benvolio! The three of you get into all sorts of hilarious circumstances! Valentine's a big loser though and you don't ever hang out with him.)**
- Mine uncle Capulet, his wife and daughters **(Could be anyone, really! There are a lot of Capulets running around, so it's hard to say who precisely these people are without knowing who wrote this letter in such fancy language.)**
- My fair niece Rosaline and Livia **(ROSALINE! We know her! So this must be a list composed by Rosaline's aunt or uncle, I guess?)**
- Seigneur Valentio and his cousin Tybalt **(What, there's a Valentine and a Valentio? Geez. That'll be confusing, so as a personal favor I'll cut both of these guys out of this story as of right now. Later, dudes! Anyway, Tybalt's a good guy to avoid. He's totally racist against Montagues, so heads up.)**
- Lucio and the lively Helena **("Lively" seems like a weird adjective to attach to someone on a list like this but oh well! It's not like I wrote it, right??)**

You read the names out loud to Peter and ask him what the deal is with this list. He explains that he works for the Capulets, who are throwing a party tonight, and this is a partial list of guests he needs to invite. He stands up, saying he needs to go track them down, and heads out of the alleyway. Before he steps out into the street, he turns back to you and shouts, "You should totally come! As long as you're not Montagues, of course. Hah hah, what a silly thought. Anyway, later!"

"DUDE," Benvolio says. "WE JUST MADE A FRIEND IN AN ALLEY."

"I KNOW, IT'S SO GREAT," you reply. "HIS NAME, PETER, IS DUMB THOUGH, SO WE'LL CALL HIM ALLEYPAL."

"Agreed!" Benvolio says. "Hey, you know what? We should crash Alleypal's party! Rosaline will be there, which means you'll be able to directly compare her to other hotties there, and when you do that you'll DEFINITELY want to trade up. Her body will not compare to the bodies of strangers."

"Hmmm . . . ," you say. "A woman fairer than Rosaline? No offense, but I'm PRETTY SURE she's got the rockingest bod the all-seeing sun ever saw since the world began, an event that, as nobody could possibly know this information, I can only wildly guess was somewhere around 4.57 billion years ago."

"Wow, and she just HAPPENED to be born in your hometown, huh?" Benvolio says.

"Yes," you say. "It was quite lucky," you say.

Go to the party: Rosaline might be there! *Turn to 43.*

Skip the party: Rosaline might be there! *Turn to 34.*

You know what? While you're here trying to decide whether or not to go to some dumb party, that woman I mentioned a few choices back has finished cleaning her room and is now working out. She's GETTING STUFF DONE. Maybe you should be her for a while! I'll sweeten the pot: right now she's wearing workout clothes. You probably find that sexy, yes? Humans like clothes that are different from regular clothes, yes? *Turn to 8.*

51
You and your friends are making your way towards the ball, and I like you, Romeo, but I gotta say: the whole way there you're thinking about your love for Rosaline and being a complete pill about it. You're saying things like "You guys go on ahead, I'll just sit outside by myself, it's cool," and your friends are replying with things like "Oh my gosh, for serious just shut up and try to enjoy yourself for once."

There are a few memorable points during the trip. One is where your bud Mercutio talks about someone called Queen Mab. The other is where you straight up, say "I've got a bad feeling about this," and predict your own upcoming death, and hah hah hah what the heck are you doing, Romeo?? That's like naming a boat the *Good Ship 100% Invincible, Especially from Icebergs* or the *SS Not Even God Could Sink This Boat*, which is to say, IT IS GENERALLY A BAD IDEA.

If you'd like to go back and complete the *Listen to What Mercutio Said* sidequest, that's an option. But if you're adult enough to take my word for it when I say what was said there isn't super important, then let's party already!

 Complete the *Listen to What Mercutio Said* sidequest (0 points): *turn to 73.*

Arrive at the party (100 points): *turn to 61.*

52

"Sure it's possible. Just overwrite the memory of her by looking at other ladies," Benvolio says. "You know. Peep on the mad hotties."

You try to imagine a mad hottie in your mind, but she's still basically Rosaline. "It's still not possible!" you say, throwing your hands up in the air. "Anyone else's beauty only reminds me of hers. You know how blind people are sad all the time because of all the eyesight they've lost? That's me, only instead of eyesight, I've lost DESIRED POTENTIAL FUTURE SMOOCHING!"

"I'm not sure any of that is actually the case," Benvolio says. He pauses, thinking, and then continues. "Dude, listen, real talk: I am going to teach you how to forget Rosaline or die trying. Right now. And as it is really unlikely that teaching you emotional coping techniques will result in my death, I'm pretty sure you're gonna learn this lesson."

Alright, Romeo! Do you want to get a lecture on relationships (boooo) or instead, do you want to get to BE a fun lady with cool muscles (yaaay)? Come on. You're big into women, Romeo: it's probably because you've always secretly wanted to BE ONE, right?? Right now the particular woman I have in mind is being told by her mom to clean her room. Doesn't that sound fun? Wouldn't you rather do that than talk about feelings?

 Listen to Benvolio lecture you about feelings: *turn to 19.*

As a matter of fact, yes, I would rather abandon my identity as Romeo and be forced to clean a room than listen to a single conversation about feelings: *turn to 6.*

53

You knock on the front door of Capulet Castle and a servant answers. "Hello, I was wondering if I could call on Juliet? I'm an eligible suitor and this call is regarding marriage."

"But of course," the servant says. "Juliet and her parents are upstairs." The servant indicates the appropriate room and leaves you to it. You adjust your hair, take a deep breath, then go for it.

"Hello, everyone!" you say, pushing open the door and walking into the room. "Even though I love someone else, I heard there was a stone-cold fox of marriageable age here and decided I was willing to be persuaded!!"

As you step into the room, you see a woman: Lady Capulet. Beside her is an older man, her husband, Lord Capulet. And beside them you see . . .

. . . you see the most beautiful woman you've ever met. You instantly forget all about Rosaline. Juliet is staring at you, her mouth slightly open, like she's shocked too. And Romeo, I like you, so I'm gonna let you in on a little secret. This whole "love at first sight" thing you're feeling right now? She feels EXACTLY the same way.

"I—" you say. "I'm—"

Juliet's parents turn to look at you.

"I . . . I'm a twin," you say. "Which is to say, I have a brother who looks just like me. The only difference is that I am the dumb loudmouth one who walks into rooms saying things he regrets. Hold on, let me go get my much cooler twin brother before disappearing forever."

You close the door, take a step sideways, and softly bang your head against the wall. Smooth move, Romeo. It's insane how attractive Juliet is. You didn't know it was POSSIBLE to desire someone so badly.

The door beside you opens, and Juliet steps out of it. She closes the door behind her and looks at you shyly.

"My name's Juliet," she says. "I'm sorry, but—I couldn't stop looking at you. I've never felt like this about anyone before."

You smile. "You should know I'm not really a twin," you say. "I'm just stupid. Forget all that stuff I said about loving someone else. That's . . . well, it's not true. Not anymore."

She runs a hand through your hair. "Good," she says, and smiles.

"I'm Romeo," you say. "Listen, I don't normally do whatever this is, but I need to tell you something. Two things, actually." You take a deep breath, drop to one knee, take her hand, and say the bravest thing you've ever said.

"If I profane with my unworthiest hand this holy shrine," you say, "the gentle sin is this: my lips, two blushing pilgrims, ready stand to smooth that rough touch with a tender kiss."

She smiles down at you.

"Hey uh also I'm kinda a Montague," you say.

She gasps and yanks her hand away. She turns to run back into the room but stops with her hand on the door. She's motionless for a few seconds, and then, without turning, she speaks.

"My only love sprung from my only hate," she says, sighing. Her hand hovers above the door handle. Then she turns back, takes your head in her hands, and kisses you hard.

"Though meeting you like this feels much like fate," she whispers between smooches.

Kiss her back: *turn to 69.*

54 You stroll confidently to your parents' house, walking in the front door without even knocking.

"Mom? Dad? It's me, Romeo! I decided to drop by and pay you a visit for no reason!"

Your parents don't answer. You quickly ascertain that they're out of the house right now. The perfect chance to go through their documents to learn more about them!

Half an hour later, you have determined most of your parents' documents are super boring. There's only one document in particular that stands out. It reads as follows:

THE SECRET HOPES, DREAMS, DESIRES, FEARS, AND WEAKNESSES OF MRS. MONTAGUE

by me, MRS. MONTAGUE

PRIVATE!!!!!

MY HOPES: that Romeo lives in Verona forever so he can come and visit us whenever he wants/all the time.

MY DREAMS: mainly of my beloved only son, Romeo, coming to visit me all the time.

MY DESIRES: that my hopes and dreams are fully realized. Duh.

MY FEARS: for example, and I know it's ludicrous, but sometimes I worry about what would happen if Romeo was banished from Verona and could never visit me again??

MY WEAKNESSES: if Romeo got banished then I'm pretty sure that grief of my son's exile will hath stopp'd my breath!!!

"Well," you say, folding up the piece of paper and putting it in your pocket, "that just saved me a lot of time."

You meet up with Benvolio that evening. He reports that he disguised himself as a maid and it was kinda flirty and fun and he had a great time. He also reports that while cleaning the room the Capulets were in with their daughter, Juliet, he found a note! He passes it to you, and you pass him the note you found in exchange. You examine the new note, which reads:

THE SECRET HOPES, DREAMS, DESIRES, FEARS, AND WEAKNESSES OF MRS. CAPULET

by me, MRS. CAPULET

DO NOT READ!!!!!

MY HOPES: now only that Juliet marries a cool dude of my choosing.

MY DREAMS: I dream of my beloved only daughter Juliet marrying a cool dude of my choosing. It's that same dream over and over every night, and now when I wake up in the morning I'm more tired than when I went to bed! Hah hah hah WHY??

MY DESIRES: Juliet marries a cool dude of my choosing! Maybe then the dreams will, at long last, stop?

MY FEARS: that Juliet won't marry a cool dude of my choosing and my dreams will punish me more.

MY WEAKNESSES: if Juliet died without marrying the cool dude of my choosing I don't know what I'd do!! Probably I'd raze Verona to the ground, or build a solid-gold statue in her honor. Either one, really??

You look up at Benvolio. "Okay," he says, "so now we know their weaknesses: your mom will die if you get banished, and Juliet's mom will either kill everyone or commission new statuary if Juliet dies without getting married first."

"Right," you say. "But I feel like I should stress that we want to get these two families together without killing my mom and/or everyone else at the same time, right?"

"Right," Benvolio says. "So how do we do this? How do we use these weaknesses to stop these two families from fighting?"

You think for a moment, then Ben snaps his fingers. "I have the perfect scheme," he says. "First, you get sentenced to banishment, but then at the last moment the Capulets swoop in and commute your sentence. That'll make the Montagues like the Capulets for sure!"

"Sure, but the Capulets would never do that," you say. "Why would they want to prevent the son of their worst enemy from being banished?"

"BECAUSE," he says, "at the same time, we get some Montague cousin to marry Juliet."

"I see where you're going with this," you say. "But it doesn't work. I only escape banishment if the Capulets like the Montagues, but that only happens if Juliet and a Montague marry, but that only happens if the Montagues like the Capulets, but that only happens if I escape banishment because the Capulets like me."

"Right," Benvolio says. "Montague won't marry Capulet because Montague hates Capulet, and Capulet won't rescue Montague because Capulet hates Montague." He smiles at you. "Geez, Romeo, if only there was some force stronger than hatred to break this stalemate! You know, a force so strong that we'd have no choice but to call it, oh I don't know . . . LOVE??"

"Love," you echo.

"Yes, love! If Juliet and a Montague LOVE each other, they'll want to get married. Nothing will stop them. And that marriage brings the two houses together. Tensions fade, you get banished, the Capulets rescue you, and that just seals the deal! Everyone's happy and peace comes to Verona forever, THE END."

You shrug. "Right, so all we need is a man who Juliet will fall in love with on sight while he, SIMULTANEOUSLY, falls in love with her. How hard could it be, right??"

"Look, we're both classy guys, and she's probably nice. One of us should be the one to go meet her and do his level best to make her fall in love with him. You or me," Benvolio says, "and I nominate you."

"Well I nominate YOU," you say. "I'm in love with Rosaline, remember?"

"Yes, I haven't forgotten," he says. "And you haven't forgotten, Romeo, that there's only ONE way to settle a dispute like this?"

You nod. "I'd expect nothing less," you say.

"Good," Benvolio says. You lock eyes with him, curling your left hand into a fist. His does the same. The air between you crackles.

"Rock paper scissors," you whisper.

Three . . . two . . . one . . .

Choose rock: *turn to 64.*

Choose paper: *turn to 41.*

Choose scissors: *turn to 83.*

55 You make sure nobody is around, then sneak into Capulet Castle. You consider pressing up against an existing wall for your "wall disguise" but realize that even in the best case it'll attract attention because people will wonder why there are two walls back-to-back in that one section of hallway. You're too smart to make THAT beginner's mistake!

Instead you stretch your arms out and up and stand really still, and pose as a new wall, placed directly in the middle of a hallway.

It is a terrible disguise, and when Mr. and Mrs. Capulet discover you standing in their hallway, that's basically what they say before they kill you! Y'all are enemies, remember?

"I thought Romeo was smarter than this," they say as they perform a murder on you, "though, for the life of me, I cannot remember why."

THE END

56 Yeah, this is clearly the wrong choice. You're cleaning a random room, nobody's in it, there are no documents to snoop through, and you're learning nothing.

Clean Mr. and Mrs. Capulet's room; maybe they'll be there: *turn to 89.*

Clean some other random room: *turn to 65.*

57 To your left is a young blond-haired guy and listen, I'm going to cheat and tell you stuff so you can get to know these guys faster. THIS dude's name is Yolo Brewski, and his interests include sports, playing sports, and yelling sports advice at other people playing sports.

FUN FACT: I don't know a lot about sports, so try to imagine I described Yolo's interests in a way that sounds really cool and informed!!

To your right is another young guy, only he's got brown hair and he's named Jaques. But instead of saying it like "Jack" he pronounces it like "Jake Wheeze." Jake Wheeze here is a melancholy guy whose interests include not having fun, interrupting jokes to say, "You know what's really funny? How all our bodies will inevitably betray us as we age," and reading books about why sadness is cool.

FUN FACT: I don't know a lot about melancholia either, because, as an author, my life is totally fun 100% of the time and never sad!!

Who do you want to talk to?

Talk to Yolo Brewski: *turn to 92.*

Talk to Jake Wheeze: *turn to 63.*

58 You enter the party and everyone is wearing masks. This is so dumb. Also, you don't have a mask, so you have to borrow one from the freebie pile. It's a horse mask with a real horsehair mane. You put it on.

You are now dressed as a horse. Your mask's wide-eyed stare greets the partygoers with a perpetually startled expression. You can see through holes in the nostrils. Everyone is looking at you, unsettled. You're not sure what Tom Paris looks like, but hopefully he's totally turned off right now.

You make your way to the dance floor and soon you're dancing, lost in the deafening throb of the aria that fills the air. You start throwing down with some random dudes, and it's actually pretty nice. You're dancing your way through your frustration with your mom and life in general when it happens. You glance out from the dance floor, and magically the crowd seems to part to allow your gaze through. There, at the other end of the ballroom, is the most beautiful man you've ever seen.

You have no idea who he is. He's wearing a unicorn mask, which isn't helping.

You see him glance your way and before you know what you've done you've looked away, blushing. You keep dancing, but you can't focus on anything except this guy. You steal another glance at him, and you almost want to roll your eyes. It's ridiculous how attractive that guy is. It's honestly ridiculous.

And I'll tell you what: I'll make this easy for you. You already know that YOU want to chat this guy up, so . . . what if you played as him, and then made him want to chat you up too?

Dude. You could seduce YOURSELF.

That honestly seems like a real time-saver to me!

Be the hot dude, chat myself up: *turn to 74.*

No, keep being myself, talk to him. I got this: *turn to 68.*

59 A day goes by.

Time passes: *turn to 47.*

60 You choose paper, and Benvolio chooses scissors. The only thing is, he seems to throw his hand down a split second after you.

"Scissors beats paper. Sorry, Romeo," he says, smiling.

"Come on, Ben, you cheated there," you say. "You waited to see what I was gonna throw."

"Romeo, I resent these scurrilous allegations! You lost fair and square. And now you have to go meet Juliet and make her fall in love with you."

He pats you on the back and shoves you in the direction of Capulet Castle.

"Best hop to it, cousin!" he says.

Become aware of the idea dancing at the edge of your consciousness that Benvolio may have set this whole zany scheme up simply to get you to go meet someone who isn't Rosaline, and go see Juliet: *turn to 53.*

He cheated at rock paper scissors!! DESTROY HIM! *Turn to 102.*

61 You and your friends enter the party, and the muffled music from the dance floor is already audible. At the entrance is a table full of masks, and everyone grabs one. Benvolio pulls one of those big-grin

comedy theater masks over his head, Mercutio grabs a black cowl that makes him look like some sort of "bat man," and you grab a rainbow unicorn mask.

You are now dressed as a rainbow unicorn.

As you move forward, you see that Lord Malcolm Capulet is at the end of the entryway, greeting his guests. You've never seen your family's archenemy in person before, and he seems pretty . . . normal? He's just this regular dude trying to be a good host. The three of you walk up to say hello.

Lord Capulet, not recognizing you but trying to make you feel welcome, loudly shouts that you'll have every lady with sexy feet dancing with you tonight. Then he grins and elbows Mercutio and says every woman will want to dance with you three now, because otherwise they'll be admitting their feet are not super sexy and may, in fact, be mad vile.

"Okay cool thanks," you say, and move into the party.

As soon as you enter the ballroom the music swells in your ears. In front of you is a ballroom full of people dancing hard, a whirlwind of bodies moving in time to the intense, block-rocking beats of a lute and harpsichord ensemble. Benvolio and Mercutio are instantly lost among the crowd.

As you look around the dance floor, the aria for strings pounding so loud you can feel it in your chest, you start to feel like anything could happen tonight. It's silly, but you feel like your next action, no matter how small, might forever affect the course of the rest of your life. The world is full of potential, Romeo, and you're just getting started. What'll it be?

Look to your left: *turn to 100.*

 Look to your right: *turn to 116.*

Look behind you: *turn to 80.*

62 You took too much!!

Geez, Romeo! You've been out for days and days, and in that time your friends have discovered your body, held a funeral, and buried you in the ground.

Your greatest fear was to be buried alive, but good news: you would've thirsted to death long before you had a chance to wake up and realize your predicament!

Your second-greatest fear was thirsting to death, but again: no worries! You would've suffocated in this coffin long before any thirst could get you.

Your third-greatest fear was suffocation.

THE END

P.S.: Any points you have earned so far are forfeit and your final score is 0 out of a possible 5000 points, because your only goal in this story was to kiss a lady and you didn't even do that once!

Also you faked your own death SO POORLY that you died, which—and I'm saying this as your friend—definitely didn't help matters.

63 "So, what's your deal?" you ask Jake Wheeze. He looks at you, all sad eyes and stubble, and holds up one hand in front of him.

"All the world's a stage," he says. "And all the men and women merely players: they have their exits and their entrances, and one man in his time plays many parts, his acts being seven ages. At first, the infant—" he begins, and at this point you interrupt him.

"Hey. I'm Juliet," you say, holding out your hand, hoping to direct the conversation elsewhere. "My interests include muscles."

Jake barely pauses as you speak and ignores your outstretched hand. "At first, the infant," he repeats, "mewling and puking in the nurse's arms."

"I'm sexually attracted to men," you say, still holding your hand out, but this time Jake talks right over you. "And then the whining school-boy," he says, "with his satchel and shining morning face, creeping like snail unwillingly to school. And then the lover, sighing like a furnace, with a woeful ballad made to his mistress' eyebrow. Then a soldier, full of strange oaths and bearded like the pard, jealous in honor, sudden and quick in quarrel, seeking the bubble reputation even in the cannon's mouth." At this point, Jake pauses for breath.

"And then?" you ask, despite yourself, still holding your hand out for that handshake.

"And then, the justice," he says, "in fair round belly with good capon lined, with eyes severe and beard of formal cut, full of wise saws and modern instances; and so he plays his part. The sixth age shifts into the lean and slipper'd pantaloon, with spectacles on nose and pouch on side, his youthful hose, well saved, a world too wide for his shrunk shank; and his big manly voice, turning again toward childish treble, pipes and whistles in his sound. Last scene of all, that ends this strange eventful history, is second childishness and mere oblivion, sans teeth, sans eyes, sans taste, sans everything."

"I understood some of those words," you say as you shake your own hand and turn back to your drink. Now Yolo Brewski and his friend are approaching you. You could talk to Yolo, or you could ignore them both.

Talk to Yolo Brewski: *turn to 92.*

Ignore the dudes, drink alone, maybe coming to the Romeo District was a bad idea: *turn to 75.*

64 Benvolio also chooses rock.
"Tie," you say. "Let's go again."
Three . . . two . . . one . . .

Choose rock: *turn to 72.*

Choose paper: *turn to 41.*

Choose scissors: *turn to 83.*

65 Again, you clean an empty room. There's no point. You're just doing maid work for free right now, Romeo.

Maybe you want to go where the action is?

Clean Mr. and Mrs. Capulet's room. Maybe they'll be there, MAYBE they'll definitely 100% be there: *turn to 89.*

Clean some other random room: *turn to 71.*

66 You say, "No water for me, bartender!" as you leave, which wasn't necessary at all, and then jog back to the castle. You've never jogged buzzed before. It's thirsty work!

When you get there, that party your parents were having is in full swing. You're drunk enough not to care, which is great! In fact, you're precisely drunk enough to . . .

Kick everybody out: *turn to 93.*

Puke on yourself and go to bed: *turn to 78.*

67 You choose scissors, and Benvolio chooses rock. The only thing is, he seems to throw his hand down a split second after you.

"Rock beats scissors. Sorry, Romeo," he says, smiling.

"Come on, Ben, you cheated there," you say. "You waited to see what I was gonna throw."

"Romeo, I resent these scurrilous allegations! You lost fair and square. And now you have to go meet Juliet and make her fall in love with you."

He pats you on the back and shoves you in the direction of Capulet Castle.

"Best hop to it, cousin!" he says.

Become aware of the idea dancing at the edge of your consciousness that Benvolio may have set this whole zany scheme up simply to get you to go meet someone who isn't Rosaline, and go see Juliet: *turn to 53.*

He cheated at rock paper scissors!! DESTROY HIM! *Turn to 102.*

68 You walk up to the strange babe in the unicorn mask. You're more nervous than you can remember being. You cup your hands around his ear.

"Hi," you shout. He cups his hands around your ear in return.

"Hi," he shouts back.

You don't know what to do, so you reach down and take his hand.

"If I profane with my unworthiest hand this holy shrine," you shout over the music, "my hands are friggin' mooches. But my lips, two blushing pilgrims, ready stand to smooth that rough touch . . . with smooches."

The man leans in to you to say something.

"I liked how that rhymed," he shouts.

Kiss the boy: *turn to 94.*

Don't kiss him just yet: *turn to 77.*

69 The two of you kiss each other for long enough that I actually start to get a little uncomfortable.

"This is crazy," you say.

"This IS crazy," Juliet agrees. "You want to stop, Romeo Montague?"

"Not on your life, Juliet Capulet," you reply. "I don't want to stop this until the day I die." She looks at you, and you realize what you've said. And you don't care. "You know what?" you say, taking her hands in yours. "That's the truth. Let's get married, Juliet."

"Now THAT'S crazy," she says.

"I'm serious!" you say. "Let's get married. Or at least engaged. We don't have to rush into things if we don't want to, right? We can stay engaged for a while if we want."

"Pfft," Juliet says. "Engagement's for wimps. We need to have the courage of our convictions," she says. "Hey, Romeo. Watch this." And then she opens the door, steps into the room, and pulls you in behind her.

"Mom, Dad," she says, "this is Romeo Montague. We've just got engaged and we're getting married on the ASAP."

They turn to look at you, shocked.

"Sir, ma'am," you say, "I know our families have had their differences in the past, but I—"

Her mother talks over you. "Juliet," she says, "are you serious? Do you really intend to marry this Montague??"

"I do," she says. "I never believed in love at first sight before, but— whoah. Seriously, Mom. It's real, so real. I wouldn't be surprised if

Romeo and I go down as the POSTER CHILDREN for love at first sight after this."

Her parents look at each other.

"This would solve our Montague problem," Juliet's mom says. "He marries into the Capulets, we're both the same family, and bam! allies instead of enemies."

"Do you think the Montagues will see it the same way?" Juliet's dad says.

"Honey, they're not stupid," she replies. "They can see the same advantages we can. This marriage can put an end to almost seventy years of unremitting hostility between our two houses—hostility which, I remind you, BOTH sides can no longer afford."

Juliet's dad seems lost in thought, then he takes your hand in his and shakes it warmly.

"My boy," he says.

You and Juliet are married two weeks later, in front of both your houses. Benvolio is more than happy to serve as your best man.

THE END

Okay, WOW: congratulations, Romeo! You met Juliet, got married SUPER fast, ended the conflict between your two families, AND ate a fun and cool breakfast! Now, who says reading isn't fun??

70 You push open the double doors to the party room. The instant you do, the music comes to a screeching stop mid-note, and everyone turns to look at you. This is your moment!

"Great party you've got here," you say. "It'd be a shame if anyone happened to get beat up during it."

"Who are you to make threats?" someone nearby says, a young man wearing a ridiculous unicorn mask with a rainbow mane. You glance at him. You're too mad right now to be fully aware of how rockin' his bod is, if indeed his bod be rockin', but even through your anger you can tell he's at least pretty good. A solid seven out of ten.

You punch him right in the eye.

"I want everyone to know," the man says, "that this woman outpunches other women like a boxer in the middle of a ring of babies." Then he goes down hard.

You feel a little bad about it, but then you realize he's probably just like those guys in the Romeo District. If you hadn't punched him just now he'd probably have tried some dumb line on you, like "Girl, are you an orphanage, because I want to give you kids," or "Girl, are you a corn plant, because I'm stalking you," or "Girl, are you hearing my soul speak, because the very instant that I saw you did my heart fly to your service."

You look around the room. "You guys want to leave, or should I keep punching?" you shout. You swing your arms like windmills and advance on the party.

"She's drunk!" someone shouts.

"She's awesome," the man you punched whispers.

You kick him as you walk by.

The party clears out pretty quickly, the partygoers moving around you to the door like water around a rock. Pretty soon just your parents remain.

"You too," you say.

"No, Juliet, sweetie, go to bed," your mother says. "I command it."

"Oooh Juliet, go to bed," you say in high-pitched mockery, advancing towards them, your arms still spinning. "Oooh Juliet, don't leave the house ever. Oooh Juliet, be best friends with your childhood nurse because you don't know anyone else! Oooh Juliet, definitely marry this random stranger on a moment's notice!"

Your parents take a step backwards for every step you take forward.

"Well I'm not doing it, okay?" you say. "I'm done. Done with this house, done with your rules, done with you both and your stupid marriage ideas. I'm done, okay? DONE."

Your parents are still moving backwards as you move forward, now adjusting their paths so that they can back out the door. You push them outside.

"And on second thought I'm not done with the house," you say. "I'm gonna keep it." You close the door in their faces. "You guys can live in the gardening shed," you shout through the door. "It's like a three-bedroom gardening shed with a finished basement! YOU'LL BE FINE."

You hear the noise of their shuffling off, and you quickly make a lap of the house, locking all the other doors and ground-level windows. Then you go to bed.

You wake up the next morning feeling great.

You get out of bed, have a quick bath, and get dressed. When you leave your bedroom you notice a lot of the servants are there, wondering why all the doors are locked shut.

"Oh, right," you say, remembering last night. "Right, sorry. I'm the boss now, everybody. You can all come and go as you please. But nobody gets in without my permission, and that includes my parents. They live in the gardening shed now," you say.

You eventually do let your parents in for visits, and things are cordial. They're happy with their simpler retirement living in the shed, you're happy that they don't tell you what to do anymore, and your servants are happy to work for someone who doesn't regularly throw parties that a large percentage of the entire town is invited to. It's surprising how happy everyone is with this new arrangement!

Several years later you run into that dude you punched at the party. Turns out his name literally is Romeo (hilarious), but despite that he's one of the more charming people you've met. You date for several months and both your parents are against it but who cares? Everything's going great until someone new catches his eye and he dumps you overnight.

Glad you didn't rush into that one, huh??

After him you have a series of really satisfying flings with some really satisfying people, and then one day, you meet Cesario. He's not like any of the men you've met before, and while he's definitely not the kind of person you ever thought you'd find yourself falling for, life is for exploring, right?

And that's what the two of you do, together, happily ever after.

THE END

So! You avoided rushing into marriage, you knew to drink water while drinking alcohol to avoid dehydration, and you ended up in one of the few happily-ever-after endings in this whole book! I award you . . . 32,767 points.

Any more and you'd overflow our point counter!

71 Okay, you clean another random room. You're deep in the bowels of Capulet Castle, cleaning rooms you're pretty sure haven't been used in weeks. All the more dust for you to remove, right?

Tell you what, I can see you're really enjoying this. If you clean Mr. and Mrs. Capulet's room I promise you'll get to clean a bunch of other rooms first.

Okay fine, clean Mr. and Mrs. Capulet's room: *turn to 101.*

Clean some other random room: *turn to 95.*

72 Benvolio also chooses rock.

"Another tie!" you say. "Let's go again."

Three . . . two . . . one . . .

Choose rock: *turn to 64.*

Choose paper: *turn to 41.*

Choose scissors: *turn to 83.*

73 Okay, so here's how it goes down. You say it's a bad idea for you to be going to this ball, Mercutio asks why, and you say you had a dream last night. Mercutio says he dreamed too! You ask what his dream was, and he says he dreamed that dreamers often lie.

"You mean they lie in BED, while they dream the truth!" you say. Oh god. Leave the puns to Mercutio, Romeo.

"I see you've been with Queen Mab," Mercutio says.

"Who's Queen Mab?" you ask, which is convenient because I am kinda stumped on this one too.

Mercutio answers you, and he kinda goes on for quite a while. Luckily for you, I've compressed what he said into a handy point-form list:

+ she's a fairy
+ she brings love dreams to people
+ the end

WOW YOU JUST SAVED LIKE TWENTY MINUTES.

Accept that you just saved like twenty minutes: *turn to 90.*

Wait, why would you trust an author about the contents of his own book? Check out Mercutio's speech for yourself. *Turn to 112.*

74 Alright, Juliet, you are now that hot dude! Your name is Romeo and you've just noticed this incredibly hot babe (that's you, Juliet!). Furthermore, you have decided you want to chat up this megababe in the horse mask. Awesome!

Right now she's dancing, and you've decided that as soon as she stops dancing, you're going to walk right over there and try to tell her how fascinating she is. Something tells you she'll be happy to hear from you. Nice! The only question, Romeo, is what will you say?

You briefly consider introducing yourself by holding out your hand and saying, "Hey girl, will you hold this for a moment while I go for a walk?" but something in you shudders intensely and you know that'd actually be a super-terrible idea. Instead, you come up with two other ideas, and you're pretty sure they'll both work equally well! Like, precisely equally well!

Walk up, take her hand in yours, and say, "Hey girl, if I profane with my unworthiest hand this holy shrine, the gentle sin is this: my lips, two blushing pilgrims, ready stand to smooth that rough touch with a tender kiss": *turn to 96.*

Walk up, take her hand in yours, and say, "Hey girl, if you don't like to be touched I can totally kiss you instead": *turn to 96.*

75 You ignore the dudes. They ask you how you're doin', and then they ask you if you know what their shirts are made of, and then they tell you they're made of "boyfriend material," and then they ask you if your daddy is a baker because you've got some hot buns, and then they go away.

When you're done with your drink you order another, and at the end of your fifth you've decided, hey, why are YOU the one running away from home? Your parents are the ones who are freaky marriage-happy weirdos! YOU should be the one kicking THEM out!! Right?

RIGHT??

Right!

So you slam down some money to pay for your beers. You're about to leave when you think, "Hey, whoah, maybe I should actually drink some water before running back home super drunk."

Do you?

Drink the water: *turn to 84.*

Well, actually, water in this time period isn't always the cleanest and is usually drawn from the same sources we put our sewage in. In contrast, the water used in beer has been boiled. And the alcohol in it can kill bacteria, so yeah, I think beer's fine. *Turn to 66.*

76 "Okay Tom," you say. "What do you like?"

"I meant interests in the business sense," he says. "I'm engaged mainly in the mercantile arts, trading mainly in sculpture and the sculpture-adjacent. I have a mature business with few liabilities, great leverage potential, and stable income opportunities. What you need to understand, Jilliet—"

"Juliet," you say.

"Juliet," he says, "what you need to understand is that I have the means to take care of you. As you can see, there are reasons for us to be married."

"I'm only sixteen years old," you say.

"Like I said," he replies as he takes a long sip of his drink, never breaking eye contact, "there are reasons for us to be married."

Ew.

Agree that this sounds like a good idea, and be with Tom Paris: *turn to 115.*

Throw your drink in his face: *turn to 98.*

77 You want to kiss this guy, and you're betting this guy is down to kiss you too, but you don't want to rush things. Also, you don't even know what he looks like, since you're still wearing masks.

You pull off your mask and smile, and he pulls off his. His face is just as attractive as the rest of his body, which is awesome and also a relief. He seems to like what he sees too. This is going great!

"You were mentioning smooches earlier?" he shouts over the music.

Kiss him now: *turn to 104.*

Play hard to get: *turn to 88.*

78 You push open the double doors to the party room. The instant you do, the orchestra stops mid-note, and everyone turns to look at you. This is your moment!

"Hey everyone, I'm back!" you say. "It's me, Juliet!"

Someone coughs.

"Bleh!" you say, throwing up on yourself in one giant load. It takes about thirty seconds. During this time your mother takes her mask off and steps forward to comfort you, but you hold your hand up.

"No. NO. This is what I wanted," you say through a mouthful of vom.

Realizing that today isn't gonna get any better from here on out, you decide to bail on it. You head upstairs, leave your dress in a pukey pile, and go to bed.

Wake up the next morning: *turn to 86.*

79 You choose rock, and Benvolio chooses paper. The only thing is, he seems to throw his hand down a split second after you.

"Paper beats rock. Sorry, Romeo," he says, smiling.

"Come on, Ben, you cheated there," you say. "You waited to see what I was gonna throw."

"Romeo, I resent these scurrilous allegations!" he says. "You lost fair and square. And now you have to go meet Juliet and make her fall in love with you."

He pats you on the back and shoves you in the direction of Capulet Castle.

"Best hop to it, cousin!" he says.

Become aware of the idea dancing at the edge of your consciousness that Benvolio may have set this whole zany scheme up simply to get you to go meet someone who isn't Rosaline, and go see Juliet: *turn to 53.*

He cheated at rock paper scissors!! DESTROY HIM! *Turn to 102.*

80 You look behind yourself and notice a bar and bartender there, right beside the entrance. Dude, holy crap, it's an open bar!

You mosey your way over to the bar. It's a bit quieter here, so you don't need to shout, but your unicorn mask is emboldening you. You lean on the bar in a way you think is cool and pound your hand on the table.

"Bartender! Drink! Gimme drink!!" you shout.

"Here's drink," says the bartender sarcastically, passing you a shot glass full of some dark, enticing liquid.

"I drink to thee," you say, tilting your mask up and throwing it back. Wow, that was actually really good! But the thing is, Romeo, you're not really good at the whole "delayed gratification" thing. When you were a kid, a professor at a local university got a bunch of kids together and put a marshmallow in front of each of them. He said anyone was allowed to eat one marshmallow now, but whoever could wait fifteen minutes would get TWO marshmallows instead.

As soon as he was out of sight you jumped up, gobbled your marshmallow, then pushed all the other kids out of the way so you could cram all their marshmallows into your mouth as quickly as you could. Then you rolled around on the floor holding your belly, and then you threw up.

The research paper that came out of this experiment ended up being titled "What the Heck, This Kid Ate All My Marshmallows: Experimental Techniques Exploring the Cognitive Mechanisms Involved in Delayed Gratification, and This One Weird Kid Who Ruined Them."

I mention this now so that you'll understand when I say the open bar you're at is a whole spectrum of new and exciting marshmallows that make you feel real fun, and within fifteen minutes you're in about the same position you were so many years ago: full of something you shouldn't have put inside your body and ready to spew.

You stagger up from the bar and rejoin the party.

Look drunkenly to your left: *turn to 103.*

Look drunkenly to your right: *turn to 87.*

81 You and Benvolio go to the sword store together. The attractive window display features sharply dressed mannequins using swords for all sorts of purposes: opening up cans, trimming Christmas trees, as wickets in a game of cricket, etc. All the swords look so shiny and new that you instantly toss your old sword over your shoulder in disgust.

"I'm getting a new one too," you say as you go inside. A little bell rings as you open the door. Everything's so cute here!

A woman comes out of the back of the store and smiles at you. "How can I help you?" she asks.

"We're looking for cool new swords," you say. "Um, two of them actually. One for each of us."

"Well, you're in the right place," she says. "What kind of sword do you want, specifically?"

"I don't know," Benvolio says. "I didn't know there was actually more than one kind."

"Oh, there are dozens," she says. "We've got longswords, shortswords, mediumswords, locally sourced basket-hilted swords, the works. It all depends on what you want to do with them." She puts a sword into your hands. You turn it over experimentally. It's nice, I guess!

"What DO you want to do with them?" she asks.

"Duels," you say. "DEATH DUELS."

The woman looks crestfallen. "Oh no, the two of you? Really? But you look like such good friends!"

"Yeah, well, he cheated at rock paper scissors," you say. "You know how it is."

"Listen, boys," the storekeeper says, "if you really want to swordfight each other to death, I can sell you swords for that." She puts a hand on each of your shoulders and smiles. "But I'd really recommend that instead of buying swords, the two of you go outside and figure out if this is what you really want. When you're an old man, do you want to look back on your life and say, 'Hey, remember that time when I was a LITERAL TEENAGER and murdered my friend over A BABY GAME invented for people who can't decide who gets the last piece of cake?'"

"Yes," you say, "that actually sounds awesome."

The shopkeeper sighs. "Well whatever, I lied and I'm not selling you swords," she says. "Get out of here."

She kicks you both out of the store and, once you're out, flips the sign hanging on her door from OPEN to OPEN (NO TEENS THOUGH).

"Maaaaan," you say.

"I know," Benvolio says. "I was totally going to win that fight too."

And since I know you're feeling robbed that you chose the swordfight option and didn't get a swordfight, I've pulled a few strings and have some good news for you! In a few minutes when you both wander off frustrated into the woods, you'll find some sturdy branches perfectly sized for jousting. You'll decide to joust each other to the death instead of swordfighting, and on your first attempt you'll run towards each other at full speed and somehow each manage to impale the other right in the eye! And then the two of you will roll around clutching your face and screaming until you pass out from blood loss and die!

It's just what (I imagine) you wanted!!

THE END

82 "No thanks," you say, getting up. Tom shouts something rude to you as you leave, but you pretend you didn't hear it, and I do the same.

You go back to the party and find your mom. She's sitting at a table with your dad.

"Tom Paris is a psycho," you shout over the music.

"That's just his way," they shout back.

"Pretty sure that doesn't mean he's not a psycho!" you shout as you leave. You return to your room, the muffled sound of string music still audible through three floors of castle, and fall into an angry sleep.

The next morning your mother informs you in no uncertain terms that there will be another party tomorrow night with Tom Paris, and the night after that, and the night after that, and there are going to keep being parties with Tom Paris until you are married to Tom Paris or he's dead, whichever comes first.

"That can be arranged," you say.

"Your marriage? Yeah, that's what we're trying to do here."

"No," you say. "HIS DEATH."

Kill Tom Paris: *turn to 117.*

Haha, what? Don't kill anyone. Just refuse to marry the dude! *Turn to 107.*

83 Benvolio chooses rock. He taps his fist against your fingers.
"Rock smashes scissors," he says. "Rock wins again!"
"FINE," you say. "I'll go chat up Juliet, WHATEVER."

Go make Juliet fall in love with you: *turn to 53.*

84 You order a pitcher of water, chug that back, and jog back to the castle. You've never jogged buzzed before. It's pretty nice!

When you get there, that party your parents were having is in full swing. You're drunk enough not to care, which is great! In fact, you're precisely drunk enough to . . .

Kick everybody out: *turn to 70.*

Puke on yourself and go to bed: *turn to 78.*

85 You make your excuses and leave the lady alone. That lady was hot, but crazy, and the two rules you live by are (a) never press your lips against the lips of crazy and (b) always make irrevocable snap decisions about other humans!

The party eventually ends. Mercutio's already left with someone else, so you and Benvolio walk home alone.

"See, Romeo? I told you you'd meet someone new," he says.

"Yeah, but she was crazy," you say. "I want someone whose MIND is as hot as her BODY, you know?"

"Really," says Benvolio.

"Okay," you concede, "but seriously, two sentences in and she was already talking about me devoting myself to her. Most attractive woman I ever met, but I'm sorry: you start talking marriage too soon and I'm out. And I file 'at the very start of our first conversation' under WAY TOO SOON." You sigh. "She WAS hot though. Dang."

You're close to your house now, so you wish Benvolio good night and go to bed. You didn't meet anyone interesting at the party, but at least you feel like you could love other, non-Rosaline women now!

You spend the next few days crashing other parties, hoping to meet someone who is (a) new, (b) super hot, and (c) not that into commitment. And you do! Her name is Amelia and she is pretty great. You fall for her quickly (AS PER USUAL) and she falls for you just as quickly (A NICE

CHANGE) and she says she likes you but doesn't want to rush into anything serious right away (COOL) but that she'll still kiss you (HAHA PERFECT).

There's just one problem: her full name is Amelia Ameliason, and the Ameliasons have been staunch allies of the Montagues for generations. As soon as your parents get wind of this, they become extremely interested in the two of you getting married right away. Amelia's parents are the same. Worse, actually.

It's impossible to have a normal relationship with someone under these circumstances. After every date your parents ask you how it went and are waaay too interested in the specifics.

"How long did you kiss for?" they ask. "How erotic was the experience? Did you suspect she'd evaluate the experience in the same way?"

It all becomes too much, and the two of you break up—but secretly, so your parents won't find out and become even more annoying trying to get you back together. But it turns out fake dating with parental pressure is even worse than actual dating with parental pressure, so eventually you let slip that you've gone your separate ways, hoping that this will, at last, be the end of it.

It's not.

Everyone insists you get back together right away. Your parents send you little notes of encouragement and pickup lines they think might work. Her parents write love notes addressed to you for her, to send along "just in case." It's ridiculous.

You and Amelia meet in secret and decide the only way out of this is for Amelia to fake her death. That'll end this talk of marriage once and for all! Everyone will think she's dead, they'll put her in the crypt, and then a few days later you'll come by and help bust her out, and she'll be able to start over in a new town somewhere, finally free of her parental meddling. It's the perfect plan!

Or at least it would've been, if both your parents hadn't been so into your marrying her posthumously "as a sign of respect." You barely escape and are forced to run away from home to live in Mantua, a nearby town.

You haven't been there one day before letters from your parents arrive, telling you to marry Amelia before she decays so much that the wedding guests will get uncomfortable. When you sneak back to Verona to rescue Amelia from the crypt, you get there too late: her parents are already there, waiting. And yours are too.

"We'd hoped you'd come here to marry her," all four parents say in unison, their voices calm. "We're glad you did."

Amelia revives, sees how her parents are still pressuring her into marrying you, rolls her eyes while saying, "Oh my god screw this," and stabs herself to death. You do the same. It's the only way out.

Parents, man.

THE END

P.S.: I'm pretty sure they married your corpses to each other anyway—sorry, guys!

86 You wake up the next morning hungover. Your first thought is, "Aw man, did I drop a vom last night?" Your second thought is, "Wait, did dropping voms actually solve my problem??" And it turns out it did! You threw up, you looked unattractive, and the dude your parents wanted you to marry didn't want anything to do with you. Mission successful, Juliet! And it's the perfect passive-aggressive technique to stand up to your parents' controlling ways.

Your parents quickly arrange another party, this time inviting a whole new subset of Verona, and you again ensure that you vomit right in front of everyone. You take careful attention to throw up on whoever they want you to marry this time, who it turns out is one Sir Andrew Aguecheek.

Well. He's Sir Andrew Agooeycheek now.

Your parents keep arranging parties to marry you off, and you keep vomiting on whoever they choose. You eventually get tired of that so you start paying a local boy to puke on people after saying, "This is from Juliet Capulet." It is as effective as it is gross-nasty, which is to say: extremely.

A few years later, you meet someone you don't want to instantly vomit on. His name's Orlando, and he's easygoing and fun and he's actually done what you almost did a few years ago: run away from home. He ran out his front door, right through the Forest of Arden, and only stopped when he reached Verona.

And it doesn't hurt that he's absolutely ripped, and absolutely gorgeous.

The two of you get along really well! He's a terrible poet, but an enthusiastic one, and he tags all the trees in Verona with poetry about you. You walk past a tree one day that has "Her worth, being mounted in the alphabet / through all the world bears Juliet" carved into it. You pass another that reads, "All the fairest pictures a dude can get / Are but black to Juliet." A third reads, "But, O, how wonderful a thing it is to look into happiness through my own eyes! (I'm talking about Juliet here btw)."

It's ridiculous. It's stupid.

You love it.

He joins you in your daily workouts, and it's almost too much of a good thing. Your heart feels like it's going to burst. You marry each other, and you're happy with each other, and later on the two of you save his brother's life by literally wrestling a lion (I PROMISE I'm not making this up).

THE END

P.S.: You wrestled a lion and won, so your final score is "holy crap that's awesome" out of 1000!!

87

You glance to your right and lay eyes on—someone new. She's wearing a mask, but even without it you'd be sure you've never seen her before. You have no idea who she is.

She's the most beautiful woman you've ever seen in your entire life.

As you stare at her, your pupils turn into little hearts, and I'd really like to say that's figurative, Romeo. She's so gorgeous that it takes serious effort for you to tear your gaze away from her and the man she's dancing with. You grab the arm of a passing servant and ask him who that woman is. You don't want to mess this up. You want to sound really classy to anyone who might possibly know her.

This is what you intend to shout into his ear: "What lady is that which doth enrich the hand of yonder knight?"

This is what comes out: "Hey, how come that woman is here? No, I mean, does she have, like, a name?" You pause, then regroup. "I-I want to know that woman??"

The servant takes one look at you and then cups his hands around your ear. "I think you've had enough, sir," he says. He starts to push you towards the doors.

"No, wait!" you shout, breaking out of his grasp and running towards the megababe. "This is really important!" When you reach her you try to say "Hey megababe" but instead of words appalling vomit comes out of your mouth and goes all over her.

Needless to say, bouncers kick you out, and Benvolio and Mercutio carry you home out of some bizarre sense of responsibility. They hold your hair out of your face as you throw up some more on the way home, dump you into bed, and leave.

The next morning you wake up to a knock on your door. Hungover, you open it for a messenger from that hot lady, whose name it turns out is Juliet, saying she never wants to see you again. You've just closed the door to go back to bed when there's a second knock.

This time when you open the door you see a lineup of messengers, extending out past the bend in your driveway. They're all from people who want to make it very clear they never want to see you again. Rosaline is among them. Guess she was at the party too, or at least heard about it!

Dang, Romeo! You messed up big-time, huh??

You decide that since everyone hates you now, your only option is to start over. But moving to a new town is expensive and annoying! So instead, you go to the graveyard, dig up a shallow grave, dress the body in your clothes, and put it in a buggy. Then you get dressed in a barrel held up by suspenders (because the corpse is wearing your only set of clothes) with a cloth bag over your head (because you want to disguise your identity).

You wheel the buggy to the edge of a cliff and start shouting, "Hey, is that Romeo in a buggy??" really loudly until a crowd forms. Then you discreetly push the buggy off a cliff.

"Wow, I really think he's super dead now!!" you say as the buggy and exhumed dead body hit the rocks below. "He might even have been that way for a while, actually!"

The crowd spreads the word that Romeo died, and you're free to start a new life under a new identity. "Romeo" means "from Rome," but since you're actually from Verona, you start going by "Veromeo" instead. But it doesn't really matter because the next day your suspenders break and you get arrested for public nudity, criminal negligence causing public nudity, AND incitement to commit gross public nudity.

Your punishment is four consecutive life sentences (it didn't help that your suspenders broke again during your trial) (thrice) and you go to jail. While imprisoned you fall in love with the jailer's daughter (because of course you do) but she says she'd have to be crazy to fall for you, the weird barrel guy in jail. So she doesn't!

THE END

P.S.: Many years later you die of old age, and soon after that your flesh rots away and reveals . . . a spooky skeleton?

OH MY GOD.

It was living inside you THE WHOLE TIME, Romeo!!

88

"Maybe I was and maybe I wasn't!" you shout to him over the music. "MAYBE saints have hands that pilgrims' hands do touch, and palm to palm is a holy palmers' kiss!"

You finish; he nods, then cups his hands around your ear in return. "Huh?" he shouts.

"I SAID," you reply, "MAYBE saints have hands that pilgrims' hands do touch, and palm to palm is a holy palmers' kiss!"

He nods again, and cups his hands around your ear again.

"OKAY COOL," he shouts.

He clearly has no idea what you're talking about, which actually makes two of us. You're getting nowhere with this, Juliet, and you want to kiss him, and you're pretty sure he wants to kiss you too, so frig! Go ahead and kiss him already!

Kiss him: *turn to 113.*

No, HE has to kiss ME, that's how this works: *turn to 97.*

89

You push open the door of the Capulets' room and step inside, focusing your attention on dusting the mantelpiece near the door. You figure the more you act like a maid, the less you'll look NOT like a maid, which can only help your disguise. Therefore, it's a few seconds later when you manage to glance at the room. You see an older man, Lord Capulet. You see his wife, Lady Capulet. And beside them you see . . .

. . . you see the most beautiful woman you've ever met. You instantly forget all about Rosaline. Juliet is staring at you, her mouth slightly open, like she's shocked too. And Romeo, I like you, so I'm gonna let you in on a little secret. This whole "love at first sight" thing you're feeling right now? She feels EXACTLY the same way.

"I—" you say. "I'm—"

Juliet's parents turn to look at you.

"I, the maid, am going to go clean the room next door," you say, slipping out of the room and into the hallway. You lean against the wall, your eyes closed. It's insane how attractive Juliet is. You didn't know it was POSSIBLE to desire someone so badly.

The door behind you opens, and Juliet steps out. She closes the door behind her and looks at you shyly.

"My name's Juliet," she says. "I'm sorry, but—I couldn't stop looking at you. I've never met a man dressed like you before."

You glance down at your maid's outfit. "Oh, this old thing?" you say. She laughs.

"I'm Romeo," you say. "Listen, I don't normally do whatever this is, but I need to tell you something. Two things, actually." You take a deep breath, drop to one knee, take her hand, and say the bravest thing you've ever said.

"If I profane with my unworthiest hand this holy shrine," you say, "the gentle sin is this: my lips, two blushing pilgrims, ready stand to smooth that rough touch with a tender kiss."

She smiles down at you.

"Hey uh also I'm kinda a Montague," you say.

She gasps and yanks her hand away. She turns to run back into the room but stops with her hand on the door. She's motionless for a few seconds, and then, without turning, she speaks.

"My only love sprung from my only hate," she says, sighing. Her hand hovers above the door handle. Then she turns back, takes your head in her hands, and kisses you hard.

"Though meeting you like this feels much like fate," she whispers between smooches.

Kiss her back: *turn to 69.*

90
Well. Good. Then we're all in agreement.

Anyway you're almost at the party! All you can do now is:

Predict your own demise (1 point): *turn to 99.*

Arrive at the party (100 points): *turn to 61.*

91
"Forget it," you say, "we'll just punch each other to death!"

"That sounds painful," Benvolio says. "I'm not sure if I—" and at this point you punch him right on the chin.

"Friggin' ow!" Benvolio says, clutching his chin. You pop him another one.

"I SAID, friggin' ow!!" he says again, now touching his cheek gingerly. You pop him further ones.

"Alright," Benvolio says. "SO BE IT." And Benvolio unlocks something deep inside himself—if I were to guess, it'd be the frustration of trying to keep the peace in a place like Verona where everyone fights to the death in the street all the time over things like "who bit whose thumbs at whom"—and winds up to attack you with a terrific flurry of blows.

Hmm . . . how best to describe what's about to happen? I guess imagine that a tornado tore through a fist warehouse and scooped up a bunch of fists, and then the tornado parked right beside your head so all the fists kept hitting you in insanely rapid succession. Yeah. Yeah, that's pretty good, actually. If you want a picture of your future, imagine a tornado of fists hitting your human face—forever.

Anyway, turns out this is fatal!

THE END

92

"So, what's your deal?" you ask Yolo Brewski.

"My interests include sports and going to my cabin on Brewski Island! That's where I'm back from today, actually," Yolo says. He sticks out his hand to you. "Hi. I'm Yolo Brewski."

"Juliet Capulet," you say as you shake his hand. "So wow: do you OWN Brewski Island?"

"No, but my parents have this cabin there. We call it Brewski Island because me and my friends go there all the time to party, and when we party we like to drink brewskis. It's pretty great," he says.

"I bet," you say.

"Oh, it is!" he says. "There's only one rule on Brewski Island: take only pictures, and drink only brewskis!" He holds up his glass to you. You cheers him, and you both take a swig of beer.

"By 'take only pictures' I of course mean 'take only drawings, sketches, or perhaps paintings that you paint yourself,'" he says. "Because that's what the word 'picture' means right now."

"Of course," you say, draining the last of your beer.

You chat for about an hour, and it's the exact opposite of what you were running from at home. It's really pleasant. After a while he invites you to come back to his Brew Pad and you think that sounds like a real good idea!

The next morning you're a little surprised at yourself for going home with someone you just met, but you're also pretty sure you like Yolo quite a lot. He's fun! You use most of your money to rent a tiny apartment and then get a job as a personal trainer for knights at a gym a few days later, which allows you to continue renting your apartment, which is great. You've got your own little life going now, Juliet! And a few months after that, you give up your apartment because you and Yolo are moving in together. The two of you date for several years before the relationship ends mutually.

It's sad, and you're sad, but as you reflect on the three wonderful years you shared you begin to realize that relationships can be a success even if they end in a breakup. They have to, right? Otherwise every relationship you've ever had and ever will have will be a failure unless one or both of you DIES, and that's baloney. That's straight-up baloney sandwiches.

Anyway you never do end up marrying anyone, but that has precisely zero bearing on how happy you are!

THE END

P.S.: Oh, guess what? You also become a pirate!!

93 You push open the double doors to the party room. The instant you do, the orchestra stops mid-note, and everyone turns to look at you. This is your moment!

You open your mouth to kick everyone out, but instead of words, vomit comes out!

So gross!! That's what you get for drinking a bunch and then running home and never once taking a drink of water, Juliet!

You vomit again in response to my criticism of your choices just now, which is even grosser!

Okay listen, Juliet. This vomit isn't stopping, like, at all, so you'd better make your exit. You vomit your way up the stairs, change out of your vomit-soaked clothes, vomit on them, and get into bed.

Wake up the next morning: *turn to 86.*

94 You lean in quickly for a kiss, but it's too soon, Juliet! You rushed into things and forgot to take off everyone's masks!

Your giant horse face hits his giant unicorn face, and you've been working on your lats lately so you really slam into him pretty hard. You basically just head-butted him.

"Argh!!" he screams, terribly loud. The music comes to a screeching halt as the man pulls off the mask and you can see his nose is now set at an impossible angle. It's clearly broken.

He's still a looker though.

"Aw geez! My nobe!" he screams as blood pours from his nostrils. "You brope my nobe!!"

"Sorry sorry sorry!!" you say, but it's too late. The man is running from the party. Two other people chase after him, probably his friends. After they watch them leave, the entire party turns their gaze towards you. You're mortified. But then you realize you're still wearing your mask! This is your chance, Juliet!

"Hello everyone. My name is Bianca. Bianca . . . Horse . . . worth. I am new in town, which is why none of you know me. And now I'm leaving town forever, which is why none of you will ever see me again."

A murmur goes through the crowd. It sounds like a murmur of . . . credulous acceptance?

"Well bye," you say, running out of the party.

Once outside, you pull off the stupid horse mask and regroup. You just blew it with that hottie, sure, but nobody knows it was you. You can still pull this off.

You enter the party again, this time grabbing a cat mask but not putting it on. When you get to the dance floor, the musicians haven't resumed playing yet. "Hi everyone, it's me, Juliet!" you announce. "Sorry I'm late. What'd I miss??"

"A horse just head-butted a unicorn!" someone shouts. "This party is awesome!!" With that, the music starts up again, and people start dancing. Your mom pushes through the crowd and grabs your wrist. She pulls you back towards the bar, where it's quieter.

"Juliet," she says, "I want to introduce you to Mr. Tom Paris, Esquire. He's the gentleman I was telling you about." She taps an older man—a much older man—sitting at the bar on the shoulder. "Mr. Paris, this is my daughter, Juliet."

Mr. Paris turns around, pulls up his crappy cutout dog mask that doesn't even fit him right, says he's pleased to meet you, and shakes your hand. You give him the once-over. Here are the results: the dude's at least 50 and dresses like a square from the Middle Ages, which is SUPER uncool, especially since we're in a little something called "the Renaissance" right now. You decide you definitely don't want to marry him. You smile politely at your mother, sit down next to Tom, and ask if maybe she could leave you two alone. She gives you an encouraging look and leaves.

"Tom," you say once she's gone, "I'm not going to marry you." Tom's smile instantly falls from his face. In its place is a hard, calculating look that you're not sure you like.

"Your mother promised you would," he says quietly and evenly. He makes it sound like a threat.

"She's not the boss of me," you say. "She used to be. But tonight I've decided I want to live my own life, and one of the things I want to do in it is not marry strange men I just met."

"Well, get to know me!" he says, his mood instantly changing. Suddenly he's warm again. "Let's go on a date." He quickly signals the bartender and orders two drinks, then turns to you and smiles.

"Ask me about my interests," he says.

Ask him about his interests: *turn to 76.*

Do not ask him about his interests: *turn to 82.*

95

You clean the room. And you know what? You keep cleaning other rooms. It turns out Capulet Castle is big enough and deep enough that there are enough dusty abandoned rooms for you to travel around cleaning rooms every day, and by the time you do finally loop back to where you started, they're dusty again. It's a perfect, endless supply of work. You keep to yourself, staying out of sight, stealing food from the castle galley when you're hungry, and sleeping in a forgotten but now impeccably clean bedroom you've discovered.

I don't claim to understand this, but you don't need my understanding. You've found something that you enjoy doing, that you're good at, and that affords you a comfortable life. Not many of us can say that. So good work, Romeo: you live a long and deeply satisfying life, get to wear some cool clothes, and these forgotten castle rooms have never been tidier.

THE END

96 Amazingly, that works! She smiles and squeezes your hand a little and shouts over the music that you don't give your hand enough credit.

You both pull off your masks. Her face is just as attractive as the rest of her body, which is awesome and also a relief! She seems to like what she sees too. This is going great!

She pulls your hand to her cheek and shouts that by holding her hand you're showing devotion, just like a religious pilgrim would show devotion to their god. And religious pilgrims often touch their hands to statues of saints, so pressing one hand against another is basically like a kiss!

Haha WOW this is your first conversation with her and she's already bringing up religion and being devoted to her eternally. You wanna bail, Romeo?

Shout, "Hah hah right um I'm gonna go over there, bye" into her ear and bail: *turn to 85.*

 No way, this lady is packed and stacked, especially in the back! Keep chatting her up. *Turn to 111.*

97
Fine. No rush, right? You say nothing, and after a few seconds Romeo seems to actually figure out what you were saying.

"HAVE NOT SAINTS LIPS, AND HOLY PALMERS TOO?" he shouts.

"AY, PILGRIM," you shout back, instantly cursing yourself for saying "Ay, pilgrim" in front of a boy you like and wondering where that even came from, "LIPS THAT THEY MUST USE IN PRAYER."

He smiles. "THEN LET LIPS DO WHAT HANDS DO," he shouts.

That's your opening, Juliet!!

Kiss him: *turn to 113.*

No, don't kiss him, stand perfectly motionless so HE can kiss ME: *turn to 141.*

98
You stand up and throw your drink in his face. He's startled but recovers quickly. Without looking at you, he takes a kerchief out of his pocket and dabs his face methodically, then folds it carefully and puts it back in his pocket. Only then does he meet your gaze. "You will live to regret that," he says evenly, a polite smile on his lips.

"Pretty sure I won't," you say. You go back to the party and find your mom. She's sitting at a table with your dad.

"He's a psycho," you shout over the music. "I threw my drink in his face and I'm pretty sure he threatened to kill me."

"That's just his way," they shout back.

"You guys are the worst parents ever in time!" you shout. You storm back to your room, the muffled sound of lutes and harpsichords still audible through three floors of castle, and fall into an angry sleep.

The next morning an envelope is slid under your door. When you open it, a single card falls out. On it is Tom Paris's signature, and a single question above it: "WOULD YOU LIKE TO SPEND AN EVENING . . . IN PARIS?"

Kill Tom Paris: *turn to 117.*

Haha what? Don't kill Paris just because he's bad at being a reasonable man. Just ignore him! *Turn to 107.*

99

You stop walking towards the party and grab Benvolio and Mercutio's arms.

"Guys, I'm worried that a consequence yet hanging in the stars shall expire the term of a despisèd life closed in my breast, perhaps even by some vile forfeit of untimely death!" you say.

"Okay that's great let's keep moving please," says Benvolio, shoving you forward.

And before you know it, you're at the party!

 Arrive at the party: *turn to 61.*

100

You look to your left, and magically, the crowd seems to part to allow your gaze through. There, at the other end of the ballroom, is the most beautiful woman you've ever seen.

Rosaline.

You recognize her despite the fish mask she's wearing, mainly because you've memorized the precise dimensions of her body. You push your way onto the dance floor, grab Benvolio, and bring him back with you. You direct his gaze towards Rosaline, then lean towards his ear. "Told you she was hot," you shout.

"OH MY GOD, LOOK LITERALLY ANYWHERE ELSE," he shouts in reply, cupping his hands around your ear. "Right now we are PHYSICALLY SURROUNDED by babes who want to party. Go talk to any of them, please, Romeo. Just one. PLEASE."

It's good advice. Instead of taking it, you stalk Rosaline for the rest of the party! You peer around a marble column as she helps herself to food from the snack table. You hide under the drinks table as she gets a glass of wine. You press one eye up to the fish tank as she's standing on the other side, horribly distorting your face.

You embarrass yourself and accomplish nothing, and at the end, when she takes off her mask, you realize she wasn't even Rosaline in the first place! She was just some other woman in a fish mask with a similarly rockin' bod!

The party eventually ends. Mercutio's already left with someone else, and Benvolio's too mad at you to walk you home, so you walk home alone.

Well that party was a complete waste of time, wasn't it? You go to bed, cry yourself to sleep, and wake up the next morning having accomplished almost nothing, and feeling like an idiot! You ruined your whole night at that party because you couldn't stop obsessing about Rosaline. Maybe Benvolio was right. Maybe you should try to forget her.

And maybe you know just the guy to help you with that.

Go to Friar Lawrence's house: *turn to 24.*

101 You decide to make your way to Mr. and Mrs. Capulet's room. You clean a bunch of other rooms on your way there, and in doing so you achieve lots of whatever it is you find SO FASCINATING about this cleaning thing. You're super happy about this whole cleaning situation, so I guess I'm happy for you too! Keep it up, buddy!

Arrive at Mr. and Mrs. Capulet's room: *turn to 89.*

102 You turn around. "No," you say. "Not this time, Benvolio. You can't cheat and manipulate me. You're supposed to be my FRIEND."

"I am your friend," he says. "I-I was cheating at rock paper scissors because I was hoping to get you to meet someone new and fall in love with her and forget about Rosaline."

"THAT'S STILL CHEATING AT ROCK PAPER SCISSORS," you say. "And if there's one thing I am strangely hard-line on, it's that everyone who cheats at rock paper scissors must be destroyed."

"Okay," he says. "I guess—I guess we gotta fight to the death now?"

"Yes," you say. "With swords. This is my choice."

"Alright." Benvolio shrugs. "Your funeral."

You get into what you call your "ready for swordfights" position.

"I don't have a sword," Benvolio says. "Um, I think I left it at home."

Go to the sword store with Benvolio: *turn to 81.*

Forget it, just punch each other to death: *turn to 91.*

103 You glance to your left. Rosaline is here! She's so great. You're totally obsessed with her, and in your drunken state you're instantly convinced she wants a surprise hug from behind. And that's the reason why you're currently running up to her and about to jump on her back from behind!

"Rosaline!" you shout as you land on her back, but it comes out as "Rosaleeeppphhh" because you're actually puking down the back of her dress as you talk. She screams and falls forward. When you hit the ground she quickly squirms out of your grasp, slaps you across the face, and runs out of the party. What happens next is kind of a blur, but you're pretty sure bouncers kick you out and Benvolio and Mercutio carry you home out of some bizarre sense of responsibility. They hold your hair out of your face as you throw up some more on the way home, dump you into bed, and then leave.

The next morning you wake up to a knock on your door. Hungover, you open it for a messenger from the woman you puked on—who it turns out wasn't even Rosaline in the first place—who says she never wants to see you again. You've just closed the door to go back to bed when there's a second knock.

This time when you open the door you see a lineup of messengers, extending out past the bend in your driveway. They're all from people at the party who witnessed your becoming a social pariah and who want to make it very clear to you, and to everyone else, that they never want to see you again.

Dang, Romeo! You messed up big-time, huh??

That afternoon, when you've finally made it through all the messengers, you sit and reflect on your life. Sure, your reputation is ruined here in Verona, but there are plenty of other fish in the sea, and by "fish" you mean "towns, villages, or hamlets"!

So you move to Denmark to start over. You end up in this oddly empty town, and when you make your way to the castle at its center you run into one Queen Ophelia, who seems to have taken over after the suspicious deaths of literally everyone else who lived there! Ophelia makes it clear she wants nothing to do with you. She says if she sees you in her town again she'll be forced to murder you. She says she's been getting real good at it.

That night you get drunk and return to the castle to ask her for a date, because obviously you would do that, and true to her word she kills you using some impressive hand-to-hand-combat ninja skills that she's developed over the past several weeks.

Wow! I guess that, in the end, your adventure in Denmark was . . . not to be??

THE END

104 "Yeah, I'd be down with that!" you say. "The kissing!"

"WHAT'S THAT?" he shouts in reply. You cup both hands around his ear.

"I'd be down with that!" you shout over the music.

"YOU'VE COME DOWN WITH WHAT?" he shouts back. You cup your hands around his ear and shout as loud as you can.

"I DON'T NORMALLY DO THIS BUT I WOULD LIKE TO KISS YOU," you shout.

"YOU DON'T NORMALLY POO BLISS BUT YOU WANT TO KISS SHOES??" he shouts in return. "I DON'T UNDERSTAND. THE WORDS I KNOW BUT I'VE NEVER HEARD THEM ARRANGED IN SUCH A WAY BEFORE. I DON'T KNOW IF I'M EVEN PARSING THEM RIGHT."

This is ridiculous. Instead of shouting anything, you place a finger on his lips, as if to shush him. Then you stroke his chin, bring your other hand to his cheek, and kiss him.

Kiss the boy: *turn to 113.*

105 You decide to stab ol' Tommy Paris. You wake up the next morning and loudly shout, "I'M GOING TO STAY IN BED TODAY, EVERYONE NOTICE THIS OKAY??" and then sneak down from your balcony into the kitchen, grab the biggest ol' knife they have, and tiptoe out of the house.

You make your way to Paris's house, where you knock on the door and say, "Hey Tom, I reconsidered and want to marry you now! Can we have some tea to celebrate? I think that'd be really . . . KNIFE??"

"I don't see why not," Tom says. "Though the way you said 'nice' sounds a little like 'knife'?"

"YOU MAY HAVE A POINT," you say, stabbing him with the point of your knife so it's funny.

Tom Paris is now dead! And I don't know what Paris ate back in his living days but it seems to have been, like, red and water? His body behaves like it's this high-pressure container for blood and now that you've put a hole in it, blood is spraying EVERYWHERE. It's on the walls. It's on the ceiling. You're coated in it, Juliet.

Aw gross, some went in your mouth! Juliet! It's still going in! Close your mouth!!

When police show up later they can easily follow the bloody footprints back to your house and arrest you for attempted murder, successful attempted murder, and also for being bad at murder.

"I would've at least washed myself in a stream," one of the cops says.

"I did," you say. "I seriously did." You shrug. "You have NO IDEA how much blood got on me."

You end up getting sentenced to be "hanged from the neck until you be dead," but there are no gallows set up, so your executioner just alters that to "be thrown from a cliff until you be dead."

It takes a few tries, I'll tell you what!

THE END

---

106 You climb into bed, happy that you met such a hunk, but also kinda sad that he's supposed to be your mortal enemy. You hear some noises outside as you're lying in bed—an animal rooting around in the bushes, maybe?—but it's not enough to keep you from sleep.

When you wake up the next morning, you go downstairs and declare to your parents that you've fallen in love with Romeo Montague, and there's nothing they can do to stop you. "I'm going to run away with him," you say, "and I don't care if my parents hate his parents. In fact, that actually makes it kind of better." A new feeling of rebellion runs through you. It feels good.

"Juliet," your mother replies, "you've spoken with him for all of three minutes, and you only know his name secondhand. How much could you really love this guy?"

"Well, I do, so . . . ," you say, unsure how to finish that sentence. "So that's that," you finish weakly.

"Julie, sweetie," your father says, "you don't know him at all. You're attracted to him, and that's great! It's great that you're exploring your new interests as a teen, and in doing so discovering what sexually interests you. I—"

"OH MY GOD, DAD," you say, "I DON'T WANT TO HAVE THIS CONVERSATION WITH YOU, OKAY?"

"Well it's happening," he says. "You're not a little girl anymore, and if you're going to be interested in boys I want to talk to you about the mechanics, risks, and yes, the great pleasures of performing sexual acts with a reproductive partner."

"OH MY GOD WE'RE NOT TALKING ABOUT THIS," you say, clapping your hands over your ears.

"Your father and I perform many sex acts with each other," your mother says. "Often to completion."

"AHHHHHHH," you say.

"It's perfectly natural," your dad says, "but as a sexual being, you do need to know how to do it safely. Now, Juliet, you may have noticed your—"

"IF I STOP SEEING ROMEO CAN THIS CONVERSATION END PLEASE," you say.

"Absolutely!" they say. "Because you won't need to have this talk with us until of course you start hanging out with boys, or more precisely, until we become aware that you are hanging out with boys."

"FINE IT'S A DEAL," you say, running back to your room. Your parents know about Romeo so he's ruined for you forever now, but there are plenty of other fish in the sea. You send a messenger to tell Romeo that you're sorry but you can't see him anymore, and sure enough a few months later you meet someone new: one Harry "Hotspur" Percy. He's a KNIGHT. You have the same visceral, instant attraction to him. Only this time you don't blab to your parents right away!

Since you have no sexual education your first sexual encounter with him is frustrating, confusing, and not exactly fun. And yep, you end up pregnant! You and Percy break up a few months later ("I don't even belong in this place," he says, confusingly) and you never see him again.

You give birth to a wonderful baby girl, whom you name "Juliet Junior" and whom you love fiercely. Life as a single mother obviously isn't the easiest thing in the world to pull off, but all the money and servants you have help quite a bit actually.

You make sure she grows up knowing exactly how, why, and where babies come from, all the same.

THE END

107 You decide to ignore all further communication from Paris. If you see him at a party, you walk in the other direction. If you see him in the street, you cross to the other side. If you see him on a waterslide you say, "Oh wow cool a waterslide," and push him out of the way so you can start enjoying the waterslide right away without him.

Your parents eventually give up on Tom Paris and try to hook you up with a new person, Billy Belgrade, but that goes even worse and you end up throwing both your drink and a plate of spaghetti into his face. Eventually the arranged marriage attempts stop, and you're left on your own. Instead of getting married, you decide to go off to university! You get a degree in kinesiology and a job as a swimming coach. You have a really successful professional life and none of your kids ever drown, which, while a baseline measure of success for a swim coach, is still really satisfying.

I forget if you ever do get married or not, so let's say . . . MAYBE?? In fact, let's say that your choice here depends on whether you, the reader, are or ever get married IN REAL LIFE.

This is awesome! Juliet's love life will now depend entirely on your own. And the only way to choose Juliet's adventure . . . is to choose your own. Go get 'em, tiger!

THE END

P.S: If you marry a woman I guess that means Juliet was into ladies all along; THAT'S COOL TOO.

P.P.S: She might even be poly! Something to think about, huh??

108
You look up to the balcony. A light is on inside!

"But soft! What light through yonder window breaks?" you whisper, holding one hand out in front of you.

A naked old dude steps out from the light onto the balcony. He's smoking a cigar. His naughty bits are dangling in the breeze. Aw gross, I think that's her dad!

"AW GROSS, I THINK THAT'S HER DAD," you say, moving away to investigate another balcony. "NICE WEEN THOUGH."

Might as well examine the only balcony left! *Turn to 121.*

109
You look up to the balcony. A light is on inside!

"But soft! What light through yonder window breaks?" you whisper, holding one hand out in front of you.

A lady in a nightgown steps out from the light onto the balcony, brushing her hair. She's . . . wrinkled? She looks like the woman you met at the party, but like, aged?

"Oh geez I think it's her mom," you say, moving back to investigate another balcony. "PASS."

I guess examine some other balcony, like maybe THE ONLY BALCONY LEFT? *Turn to 121.*

110

"But soft! What light through yonder window breaks?" you ask yourself again. You decide to answer your own question out loud.

"It is the east, and Juliet is the sun," you explain to yourself. You hold out one hand in front of you. "Arise, fair sun, and kill the envious moon, who is already sick and pale with grief, that thou, her maid, art far more fair than she! Be not her maid since she is envious: her vestal livery is but sick and green, and none but fools do wear it. Cast it off!" Classy, Romeo!

At this point Juliet says something, but you can't quite make it out. It seems like she's talking to herself too?

"It is my lady," you go on, staring at her, your one arm still upraised in front of you. "Oh, it is my love. Oh, that she knew she were! She speaks, yet she says nothing. What of that? Her eye discourses. I will answer it!"

You lower your arm and step forward. You suddenly realize that being surprised after dark by a dude trespassing in her garden might not be something she responds well to. You creep back into the bushes.

"I am too bold," you say, raising your arm up again. " 'Tis not to me she speaks. Two of the fairest stars in all the heaven, having some business, do entreat her eyes to twinkle in their spheres till they return. What if her eyes were there, they in her head? The brightness of her cheek would shame those stars as daylight doth a lamp. Her eye in heaven would through the airy region stream so bright that birds would sing and think it were not night."

Juliet leans, resting her cheek in her hand.

"See how she leans her cheek upon her hand," you say to yourself. "Oh, that I were a glove upon that hand that I might touch that cheek!"

Actually wish to be a glove upon that hand: *turn to 157.*

 Keep staring at her: *turn to 142.*

111 The music here is so loud. You raise your voice even more to be heard over it.

"UM, DON'T RELIGIOUS PILGRIMS HAVE, LIKE, LIPS TOO?" you shout over the noise.

"SURE," the woman shouts back. "LIPS THEY'RE FORCED TO USE ONLY IN PRAYER."

"OH. THEN MAYBE YOU'LL LET MY LIPS DO WHAT HANDS DO, IN THIS METAPHOR WE'VE CONSTRUCTED? CAN I . . . CAN I KISS YOU?"

She looks at you, a small smile on her lips. You cup both hands around her ear.

"I PRAY THEE, PLEASE GRANT MY REQUEST," you shout, smiling, "BEFORE THIS PILGRIM'S FAITH TURNS INTO DESPAIR." She smiles a little more, like you're missing something. She holds your gaze for a long moment.

"SAINTS DON'T MOVE, EVEN WHEN THEY'RE GRANTING PRAYERS," she hollers.

"THEN DON'T MOVE," you shout. "BECAUSE I'M ABOUT TO MAKE MY PRAYER COME TRUE." And then you kiss her.

She kisses back. Hard.

You pull back and whisper in her ear, "Your lips have purged the sin from mine," and yeah it's a weird thing to say, but it works in the moment.

"Then my lips have your sin now?" she whispers back. At last, you're close enough to hear her without shouting.

"I guess so," you say, your lips brushing hers.

"Well you'd better take it back," she breathes.

And then you're kissing again.

 Somewhere, a clock chimes midnight: *turn to 120.*

112 Haha OKAY HAVE FUN, CHUCKLES.

So you've asked Mercutio about Queen Mab. In response, he holds out one hand in front of him and begins to talk in, swear to God, improvised iambic pentameter:

> *She is the fairies' midwife, and she comes*
> *In shape no bigger than an agate stone*
> *On the forefinger of an alderman,*
> *Drawn with a team of little atomi*
> *Over men's noses as they lie asleep.*

Her wagon spokes made of long spinners' legs,
The cover of the wings of grasshoppers,
Her traces of the smallest spider's web,
Her collars of the moonshine's watery beams,
Her whip of cricket's bone, the lash of film,
Her wagoner a small gray-coated gnat,
Not half so big as a round little worm
Pricked from the lazy finger of a maid.
Her chariot is an empty hazelnut
Made by the joiner squirrel or old grub,
Time out o' mind the fairies' coachmakers.
And in this state she gallops night by night
Through lovers' brains, and then they dream of love;
On courtiers' knees, that dream on curtsies straight;
O'er lawyers' fingers, who straight dream on fees;
O'er ladies' lips, who straight on kisses dream,
Which oft the angry Mab with blisters plagues,
Because their breaths with sweetmeats tainted are.
Sometime she gallops o'er a courtier's nose,
And then dreams he of smelling out a suit.
And sometime comes she with a tithe-pig's tail
Tickling a parson's nose as he lies asleep,
Then he dreams of another benefice.
Sometime she driveth o'er a soldier's neck,
And then dreams he of cutting foreign throats,
Of breaches, ambuscadoes, Spanish blades,
Of healths five fathom deep, and then anon
Drums in his ear, at which he starts and wakes,
And being thus frighted swears a prayer or two
And sleeps again. This is that very Mab
That plaits the manes of horses in the night
And bakes the elflocks in foul sluttish hairs,
Which once untangled, much misfortune bodes.
This is the hag, when maids lie on their backs,
That presses them and learns them first to bear,
Making them women of good carriage.
This is she—

—and this is the point where I literally force you to say, "Enough, enough, Mercutio, enough! You're talkin' garbage!" and HOORAY, WE CAN ALL MOVE FORWARD WITH THIS STORY NOW.

Now we can finally get to the party, which is already SUPER DELAYED. Seriously, we're already neck-deep in this story and you haven't even met Juliet yet! What are you even doing? She's the other person whose name is in the title; PROBABLY she's pretty important??

At this point you can make your way to the party, OR, for some reason, you can delay just a little bit longer to predict your own death!

 Predict your own demise (−10 points): ***turn to 99.***

Arrive at the party (only 50 points now, that's what you get for delaying): ***turn to 61.***

113
You kiss him. He kisses back. Hard.

You pull back and he whispers into your ear, "Your lips have purged the sin from mine," and yeah it's a weird thing to say, but it works in the moment.

"Then my lips have your sin now?" you ask. At last, you're close enough to hear her without shouting.

"I guess so," he says, his lips brushing yours.

"Well you'd better take it back," you breathe.

And then you're kissing again.

Somewhere, a clock chimes midnight: ***turn to 120.***

114
"O Romeo," you sigh, then raise your arm out in front of you. "Romeo! Wherefore art thou Romeo? Deny thy father and refuse thy name. Or, if thou wilt not, be but sworn my love, and I'll no longer be a Capulet!"

Something shifts in the bushes below. Probably a raccoon. Nothing to worry about.

" 'Tis but thy name that is my enemy," you reason. "Thou art thyself, though not a Montague. What's Montague? It is nor hand, nor foot, nor arm, nor face, nor—"

You look around to make sure nobody is listening in. The coast is clear!

". . . nor any other part belonging to a man," you whisper.

Nice!!

"O, be some other name!" you cry, straightening up and pacing back and forth. "What's in a name? That which we call a rose by any other word would smell as sweet."

I want to mention calling them "Grossweed Stankblossoms" here, but that'll kill the mood, so let's just proceed.

"So Romeo would," you say, "were he not Romeo called, retain that dear perfection which he owes without that title. Romeo, doff thy name, and for that name, which is no part of thee, take all myself."

Suddenly, a dark shape steps out of the bushes beneath your balcony. "I take thee at thy word," the shadowy man says, his hand raised up towards you. "Call me but love, and I'll be new baptized. Henceforth I never will be Romeo!"

Whoah, what the hell? What man art that thus bescreen'd in night, so stumblest on your counsel??

"Whoah, what the hell?!" you shout, startled. "WHAT MAN ART THAT THUS BESCREEN'D IN NIGHT, SO STUMBLEST ON MY COUNSEL??"

Call for your parents to help: *turn to 153.*

No, it's fine. Instantly calm down and chat up this strange man instead. *Turn to 163.*

115

"Tom Paris, I have considered this matter, and upon inspection I believe I was waiting for an older man to come into my life and purchase me," you say. "Yep! That's what I want!"

"Good, good," Tom says. "Well, that's this matter closed. We'll have the marriage this week, and you'll move in that night. I'm expecting a return on my investment within nine months, Juliet."

"Can't wait!" you say, and give him a thumbs-up.

And that's how it goes. Nine months later you give birth to an unpredictable combination of your and Tom's genetic code, which soon begins to suck nourishment out of your body via your chest.

Ah yes: motherhood. It's what you wanted!

THE END

116 You look to your right, and magically, the crowd seems to part to allow your gaze through. There, at the other end of the ballroom, is the most beautiful woman you've ever seen. You have no idea who she is. She's wearing a horse mask, so you can't see her face, but her body is really cool and neat.

You grab a passing servant by the hand, and just as you're about to say, "Hey, who IS that chiseled ultrababe?" you realize there's a chance this person might know her, so instead you try to sound as classy as you can.

"Excuse me, sir! Uh, what lady is that which doth enrich the hand of yonder knight?" you shout into the servant's ear.

"Dunno," the servant shouts in reply, pulling his hand free from yours.

"Oh wow, she's so hot! SO HOT," you shout. "In fact," you say as you cup one hand around the servant's ear while holding the other one out in front of you, "her beauty's too rich for use, for earth too dear. So shows a snowy dove trooping with crows, as yonder lady o'er her fellows shows. The measure done, I'll watch her place of stand, and, touching hers, make blessèd my rude hand. Did my heart love till now? Forswear it, sight! For I ne'er saw true beauty till this night."

"Okay," the servant shouts in reply. "I still don't know who she is."

You lean back against a marble pillar to watch this woman dance. You feel like you're in a trance: your whole body feels hot. Your face is flushed. Your ears are burning. You are now obsessed with this woman!

You help yourself to a drink of cold water to calm down and promise yourself that when this dance ends, you're going to talk to her. You're going to do this, Romeo. You're going to go hit on this stranger.

Hey, along those lines, I've got some good news: this song is actually going to end in a little under six seconds, and then the band is going on break! So that's great, right? You'll actually be able to talk to her!

You start to panic, thinking a few seconds isn't enough time to think of what to say. You can't think! You can't think of a single thing to say!!

I try to calm you down, but it's no good: you're still panicking. You're looking around wildly, trying to find inspiration. How many seconds have you burned through already? How many seconds are left??

ROMEO, listen to me! Here's a secret: you can take your time with your choice here. There's no rush! Keep this between you and me, but I programmed the book such that Juliet will keep dancing until you decide what to say, and then the second you do, she'll stop dancing and respond. It's a little unrealistic, but it does save us from having to go through pages and pages of waiting until this song ends!

You thank me for giving you this straight talk and agree that your suspension of disbelief is done willingly!!

Alright, Romeo. It's all up to you now. Here are your top three options—and just between you and me, two of them will get the same result, and one will get a different one. BUT WHICH IS WHICH??

Walk up, hold out your hand, and say, "Hey girl, would you hold this for me while I go for a walk?" *Turn to 123.*

Walk up, take her hand in yours, and say, "Hey girl, if I profane with my unworthiest hand this holy shrine, the gentle sin is this: my lips, two blushing pilgrims, ready stand to smooth that rough touch with a tender kiss": *turn to 96.*

No need for that pilgrim talk! Just walk up, take her hand in yours, and say, "Hey girl, if you don't like holding hands I can totally kiss you instead." *Turn to 96.*

117 Alright! How?

Poison him: *turn to 145.*

Stab him: *turn to 105.*

118 Juliet sighs loudly. "Aw dangs," she mutters. You can't tell what she's talking about.

"Say it again!" you say. "You look glorious tonight. Like an angel, basically! You're an angel flying high above me, and all I can do is lie down on the grass and stare at you."

She can't hear you, dude. You know that, right? And that's good, because she's just started talking again and she's talking about you!

"Oh, Romeo," she sighs. "Romeo. Why do you have to be a Romeo? Change your dang name. Or I could change mine. Either works, and both would solve our problem."

You ask yourself (out loud for some reason) if you should keep spying on this woman you just met. You decide you definitely should.

"It's just your stupid name that's the problem," she reasons. "You'd still be yourself even if you stopped being a Montague. What even IS a Montague anyway? There's nothing intrinsically Montague to a Montague hand, or Montague foot, or Montague arm, or Montague face, or Montague—"

Juliet looks around to make sure nobody is listening in.

". . . Montague peener," she whispers.

"Anyway," she says, straightening up and pacing back and forth on the balcony, "take some other name! Names are dumb. Roses would smell just as nice if we called them 'Grossweed Stankblossoms, the Hideous Toxic Plants That Are Worse Than Dog Farts, You Don't Even Know.'"

She pauses, considering her own words. She seems to conclude that what she just said was an accurate statement.

"So in conclusion, Romeo," she says, "trade in your name, which I remind you really has no intrinsic value, and I'll give you ME in exchange."

"Okay, that actually sounds really cool to me!" you say, stepping out from the bushes.

"WHOAH, WHAT THE HELL?" Juliet shouts, startled and freaking out. "Mom! Dad! THERE'S A STRANGE DUDE HERE HIDING IN DARKNESS AND SPYING ON ME!!"

Haha wow who could've predicted hiding in the bushes outside the house of someone you just met would go really poorly? If you don't want to get arrested here, Romeo, I think your only option is to be Juliet for a bit and decide to calm yourself down!

Be Juliet for a bit, decide to calm down: *turn to 163.*

Hide in the bushes; nobody will ever think to look for a creepy man in the bushes: *turn to 150.*

119
You look up to the balcony. A light is on inside!

"But soft! What light through yonder window breaks?" you whisper, holding one hand out in front of you.

A lady in a nightgown steps out from the light onto the balcony, brushing her hair. She's . . . wrinkled? She looks like the woman you met at the party, but like, aged?

"Oh geez I think it's her mom," you say, moving back to investigate another balcony. "PASS."

Examine that wood balcony: *turn to 108.*

Examine some other balcony instead: *turn to 167.*

Continue as the boy: *turn to 148.*

Continue as the girl: *turn to 154.*

121 You look up to the balcony. A light is on inside! "But soft!" you whisper. "What light through yonder window br—"

Just then, the light inside goes out. Clearly whoever was inside has gone to bed for the night.

"Aw poots," you say. "It was a candle, but Juliet's gone to bed now. Well, that's the end of that."

You are pretty sure that this is Party Babe Capulet's balcony though, so you start climbing up the outside of the building. You're going to surprise her in her darkened bedroom with a kiss! That's totally reasonable behavior for someone who just met her!

You've climbed only a few feet up when you're hit on the head from behind. When you come to, you're moving through the forest, carried above someone's head like a log. You look down, and Naked Old Man Capulet is the one carrying you as he runs. He notices that you're awake.

"Saw you creeping around in the bushes. Kept an eye on you. Was waiting for you to make your move and climb up," he says. Your eyes travel down a little lower on his frame, and Mr. Capulet notices. "Had to go attack you right away, no time to get dressed," he explains.

"C'mon man, I just wanted to kiss her," you say. "Hey, we met at your party. I'm Romeo, remember? The son of your most hated enemy?"

"I remember," he says, and hits you on the head again.

When you come to, you're still being carried by Naked Old Man Capulet, but now you're out of the forest and entering a clearing. You struggle, trying to free yourself from his grasp, but it's no good. This dude is kinda ripped.

"You're really strong," you say. "Just like your hot daughter!"

"See this is the reason I'm really happy that I'm about to throw you off the cliff I've been running towards for the past fifteen minutes," he says. Then he grabs you by the feet, spins you around a few times to gain momentum, and sends you flying off the cliff.

"I regret only my inability to get with your hot muscley daughter!!" you say as you fly over the edge, and that's what they paraphrase on your gravestone.

"Here Lies Romeo Montague," it reads. "'My One Regret Is I Never Made It with More Babes.'"

Your gravestone keeps getting stolen by teens because honestly, it's pretty amazing.

THE END

122 "Hey guess what? My love for you is as boundless as the sea, and twice as deep," you say.

"Cool!" he says. "Mine too." Just then you hear Angelica calling for you. Perfect timing. You tell Romeo not to go anywhere, run back into your room, and open the door for Angelica.

"I'M SLEEPING, GOTTA GET BACK TO IT NOW, LATER, ANGELICA," you say, then close the door on her before she can get a word in edgewise. You run back out to the balcony. "Okay seriously, three words and then it's good night for real this time," you say. You pause for a moment, trying to compress that relatively complex sentiment down to three words.

"Marry now, please," you say. Just then, you hear your nurse calling for you. "Oh my god, just a second, a thousand times good night," you say, and rush back indoors. "I'M STILL FAST ASLEEP AND I SHOULD REALLY GET BACK TO BED FOR IT, LATER," you say, then close the door on her again.

You go back out to the balcony. Romeo was about to leave, but you call him back. "Nurses," you say, rolling your eyes. "Anyway, listen, I'm trapped here so we can't get married right away, but I'll send my nurse as a messenger tomorrow, cool? Incidentally, if I could, I'd make it so the goddess Echo repeated 'My Romeo' until she was more hoarse than me."

"Neat," Romeo says.

"What time should I send her tomorrow?" you ask.

"Wait, hold on," Romeo says. "It's past midnight. Do you mean tomorrow as in Tuesday, or tomorrow as in today?"

"Oh," you say. "Monday. Today. Let's get married today," you say.

"Okay," Romeo says. "On weekdays I'm normally up around eight, eight thirty, so any time after nine is good."

After working out these logistics, the two of you spend what turns out to be a really long while telling each other how much you love each other until it's almost morning.

"Whoa, it's almost morning," you say. "I'd let you go, but I'm like a kid with a bird tied to a string who keeps monstrously pulling her back whenever she tries to escape."

"I wish I were your bird," Romeo says.

"I'd literally pet you to death," you say, smiling and shrugging. "Anyway, good night! Parting is such sweet sorrow that I shall say good night till it be morrow!"

"Right back atcha!" Romeo says.

You go to bed and toss and turn, too excited for sleep, until finally it's late enough in the morning that Angelica should've shown up for work by now. You put on a fresh change of clothes and rush downstairs, trying to find your nurse. You locate her in the nursery.

"Angelica, can you do me a favor?" you ask. "I got engaged last night to someone that I just met. Can you find Romeo Montague and tell him that even though it's already been several hours since I last saw him, I'm STILL not having second thoughts and want to get married right away?"

"Ah, young love," your nurse sighs happily. "I will absolutely do this! Only son of your family's greatest enemy, right?"

"Right," you say. "Great. I said I'd call for him at nine, and it's eight thirty now, so you should probably leave now so you can get him by then. I will wait for your return!"

"I think this is a really good idea!" she says, rushing out the door.

You slam down a protein shake for breakfast and go to the gym. Nothing to do but wait now!

Work out to pass the time: *turn to 169.*

 Instead of waiting, be Romeo! I'll make sure to find the nurse and get this whole situation taken care of pronto! *Turn to 178.*

Instead of waiting, be the nurse! I'll get this whole situation taken care of, and ALSO, please make the nurse's adventures into this whole separate sidequest thing. *Turn to 217.*

123 Surprisingly, that amazing line somehow fails to deploy properly!

"I'd rather stay here and party, even if this party is infested with strangers who think it's a good idea to introduce themselves by asking me for a favor," the woman says, pulling her hand back.

"Um, what's your name?" you say.

"Juliet," she says.

"I'm Romeo," you say.

"It was nice to meet you, Romeo," she says, spinning on her heel and returning to the dance floor.

You blew it, dogg! You go home and go to sleep, sad that you've fallen for two women in a row who don't even want to kiss on you. You cry a little; I'm not gonna lie. And you wake up feeling like an idiot. Once again you've gotten instantly obsessed with someone and once again it didn't work out.

"Man, forget her and her hot body!" you tell yourself in the mirror. "I'm sticking with Rosaline. After all, better the hot body you know than the hot body you don't!" you say, smoothly updating a famous proverb about devils so it applies to sweet babes instead.

You are now obsessed with Rosaline again. She still wants nothing to do with you, dude!

"I'd be happier if only I could just forget Rosaline," you mutter. "If only—IF ONLY—I could take a drink of something and all my emotional problems would be solved!"

Just then, you remember that there might actually be a way to make that happen!

Go to Friar Lawrence's house: *turn to 24.*

124 You check out the sweet cover, then turn the page . . .

You are Robin "Puck" Goodfellow, a fairy! Exciting, right? You are a tiny person with wings who could be killed by a flyswatter, but on the plus side, you can fly and have spooky magical powers. You are a shrewd and knavish sprite, which is to say, you can be a bit of a jerk sometimes but at least you have fun doing it.

You have a job working for your boss, Oberon. He's the king of the fairies. He and his wife, Titania, are estranged, because Titania stole someone else's baby. That's not what Oberon's mad about, though: he wants the baby for himself so he can raise it to be his henchman. Titania is against that and wants to raise the stolen baby herself.

Your boss and his wife are awful people! They're even jerkier than you are!

You're standing outside your boss's office, where scant minutes ago, your boss gave you a mission. He wants you to:

- invent a love potion
- make it so that when the potion is applied to the eyelids of a sleeping person they'll fall in love with the first person they see when they wake up
- and apply it to his wife because she sleeps in the woods so this way she'll wake up and fall in love with a woodland animal and then when he negates the love potion's effects she'll be so embarrassed that she'll give him the baby

You're trying to decide what you should do. Should you go along with your boss's crazy scheme, or should you refuse to help him with his personal life, which isn't even part of your job description anyway?

Oh! And I should tell you it's dusk in the middle of summer right now, so this is the eponymous midsummer night's choice you were waiting for. Right here on the first page! Talk about a book that hits the ground running!

Oh! I should also hint that maybe dying in this book carries terrible, real-life consequences, which is hilarious from my perspective, because basically every second option here kills you. So, consider yourself hinted, Puck! Now, what's it gonna be?

Tell your boss this is a stupid scheme and you're not going to drug his wife so that he can steal a child: *turn to 128.*

Whatever, go invent a love potion: *turn to 127.*

125
You're about to give up when you decide to search in the meadow one last time. And guess what: you come across two humans sleeping, a boy and a girl. They're sleeping apart so clearly this is a good place for a love potion to intervene!

You stick some potion on the human dude's eyelids and return to Oberon. On the way back you run into another human and you turn him into a half-man half-donkey hybrid because hah hah hah why not.

Oberon is happy to see you: your potion worked perfectly on his wife, and she's now fallen in love with what Oberon describes as a "half-man half-donkey hybrid." You are pleased that your capriciousness has paid off so quickly.

Just then, two humans come by: they're the ones you saw earlier! But they're fighting with each other.

"Puck," Oberon says, "I know your potion works because I used it on my wife. Are you SURE you dosed the right humans?"

"I have absolutely no idea if I did," you say. "I dosed him simply because he was wearing Athenian clothes. As we are in a forest OUTSIDE ATHENS, I'd actually say there are pretty good odds this isn't the right guy."

"Right," Oberon says. "Alright, well, the only way to correct a love potion incident is with another love potion incident. Go find the right guy and dose him this time."

"Won't that result in two human men fighting each other over the same human woman?"

"HOW SHOULD I KNOW?" Oberon says, annoyed. "Are humans monogamous? MAYBE?? But maybe they're not, and maybe I'm getting tired of talking about human social structures. Dose him and let me know!"

You return to the forest, search some more, and finally find another sleeping human man to drug. There, now he's drugged! This will definitely solve your problems forever!

Unfortunately, the human man is woken up by the noise of the other two humans arguing, and he sees the woman first, so now BOTH drugged human men like the same human woman and they want to fight about it. And the human women are fighting too, each thinking the other is behind this somehow.

You have messed this up but good, Puck!

It was a mistake to try to solve my problems with drugs in the first place, separate everyone and restore them back to normal: *turn to 130.*

Man this is taking forever and I'm getting nowhere, just convert the potion to an aerosol and spray it across the entire forest: *turn to 133.*

126
You decide that one more test is required and apply your potion to your own eyelids. You close your eyes, spin around, and get back up again.

The first thing you see is a cloud! It's the most beautiful cloud you've ever seen. You follow its shadow across the grass and trace its path across the forest floor. Soon you're in a part of the forest you don't recognize, lost. And as you watch, your beloved cloud begins to dissipate. You try to fly up to it, but it's too far away, and as you watch, your beloved dies and there's not a single thing you can do. Nothing has ever hurt you so much, and nothing will again. You know you'll never be able to love another person, place, or thing as much as you loved that cloud.

You sink into a deep depression, never trying to find your way back, withdrawing from life and spending most of your time inside a dark and smelly hole in the base of a tree. You become weird and unsocialized. The local kids soon tell stories about Ol' Mr. Goodfellow, and dare each other to come up and knock on your door.

You die a few years later a deeply sad, deeply broken old-man fairy.

On the plus side, dude, your potion worked really well! AND YET LOOK AT THESE TRAGIC CONSEQUENCES, IF ONLY THERE WAS A MORAL HERE HUH??

The End

P.S.: In real life you don't die a deeply sad, deeply broken old-man fairy. Instead, you die as a young human with his whole life still ahead of him! That's even MORE tragic!

Sheesh!!

127
Sure, why not? Inventing a love potion is no big deal for you, thanks to your +1 shrewdness and +2 knavishness perks.

You decide to use a flower called "love-in-idleness"[1] as your base: its milk-white petals turn purple when struck by one of Cupid's arrows, who by the way is real in this story. Anyway this makes harvesting the affected flowers really easy, especially since Cupid got bored with mortals and started a fruitless regime of trying to make flowers fall in love with each other.

You harvest some flowers, fly them home, and grind them up into a paste, which you cut with water. Tada! For good measure, you pour your slurry into a heart-shaped jar. There: that's DEFINITELY a love potion.

---

1 ASIDE TO EDUCATORS—TEENS, DON'T READ THIS: don't worry, these flowers aren't really drugs in real life and if you see teens trying to ingest them, all that tells you is that you are looking at stupid teens.

The only question is, do you test it out first, or do you bring this potion to Oberon untested?

Test it out: *turn to 132.*

I'm sure it's fine: *turn to 136.*

128

You go back into Oberon's office and tell him you won't do it. Oberon flies into a rage. "Are you suggesting," he says, "that drugging people without their consent is somehow OBJECTIVELY TERRIBLE??"

"Yes," you say.

"And are you suggesting," Oberon shouts, again really angrily, "that you know drugs are bad and didn't need a book to illustrate it for you, much less one where if you die in the book you die in real life??"

"Yeah, I think so," you say.

"NOPE NICE TRY BUT OBVIOUSLY YOU HAVE BEEN FED THOSE LINES AND ARE JUST TRYING TO GET OUT OF LEARNING A COOL LESSON ABOUT DRUGS," Oberon shouts, and then he bites off your head. Fairies have mouths crammed full of way too many sharp little teeth, did you know that? Sorry, I really should've mentioned this sooner! They're just vicious little beasts. Monsters, really.

Anyway, you are a dead body now! You're out of luck, Puck!

P.S.: Oh, also, you died in real life too of unrelated acute total body failure.
P.P.S.: Surprise??

The End

129 You produce a new version of your potion, less dilute, and sit down across from your sandwich again. You put a dab of it on each of your eyes and stare at your sandwich.

After a moment, you write down some notes, which read:

WHAT I WANT:

- to do activities with this sandwich
- to share a meal in a group with this sandwich
- i would NOT forget this sandwich's birthday

Better! You label this bottle "Let's Hang Out Sometime Potion" and turn your attention to producing an even more concentrated version. You then dose yourself again, and this time, you find yourself big into your sandwich. Your notes read as follows:

WHAT I WANT:

- to kiss this sandwich!!!!
- i want this sandwich inside me via my mouth (eating)!!
- i will possess this sandwich, digest its essence, turn its best parts into my very flesh and organs!!!

PERFECT. You label this potion "Puck's Love Potion DO NOT DRINK / APPLY TO EYELIDS," slip it into your pocket, cram the sandwich into your face, sigh contentedly, and return to your boss.

Return to Oberon: *turn to 135.*

What if . . . what if I drank it and/or applied it to my eyelids though? *Turn to 126.*

130 Yes! YES, this is the lesson we were trying to teach you the whole time. YOU CAN'T SOLVE ALL YOUR PROBLEMS WITH HOMEMADE EXPERIMENTAL DRUGS. It's a lesson that seems really obvious in retrospect, but apparently you needed to learn it. Remember: the only good drugs are serotonin and dopamine, and then ONLY if they squirt out of your organs naturally!

Now unfortunately for the moral we're trying to convey here, the only way to solve this PARTICULAR problem is with more homemade experimental drugs. You rush home to make a "reverse the effect of the previous potion" potion, then return to the forest, dose all the humans there, and apply it to Titania, too, for good measure. As you're doing so your boss, Oberon, shows up, and surprisingly, he's happy to see you doing this!

"I already confronted her about sexing up that half-man half-donkey thing," he says. "Made fun of her for hours as she was looking for presents for him. She begged me to leave her alone, and I said I'd do it if she gave me the child. Titania went for it! So we're done here. Your reversal potion makes the people affected think it was just a dream, right?"

"Right," you say.

"Perfect," Oberon says. "The perfect crime."

"Um, she's eventually gonna notice her kid is missing and living with you though," you say.

"DOESN'T MATTER, I GOT THE KID," Oberon says, and leaves.

Your jerky boss got what he wanted after all! You wisely conclude that even if you have the absolute best of intentions, drugs can still lead to bad things happening. You're about to conclude that hey, wait a minute, that conclusion ALSO applies to pretty much every single thing in the entire universe, but at that point I cut you off and say nevermind that because guess what, Puck! You won this book!

Hooray!!

The humans are going home and along with them goes the formerly half-donkey dude—you turned him back to normal too. This "dream" has inspired him to write a book about star-crossed lovers! Well, less a "book" and more a "four-page minicomic." It's called *The Most Lamentable Comedy and Most Cruel Death of Pyramus and/or Thisbe.*

Do you want to read it? It's included for free in this book as a special bonus, to make learning fun!

I guess: *turn to 138.*

No, I'm good, I think I'm done here, let's just end this: *turn to 396.*

131

See? YOU SEE WHAT HAPPENS?? You started "experimenting" with drugs at the start of this and now, barely six choices later, you already want to commit the murder crime. And committing the murder crime on someone is one of the worst crimes you can do!

You agree you've learned a very valuable lesson about drugs.

You go on to wonder if maybe you can kill Oberon anyway; since this whole story was supposed to be against drugs and you've already learned that valuable lesson, maybe we could slip in some violence too? Like, maybe you could attack Oberon with scissors and cut his head off?

And I hem and haw but finally I'm like, "Okay FINE, just don't do any drugs while you're at it," and you're like, "Cool, this is why I read books."

You cut off Oberon's head with a pair of scissors, mount it on a spike, and while I'm not looking do some cool drugs too.

HEY!!

P.S.: The drugs kill you, OBVIOUSLY, and you die in real life too, OBVIOUSLY.

The End

132 You don't want to go around giving strange potions to other people, so you have no choice but to test this potion out on yourself. It's designed to make you fall in love with the first thing you see when you open your eyes, so you'll need a target.

There are no people nearby, but you do have the delicious ham sandwich you packed for lunch. While you are excited to eat it, you have little to no romantic attraction to it, mainly because it's your ham sandwich. Perfect!

You open up your lunchbox, place it on your desk, and sit down in front of it. On a pad of paper, you write:

BEFORE FEELINGS:

- it's an okay sandwich
- i'm kinda hungry??

You put your pencil down, dip your fingers into the potion, close your eyes, and apply it to your eyelids. Then you open your eyes and look at your sandwich again. You consider the sandwich carefully, then take some more notes:

AFTER FEELINGS:

- ◆ man i did a real good job on that sammich
- ◆ i like this sammich!!!

Your heart sinks. Dang it, Puck, this isn't a love potion! It's only a LIKE potion!

Make a new potion, more concentrated this time: *turn to 129.*

Naw, this is good enough for me! *Turn to 136.*

133
You find a spritzer, put your potion inside, and fly up into the air. You start spraying while flying in an expanding spiral, covering the largest amount of ground as efficiently as you can. Every fairy and human in the forest gets doused in your love potion. The next time they close and open their eyes— i.e., the next time they blink—they'll fall in love with whatever they're looking at.

Needless to say, this completely destroys fairy society as you know it. Most of your fellow fairies happened to be looking at trees, so there are a lot of people in love with the leaves or particular squirrels. Not to mention the fairies talking to a group of other fairies who now love every single member of that group, or the fairies who happened to be looking in a mirror. There are a lot of nontraditional relationship arrangements created here is what I'm trying to say.

You return to a fairy culture in chaos. Over the next few weeks the fairy community rebuilds itself, with the idea that "falling head over heels for your true love" is something instant, unpredictable, and always correct being foundational to this new society.

This is great for your friends—they're now absolutely convinced they're with the perfect life partner 100% of the time—but when they start having children this messes them up but good. These undrugged children enter a world that's a lot more complicated for them than for their parents. Their entire society tells them over and over that their one true love is out there, and that they'll "just know" it when they first meet them, and when it does it'll be perfect forever.

But of course it isn't.

These children grow up and love a bunch of different people in a bunch of different ways and this idea of "the one" ends up being toxic: whenever they have a fight with their partners, they assume they're not meant to be together, because you wouldn't have a fight with "the one," right? The one you're meant to be with is perfect, and you're perfect together, and settling for anyone else is compromise. A second-place consolation prize until The One shows up.

Those who do not outgrow these teachings tend to end up being pretty unsatisfied little fairies.

SPRITZ!
SPRITZ!

The End

P.S.: I almost forgot about the humans in the forest! They happened to be talking to each other in a group, so they entered into a polyamorous relationship that they are all really satisfied with, so good work there I guess? Some humans had some really fun sex because of you!!

P.P.S: Oh also I got so carried away in my relationship-politics screed that I forgot this story was supposed to have an antidrug moral, so, um, if anyone asks tell them I said drugs were bad, okay?? Like, super bad. Just the worst.

P.P.P.S: Oh also one more thing YOU'RE DEAD, OH WELL.

134 Yes! YES, this is the lesson we were trying to teach you the whole time. YOU CAN'T SOLVE ALL YOUR PROBLEMS WITH HOMEMADE EXPERIMENTAL DRUGS. It's a lesson that seems really obvious in retrospect, but apparently you needed to learn it. Remember: the only good drugs are serotonin and dopamine, and then ONLY if they are produced AND consumed inside your own body!

Now unfortunately for the moral we're trying to convey here, the only way to solve your PARTICULAR problem is with more homemade experimental drugs. You rush home to make a "reverse the effect of the previous potion" potion, then return to the forest and begin to apply it to Titania. As you're doing so your boss Oberon shows up, and surprisingly, he's happy to see you doing this!

"I already confronted her about sexing up that half-man half-donkey thing," he says. "Made fun of her for hours as she was looking for presents for him. She begged me to leave her alone, and I said I'd do it if she gave me the child. Titania went for it! So we're done here. Your reversal potion makes the people affected think it was just a dream, right?"

"Right," you say.

"Perfect," Oberon says. "The perfect crime."

"Um, she's eventually gonna notice her kid is missing and living with you though," you say.

"DOESN'T MATTER, I GOT THE KID," Oberon says, and leaves. Annoyed, you restore the half-man half-donkey to his previous full-man zero-donkey status. Your jerky boss got what he wanted after all!

You wisely conclude that even if you have the absolute best of intentions, drugs can still lead to bad things happening. You're about to conclude that hey, wait a minute, that conclusion ALSO applies to pretty much every single thing in the entire universe, but at that point I cut you off and say nevermind that because guess what, Puck! You won this book!

Hooray!!

The humans are going home (you kinda forgot to restore them, but they're in "love" so no harm no foul right?) and along with them goes the formerly half-donkey dude. This "dream" has inspired him to write a book about star-crossed lovers! Well, less a "book" and more a "two-page minicomic." It's called *The Most Lamentable Comedy and Most Cruel Death of Pyramus and/or Thisbe*.

Do you want to read it? It's included for free in this book as a special bonus, to make learning fun!

I guess: *turn to 138.*

No, I think I'm done here, let's just end this: *turn to 396.*

135 You return to Oberon with the potion.

"Perfect," he says. "This is just what I need to alter the emotions of my wife to gain control of her child."

"Cool," you say.

"Oh also, I spied on some humans while I was waiting and they seemed upset about relationship junk," he says, "so while I'm busy with my wife, I want you to take some extra potion and drug them too. I'm terrible with names, but there was a boy human and a girl human. Drug the boy human."

"The boy human?" you ask.

"Yes, the boy human!" he says, annoyed. "They look like girl humans but with deeper voices! He was wearing Athenian clothes. Drug him!"

"Okay," you say, and set off into the forest to look for them.

After several hours, you conclude that there are like zero humans in this stupid forest.

Look once more by the pond before giving up: *turn to 137.*

Look once more by the meadow before giving up: *turn to 125.*

136

When you get to Oberon—sooner than he expected!—he thanks you and takes the potion to drug his wife.

"Thanks," he says. "I was getting bored waiting and was about to take an interest in what those humans over there were doing, but now I don't have to."

"Cool," you say.

Unfortunately for you, whatever your potion is, it isn't a full-strength love potion! Titania wakes up super cheesed that her eyelids smell like dried potion and quickly deduces what her estranged husband attempted. She takes revenge by having HER fairies make a death potion, which is really easy because all drugs kill you,[1] and pours it on top of Oberon. All Oberon has time to say before he dies is "No fair, Puck's the one who made the potion," which of course leads Titania to murder you in the exact same way.

Interestingly enough, her potion was really well tested and worked perfectly!!

P.S.: Later on, Titania uses the potion to control weeds in her garden.

P.P.S.: Later on after that, Titania uses precise drops of the potion to control the spread of disease in the body and help cure tumors.

P.P.P.S.: None of this affects you because you're a skeleton now though.

P.P.P.P.S: In real life too, sorry, pal!!

The End

---

1 You know, EVENTUALLY.

137

You're about to give up when you decide to search by the pond one last time. And guess what: you come across two humans sleeping, a boy and a girl. They're sleeping apart so clearly this is a good place for a love potion to intervene!

You stick some potion on the human dude's eyelids and return to Oberon. On the way back you run into another human and you turn him into a half-man half-donkey hybrid because hah hah hah why not.

Oberon is happy to see you: your potion worked perfectly on his wife, and she's now fallen in love with what Oberon describes as a "half-man half-donkey hybrid." You are pleased that your capriciousness has paid off so quickly.

Just then, two humans come by: they're the ones you saw earlier! And whatever problems Oberon saw seem to have evaporated: they're totally in love now, fawning over each other.

"Huh," you say, "apparently the problems in that relationship were entirely on the man's side, since adjusting him was all it took to solve them."

"I guess," says Oberon. "I dunno. Could be they'll just have more problems. Real talk, Puck: sometimes you can love each other with all your heart but still be terrible for each other. Sometimes love is a destructive, awful thing."

"This is depressing," you say.

"Alright!" Oberon says, clapping his hands together. "Now to go see my chemically altered wife and convince her to give up her adopted child to me!"

You are suddenly aware that you've been aiding and abetting a monster.

It was a mistake to try to solve my problems with drugs in the first place. Restore Titania to normal: *turn to 134.*

Nevermind that, just kill Oberon, that'll solve my problem way easier: *turn to 131.*

P tosses the sword away and attacks the lion with his bare hands, which the lion obviously bites off super quickly. T follows and gets her hands bit off too. Then the lion bites off the rest of them and goes home, super full of deer and teens, to lie down for a bit. A lot of things have happened to this lion in a very short period of time: she killed a deer, she ate the deer, then she was attacked by teens who loved each other and ate them too! It's a lot to take in.

You might even say . . .

. . . it's a lot to digest??

THE END

P's like, "Haha can't believe I forgot I had a sword," and T's like, "Okay we can laugh about this later let's kill this lion first," and T stabs the lion right in the body like eighty times! The lion dies and then P and T take the lion back into town expecting to be hailed as heroes. Instead, their parents are hailed as drastically deadbeat parents who allow their teen children to go play in LITERAL LION FIELDS, and so they lose custody. P and T are adopted by other people who don't mind if they date each other and so they live happily ever after! They get married and stab any lions who get in their way for the rest of their days.

THE END ❤

Check out the other books in my INSPIRED BY A NIGHT I SPENT ALONE IN THE FOREST series!

Titles Include:

ANTHONY AND/OR CLEOPATRA

MUCH ADO ABOUT CHOICES

OTH AND/OR ELLO

When you're done reading, *turn to 396.*

139 "Oh, Romeo," you sigh. "Romeo. Why do you have to be a Romeo? Change your dang name. Or I could change mine. Either works, and both would solve our problem."

Something shifts in the bushes below. Probably a raccoon. Nothing to worry about.

"It's just your stupid name that's the problem," you reason. "You'd still be yourself even if you stopped being a Montague. What even IS a Montague anyway? There's nothing intrinsically Montague to a Montague hand, or a Montague foot, or a Montague arm, or a Montague face, or a Montague—"

You look around to make sure nobody is listening in. The coast is clear!

". . . Montague peener," you whisper.

Nice!!

"Anyway," you say, straightening up and pacing back and forth on the balcony, "take some other name! Names are dumb. Roses would smell just as nice if we called them 'Grossweed Stankblossoms, the Hideous Toxic Plants That Are Worse Than Dog Farts, You Don't Even Know.'"

I totally agree with you, Juliet!!

"So in conclusion, Romeo," you say, "trade in your name, which I remind you really has no intrinsic value, and I'll give you ME in exchange."

Suddenly, a dark shape steps out of the bushes beneath your balcony. "Okay that actually sounds really cool to me!" the shadowy man says.

Whoah, what the hell??

"WHOAH, WHAT THE HELL?" you shout, startled and freaking out. "Mom! Dad! THERE'S A DUDE HERE HIDING IN DARKNESS AND SPYING ON ME!!"

Keep calling for your parents: *turn to 153.*

Calm down and chat up this strange man instead: *turn to 163.*

140 "Lady," you say, "I swear by yonder blessed moon, that paints the top of the fruit trees in silver light, and—"

Juliet interrupts you. "I'm looking for something a little more consistent here than the constantly changing moon."

No dice, Romeo.

"Um, what should I swear by?" you ask.

"Swear by your wonderful self, which is my new god, my new idol, and I'll believe you," she says.

Whoah! Juliet's got it bad!

Swear on yourself: *turn to 158.*

On second thought, tell her that things are moving a little fast, and while it's flattering she worships you like a god, maaaaybe the two of you should move a bit slower before you both start saying things you can't really mean yet: *turn to 187.*

141

You close your eyes and stand perfectly motionless. Romeo stares at you, confused. After a long moment, you peek one eye open.

"SAINTS DO NOT MOVE," you shout, "THOUGH GRANT FOR PRAYERS' SAKE."

Romeo is still confused.

"BY THAT I MEAN," you say, "THAT SAINTS DON'T MOVE EVEN WHEN THEY GRANT PRAYERS."

"OH," Romeo shouts. "NEAT. I DIDN'T KNOW THAT ABOUT SAINTS."

And then he kisses you.

Finally!! Kiss the boy! *Turn to 113.*

142

Juliet sighs loudly. "Ay me!" she mutters. You can't tell what she's talking about.

"O, speak again, bright angel!" you say. "For thou art as glorious to this night, being o'er my head, as is a wingèd messenger of heaven unto the white, upturnèd, wondering eyes of mortals that fall back to gaze on him when he bestrides the lazy-puffing clouds and sails upon the bosom of the air."

She can't hear you, dude. You know that, right? And that's good, because she's just started talking again and she's talking about you!

"O Romeo," she sighs, then raises her own arm out in front of her. "Romeo! Wherefore art thou Romeo? Deny thy father and refuse thy name. Or, if thou wilt not, be but sworn my love, and I'll no longer be a Capulet!"

"Whoah I could totally do that," you whisper to yourself.

"'Tis but thy name that is my enemy," Juliet reasons. "Thou art thyself, though not a Montague. What's Montague? It is nor hand, nor foot, nor arm, nor face, nor—"

Juliet looks around to make sure nobody is listening in.

". . . nor any other part belonging to a man," she whispers.

"O, be some other name!" she cries, straightening up and pacing back and forth. "What's in a name? That which we call a rose by any other word would smell as sweet." (She has obviously never considered "Grossweed Stankblossoms, the Hideous Toxic Plants That Are Worse Than Dog Farts, You Don't Even Know.") "So Romeo would," Juliet says, "were he not Romeo called, retain that dear perfection which he owes without that title. Romeo, doff thy name, and for that name, which is no part of thee, take all myself."

"I take thee at thy word," you say, stepping out of the bushes raised hand first. "Call me but love, and I'll be new baptized. Henceforth I never will be Romeo!"

"Whoah, WHAT?" Juliet shouts, startled, freaking out. "WHAT MAN ART THOU THUS BESCREENED IN NIGHT, SO STUMBLEST ON MY COUNSEL??"

Haha wow who could've predicted hiding in the bushes outside the house of someone you just met would go really poorly? If you don't want to get arrested here, Romeo, I think your only option is to be Juliet for a bit and decide to calm yourself down!

 Be Juliet, calm yourself down, and chat up this strange man instead: *turn to 163.*

No man, talk your way out of this as Romeo: *turn to 170.*

Hide in the bushes; nobody will ever think to look for a creepy man in the bushes: *turn to 150.*

143 The bedknob impacts against the stone walls of your room and smashes into smithereens. It's REALLY SATISFYING. You probably could've aimed at the wall a little farther away from Angelica's head, but oh well!

The largest chunks land at Angelica's feet and roll for a few seconds before settling. She stares at them, her eyes wide. I think she got your message, if the message you meant to send was "I'm not in the mood for jokes, wordplay, or a comic scene demonstrating the effect young love has had on me and your happiness at seeing me so taken by it."

She looks up at you and swallows. "Romeo's still down to marry you and he's expecting you at Friar Lawrence's house at two thirty this afternoon and you can make it if you tell your parents you're just stepping out to take confession," she says.

"Nice," you say. You walk into your closet and slip into your best "gettin' married" dress.

"I can't come because I have to go wait in an alleyway to meet up with an associate of Romeo's who'll be delivering a rope ladder so that Romeo can climb in here," Angelica says as you change. "So that way you can sex each other up tonight all you want."

"NICE," you say, stepping out of the closet. Whoah, Juliet. You look AMAZING. You're about to make your way downstairs, but something makes you stop halfway through the doorway. You turn back towards Angelica. She looks up at you, uncertain. You smile.

"Wish me luck," you say.

Go get married: *turn to 160.*

144

You hang out on your balcony for a bit, thinking about Romeo. He's so great! He's hot, and . . . well, that's all you know about him for sure.

But.

But PROBABLY he's really nice and smart and great to talk to, and intuitive, and understanding, and considerate. PROBABLY he'll make sure to communicate with you every day, even if it's just a quick note to say he loves you. PROBABLY his favorite food is a nice fillet of salmon for two by candlelight, and he loves horses, and even though he won't admit it to his guy friends he's got this secret soft spot he only shares with you for romantic comedies, and every year on your birthday just the two of you will go to see your favorite play, *10 Things I Hate About Thou.*

You sigh happily. "Romeo's so great," you say.

Well, that was fun but it's getting late! Time for bed. *Turn to 106.*

Keep puttering around on the balcony for a bit longer: *turn to 159.*

145

You decide to poison ol' Tommy Paris. The next morning you sneak out of your house and go into town, where you meet up with Friar Lawrence. Friar Lawrence is a friend of yours. He's always ready with a sympathetic ear and a toxin-based solution to any of life's challenges.

You spend a few minutes catching up, then he asks you to what he owes the pleasure of your company.

"Friar, I want to kill a man," you say.

"Juliet!" he says, shocked. "You shouldn't kill anyone! Murder is a mortal sin!" He starts pacing the room, agitated. "As you know, Juliet, I am a Franciscan friar: a member of one of the three major orders living according to the Rule of St. Francis."

"I do know this," you say.

"And that means that we're not allowed to wear shoes or ride horses," he says. "OR MURDER OTHER PEOPLE."

"Fine," you say. "I want to kill myself then."

"Oh in that case no problem," the Friar says, sitting down and happily pushing a small bushel of herbs into your hands. "Make tea from this, and drink it. You'll be dead within forty-six minutes."

"Thanks, Friar!" you say.

"Ta!" Friar Lawrence says, shoving you out the door. "I believe in a radical form of self-realization and think no one should have dominion over your body, whether it's other people or even the state!"

"I know, that's really convenient!" you say.

The next morning you loudly say, "I'M GOING TO STAY IN BED TODAY, EVERYONE NOTICE THIS, OKAY??" and then sneak down from your balcony and out of the house. You make your way to Paris's house, where you knock on the door and say, "Hey Tommy, I reconsidered and want to marry you now! Can we have some tea to celebrate?"

"I don't see why not," Tom says. Forty-six minutes later, he's lying dead at your feet, and you can finally spit out the tea you've held in your cheeks without swallowing for that entire time. You spit it out into a napkin. It's the one you wrote on and held up when Paris asked you why you weren't swallowing your tea. "Oh I'm just not thirsty yet" it says.

You sneak out, return to your house, loudly say, "I CHANGED MY MIND AND I'M LEAVING MY ROOM NOW," and get on with your life.

The next day, news spreads that Paris is dead and you end up getting away with it, due to cops being bad at this point in time, and also science not being invented yet. That was actually fairly easy, and you kinda fall into the trap of murdering everyone who hits on you poorly (such an easy trap to fall into, you know?) and before long you have the nickname "Black Widow" and nobody wants to date you.

And because of that, you never get married.

And because of that, you spend the rest of your life alone.

And by "alone" I mean "surrounded and supported by a large and ever-expanding network of terrific friends who only want the best for you, who love you, and whom you love in return!"

Aww, that's really nice! Congratulations, Juliet!

THE END

146

You enter downtown Verona but find any further progression blocked by a giant clockwork arm extending across the road. You turn around to find another path but discover that giant clockwork arms are now blocking those ways forward as well. The only place you can move is back towards the gatekeeper, and Romeo's not there!

A Veronan runs up to you. "It's a new security measure," he explains. "It keeps out anyone who doesn't know the passphrase."

"OH MY GOD," you say. "THIS FRIGGIN' TOWN."

"But there's some good news," he says. "You don't need to know the passphrase to get past! You just need to know the decryption key. That'll decrypt the passphrase and let you through."

"What's the decryption key?" you ask.

"Beats me," he says. "I've been trying to get past here for hours. You wanna try?"

The only exit is to the south.

Look machine: turn to 227.

Go south: turn to 236.

147 "But soft! What light through yonder window breaks?" you ask yourself again. You decide to answer your own question out loud.

"Oh, it's Juliet," you say. "She's east of me, so I'm metaphorically treating her as the sun. And what a sun! She's a sun SO SEXUALLY ATTRACTIVE that even the moon is jealous of her. She should kill that moon. Also, she should stop being a virgin. I should help her stop being a virgin.

"Virgins are losers," you say.

You don't know this, but in Roman mythology the goddess of the moon is the same person as the god of virginity (Diana!), so this horny metaphor you've been building is actually working out pretty well. Work in birthing and hunting and you'll hit all of Diana's interests, Romeo!

At this moment Juliet says something, but you can't quite make it out. It seems like she's talking to herself too!

"There's Juliet," you say, staring at her in secret from the bushes outside her window. "I love her and want to kiss her. Also, I can't hear what she's saying right now BUT WHO CARES, because her eyes alone do talking enough for me." You pause, lost in her eyes.

"Screw it," you say. "I'm talking to her." You step out of the bushes and instantly lose your nerve.

"Naw," you say, retreating back into the shrubbery.

"Still! Those eyes, man," you say to yourself. "I'm serious. It's like the two prettiest stars in the sky went on break and asked her eyes to fill in for them until they get back. Wow, imagine if her eyes were in the sky, and therefore the stars would be INSIDE HER HEAD??" You pause again, considering it.

"That'd be pretty crazy, actually," you conclude. "Her cheeks would be LIT UP. They'd be so bright that night would seem like day. Birds would get all messed up."

Juliet leans, resting her cheek in her hand.

"Frig, man, I sure wish I was that glove," you say.

Actually wish to be that glove: *turn to 157.*

Keep staring at her: *turn to 118.*

148 The chimes stop, the band quiets, and the woman you met literally three minutes ago, whom you're already kissing on and whose name you don't even know, pulls back a little.

"You kiss by the book," she says, and you're instantly wishing you'd cleaned up before you headed out tonight. The books stacked beside your bed right now include *Kiss It Better! What YOU Can Learn from the World's Greatest Kissers, Reminiscing About Kissing: Sixty-Six Years of Sexy Smooches, Basorexia!*, and *How to Press the Bacteria-Rich Outer Edge of Your Digestive Tract Against the Bacteria-Rich Outer Edge of Someone Else's Digestive Tract and Exchange Fluids.*

"Oh hah hah, that's weird," you say. Before she can say anything, a woman in a nurse outfit walks up and says, "Hey, your mom wants to talk to you."

"Yes, Angelica," she says, and takes your hand. "Sorry," she says. "My parents are really controlling. I'll be back soon. Promise."

She leaves, and you turn to the nurse lady. You're still a little stunned from meeting that woman and how SUPER RAD your kisses were though, so when you try to say, "Who was that woman?" it accidentally comes out as "What . . . is her mother?" which is barely even grammatical.

She smiles. "Her mother's the lady of the house," she says. "Lady Capulet. And I'll tell you what, whoever puts a ring on that is gonna be loaded."

You take a step sideways in shock, which is what humans do in real life when they encounter information they were not expecting. The woman leaves you, unconcerned.

"I, Romeo Montague, cannot believe that she's a Capulet," you say to yourself, unbelieving. "She's my worst enemy! How could this have happened? How is it possible that I would meet a Capulet, at a party hosted by the Capulets, here at Capulet Castle, situated as always at One Capulet Lane??"

Benvolio and Mercutio emerge from the crowd. "Let's bounce, bro," Benvolio says. "Always leave a party early. That way, you don't have to help with cleanup."

"OBVIOUSLY," you say. "But we just got here! Also, I think I'm in trouble."

Benvolio is already pulling you to the exit. You're almost out of the castle when the nurse lady catches up to you and asks you what your name is.

"Romeo Montague," you say. She gasps and brings a hand to her mouth. "It's okay," you say, trying to calm her down. "Yes, we crashed the party. But we're leaving now, okay? We don't want any trouble."

"Daaaaang," she says, taking a few steps backwards. She still seems shocked, but whatever.

You and your friends leave the party. Benvolio and Mercutio are talking to each other, laughing, gossiping, making fun of the people there. You don't hear a word of it. All you can think about is that woman, this mysterious Hottiebabe Capulet. You don't even know her name! For all you know, it could actually be "Hottiebabe Capulet." On the other hand, it could be something less attractive, like "Stinkums Dentalplaque Capulet."

"I have to go back," you say out loud. Your friends look at you in surprise.

"What?" they say. "Romeo, wait!"

You realize you're already running back towards Capulet Castle. "How can I leave while my heart's rooted here?" you shout over your shoulder.

You hear your friend shouting after you (something about having sex with ghosts, and also fruit? Probably you misheard that, right?) but you don't stop, and before long you've hopped the castle fence and made your way to the castle proper. It's quiet: looks like the party's ended. You're crawling around in the bushes trying to figure out which room is hers. There are several balconies attached to the house. Could be any one of them, actually!

Examine the nearby stone balcony: *turn to 119.*

Examine the nearby wooden balcony: *turn to 155.*

 Examine some other balcony instead: *turn to 167.*

149
You're about to shove him away when you realize you can distract him using your one strength (words!) and his one weakness (FREE FOODSTUFFS). "Oh hey, my dad invited us over for lunch," you say. "He wants to give us a free lunch."

"No such thing," Mercutio says suspiciously. "There are even aphorisms about it."

"I'm serious," you say. "He said he bought too much lunch by mistake, so now he has to eat his way out of this problem, and he could use some help."

Mercutio looks at you. You can see hope growing in his eyes.

"I'm just saying, he asked me if I knew anyone," you say, smiling.

Mercutio instantly grabs Benvolio by the wrist and drags him towards your father's house.

"Okay so I'll catch up with you later!" you shout after him, but they're already gone. You turn to the nurse and apologize. "Sorry my friends are tools," you say. She takes you by the hand and leads you into a more private area of the town square.

"If your intentions towards Juliet are anything less than honorable, I will cut you," she says.

"I love her, I swear it," you say, "I still want to marry her. Tell her that," you say. "And tell her if she comes to Friar Lawrence's house this afternoon at two thirty, I'll prove it. We'll totally get married."

The nurse seems satisfied and turns to leave. Just then, you realize that once you're married, you'll probably get to have sex with Juliet! That'll be pretty neat, right? You could do it at your place or hers, but either way someone is going to need a way to sneak in or out of her house without being noticed.

"Wait, wait," you say. "In an hour a friend of mine's going to drop off a rope ladder. If you set it up, I'll use it to meet Juliet in secret tonight."

"Okay," she says.

"For sex," you say.

"Okay," she says.

"I'll pay you money to do this," you say.

"No, it's okay," she says. "You don't have to make it weird. I'm down with this plan. I've kinda spent three hours trying to find you, so yeah, I'm just happy to see this concluded."

You press some Veronabucks into her hand. "Here's some money. Commend me to Juliet, okay? Tell her I'm handsome, and also, have money."

"Got it," she says. She puts the money in her pocket and turns to you. "So! You have kinda just paid for a few moments of my time. Do you want to talk about dogs and rosemary for a bit? I could also mention toads or spelling."

"No, that sounds like a needless waste of my time," you say, waving to her. "Okay bye!"

With that, she leaves. You stop by Benvolio's house and have him send over your rope ladder ("because of a secret," you say), and then you head back to your place.

Alright, Romeo: you've got two hours to make it over to the Friar's house for your wedding. That's only two hours to figure out what you're going to wear! Luckily for you the decision is really easy (you look in your closet and decide to go in your "Romeo clothes" that you've been wearing all week), so you mosey on over to the chapel in plenty of time.

Now's the time, Romeo. It's the day, the very hour of your wedding. It's one of the most important days of your entire life. It's what you've been working towards this entire book, mostly!

This is YOUR day, Romeo.

Get married: *turn to 192.*

 On second thought, as fun as a wedding might be, it might be even more fun to be my bride and get married to MYSELF. Get married as Juliet! *Turn to 166.*

Actually, on third thought, weddings are OH MY GOD so boring. Can we skip over the wedding? Please? *Turn to 156.*

150 You creep back into the bushes to hide, but Juliet keeps screaming, and a few seconds later Juliet's dad runs out with a pile of swords, naked and angry.

"Man, ain't no way he's gonna stab me with those swords," you say.

Years later, strangers wandering Verona's peaceful, picturesque graveyard will find those exact words—engraved beneath your name on your headstone—to be a particular highlight of the tour.

THE END

151 "Oh," Romeo says, clearly disappointed. "I mean, yeah I guess that's fine. So can I see you tomorrow or what?"

"Give me some time, dude. I'll call you later in the week, okay? Maybe we could go see a play."

"Okay," Romeo says. "Okay, yeah, that sounds nice. I will wait for you, my love!!" Your nurse calls for you again, and you climb into your bed. "SORRY, CAN'T ANSWER, TOO BUSY SLEEPING," you shout at the closed door.

Less than two days later, you send a messenger to Romeo's house to confirm a time for your date, but Romeo has literally already married someone else.

"I don't know what to tell you," the messenger says.

Two days after that, they're both dead: they killed themselves! Romeo drank poison and the poor woman stabbed herself to death with his knife. Wow.

"I, for one," you say, "am certainly glad I didn't jump into bed with THAT."

You live to a really old age and never end up having to stab yourself to death for any reason, which is actually really nice!

THE END

152 You quickly punch in the date. "November 12, 1955," you say.

"Wait, what?" Juliet says. "We're long dead then. What could we possibly change?"

You're not sure why you chose that date. "I don't know," you say. "It could be that that point in time inherently contains some sort of cosmic significance, almost as if it were the temporal junction point of the entire space-time continuum. On the other hand, it could just be completely random."

You take her hand.

"Let's find out," you say. The two of you step into the quantum-leap accelerator and vanish.

Arrive in the past: *turn to 164.*

153 You call for your parents, and soon you see your dad running out the front door, carrying about fifteen different swords in his arms as he runs, the extras falling off behind him. He lives for attacking trespassers at night!

Also he sleeps in the buff, so he's naked right now. Geez, Dad.

Your naked dad catches up with the shadowy figure and puts his favorite few swords into his belly and moves them around a little, which kills a human.

"That's what you get for creeping in the bushes," your dad says, pulling the body of the interloper out into the light. And—oh no. I'm so sorry, Juliet. It was Romeo.

You're really upset that your dad killed your boyfriend, and so you go into mourning. You dress in black and yell at your parents a lot, but eventually you start to think, hey, it was weird that he was hiding outside your house in the middle of the night, spying on you. You begin to realize that you didn't actually know him at all. And you begin to feel less hurt.

You also begin to realize that this black veil you've been rocking actually looks really awesome! You start wearing a lot of black lace and black nail polish all the time and LONG STORY SHORT you end up inventing a really cool look several centuries ahead of schedule, and as a result of your influential style everyone in the 1600s dresses Goth all the time, which honestly makes history WAY more cool-looking.

THE END

154 The chimes stop, the band quiets, and the man you met literally three minutes ago whom you're already kissing on and whose name you don't even know pulls back a little. His smooching was pretty good! Certainly competent, with no small amount of passion, though also strictly according to the beats and patterns laid out in *Kiss Me, Kate: Kate "Kissable" Minola Reveals Her Ten Steps to Perfect Kissing Every Time.*

"You kiss by the book," you say.

"Oh hah hah, that's weird," he says. Before you can say anything, Angelica sidles up to you and tells you your mom would like to have a word.

"Yes, Angelica," you say as she takes your hand. You turn back to your kiss partner.

"Sorry," you say. "My parents are really controlling. I'll be back soon. Promise." Then you go find your mother sitting in the back of the room and ask her what she wants.

"I want to know why you're talking to that ridiculous unicorn instead of talking to Paris," she says. "He's the dog sitting at the bar. I think he even made his own mask at home," she says, clearly impressed with him.

"That's dumb, and I'm not talking to him," you say. "Besides, I just met someone new and already kissed him twice, so I guess you could say things are getting pretty serious."

"What's his name?" your mother asks.

"OBVIOUSLY I DON'T KNOW THAT YET," you say, storming off. You're making your way back to him through the party when you bump into Angelica.

"Angelica!" you say, pulling her to you. "Do you know who that hunky dude is?"

"Which one?" she asks.

"The one I was just kissing!" you say. "The dude you literally just saw me kissing." She stares at you, uncomprehending. "The boy I was kissing under a minute ago is the one I am interested in right now," you say.

"Ohhhhh," she says. "I'ma go find out."

You watch her leave. "If he be married, my grave is like to be my wedding bed," you say to nobody in particular, holding one hand out in front of you.

She returns shortly. "He's Romeo Montague," she says. "The only son of your great enemy." You stagger to the side, shocked. He's a Montague? But Montagues are the sworn enemies of the Capulets, and that applies especially to you, Juliet Capulet!! You're not sure what to say.

"My only love sprung from my only hate!" you whisper. "Too early seen unknown, and known too late!" Hey, rhyming couplets! Not bad, Jules! Got any more?

You stare at Angelica, wild-eyed. "Prodigious birth of love it is to me, that I must love a loathèd enemy!" you say. Two in a row!

First one was better though.

". . . What?" Angelica asks.

"Nothing," you say. "It's nothing. It's just a rhyme someone I danced with tonight taught me."

Your mother calls you, and you and your nurse head over. She says you definitely have to go talk to Tom Paris now. Instead of doing that, you say, "NOOOOOPE," and then you say, "LEAVE ME ALONE, MOM," and then you go up to your room.

Go to bed: *turn to 106.*

Putter around on the balcony for a while: *turn to 144.*

155 You look up to the balcony. A light is on inside!

"But soft! What light through yonder window breaks?" you whisper, holding one hand out in front of you.

A naked old dude steps out from the light onto the balcony. He's smoking a cigar. His naughty bits are dangling in the breeze. Aw gross, I think that's her dad!

"AW GROSS, I THINK THAT'S HER DAD," you say, moving away to investigate another balcony. "NICE WEEN THOUGH."

Examine the nearby stone balcony: *turn to 109.*

Examine some other balcony instead: *turn to 167.*

156 What? Romeo, this is your WEDDING. This is the natural culmination of the romance you've been having with that woman you spied on in the bushes! Your ENTIRE STORY[1] has been leading to this moment!

But you know what? Sure, why not? I wrote a really sweet wedding scene, but come on, it's not like I wrote this book because I ever wanted anyone to, you know, READ IT.

Um okay geez calm down I'll go to your/my dumb wedding: *turn to 192.*

Okay perfect, glad we can skip the wedding and all the speeches or whatever: *turn to 199.*

157 "Dang, I REALLY wish I was that glove," you say.

Once in a very long time, the universe grants wishes. It doesn't happen often, but you're so in love with this woman, so fervent and obsessed, that your wish takes on the character of, for example, the wish of a parent hoping for their drowning child to be saved from a torrential flood. And because of that, a miracle happens: your wish is granted. That kid drowns now, incidentally.

You are now a glove!

A glove (from the Old English "*glof*") is a garment covering the hand, with separate openings for each finger and the thumb. Gloves are typically worn to protect and comfort hands against cold, heat, friction, abrasion, chemicals, or disease. Gloves are an early invention, attested to as early as the eighth century BC, when they are mentioned in Homer's *Odyssey*.

Gloves are not capable of sentient thought.

---

1 On this particular run-through.

THE END

158 "I swear on my own awesome bod—" you begin, but Juliet interrupts you.

"You know what? This is crazy. It's too rash, too unadvised, too sudden," she says. "How about this: we say good night, and we meet again tomorrow. Sound good?"

"I was hoping I'd get to sex you," you say.

"What?" Juliet says.

"Um, I was hoping we could make . . . PROMISES of love?" you say.

"Better," Juliet says. "Okay, I'll go first: my love for you is as boundless as the sea, and twice as deep."

"Cool!" you say. "Mine too." Just then Juliet hears someone calling for her, and she disappears into her room.

"I'm afraid that since it's night this might all be a dream," you say out loud to yourself, but Romeo: don't worry about it. Worry you're trapped in a dream if you suddenly find yourself back in school and your parents teach every class and also you're naked. The fact that it's dark out is actually totally fine and not indicative of anything except that you stayed up past your bedtime.

Just then, Juliet runs back out onto the balcony!

"Okay seriously, three words and then it's good night for real this time," she says. She pauses for a moment, clearly trying to compress the relatively complex sentiment she's feeling down to three words.

"Marry now, please," Juliet says. Someone calls for her again. "Oh my god, just a second, a thousand times good night," she says, and rushes back indoors.

You've got another chance to say something she won't hear, so you hold your hand out in front of you and say, "Love goes toward love as schoolboys from their books, but love from love, toward school with heavy looks."

By that, you're pretty sure you mean that lovers run towards their partners in the way schoolboys do when it's time to go home (i.e., enthusiastically), and that, in contrast, lovers leave their partners in the same way schoolboys go to school, which is to say, sadly and reluctantly because school is just the WORST, am I right?? Man I just hate how we have a civilization's worth of information written down for us and also have the infrastructure in place so that this information can be studied and learned from as early in life as possible. WHAT A FRIGGIN' DRAG.

Anyway nobody hears you and you're about to leave when Juliet comes running back out.

"Nurses," Juliet says before you can say anything. "Anyway, listen, I'm trapped here so we can't get married right away, but I'll send my nurse as a messenger tomorrow, cool? Incidentally, if I could, I'd make it so the goddess Echo repeated 'My Romeo' until she was more hoarse than me."

"Neat," you say.

"What time should I send her tomorrow?" she asks.

"Wait, hold on," you say. "It's past midnight. Do you mean tomorrow as in Tuesday, or tomorrow as in today?"

"Oh," she says. "Monday. Today. Let's get married today," she says.

"Okay," you say. "On weekdays I'm normally up around eight, eight thirty, so any time after nine is good."

After working out these logistics, the two of you spend the next several hours telling each other how much you like each other until it's almost morning. And yes, I just smoothly shifted events ahead so we don't get to hear your love poetry! You seriously expected us to stick around for it after you opened up with your "love is like school" verse? Because if so, bad news, it's not happening!

"It's almost morning," Juliet says. "I'd let you go, but I'm like a kid with a bird tied to a string who keeps monstrously pulling her back whenever she tries to escape."

"I wish I were your bird," you volunteer.

"I'd literally pet you to death," Juliet says, smiling and shrugging. She looks so cute when she does that!

"Anyway," she says, "good night! Parting is such sweet sorrow that I shall say good night till it be morrow!"

"Right back atcha!" you say.

Whistling happily, you make your way home to bed.

Go home and go to bed: *turn to 178.*

159

You sigh a bit more, leaning on your balcony, supporting your head in your hand.

You decide you want to talk to yourself about Romeo. Maybe you'll be able to reason your way through this, right? You don't have many friends, so by now Conversation for One is a game you're pretty used to.

Talk to yourself in fancy language: *turn to 114.*

Talk to yourself in regular human language: *turn to 139.*

160

You run into Friar Lawrence's house and find your beloved Romeo already there, chatting with the Friar.

You run up to Romeo and hug him. As you hug, the Friar stands to your side, watching.

"I'm not going to leave you two alone until you're married," he whispers.

"Gross," you and Romeo say in unison. You pull back from the hug. "Alright!" you say, slapping Romeo on his shoulders. "Let's get married, shall we?"

Get married: *turn to 203.*

On second thought, weddings are OH MY GOD SO boring. Can we skip over the wedding? Please? *Turn to 172.*

161

You head north to Capulet Gate. A gatekeeper stops you.

"Sorry," he says, "but we've tightened security after the party last night. Anyone going in or out needs to know the passphrase."

"What passphrase?" you say. "I don't know any stupid passphrases."

"Honey," he says, "if you're trying to get through these gates, you'll need something better than that." He pushes you back towards the south.

Go south: turn to 173.

162 This is the ending you wanted, huh? Two senior-citizen ghosts, in love but kinda bored, deep inside the dying heart of a red-giant sun? Well, good news! Against all odds, you found it in this book, a book that was originally titled *OH COOL, RICH HETEROSEXUAL TEENS IN LOVE.*

You and Juliet stretch out and relax inside the red-giant sun. The torrent of flame around you is nice. It's nice!

"I finally don't feel so COLD all the time," you say.

THE END

163 Juliet, you instantly calm down. It's entirely reasonable that a man you just met at a party would now be lurking in the bushes outside your house! It's nice! This is what romance looks like!

"It's me, Ro—" the man starts, then stops. "Wait, no, I don't want to use my name. I hate my name now, because you hate it."

"Romeo?" you ask. "Is that you? I mean, I haven't even heard you say a hundred words yet, so it's a little hard to recognize you by your voice. But you're Romeo, right? A Montague?"

"I'm neither if you don't like 'em," the man says.

"How'd you get in here?" you ask. "The walls surrounding our property are pretty steep, actually." The man steps forward, and you can see him. You remember that sweet bod from earlier tonight. It's definitely Romeo.

"If my dad finds you here he'll kill you," you say.

"One angry look from you would be worse than twenty of your homicidal relatives," he says. "Look at me with love in your eyes and I will be invincible!"

"I'm serious, dude," you say, "my dad will murder you."

"I'd rather die than live a second more without your love!" Romeo says.

"He owns like thirty swords," you say.

"Oh," Romeo replies. "I didn't realize it was that many."

He looks like he's about to leave, and you're suddenly aware that you don't want this guy to go anywhere, so you instead lower your voice and hope it'll be enough not to attract your father.

"How did you even find me?" you ask.

"Love guided me to you," he says.

"Seriously though," you say. There's a pause.

"I would sail to the farthest sea to be with you," he volunteers.

"Huh," you say. And then you decide: enough messing around. You'll just tell him how you feel. "Okay," you say, "cards on the table, Romeo: I like you. A lot. And I know you're probably thinking I say this to all the guys, but I don't. This level of attraction is new to me. But if this is going to work—if there's going to be an 'us' here—then I need to know that you love me too."

"Oh I totally do," Romeo says. "Seriously."

"Too easy," you say. "Prove it. Convince me you're telling the truth."

"I love you! I, um, I swear on the moon!" Romeo says. "The moon is that thing in the sky that reflects light towards us, which we can then observe on the surrounding trees."

"The moon comes and goes in phases, Romeo," you say. "I'm looking for something a little more consistent here."

"I love you and I swear . . . on myself?" Romeo says. He says it so earnestly, so eagerly, that you're suddenly acutely aware of what you're asking this stranger to do.

"You know what?" you say. "This is crazy. This whole swearing thing is crazy. We've just met and I'm already asking you to commit to me. I'm ridiculous. You should go."

"You'd really leave me so unsatisfied?" Romeo says, and this kid's got nerve, I'll give him that!

"Oh, tell me, precisely what satisfaction are you looking for tonight?" you ask. Romeo surprises you by saying he just wants to tell you that he loves you, and to hear you say the same in return.

And you surprise yourself by being tempted to tell him exactly that.

 Confess your love to Romeo: *turn to 122.*

Tell Romeo you like him, but you've just met, so let's hold off on this love talk for at least a couple of weeks: *turn to 151.*

164

You've spent thousands of years living in an incorporeal body that doesn't have to worry about things like "muscles" or "bones" or "which way arms can bend without hurting" and in that time you kinda forgot how to live inside a physical body. I say "kinda" but that's a bit of a lie, so I'll tell you the truth: you absolutely and completely forgot how to drive a human body, Romeo.

You and Juliet materialize into bodies that aren't yours and instantly fall to the ground. It's a different brain, and a differently shaped body, and you have no idea how to work the controls. A baby might figure it out in a few months, but you're not a baby anymore. Babies are way smart, Romeo. They can learn an entire language just by listening to it for a few years! In contrast, you spent seven years studying French, and all you had to show for it at the end is the ability to say "Yes, I am a werewolf."

Bien sur, je suis un loup-garou.

Anyway, none of that can help you now! You've both flopped over and peed your pants. You can feel your host beginning to reassert himself. He's wondering why he's on the floor with peed pants. He's pretty embarrassed about it. Juliet's host is probably in pretty much the exact same spot.

Both your and Juliet's host bodies get up, look at each other, and run to the bathroom. It turns out you were at a high school dance, and this was the first dance these two people—George and Lorraine are their names—were going to share! But now they've both peed themselves and are too mortified to talk to each other ever again. They never fall in love, they never get married, and they never have any kids with each other. All because of you.

But come on, this is high school! Only a few people will love only one person their entire lives, and even fewer meet that one single person they'll ever love in HIGH SCHOOL. George and Lorraine graduate and go out into the world and fall in love and get married and have kids with other people. And that's fine! They're just as happy in some ways, they're happier in other ways, and they're less happy in some third ways, and it's a VERY REASONABLE ENDING, all things considered.

Lorraine and George never do find out that the reason their lives turned out the way they did is that, hundreds of years before they were born, two horny teens decided to take it slow, then they died, then they became ghosts, then they decided to change their past with a ghost time machine of their own construction, then chose a date at random instead of changing their past after all.

Honestly, I'm not sure they would've believed it anyway.

THE END

165 "I do," you say. You love her more than ever.

"You may kiss," Friar Lawrence says, and you do, and it's perfect. It's absolutely perfect.

Congratulations, Romeo! You have gotten married. And now you're kissing a woman too! I guess, in the end, everything worked out super well for you after all. Nicely done!

I award you 1000 out of a possible 1000 points.

THE END

Wait, what the heck? There's a zillion more pages in this book! HELLO, I DEMAND MORE STORY. LIKE, AT LEAST A HUNDRED PAGES' WORTH. *Turn to 177.*

No, I'm good! This was an entirely satisfying story and I'm sure that here, just as in real life, stories never really end and instead just go in different directions that I might end up not liking, and things are actually pretty great right now, so I'm content to put this book down and say, "Good enough for me!" *Turn to 235.*

166 Okay, we can do that! After all, the book's called *Romeo and/or Juliet*; it would hardly be fair if I didn't let you be Romeo and/or Juliet!

You are now Juliet! And you are about to get married. Exciting times!

 Go get married: *turn to 160.*

167

You look up to the balcony. A light is on inside!

"But soft! What light through yonder window breaks?" you whisper, holding one hand out in front of you.

A lady in a nightgown steps out from the light onto the balcony, brushing her hair. She's . . . super hot! It's the same lady, Romeo!

And here I want to pause to say, honestly, I thought you'd find out this woman's name by now. I really did. But that hasn't happened, and I guess I have nobody to blame but myself. Anyway, her name is Juliet. Juliet Capulet. Surprise! IT'S THE WOMAN WHOSE NAME IS ON THE COVER OF THIS BOOK. And I get that my just telling you now introduces a continuity error here, but just forget it. Nobody will ever notice you suddenly know who she is, unless they're forced to study this book in great detail, and even then I'm sure their teacher will just say, "Oh Romeo probably saw her name on the house directory on the way out. That's a thing houses have so it's not a problem, the end!"

Alright, so Juliet's here! You're staring at her from the bushes you're hiding in, and you are REALLY feeling like talking her up to yourself. How you wanna play this, Romeo?

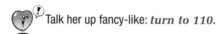Talk her up fancy-like: *turn to 110.*

Talk her up normal-like: *turn to 147.*

168

You draw your sword.

"I will stab this sword into your mouth," you say. "That should shut you up."

"Oh, we're really gonna do this?" Mercutio says. "We're really gonna fight to the death right here in the middle of every—"

(At this point, you stab your sword into his mouth, which is why he stopped talking suddenly.)

Everyone is really surprised that you did this, especially you, which is dumb because you're the one who decided to do this in the first place. Police quickly arrive and arrest you, many citizens testify you attacked him unprovoked (you discover "He was making fun of the nurse of a lady I'm trying to impress" doesn't count as provocation), and because of your murder trial you miss out on your wedding. Also the trial ends in your being sentenced to death, so you also miss out on your continued existence.

Your death sentence is carried out by lethal injection, which in this time period involves cutting a hole in your skin and stuffing bugs inside of it! Oh, gross. Romeo, you have unlocked the GROSS ENDING.

Your gravestone reads as follows.

HERE LIES ROMEO MONTAGUE

Good friend, for heaven's sake forebeare
To digg the dust enclosed heare;
Because it's grosse and full of bugges
Life's crazy, I don't know, *shrugges*

THE END

169
You do an hour of cardio, which brings you to 10 a.m. Your nurse still isn't back, Juliet, so you decide to do some muscle building, focusing on your 'ceps: bi-, tri-, and quadri-. An hour later it's 11 a.m. and your 'ceps are all totally blasted, but your nurse still isn't here. "What's taking so long?" you mutter as you wipe down your weights and also muscles. "This is ridiculous."

You spend another hour doing more cardio, turning the castle hallways into a 2K course that you lap until your legs feel like jelly. And she's STILL not here. "She said she'd be back in half an hour, THREE HOURS AGO," you mutter as you jog. "Ridiculous. Totally ridiculous."

You decide to hit the showers. She's still not here. "If she were young and in love like me she'd be back already," you mutter as you lather up your hair. "I'm fast and awesome."

You decide to head back to your room. She's still not here. "You know what ALL SENIOR CITIZENS EVER are?" you say as you flop down onto your bed. "Sluggish." After a moment, you prop yourself up on one arm to address an imaginary audience. "Oh I'm sorry, is that ageist? OH WOW IF ONLY A SENIOR CITIZEN COULD SHOW UP HERE TO TELL ME THAT IN PERSON, AND PERHAPS OTHER NEWS AS WELL."

You decide to sign a piece of paper that reads, "I hereby declare that Angelica Nurse is the worst nurse ever; I can never take this back," but your nurse pokes her head in your bedroom doorway before you can find a blank scroll.

"Hey Juliet," she says, completely neutrally.

Ask her if she got ahold of Romeo: *turn to 194.*

Casually walk over to your bed, break off a bedknob with your bare hands, toss it a few times as if to test its weight, then throw it at the wall as hard as you can before asking her if she got ahold of Romeo: *turn to 143.*

170

You take a step towards Juliet. This will require all your smooth-talking skills, but you feel like you're up to the task. "My name, dear saint," you say, "is hateful to myself, because it is an enemy to thee. Had I it written, I would tear the word." You look around for a piece of paper. "I'm serious," you say. "I'll write it down and tear it up right now."

"Romeo?" Juliet says. "My ears have not yet drunk a hundred words of that tongue's uttering, yet I know the sound. Art thou not Romeo, and a Montague?"

"Neither, if either thee dislike," you say, keeping your language as classy as hers. This is going really well! Juliet asks you how you got past her security system and you reply, "With love's light wings did I o'erperch these walls, for stony limits cannot hold love out," which was ABSOLUTELY the right thing to say. You both lower your arms and stare at each other happily. Words aren't necessary right now. But then Juliet seems to remember something.

"If my relatives see you they'll totally murder you," Juliet says.

"I'm not going anywhere," you say. "One look from you and I'm invincible against any wack relatives."

Juliet sighs happily. "I'd give anything for them to not find you," she says.

"I'd rather die by their hate than live without your love," you say. Juliet smiles, then frowns again.

"How did you even find me?" she asks suspiciously.

"Love guided me to you," you say.

"Seriously though," she says. You pause.

"I would sail to the farthest sea to be with you," you say.

Again, it seems to have worked. Juliet raises her arm out in front of her and says the following speech, not letting you get a word in edgewise:

> Thou know'st the mask of night is on my face,
> Else would a maiden blush bepaint my cheek
> For that which thou hast heard me speak tonight.
> Fain would I dwell on form. Fain, fain deny
> What I have spoke. But farewell compliment!
> Dost thou love me? I know thou wilt say "ay,"
> And I will take thy word. Yet if thou swear'st
> Thou mayst prove false. At lovers' perjuries,
> They say, Jove laughs. O gentle Romeo,
> If thou dost love, pronounce it faithfully.
> Or if thou think'st I am too quickly won,
> I'll frown and be perverse and say thee nay,
> So thou wilt woo. But else, not for the world.
> In truth, fair Montague, I am too fond,
> And therefore thou mayst think my 'havior light.
> But trust me, gentleman, I'll prove more true
> Than those that have more coying to be strange.
> I should have been more strange, I must confess,
> But that thou overheard'st, ere I was 'ware,
> My true love's passion. Therefore pardon me,
> And not impute this yielding to light love,
> Which the dark night hath so discovered.

Okay honestly you didn't even catch all of that, but it doesn't matter, because you caught enough to know that she's big into you!! This is perfect. All you need to do is swear your love to her and you've sealed the deal!

Swear your love by yonder blessed moon: *turn to 140.*

Swear your love by your gracious self: *turn to 158.*

Tell her that you're really attracted to her but you can't really say you love her yet. But you really want to get to know her, and can't wait for that to happen! *Turn to 187.*

171 Ghost You and Ghost Juliet watch space for a timeless age, considering all that you've seen and all that you can learn from that. At last, finally, you realize you've seen enough to do what you need to do. You stop watching.

And you start working.

It takes centuries—you're not sure how many—but finally out of ectoplasm and your own ingenuity you and Juliet construct your greatest work: a ghost time machine. You can't send your body back in time (not that you have one in the traditional sense of the word but WHATEVER), but you can send your consciousness back in time, leaping from this life to that one, perhaps even putting things right that once went wrong.

There's just one catch: a human mind can't hold the millennia of memories you've accumulated as a ghost. When you leap back, you'll only have a few seconds at most to make a difference before you forget all about your lives as ghosts—forever.

Juliet places her ghost hand in yours and smiles.

"Let's do it," she says.

What do you set the temporal controls for?

Monday, July 22, 1585—12:35:44.59 a.m.: *turn to 202.*

Saturday, November 12, 1955—9:10:00.00 p.m.: *turn to 152.*

Sunday, December 25, 0000—8:23:12.45 a.m.: *turn to 185.*

172 What? Juliet, this is your WEDDING. This is the natural culmination of the romance you've been having with that dude hiding in your bushes! Your ENTIRE STORY[1] has been leading to this moment!

But you know what? Sure, why not? I wrote a really sweet wedding scene, but come on, it's not like I wrote this book because I ever wanted anyone to, you know, READ IT.

So! Anything else you want to skip while we're at it?

Um okay geez calm down I'll go to your/my stupid wedding: *turn to 203.*

 No, just skipping the wedding is fine. Let's jump ahead to the point where we're married and/or smooching. *Turn to 188.*

You know what? Yeah, actually. Let's skip ahead to whenever the next fight scene is. THANKS IN ADVANCE, BOOK, THIS IS GOING TO BE REALLY COOL. *Turn to 184.*

---

1 On this particular run-through.

173

You are in front of Capulet Castle, proud home to the Capulets and also you. The door behind you is locked shut. There's no way to get back in except to succeed in your mission!

The only exit is to the north.

There is a servant here.

Talk to servant about gatekeeper: turn to 179.

Go north: turn to 164.

174

"Look, let me—let me put that another way," you say. "I'm sorry, but it's like—you ever walk near a cliff or something and you think, 'I could jump right now'? Or, like, you're driving your horse with some friends and out of nowhere you think about how you could drive that horse right into a tree?"

Juliet nods. "You're suddenly aware of how you could drive that horse into a tree at a full one horsepower and how everyone would be instantly inconvenienced on impact," Juliet says. "I mean, assuming the horse doesn't naturally dodge the tree, you could really bruise someone you care about."

"That's kinda how I feel now," you say. "Like I'm standing on the edge of that cliff, only the cliff is labeled 'MARRIAGE' and the rocky shoals at the bottom are labeled 'RESPONSIBILITY' and there's an arrow pointing to me labeled 'FORTUNE'S FOOL.' You know?"

"Sweetie, we don't have to get married today," Juliet says, squeezing your hand. "We've got the rest of our lives for that. Besides, if we wait, we could have a ceremony our families could attend. BOTH our families."

"Yeah right," you say. "Our two families who hate each other. They're definitely going to all want to cram into this church to watch us kiss on each other."

"Well," Juliet says, "they WOULD be separated on different sides of the aisle."

And I want you to look at those empty seats right now, Romeo, because very soon I'm going to do a clock wipe to this exact same scene, three years later. As you watch, those empty chairs will be filled with friends and family, Montagues and Capulets, and while that aisle WILL separate them during the ceremony, they're going to dance and laugh and toast each other at the reception. It's going to be that way because you and Juliet are going to spend the next three years getting your parents to talk to each other, making them realize that as much as they hate each other, they love you both even more, and your love can beat up their hate any day.

You're going to love each other so fiercely, Romeo, so completely. Your two houses will have no choice but to start liking each other, because you and Juliet won't accept anything less. You're going to be the change you want to see in the world, and you're going to do it all by loving this woman with everything you've got and by her loving you just as hard in return.

Ready, Romeo?

Here goes.

THE END

175 "What?" Romeo says.

"I just met you, dude!" you say. "Yesterday. At, like, midnight. I've known you for less than twenty-four hours."

"But I love you! This is romance! I love you and I love romance!" Romeo says, a little frantically.

"I like you too, Romeo, but I can't marry you today. So, um . . . sorry?" you say.

"You were going to marry me a second ago," he says.

"Changed my mind," you say, and kiss him on the cheek. "If you love me this won't be a huge deal, okay? Come on man, it's not like I'm running out on a wedding we've been planning for months. I'm running out on a wedding you got my nurse to invite me to a few hours ago."

"IT IS A HUGE DEAL!" Romeo shouts. He jumps down into the audience area and kicks over a chair. "I was gonna get married!!"

"Romeo, buddy, calm down," you say.

"YOU calm down!" he says. "You—you can't say you'll marry someone and then not marry them!"

"So we should get married out of—what, inertia? OBLIGATION?" you say.

"YES!" Romeo shouts.

"Look, you're obviously not yourself, and I didn't think you'd get this upset," you say. "I'm sorry, but I'm going home. We can talk about this later."

You leave Romeo there. When you get home you explain what happened to Angelica, who honestly kinda seems more upset about it than you are.

The next morning, the word "HARLOT" is mysteriously painted on your castle's exterior walls. The day after that, "JULIET IS A" is added above it. The day after that "LET ME BE CLEAR, WHEN I SAID" is added before it, and "I ACTUALLY MEANT THAT SHE NEEDS TO BE MORE OF ONE. SHE'S NOT ENOUGH OF A HARLOT RIGHT NOW AND I WOULD PREFER IF SHE WERE HARLOT-ER. SIGNED, ROMEO."

The day after that your dad gets the walls cleaned. He also pays a bunch of people to go over to Romeo's house and beat him up.

"OKAY GEEZ SORRY" is painted on your walls the next day. And you never hear from Romeo again.

Later on, in college, you're at a party and the conversation gets to old relationships. For the first time you decide to break out the story of Juliet and Her Romeo: AKA, That One Time I Was Engaged for Almost a Whole Day.

Your friends start giggling as you tell the story, and before long you're giggling too. Everything that happened felt so important when it was going on, but now that you've got some distance, it really does sound like a joke. Romeo left your party to hide in the bushes outside your house? He proposed to you through your NURSE? He tried to get his friends to bring over a SEX LADDER?

Your friends are laughing, and you're laughing too, and before long you're laughing so hard you're struggling to breathe. You're laughing the way people who were drowning but somehow made it back to shore laugh as they lie faceup on the beach, the blinding sun in their eyes, their muscles exhausted and screaming.

That is to say, thankfully.

THE END

176 "Hello," you say. "I'm not sure if we've met. I am Angelica Nurse, and I am on a quest. A 'nurse quest,' if you will."

The servant looks at you, uninterested.

"Fascinating," she says.

Look around: turn to 183.

Go north: turn to 164.

177 Okay later on you make some choices that it turns out were bad even though they TOTALLY seemed reasonable when you made them, or maybe not, and that gets you into trouble and you probably die.

THE END

NO. I want more story with DETAILS. *Turn to 206.*

178 Here's the thing, Romeo: after making your way home after the party last night, you couldn't sleep. In fact, you stayed up all night, and once morning comes you start to feel antsy. Instead of waiting there for the nurse Juliet said she'd send, you wander over to your friend Friar Lawrence's house. You've got the time, and there are things you need to set up if you're going to get married today!

You're inside the Friar's house now, and you've just told him you've fallen for Juliet Capulet and want him to marry you both today.

"Holy s—" he begins, then catches himself, smoothly changing the syllable into "—aint Francis! What happened to Rosaline? You were crying about her all the time only yesterday!"

"I didn't cry ALL the time," you say.

"YOU CRIED ALL THE TIME," he says. "There's literally a crusty trail on your cheek from an old tear you cried over her. Right there. See? It's right there."

"Aw geez," you say, rubbing your face and glad that at least the two times Juliet saw you last night you were either wearing a mask or standing some distance below her in some bushes.

"Listen," you say. "YOU said I should stop obsessing about Rosaline, and I have! I'm obsessed with Juliet now, okay? I've known her for less than twenty-four hours but I'm not a BABY anymore, so you know I know what I'm talking about when I say I love her and want to spend the rest of my life with her! Come on, Friar, will you marry us or not??"

Friar Lawrence looks at you for a moment. "Oh, what the hell," he says, sighing.

"Cool," you say. "Perfect. What time is it now?"

"Nine fifteen," he says.

"OH CRAP I WAS SUPPOSED TO BE HOME FOR NINE," you say. "AW GEEZ." You rush out the door but stop and run back to the Friar's house. "WE'LL BE BACK AT, I DUNNO, AROUND TWO THIRTY TO GET MARRIED," you say, then turn to run out the door again.

"Go wisely and slowly!" the Friar shouts after you.

"NO TIME FOR THAT," you say, tripping over a root outside, scrambling to your feet, and breaking into a run again. You reach your house at around 9:45 on account of how running is hard and you're not used to it. Unsurprisingly, after 45 minutes, nobody is waiting outside. You missed her. You told Juliet to send her nurse for you and then stood her up. Nice going, cool guy.

There's nothing for you to do now but grab a quick breakfast and then head downtown. Juliet's nurse will be looking for you, and downtown's the most visible place to be. She'll be sure to check there eventually. When you get there, you place yourself by the public fountain right in the middle of the square. It's got two advantages: your friends are already hanging out here, and from here you'll be able to see if any nurses wander past!

"You ditched us pretty well last night, bro," Mercutio says after you say hello.

"I had important business," you say, sitting down. Mercutio makes a bunch of gross sex puns at you, you make a bunch in return, and before you know it it's almost time for lunch. You burned the whole morning on dumb sex puns, Romeo! Literally the whole morning is gone now. And no I'm not telling you what the sex puns were, because honestly you kinda lost steam around hour two anyway.

Just then you see Juliet's nurse walking nearby. Benvolio spots her too. "Land ho!" he shouts.

Perfect. He's making fun of her weight.

"No dude, I think there are actually TWO people there," Mercutio says. Great: Mercutio's making fun of her weight too. Mercutio's not the kind of person to let a fat joke drop, and Benvolio will go along with whatever he says. You feel your stress level rising.

Surprisingly, the nurse comes over to your group. "I'm looking for

Romeo," she says. "All I know is that he's young, he wears a unicorn mask sometimes, and he's in love with—"

"That's me!" you say, interrupting her before she can reveal your big news to your friends. They give you a surprised look that seems to say, "You know this woman?" and then goes on to say, "We respect you less for knowing this woman, because we judge people by appearances."

"Um," you say, "by that I mean, this young Romeo you're looking for will be older when you find him than when you started looking. Because we're all older than we've ever been before in our entire lives, every second of every day. Yes, every day brings us twenty-four hours closer to death." Your friends turn away, satisfied that your answer is suitably sassy enough.

"Fancy words," the nurse says suspiciously.

"Fancy words," Mercutio says in a singsong mimic of the nurse, and you elbow him again to get him to shut up.

"What? Why do you keep protecting her?" Mercutio says, frustrated. He motions to her. "She's a prostitute. Her ugliness is the perfect cover, because nobody would believe anyone so homely would be SUCH AN INCREDIBLY SUCCESSFUL SEX WORKER."

You are literally from the 1500s, so you think getting paid to have sex is the worst thing in the world for a person to do. You ask him to shut the hell up.

"Make me," he says.

You place your hand on the hilt of your sword.

Fight Mercutio: *turn to 168.*

 Don't fight Mercutio: *turn to 149.*

179
"Hello," you say. "It's me, Angelica Nurse. Listen, do you know the password to get past the gate?"

The servant looks at you evenly.

"Maybe I do and maybe I don't," she says. "What's in it for me?"

Say, "I'll tell you a secret in exchange": turn to 195.

Ask, "What do you want?" Turn to 212.

End this conversation: turn to 173.

180

You wait around all afternoon until it's finally dark out. "Whew, what a day!" you tell your parents as you get up from the couch you've been sharing with them and stretch. "I'm exhausted!"

Your mom gives you a look.

"I'm exhausted from sitting around all day," you explain. "I'm definitely not exhausted from secretly getting married and THEN sitting around all day, that's for sure!"

Your dad nods. "Good, good." He stands up and stretches too. "It can be tiring to do nothing all day long, but that is the price we pay for being super rich," he says. "Good night, Juliet."

You go up to your room, put on your sexiest sleepwear, and wait for Romeo to appear.

An hour passes and you start to get bored. You're excited about tonight, but at the back of your mind you're also aware that you've never had sex before and haven't really had much sexual education! As near as you can figure it, you've got three choices:

Talk to yourself about how much you want to have sex with Romeo: *turn to 214.*

 Talk to yourself about how much you want to have sex with Romeo in the fanciest language you can muster: *turn to 197.*

Just sit quietly, I don't need to talk to myself about sex now, thanks: *turn to 190.*

181

You walk away without reacting. Behind you, the sound of swordfighting intensifies. Benvolio begins to follow you but turns back. "I need to put an end to this," he says. "I'll catch up later. Go. I'll be fine." Benvolio shakes your hand, and you watch him run back to the fight.

You return home. You sneak into Juliet's bedroom as scheduled that evening, but your plans for FUN SEXUAL ACTIVITY are postponed when she tells you the news of what's happened in the town square.

It turns out that after you left, Benvolio rushed into the fight trying to make peace and was stabbed in the guts to death by Tybalt! Mercutio, enraged, stabbed Tybalt in the guts to death too, but Tybalt in return managed to stab Mercutio in the guts to death just before he died! So they're all dead now: one Montague, one Capulet, and one blood relative to Police Chief "Prince" Escalus. Whoops.

"Whoops," you say.

The next morning the entire families of the Montagues and Capulets are all dragged into court by Escalus. You're sitting in a packed courtroom with your family while Juliet sits with hers on the other side of the aisle. You wave at her. She waves back. At some point you should probably tell your parents you got married?

Escalus says this stupid fight between your families has to end. Today. Both your and Juliet's parents protest that it was the other family's fault, but Escalus cuts them off. "I don't care, I really don't care," he says. "Get over yourselves and give me a solution," he says, "because you lot are leaving this courtroom one of two ways: by settling your dispute, or because I've banished you all to different towns.

"I swear to God I'll do it," he says. "Make you somebody else's problem for a change."

Escalus looks around the courtroom. "Well??"

Stand up and announce that you and Juliet have gotten married: *turn to 215.*

Stay quiet: *turn to 198.*

182

You stumble backwards under the force of his blow, and Tybalt gives you time to recover.

"I don't want to fight you!" he screams as you get to your feet again.

"Then stop," you say, and then you're charging him, your sword raised. You're about to bring your blade down on his neck when you feel an acute pain in your chest. You glance down and discover Tybalt has actually managed to stab you first. You crane your neck around to look behind you and see that his sword went all the way through and poked out the other side.

Gross.

"I didn't want this," Tybalt says. He starts to pull his sword out, but you scream in pain, and he stops. "I don't know what else to do," he says.

And I hate to tell this to you, Romeo, but what you have is a mortal wound, and it's going to kill you very soon. You can linger on this sentence as long as you want to draw things out, but when you reach its end, you'll also reach yours.

And there it is.

You are now dead! You were stabbed to death by Tybalt: a character so minor in this story that he's barely even gotten any lines so far. You managed to meet someone, marry her, and die in an unrelated matter in less than 24 hours.

"How did this happen?" you ask yourself, dying on the Veronan street. "Could it possibly be due to my terrible decisions?"

Quite possibly, yeah! The real downside of this is that you'll never see Juliet again. Who will apologize to her for being such a screwup?

Not you, corpsie!!

THE END

P.S.: You are later resurrected by the fates to act as a sort of Grim Reaper–style character, a ghostly apparition who tracks down people who somehow cheated their proscribed death, working to ensure that they die anyway in deliciously ironic circumstances. But that's a story for another book! One that I hope is titled, oh I don't know . . . *FORTUNE'S GHOUL*??

183 You are in front of Capulet Castle, proud home to the Capulets and also you. The door behind you is locked shut. There's no way to get back in except to succeed in your mission!
The only exit is to the north.
There is a servant here.

Talk to servant: turn to 176.

Go north: turn to 161.

184 Sure, let's do that! Let's absolutely just skip ahead to the next thing. I don't know what I was thinking with all this "romance" stuff. Screw me, right?

Alright, the next fight scene I see here is with Romeo. You are now Romeo, and your friend Mercutio is fighting your new cousin Tybalt. You and your bestie Benvolio are about to jump in and try to break it up—with swords!

Let's see what happens!!

Go fight a dude! *Turn to 193.*

185 "That's not a real date," Juliet says. "There was no year zero. If we went back to that time, we'd probably, I don't know, end up dividing by zero and find ourselves inside a black hole."

"Obviously I know that!!" you say. "Everyone knows that. I was just wondering if YOU knew that."

You quickly punch in a different date.

Monday, July 22, 1585—12:35:44.59 a.m.: *turn to 202.*

Saturday, November 12, 1955—9:10:00.00 p.m.: *turn to 152.*

186 "Here," you say, handing her your nurse hat. "Have it."

She removes her servant hat and puts on your hat. She adjusts it on her head and seems satisfied. She throws her servant hat at you in exchange. It says, "HI! ASK ME TO DO ANYTHING FOR YOU." It's gross. You hate it.

You have dropped your NURSE HAT.

You have gained a GROSS HAT.

Your score has been reduced by 1 point and is now −1 points out of a possible 1000 points.

"If you want that passphrase," she says, "you'll put it on." You sigh and put on the GROSS HAT, and she laughs at you. "Okay, now my arm hurts a little," she says. "It's a little stiff. Nurse it back to health and I'll give you the passphrase."

"Hey! You said you'd give me the passphrase if I gave you my hat!" you say.

"That was before my arm got hurt in the hat exchange," she says. "Maybe it's gonna hurt more if it doesn't get any attention. Maybe soon I'm gonna need more cool clothes to make up for it."

You sigh. "Give me your arm," you say. She holds it out, and you poke it tentatively with your finger. "You know I'm not this kind of nurse, right? You want a medical nurse," you say. "I'm the kind of nurse who feeds babies out of her chest."

"Or," she says, "instead of making dumb excuses, you could massage my arm." You do. It takes a whole friggin' hour. At the end the servant says, "Okay, thanks! My arm feels a little better, I guess."

"Well, good," you say.

"Anyway," she replies, getting up and rubbing her arm slightly, "I'm as good as my word. The passphrase you need is 'We are such stuff as dreams are made on, and our little life is rounded with a sleep.' Got that?"

"That's a stupid passphrase," you say.

"I dunno," she says. "It got my arm massaged."

Look around: turn to 226.

Talk to servant: turn to 208.

Go north: turn to 200.

187

"Oh," Juliet says. "Okay. That's reasonable and realistic." She sounds disappointed but accepts how you feel.

Over the next several months you have many secret dates with each other until you are ready to tell Juliet you love her and that you want this relationship to be more serious. But when you do, she admits that she's been seeing other people, and she's not ready to become exclusive with anyone yet.

Several months later she is ready, but by that point you've already started seeing someone new, and you've just said you'll be exclusive with her. And so it goes for years and years: you remain friends, speaking not infrequently, but things never quite work out so that the two of you can date.

Only decades later, when you're both in your eighties, do the stars finally align and the two of you finally give being together a real shot. And it's WONDERFUL. You share several great years together, but you're both old now. The two of you die in your sleep, only six years after finally getting together.

Life as ghosts is quiet, and you're happy, but you can't help but feel like you missed out on something by not getting together when you were younger and had the athleticism required to bump your neat bodies up against each other in fun and cool ways. The two of you chose the safe route, and one thing you're beginning to learn during these years spent as ghosts is that, sometimes, safety isn't the most romantic thing in the world.

"I kinda wish we'd gotten together when I was, you know, young. And hotter. And more flexible," you say to your ghost wife.

"Yeah," Juliet sighs. "Me too. And while we would've been acting in a rash manner, the upside is even if our decisions had killed us, at least then we'd have spent eternity as hot babe ghosts, instead of tired senior-citizen ghosts with sore backs. Also, I'm cold all the time."

"Me too," you say. "But if wishes were horses, we'd all be horses." You smile and offer Juliet your arm. "Juliet, my love: I'm too tired to haunt anyone, but . . . would you like to do some people-watching?"

"You know what, Romeo? I really would," Juliet says. And so you do.

You and Juliet watch. You watch as the years become centuries, and the centuries millennia. You watch as humanity leaves Earth and begins to explore the stars. You watch as the last remnants of humans left behind degrade to savagery as the ecosystem, and with it civilization, collapses. And you watch, millions of years later, as Earth herself is consumed by the flame of the ever-expanding sun, now a red giant.

End the story here: *turn to 162.*

No, what? Apply everything you saw and learned as ghosts and get out of this predicament! *Turn to 171.*

188
After a while, Romeo pulls back from the kiss.

"Okay dude, I gotta go hang out with my bros now," he says.

"What?" you say. "We JUST got married!"

"I know, it was great, and you were great! But we always hang out on Monday afternoons and I'm already late. I'd invite you, but, you know: boys only."

"Romeo," you say sadly, "I wanted us to spend the day together."

"Okay," he says, "how about we hang out tonight? I'll come by your castle at dark and we can consummate our marriage. That sounds good, right? That'll be fun, right?"

"I guess," you say, kicking at some dust at your feet.

"Hey," Romeo says. "Come on, Juliet. I promise after I'm done hanging out with my friends, I'll sneak into your house and we'll have some really cool sex."

"OKAY FINE," you say. "But you'd BETTER be there. Don't, I don't know, commit murder and get banished from Verona or anything."

"Duh," Romeo says, and then he's gone. He didn't even comment on your foreshadowing!

Oh crap! Forget I said you were foreshadowing!!

 Say good-bye to the Friar and go home and wait, I guess: *turn to 180.*

189
You break into a run, and you don't stop till you reach . . .

. . . your house: *turn to 210.*

. . . Friar Lawrence's house: *turn to 204.*

190
You sit quietly. It's nice! Sometimes sitting quietly is nice!

After a while, there's a knock at your door. I suppose the quiet time couldn't last forever, right? Besides, I did kinda promise adventure in this story, so in a way, maybe it's for the best we didn't get to sit here for too long, no matter how nice and peaceful and refreshing a change of pace it was.

OH WELL. BACK TO ADVENTURE, I SUPPOSE.

Open your bedroom door: *turn to 207.*

191
Tybalt draws his sword as you swing at him, narrowly avoiding getting instagibbed. He leaps back, holding his sword at the ready.

"I don't want to fight you, Romeo!" he shouts.

"Too bad that I do!" you reply, attacking him again. You manage to nick his arm (at which point you consider saying, "Looks like I'M the one who's better armed here," but decide not to because if you went down that road there'd be pages and pages of body-themed puns and we'd all be powerless to stop it) and in return he cuts your shoulder.

Your swords clash, and for a moment you're face-to-face, so close you can smell his breath and he can smell yours. Closer, actually. It's like you're passing the same breath of air back and forth between your two pairs of slightly opened lips.

I don't think it's supposed to be this sexy, but oh well!!

Push him back and attack: *turn to 201.*

Wait for him to push YOU back, and defend against whatever he comes at you with: *turn to 182.*

192 Friar Lawrence leads you into the chapel. You climb up onstage and take Juliet's hands in yours. The Friar stands in front of you both and speaks in his stage voice, loudly addressing the rows of empty chairs left over from a previous wedding.

"We are gathered here today to see Romeo Montague and Juliet Capulet wed in holy matrimony," he says. Then he pauses for a second, concerned. "Wait: Romeo, does Juliet have a middle name?"

"Her Christian name is Juliet Hottie Megababe Capulet," you say.

"No it's not," Juliet says, laughing. "Don't be so weird, silly! Keep that up and I might, hah hah, I might start thinking that marrying someone I've known for less than twenty-four hours is a bad idea!"

You shut the heck up.

Friar Lawrence places a hand on her shoulder. "Juliet, do you take this man to be your lawfully wedded husband?" he says.

Juliet stares deeply into your eyes as she answers. She seems to contemplate her choice for a moment, as if trying to decide between two or more options that will define her future.

"I do," she says.

"Excellent," Friar Lawrence says. He now places his hand on your shoulder. "And do you, Romeo, take Juliet to be your lawfully wedded wife?"

You look deeply into Juliet's eyes and smile.

Say, "I do": *turn to 165.*

Say, "Haha, what? No." *Turn to 174.*

193 You draw your sword.

"Come on, Benvolio!" you shout. "Let's stop this fight by joining it!"

"Yes!" shouts Benvolio as he raises his sword above him. "Fighting for peace! We have to do that!"

The two of you rush into the fight! But rather than stopping any violence, all you manage to do is stand there waving your arms between Tybalt and Mercutio, which distracts Mercutio long enough for Tybalt to stab him from under your arm. He drops his sword and clutches his chest, screaming.

"Cheese it!" Tybalt says, and cheeses it out of there.

Mercutio collapses to the ground. You kneel by him and cradle his head in your arms, which is actually a terrible thing to do to someone who has just suffered internal injuries but what do you know about medicine?

"A plague on both your houses," Mercutio says.

"Whoah, easy on the plagues there, big guy," you say.

Benvolio crouches beside you. "What, are you hurt?" he says, but his intonation is a bit off and it comes out more like "What are you, hurt?"

"Yes, a scratch, it's just a scratch," Mercutio says. He takes in air suddenly, wincing. "But it'll be enough."

Mercutio looks to be in a bad way. You want to comfort him. But you don't know what to say to your dying friend.

Tell him you love him, you'll always love him: *turn to 223.*

Tell him it can't hurt THAT bad: *turn to 241.*

Tell him, "Hey, speaking of plagues, a plague on both YOUR houses too, buddy": *turn to 216.*

194
"Where the heck were you?" you demand of your nurse. "And did you get ahold of Romeo? What'd he say??"

"Just a sec," she says, motioning towards the chair in the corner of your room. "My bones ache. I'm real tired."

"Hey! Here's an idea," you say. "I'LL TRADE MY BONES FOR YOUR INFORMATION."

"Calm down, calm down!" she says. "What's the rush? Do you not see I'm out of breath here?"

"HOW CAN YOU EVEN BE OUT OF BREATH," you say, "IF YOU CAN TELL ME YOU'RE OUT OF BREATH?? OH MY GOD. YOUR EXCUSES ARE TAKING UP MORE TIME THAN SIMPLY TELLING ME YOUR NEWS WOULD TAKE."

Angelica fans her face weakly and smiles.

"Look," you say, "just tell me if it's good news or bad news, okay? Just tell me that."

"Romeo has a handsome face and his legs are actually pretty okay," she says. "Have you had lunch yet?"

"NO I HAVEN'T HAD LUNCH YET," you say. "Also, I know all this stuff already! Does he still want to marry me or not?"

"Oh, my back!" Angelica says. "If only my back could be rubbed by someone, as I've recently learned massages can be bartered for goods and services!"

You stand behind her and massage her shoulders. "Little lower," she says. You roll your knuckles over the knots of her back.

"What'd he say?" you ask.

"Ah, that's good," she says. "Why are you so impatient?"

You push your knuckles into her back with some force. She whimpers. "What'd he say?" you ask again, ever so sweetly.

"Are you allowed to go out for confession today?" she asks.

"Yep," you say.

"Then go to Friar Lawrence's house, because Romeo's waiting there to make you his wife."

You're so happy! You wrap your arms around her in a hug.

"Go, go," Angelica squeaks out. You let her go, walk into your closet, and put on your best "gettin' married" dress.

"I've got to stay here," Angelica says as you dress. "Romeo's sending over a friend with a rope ladder, so he'll be able to get here tonight for sex times. As you can see, I've thought of everything."

You walk out of the closet, looking gorgeous. "Wish me luck," you say, and then you're out the door.

Go get married: *turn to 160.*

195 "What secret?" she says.

"Um," you say. "I haven't told anyone this before, but . . . when I was fourteen, I had a crush on my cousin."

"BORING," says the servant. "EVERYONE is mad crushing on their cousins in this stupid time period. No deal, I'm not telling you anything."

She turns away from you, ending the conversation, but something in her body language tells you she'd be willing to have this exact conversation once more.

Look around: turn to 173.

196

"I'm keeping my hat," you say.
"Suit yourself," she says, and turns away.

Look around: turn to 173.

197

You hold up one hand in front of you as you pace your bedroom. Here's what you say:

> *Gallop apace, you fiery-footed steeds,*
> *Toward Phoebus' lodging. Such a wagoner*
> *As Phaeton would whip you to the west*
> *And bring in cloudy night immediately.*
> *Spread thy close curtain, love-performing night,*
> *That runaways' eyes may wink, and Romeo*
> *Leap to these arms, untalked of and unseen.*
> *Lovers can see to do their amorous rites*
> *By their own beauties, or, if love be blind,*
> *It best agrees with night. Come, civil night,*
> *Thou sober-suited matron, all in black,*
> *And learn me how to lose a winning match*
> *Played for a pair of stainless maidenhoods.*
> *Hood my unmanned blood bating in my cheeks,*
> *With thy black mantle, till strange love, grow bold,*
> *Think true love acted simple modesty.*
> *Come, night. Come, Romeo. Come, thou day in night,*
> *For thou wilt lie upon the wings of night*
> *Whiter than new snow upon a raven's back.*
> *Come, gentle night, come, loving, black-browed night,*
> *Give me my Romeo. And when I shall die,*
> *Take him and cut him out in little stars,*
> *And he will make the face of heaven so fine*
> *That all the world will be in love with night*
> *And pay no worship to the garish sun.*
> *Oh, I have bought the mansion of a love,*
> *But not possessed it, and though I am sold,*
> *Not yet enjoyed. So tedious is this day*
> *As is the night before some festival*
> *To an impatient child that hath new robes*
> *And may not wear them.*

Referencing Phaeton AND Phoebus, huh? Classic.
Suddenly, there's a knock at your door. You lower your arm.

"Just a minute!" you say, glancing around your room to make sure there's nothing that would suggest you're planning for your husband to visit you tonight. Everything looks great, except for the lingerie you're wearing.

"Um, pay no attention to how sexy my pajamas are! I'm just super hot all the time, no big deal!" you say.

 Open your bedroom door: *turn to 207.*

198

You keep your mouth shut throughout the awkward silence that follows. "Nobody?" he says. "None of you can think of a way to end this strife? Not one. All y'all's mouths are sealed up?"

You look around. Nobody seems prepared to say anything.

"Okay, fine, perfect," Escalus says. He straightens. "Immediately we do exile you low-res bojos from Verona. Montagues go to Mantua, Capulets to Cologna Veneta."

He bangs his gavel. You hear a gasp. Someone starts to cry. Escalus is unmoved.

"I will be deaf to all pleading and excuses," Escalus says. "Now get the hell out of my town."

Leave with your family: *turn to 219.*

Hide in a closet with Juliet until everyone's gone: *turn to 211.*

199

After the wedding you remember your standing date to hang out with your bros, so you tell your bride of at least a few minutes that you'll catch up with her later. She's unhappy with this, but you PROMISE you'll come by tonight so you can have Married People Sex.

She's quite excited about the prospect of Married People Sex.

That settled, you run out of the Friar's house and make your way downtown, back to your bros Benvolio and Mercutio! When you finally find them, they're just saying good-bye to Peter (remember him? You call him Alleypal! He's the guy whom you got word of Juliet's party from, in, um, an alley) and talking to—aw geez, they're talking to TYBALT.

I'm supposed to be an impartial narrator, but dude, Tybalt's a tool! He calls himself THE PRINCE OF CATS. Do you know how many non-tools call themselves the Prince of Cats? I will give you a hint: the number involved was invented by the Mesopotamians and occupies a central role in modern mathematics, and if you somehow divide by it you can cause a black hole.

Friggin' Tybalt. Oh, and he's now your cousin by marriage too, so good work on that one, ROMEO. Real cool extended family you married into, bro.

"Hey Tybalt, what's up?" you say, trying to be polite to your new family.

"Hey Romeo," he sneers. "Thou art a villain."

Nobody talks to you like that! You're about to fight him right then and there to prove how much of a villain you're not, but then you remember your new wife and new family and decide to be the bigger man. You turn and walk away, saying good-bye to him over your shoulder. But then you still want to get him back for what he said about you, so you shout back one last zinger: "Your words can't hurt me anymore because I have a secret reason to love you now, Tybalt!"

That, uh, probably sounded more badass in your head.

You only get a few paces away before Tybalt calls after you. "What's the matter, Romeo? CHICKEN??"

You freeze in mid-step. You turn around slowly and explain, very calmly, that nobody calls you chicken.

"Chicken," he says.

"Allow me to clarify," you say. "Nobody whose opinion I RESPECT calls me chicken, but if they did, I would consider their words carefully and perhaps make a positive change in my life. However, as you are the one calling me chicken, Tybalt, I honestly don't care.

"Also," you add, "it's illegal to fight in the streets anyway, so I'm not chicken, I'm LAW-ABIDING." And with that, you walk away. You're not going to fight Tybalt today, even if he is a big loser.

Mercutio looks at you with disgust. "I can't believe you're being such a wimp," Mercutio says as you walk past him. "GOD. Man up, Romeo. Hey Tybalt, call ME chicken!"

"You're chicken," he says.

"What?! I CAN'T BELIEVE YOU CALLED ME THAT," Mercutio says, and draws his sword. He runs at Tybalt, their swords clash, and as simple as that, they're now swordfighting in broad daylight. It looks like they mean it, Romeo. I think this might be a fight to the death here!

I think . . . this book might've just gotten awesome??

Try to break up this fight to the death . . . BY JOINING IT: *turn to 193.*

Keep walking away; this is Mercutio's choice: *turn to 181.*

200

You are at Capulet Gate. A gatekeeper stops you from moving any further north.

"Sorry," he says, "but we've tightened security after the party last night. Anyone going in or out needs to know the passphrase."

"Ah, yes, of course!" you say. "And may I just say, sir, that we are such stuff as dreams are made on, and our little life is rounded with a sleep?"

"You can and did," the gatekeeper replies, tipping his hat at you.

Your score has increased by 100 points, and is now 99 points out of a possible 1000 points!

The gatekeeper begins to open the gate and chats with you as he works the machinery. "Hey, someone who looked like you but in a better hat was here earlier," he says. "She didn't know the passphrase though."

"Well," you say, "whoever she was, she sounds awesome and not at all annoyed by this entire process."

You step forward through the gate. The gatekeeper closes it behind you. As you make your way north, he shouts after you to wait. "I forgot to say," he shouts, "we're releasing the man-eating dogs now! So, uh, don't come back this way unless you can handle man-eating dogs!"

You are on the road to downtown Verona.

The only exits are to the north (ahead of you) and south (behind you).

Go north: turn to 146.

Go south: turn to 236.

201

Tybalt stumbles backwards under the force of your blow, and while he's off balance, you raise your sword, aim at his chest, and charge.

"This is for Mercutio!!" you shout. You knock his blade out of the way and experience what you will later describe as the disturbingly satisfying sensation of a sword sinking into some guts.

Tybalt looks down at the sword in his chest, going all the way through and sticking out the other side. Then he looks up at you. "I didn't want this," he says, and then he dies. Benvolio runs up to you.

"Where were YOU during this fight?" you say.

"Over there," Benvolio says, pointing to the side a little, "standing quietly. But that doesn't matter right now! You need to get out of here! YOU JUST KILLED A MAN IN BROAD DAYLIGHT. You'll get the death penalty for sure. Get out of here, cousin!!"

You look down at your sword sticking out of Tybalt. "Oh, I am fortune's fool!" you say.

"WHY ARE YOU STILL HERE?" Benvolio shouts, shoving you away.

Run away: *turn to 189*.

No man, I got perks to speech, I can talk my way out of this: *turn to 213*.

202

You and Juliet agree to set the temporal coordinates for the early morning of July 22, 1585: the exact moment when, outside her balcony, eons ago, you proposed taking it slow. If this works—and you believe that it will—you're going to propose something different: marriage.

And Juliet will be there to say yes.

You and Juliet hold hands, step into your quantum-leap accelerator, and vanish. You feel like time is passing, but you're not sure how.

You suddenly find yourself outside a balcony. It's smaller than you remember. "Hold on," you think, "what am I talking about? How would I remember a balcony I've never seen before?" Everything feels so heavy. So solid. You can feel your lungs moving in your chest. That feeling goes away, right?

Wait, which feeling?

Frantically, you realize you're already beginning to forget. If you don't talk to Juliet now you may not change anything, and thereby doom yourself to an eternity stuck in a time loop, forever returning back here, forever changing nothing, forever returning once more.

"Juliet!" you say. "Ignore all that other stuff I said. I've loved you since the moment I met you. I'll love you until the Earth stops spinning and the sun explodes, and for some reason I feel like I'm speaking with authority. Will you marry me? Like, soon? Will you marry me really soon?"

Juliet looks puzzled for a moment but then smiles. "I will," Juliet says. "I absolutely will."

"Well," you say. "Good. Is this crazy? It feels crazy."

"If this is what crazy feels like," Juliet says, "then let's go nuts. I'll send my nurse for you tomorrow at nine. We'll work out the specifics, and then . . . everything will be fine!"

"Good!" you say. "Good. Well, I'll . . . see you tomorrow!"

"You will indeed," she says. Juliet blows you a kiss and then disappears back into her room. You stand there in the darkness, watching her empty balcony for a moment, feeling your heart beating hard in your chest. You're getting married! Tomorrow! This is insane! This is exactly what you want!

You turn to leave, but stop in your tracks. You feel like you're forgetting something important, but the more you try to remember it, the more it's gone. You check your pockets for your wallet and keys, but they haven't gone anywhere. You're not forgetting anything. The feeling passes.

Whistling happily, you make your way home to bed.

Go home and go to bed: *turn to 178.*

203

Friar Lawrence leads you into the chapel. You climb up onstage and Romeo takes your hands in his. Friar Lawrence stands in front of you both and speaks in his stage voice, loudly addressing the rows of empty chairs left over from a previous service.

"We are gathered here today to see Romeo Montague and Juliet Capulet wed in holy matrimony," he says. Then he pauses for a second, concerned. "Wait, Romeo, does Juliet have a middle name?"

"Her Christian name is Juliet Hottie Megababe Capulet," Romeo says.

"No it's not," you say, laughing. "Don't be so weird, silly! Keep that up and I might, hah hah, I might start thinking that marrying someone I've known for less than twenty-four hours is a bad idea!"

Romeo shuts the heck up.

Friar Lawrence places his hand on your shoulder.

"Juliet, do you take this man to be your lawfully wedded husband?" the Friar asks you.

You stare deeply into Romeo's eyes as you answer.

"I do": *turn to 220.*

"Haha, what? No." *Turn to 175.*

204

You're in way over your head, Romeo. You just killed a dude in broad daylight in front of a whole city's worth of witnesses. You have no idea what to do.

But you know someone who might. You burst into Friar Lawrence's house, surprising the Friar in the middle of one of his experiments. In a rush, you explain what happened and beg him to tell you what to do.

"Get into my basement," he says. "We'll hide you here while we figure out what to do." He shoves you into a dark windowless room, locking the door from the outside. On the other side of the door he hisses, "I'm going into town to find out what happened. I'll be back soon. Don't make a sound!"

You sit in the dark for several hours. For the full "virtual reality" experience of this book, *turn to 218* and hold the book up really close to your face for several hours before returning here and reading the next sentence!

Hey, welcome back.

You can hear the noise of someone entering the basement. The door unlocks, and light floods the room, blinding you.

"It's me," the Friar says.

"What news?" you say. "Seriously, dude! What sorrow craves acquaintance at my hand that I yet not know?"

"Calm down, calm down," says the Friar. "I have good news. You're not being put to death, Romeo! You've only been banished!"

"Hah!" you laugh. "BANISHED? Be merciful, say 'death.' Exile's eighty billion times worse than banishment!!"

"Um," the Friar says. "Romeo, there's literally a whole world outside Verona. You know that, right?"

"Yeah, but it sucks there," you say. "Being banished from Verona is like being banished from the world, and you know what that is? DEATH. It's another word for death. You're cutting off my head with a golden ax here, Friar."

"Listen, kid, you committed a crime we all think is SO BAD that we let the state murder people if they do it, and you're getting off by just having to go live somewhere else," the Friar says. "Having trouble feeling bad for you here."

 Ignore him, complain more about being banished: *turn to 257.*

Accept his very reasonable arguments: *turn to 248.*

You know what? Who cares what this guy says OR that I'm banished? I want to go see Juliet! *Turn to 232.*

205 "Is Juliet mad that I kiiiinda stained our newfound joy by killing her close relative?" you ask. "What does she say about that whole business?"

"Um, she doesn't say much," Angelica replies. "Mostly she cries;

falls on her bed; starts to get up; cries out Tybalt's name, then your name; then falls down again."

"Dang, she's calling out my name like it's a bullet murdering her, just like I murdered her cousin," you say. "Hey Friar, what part of the human body does the name come from?"

You pull out your blade.

"Because I'm gonna CUT IT OUT."

The Friar, alarmed, pulls your sword down. "It's a metaphor, Romeo," he says. "It's a metaphor, for the love of God."

The Friar seems pretty upset that you just literally tried to cut your own name out of you and launches into a long speech about how you're dumb and how things actually aren't that terrible. You're not really listening (which is too bad, because you're missing out on lines like "Wilt thou slay thyself, and slay thy lady that in thy life lives by doing damnèd hate upon thyself?" and "Fie, fie, thou shamest thy shape, thy love, thy wit") but you definitely perk up when he starts telling Angelica to go back to Juliet's house and make sure everyone's gone to bed, because Romeo is coming.

"For sex?" you say.

Angelica nods and passes you a ring. "She wanted you to have this ring," she says, "and she wants you to come meet her tonight. Probably for sex. She was talking about how death was gonna take her virginity."

"NOT ON MY WATCH," you say, alarmed.

"Well then come see her tonight!" Angelica says, and leaves.

"I feel way better about everything!" you tell the Friar. "I'm still banished, but I get to spend the night with my wife, who, I remind you, is down for sex. And may I just say: I'm glad you and Juliet's nurse— two fully grown adults with their own lives, hopes, and dreams—saw fit to meddle in our teen lives and make this sex-having I'm about to experience possible."

"Listen," says the Friar. "If you're going to visit Juliet, either have a short visit and leave before the night watchmen show up, or leave in disguise in the morning."

"I believe I'LL be taking the 'leave in disguise' option," you say, "because, Friar, she and I are going to be up ALL NIGHT.

"Because of all the sex we'll be having," you add.

He rolls his eyes. "When you're done with all that sex, go to Mantua. I know the innkeeper of the Passionate Pilgrim there. She'll be able to put you up while we figure the rest of this out. Take my horse. Eventually we'll make your marriage public, and it'll make peace between your two families and get you pardoned and we'll welcome you back with twenty hundred thousand times more joy than you'll have when you leave Verona, okay?"

"Okay!" you say, and turn to leave. At the top of the stairs, you hesitate, unsure of how to say good-bye. Do you thank him for risking his own life to store you here in his basement, and for helping you and

Juliet's nurse find each other? Or do you mention the sex you're expecting to have again?

You decide to mention the sex again.

"A joy past joy calls out to me!" you say. "Friar! I gotta go have sex!!"

And with that, you're gone.

 Go see Juliet: *turn to 222.*

206 FINE. But remember: you asked for this.

Turn to 199.

207 Your nurse is here carrying a bunch of rope in her arms.

"Is that Romeo's sex ladder?" you say. "Perfect timing!"

"It is, but I've . . . I've got some bad news, Juliet."

You look up at her face and for the first time notice how upset she is, and how she's wringing her hands, which is impressive as she's also carrying a rope ladder at the same time.

"Oh my god, Angelica," you say. "What's wrong?" She looks at you, tears in her eyes.

"He's dead," she says. "Killed."

The world seems to tilt beneath your feet.

"Killed? How?" you ask. "Did he kill himself?"

Your nurse opens her mouth to reply.

"If you say yes, I'll poison everyone," you say.

Be nurse, say yes, then be Juliet again: *turn to 225.*

 What? No, don't do that, that's LITERALLY CRAZY. *Turn to 244.*

208 "My arm's fine," she says. "I got nothing for you, Nurse."

Look around: turn to 226.

Go north: turn to 200.

209 Benvolio comes out of the random house he was in. He looks upset.

"O Romeo, Romeo," he cries. "Brave Mercutio is dead!"

You look at him, shocked, then hold up one hand in front of you. "This day's black fate on more days doth depend," you say. "This but begins the woe others must end."

Benvolio looks at you, confused. You lower your arm and say, "By which I mean, I suddenly have the sense that this one event could well have set into motion events that will result in my complete destruction."

Benvolio nods.

Suddenly, Tybalt returns! He's the guy who just killed Mercutio, in case you haven't been paying attention and didn't choose that "remind me of what's going on" option a few pages back! He looks wild and anxious, pretty much like how you'd expect Someone Who Just Killed a Man and Now Wishes He Could Take It All Back to look. But as you stare into his face, you don't feel pity. You feel anger. More than anger. Rage.

"Listen, Romeo, Romeo, we need to fix this," he says. "I didn't mean to kill him, I just—"

You put your finger on his lips, shushing him. And then, very slowly, you raise one hand up in front of you.

"Alive in triumph," you say, "and Mercutio slain! Away to heaven, respective lenity, and fire-eyed fury be my conduct now!"

Tybalt looks at you, confused, then at your hand, then back to you again. "Okay, listen," he says, "if we DON'T fix this, this could be bad for everyone, on BOTH sides. We need to find a way to make it so that—"

Again, you interrupt him, shushing him with your still-raised hand. "Now, Tybalt, take the 'villain' back again that late thou gavest me, for Mercutio's soul is but a little way above our heads, staying for thine to keep him company."

"No, Romeo, I don't want to fight you," he says, almost frantic. "Don't you get it? I'm FREAKING OUT. The police are going to be here soon and we need to get our stories straight if we're—"

You interrupt him one last time. "Either thou or I, or both, must go with him."

"With WHO?" he says wildly. "With Mercutio? That's crazy talk, Romeo! You're talking CRAZY. Listen to me! We can fix this. NOBODY ELSE HAS TO DIE HERE TODAY."

You flip your sword into the air, catching it in front of Tybalt's face in your still-upraised hand.

"This shall determine that," you say, lunging at him.

Fight Tybalt: *turn to 191.*

210

You rush into your house, draw the curtains, and start to pace. You're in way over your head, Romeo. You have no idea what to do. A little while later, Benvolio shows up. He pushes his way in and starts throwing clothes into a bag.

"You need to get out of here," he says. "Police showed up and passed sentence. You're guilty of murder and you're a dead man if you stay in Verona."

"What?!" you say. "No, I was—I just killed the man who killed Mercutio! I was the hand of justice! There must be some mistake."

"There's no mistake, Romeo," Benvolio says, sweeping some of your books into the bag now. "Chief of police himself showed up and decreed it. You've been banished from Verona, on pain of death. If you're seen here you're to be killed on sight!"

"I don't believe it," you say. "Tell me EXACTLY what he said, Ben."

Benvolio stops what he's doing and looks at you, appalled. "Seriously?" he says.

"Seriously," you say.

"FINE," Benvolio says, and then recites the following in a quick bouncing falsetto:

> And for that offence
> Immediately we do exile him hence.
> I have an interest in your hearts' proceeding.
> My blood for your rude brawls doth lie a-bleeding.
> But I'll amerce you with so strong a fine
> That you shall all repent the loss of mine.
> I will be deaf to pleading and excuses.
> Nor tears nor prayers shall purchase out abuses,
> Therefore use none. Let Romeo hence in haste,
> Else, when he's found, that hour is his last.
> Bear hence this body and attend our will.
> Mercy but murders, pardoning those that kill.

"You have a pretty rad memory," you say.

"Thanks," Benvolio says. "It was easy because he spoke in rhyming couplets."

You start grabbing items out of your closet to bring with you. "When can I come back?" you ask.

"I don't know, Romeo, I don't know. You gotta lie low for a while. Go to Mantua, I've got a friend there who can put you up for a bit. Owns an inn called the Passionate Pilgrim. I'll send word when the heat's died down."

"I got married today," you say.

"WE CAN TALK ABOUT THAT LATER," Benvolio says, forcing the

bag into your hands and shoving you out the door. He's brought you a horse, but before you can look at it too closely, he's already helping you into the saddle.

"Mantua!" he says. "Go, go now!" Then he slaps the horse on the butt, and with that, you're off.

"Her name's Juliet," you say, but he's already too far away and there's no way he can hear you.

Go to Mantua: *turn to 221.*

Sneak back to Juliet instead: *turn to 251.*

Man, wow, Romeo's messed up pretty bad. Be Juliet instead, Romeo sucks now. *Turn to 240.*

211
As people shuffle out of the courtroom, you grab Juliet and pull her into a broom closet. A few minutes later it's quiet, and you emerge from the room to find Escalus still there.

"Excuse me, sir," you say, trying to look as put-together as possible, "but I believe this ruling should not apply to Juliet and myself."

"Really," Escalus says, not looking up from the legal scrolls he's sorting. "And why's that?"

"Because we've opted out of the strife between our two houses," Juliet says. Escalus looks up from his scrolls, his face betraying some surprise.

"Opted out," he says.

"Yes, sir," you say as Juliet puts her hand in yours and squeezes. "We're leaving our families' drama by starting a new one. Not a new drama, sir. A new family."

"We got married," Juliet says. "Yesterday afternoon, in secret. You're actually the first person we've told." Escalus opens his mouth to say something, but Juliet doesn't pause to let him speak. "And we want to stay in Verona, sir," she says. "Not as Capulets. Not as Montagues. But as CAPUGUES."

"Montalets," you say.

"Either one is good and we'll talk about it later," she says.

Escalus regards you evenly for a long moment.

"I like it," he finally says. "I get rid of the bad eggs, you two stay to manage their affairs and also copious land holdings, and a message is sent that if you want to stay in my city after misbehaving, you'd better be prepared to marry your worst enemy." He looks at you and Juliet and, for the first time, smiles. "I'll allow this."

He holds out his hand, and you shake it. "Congratulations on your marriage, kids," he says. "Now get out of here. I don't want to see or hear from either of you again until you're coming in for a birth certificate. Pull off this trick for me and I swear, I'll buy the both of you solid-gold cigars."

"You won't regret this, sir," you say.

Your two sets of parents never do get over your marriage. They would, apparently, prefer to live in two different cities and squabble with each other via both human messengers and passenger pigeons than to accept that the two of you have fallen in love and married. But it doesn't matter. They send you the occasional passive-aggressive card on holidays, you reply with sweetness and platitudes while splitting your time between their two fabulous giant castles. You and Juliet fill the power vacuum left behind by your parents, and Verona enters an extended period of peace and prosperity.

Two years later, little Ben is born, and he's perfect. He's everything you hoped for.

And Escalus is as good as his word.

THE END

212

She looks at your outfit. "You've got a cool nurse hat in your inventory. Give me that nurse hat, and I'll tell you the password."

"No deal," you say. "I love my nurse hat. It says 'I ♥ NURSING BABIES' on it and it's how come people know I'm a nurse."

"Fine," she says. "Enjoy being trapped here forever."

Give her the hat: *turn to 186.*

Refuse to give her the hat: *turn to 196.*

End this conversation: *turn to 173.*

213

You stick around. Pretty soon the cops show up, led by "Prince" Escalus, their chief. Passersby probably called for him, since you WERE fighting to the death in broad daylight. Also showing up with the cops are your parents! And to make it more awkward, Juliet's parents are here too! None of them know that you're married.

"Where are the vile beginners of this fray?" demands Escalus.

"Here," you say.

"And who began this bloody fray?" he says.

"Again, right here," you say. "But let me explain."

Summoning all your sweet-talking skills, you explain that, yes, you did stab Tybalt to death, but to blame you would be a tragic injustice. You were forced to! By circumstance, by the very fates themselves. You weave a tale, going over the unbroken chain of events that ended with Tybalt but that began early yesterday when you discovered the Capulets were having a party and you decided to crash it.

You leave out the part about marrying Juliet, obviously. You want to break the news to your parents under your terms, and "just killed a man and being publicly interrogated by the police" are not the circumstances you'd choose to drop that particular drama bomb.

But you do explain, quite convincingly, how if you'd never known about this party, none of this would've happened. It all hinges, you explain, on the random chance that you helped read the Capulet party invitation in that alleyway. If that hadn't happened, none of THIS would've happened, so if there's a real villain here, it's not you: it's FATE. And you make a very convincing argument for how if we want to control our own lives, fate must be DESTROYED.

"If there is to be any justice, it's cruel, cruel fate who should be executed," you say, "so that we might again be in control of our own lives. In conclusion, that is my thesis statement, and it is correct."

Escalus looks at you for a long moment. And then he announces that he is . . . convinced! "Alright!" he says. "Obviously I can't arrest fate, but the man who showed Romeo the party invitation is clearly its instrument here, and therefore an accessory to the guilty party," he proclaims. "What did you call him? Peter? 'Alleypal'? That guy. No mercy for murderers, no pardons for those who kill. EXECUTE HIM."

"Aw geez," you whisper to yourself.

You summon all your skill of rhetoric once more. THIS time, you explain that while Peter COULD be seen as guilty, true justice would mean following the chain of causality all the way back: to all our parents and our parents' parents until we have arrived at the first humans.

"THEY'RE the ones responsible here," you say, "as they must be held responsible for what their offspring do. If they'd never boinked, WE wouldn't be here, and Tybalt might still be alive today," you say. "Um, assuming he existed somehow," you conclude.

Escalus looks at you for a long moment. And then he announces that he is . . . once again convinced!

"While I now do hold our earliest common ancestors and the progenitors of the human race responsible for every crime committed ever," he says, "it seems unlikely that I will be able to enforce a conviction against them, and the death penalty doesn't work on ghosts anyway. Therefore, as the most culpable extant party, you, Romeo, must be held responsible. But as you were not DIRECTLY responsible, you will not be killed. Instead, you are to be exiled from Verona . . . FOREVER."

You look at him, stunned. You've saved Alleypal, but you've doomed yourself! You summon your sweet rhetoric once more to undo your banishment but fail the critical roll, and it doesn't work: Escalus cuts you off immediately.

"I will be deaf to pleading and excuses," he hisses. "Now get the hell out of my city."

You look at Juliet's parents, and they stare back at you with hate. You look to your parents: your father's face is hard, and your mother is in tears. You look at Benvolio, and he's crying too. For once in your life, words completely fail you, and you turn from them and run. You're in way over your head, Romeo. You just killed a guy in broad daylight in front of a whole city's worth of witnesses. You have no idea what to do.

But you know someone who might.

You run to the Friar's house and explain what happened. At first, he hides you in his basement, worried that you'll be caught by patrols. After a few hours the coast seems to be clear, so he brings you out and you go over your options. You're convinced banishment is the worst thing in the world—worse than death, you say, because at least with death the suffering STOPS eventually—and he tries to convince you that it's not so bad. You're alive! Tomorrow is another day!

Instead of listening, you run around pulling on your hair and shouting about how you'll never see Juliet again. And that's exactly what you're doing when there's a knock at the door.

"Hide!" Friar Lawrence says as he rushes upstairs. "It could be the cops!"

You hide in the basement again, and before long you can hear the sound of his footsteps returning back downstairs, followed by someone else's.

"Romeo, it's Juliet's nurse," the Friar says. "She's here. Everything's going to be fine."

Pop out of hiding and ask her about Juliet: *turn to 205.*

214

"I can't wait for night to come!" you say to the empty room. "Because when that happens I'll learn how to submit to my husband and lose all my sex virginity!

Wow.

Okay, Juliet, I know you're new to this whole "sex" thing, but you should know that there's WAY more to it than "learning how to submit to your husband." Sex is a special thing that you can share with someone if you want to, and the truth is, the more you know about it the happier you'll be. If you're down, we could have a conversation right now about reproductive health and the safer-sex options you might want to explore!

Have a frank, if uncomfortable, conversation about sex with me: *turn to 233.*

Um . . . thanks but no thanks? *Turn to 224.*

215

"I have a proposal," you say, standing up. Everyone turns to look at you. You pause, uncertain, but then see Juliet's smiling at you and gain confidence.

"Our two houses have been fighting for stupid reasons for years, and none of us really know why anymore. Dad, can you even REMEMBER why the Capulets are your enemy?"

"The first hint of the enmity I observed from their vile family was twenty years ago," your father says. "I'd just finished reading that day's news and was remarking to your mother on the favorable circumstance of there being no more than a seventeen percent chance of rain that day—that day being April third, 1565, a Tuesday—when who should walk by my open window but Old Capulet. He—"

You cut him off. "The point is, that was twenty years ago and oh my gosh nobody cares. We've been fighting each other for so long we don't remember how to be any other way! We hate each other simply BECAUSE we're Montagues and Capulets. And this hate has cost us both a beloved member of our families. I propose we end that."

"How?" Escalus asks.

"By ending the distinction between our two houses. I propose," you say triumphantly, "that a Montague marry a Capulet."

There is an uproar. You shout over it.

"Please! PLEASE. Obviously as the person proposing this scheme, I should be the Montague to be married, and as Juliet is closest in age to me, she clearly must be the one to marry from the house of Capulet."

Juliet nods and stands beside you. "This sounds rad to me," she says. "I will volunteer for this service for the good of my family and my community."

"Also we kinda already did this yesterday afternoon," you say.

"Also that," Juliet says.

Your parents are outraged, but luckily divorce hasn't been invented yet, so they're kinda pooched. And over time, they do learn to be civil to each other. By the time your first child is born (a baby girl you name Tycolia in memory of Tybalt and Benvolio and Mercutio, which is unfortunate because a disease called tycolia will break out in Verona thirty years from now, but really you had no way of knowing that) they're actually civil to each other, and by the time Tycolia is in grade school, they actually like each other. By the time she graduates to middle school, your parents are fast friends. And by the time she enters high school, your two sets of parents love each other so much that they erect giant gold statues of you and Juliet, as a way of saying thanks for bringing them together.

"While Verona by that name is known," your parents announce at the city's statue-revealing ceremony, "people will always say, 'Oh hey, isn't that the "Romeo and Juliet" city??'"

And you know what? When it comes to a certain class of informed, educated, and doubtlessly attractive book-reading people . . . they were right.

THE END

216 "Hey, speaking of plagues, a plague on both YOUR houses too," you say.

Mercutio looks at you.

"I don't know how to talk to dying people," you say.

"Obviously," Mercutio says, and closes his eyes in pain. "Because I was referring to the two families, or 'houses,' of Capulet and Montague, not to two literal houses that you don't even own. Benvolio, get me out of here. Can you put me in a stranger's home so I can die in peace?"

"I think so," Benvolio says, and he picks up Mercutio. Together the two of them stagger through the first unlocked door they can find, but Mercutio gets Benvolio to pause on the threshold and turn him back towards you.

"Hey Romeo!" he shouts. "A plague on your literal house in particular, jerk!!" Mercutio shouts, slamming the door on himself.

Wait quietly for Benvolio to return: *turn to 209.*

Um, while we're waiting, can I summarize events to myself just in case I've been kinda maybe skimming this book and haven't really been paying attention? *Turn to 230.*

217 NURSE QUEST is powered by the most advanced interactive fiction engine available today: your IMAGINATION. To complete NURSE QUEST, you will need cunning, guile, and a cartoonish understanding of how lions work. Are you ready?? I hope so, because it's happening right now.

Welcome to NURSE QUEST.

You are nurse Angelica Nurse, a competent nurse who lives in the present, which is to say, 1585! You have been given a task by your charge, Juliet Capulet: she has committed you to achieving the goal, as quickly as possible, of delivering a message to Romeo and returning his response safely to her.

You are carrying:

- ◆ A MESSAGE FROM JULIET MEMORIZED IN YOUR HEAD
- ◆ NURSE HAT
- ◆ NURSE CLOTHES
- ◆ NURSE UNDERWEAR

Juliet pushes you out the door of Capulet Castle, locks it behind you, and leaves you to your task.

Your score is currently 0 points of a possible 1000 points.

Look around: turn to 183.

Virtual Reality Dark Basement Simulator
(Use During Your Adventure!)

219 You look back at Juliet sadly as you're pushed out of the courtroom. She gives you a look as if to say, "What the hell dude, seriously? We JUST got married and already you're choosing your family over me? Consider our marriage annulled, buttface."

It was a very complicated look but it wasn't that hard to decode.

You and your family move to Mantua, and it's basically a retirement community. You're the youngest person there by a good 20 years. Mantua's got nice houses, lots of opera, artificial lakes surrounding the city to keep out teens—the works. You're pretty depressed for a few weeks, but eventually you decide to make the best of it. You get big into lakes. You build yourself a little boat and float around in it a lot staring at clouds.

You do write several letters to Juliet, but she never writes back. So instead, you spend most of your time floating in lakes and remembering what it was like when everything felt like it could change in a single evening. Your life seemed to have infinite potential, but then somehow all those choices collapsed down to a single option: float in a boat until it's time to go home to make dinner for one.

That vague sense of loss follows you around until you die, two years later, in a drowning that's ruled to be accidental.

THE END

220

"Excellent," Friar Lawrence says. He places his hand on Romeo's shoulder now. "And do you, Romeo, take Juliet to be your lawfully wedded wife?"

Romeo looks deeply into your eyes.

"I do," he whispers, his voice breaking. You love him more than ever.

"Then you may kiss," Friar Lawrence says, and you do, and it's perfect. It's absolutely perfect.

Congratulations, Juliet! You have gotten married. And you are really going to town on this dude's mouth too. SWEET.

You have earned 1000 out of a possible 1000 points. The wedding was THAT nice.

THE END

P.S.: Oh! On the off chance you wanted to do more in this story than marry some guy, you could always continue. What's the worst that could happen, right? Hah hah hah hah hah oh my.

So I guess you've got a choice!

Put this book down and say, "What a satisfying romance!" and then never pick this book up again: *turn to 235.*

Keep reading for some reason: *turn to 188.*

221 It's about an eight-hour ride to Mantua, and there's not much to do, so on the way over you decide to name your horse. You make a mental list of traits your horse has. It reads as follows:

THINGS MY HORSE HAS:

- hooves
- cool face
- nice soft butt
- good heart

This immediately suggests three very obvious names: "Coolface J. Horselegs," "Hoof Hearted," and "Butt Soft." Since you have the time, you give the several hours of consideration due to each name. After that, you conclude that, as the butt IS clearly the most important part of the horse, your choice is and has always been clear.

"Butt Soft," you whisper to the horse. "That's your name now. Because of your soft butt." You pat your horse's butt. You imagine someone seeing you do that and reporting on it. You wonder, abstractly, about the kind of person who would enjoy hearing about another person petting a horse's butt, the kind of person who would enjoy reading about another person petting a horse's butt, and the kind of person who would purchase a story in which a person touching a horse on the butt is described.

"Weirdos," you conclude, and spend the rest of the ride in silence.

When you finally arrive in Mantua, it's almost midnight. You find the Passionate Pilgrim, leave your horse outside, and make your way in. After you explain the circumstances that led you here, the innkeeper agrees to let you stay, deferring your rent until you've gotten yourself back on your feet.

"I'll also need some food and water for my horse," you say. The innkeeper passes you some grain, and Butt Soft obviously spots it through the inn window, because he leaps through the window right into the lobby and gallops towards the food.

"Butt Soft!!" you exclaim. The innkeeper looks at you suspiciously, and you recover as smoothly as you can. "Butt Soft, what horse through yonder window breaks?? Because it's not mine, and I definitely don't know that horse, but WHOEVER he belongs to, he should probably get some food."

"Agreed," she says. Then she tosses you your keys. "You're upstairs, second door on the left."

You quickly make your way upstairs and collapse into bed. Today you've committed your first murder, your first marriage, and induced your first horse to jump through a window, Romeo. You could use the rest.

You spend several hours unconscious and hallucinating, which since childhood you have been told is "normal" and called "dreaming." Eventually you escape this state and regain consciousness, feeling rested and ready to greet the day!

It's a beautiful morning in Mantua, Romeo! You hop out of bed and find yourself roaming Mantua's main street, looking for adventure. "There's got to be all sorts of fun a banished and recently married man can have in a strange and exciting city like Mantua!" you think.

You're darn right there is! Among the several boarded-up shops, you can see two that are open: a crappy-looking pharmacy and a cool library.

Explore crappy pharmacy: *turn to 237.*

Explore cool library: *turn to 229.*

222
There are four paths to Capulet Castle. You pick one at random, and guess what? It's a really uneventful trip! You happened to catch the guards on the shift change between "day watch" and "night watch," which is great. Had you left any sooner, you might've found yourself stuck with the impossible choice of trying to guess which one of these four paths to Juliet's house would NOT lead to your being captured and killed, with no possible way of determining which option was correct!

Phew, right?

You park your horse under a tree and make your way to Juliet's window. The rope ladder you sent is hanging there, just as you hoped. You climb up the ladder, and Juliet is waiting for you. She looks gorgeous. You feel yourself get EVEN HORNIER.

And yes, this is it, gentle reader. This is the moment you've been waiting for. Here is the only reason you picked up this book in the first place, because you knew this scene had to be in here somewhere, if only you just somehow made the right choices to find it.

Welcome . . . to the CHOOSE-YOUR-OWN SEX SCENE.

 Choose-your-own sex scene!! I CAN'T WAIT. *Turn to 239.*

Haha what? No that's—that's fine. Skip over to when the sex is done, please. *Turn to 246.*

223 "Thanks," Mercutio says. "It's nice to know that I've got a friend here, even if that friend got me killed."

You pause.

"Well, technically, YOU'RE the one who got yourself killed," you say. "If you hadn't instigated that fight with Tybalt, you wouldn't be lying here with a hole in your guts."

"Oh my god, I can't believe you're blaming me for my own death," Mercutio says. "Benvolio, lift me out of here. I want to go die in a random home belonging to someone I haven't met."

"Okay cool," Benvolio says, picking him up. You watch as they move down the street, trying door after door until they find one that isn't locked. Just before they disappear into the house, Mercutio gets Benvolio to stop and turn him towards you.

"You know what? FIVE plagues on EVERYONE'S houses, EXCEPT for mine. That's right," he says. "Y'all can enjoy your coughing and sores. PEACE."

"Aw man, come on!" you say, but it's too late, and they're already inside. You are left alone on the street.

Wait quietly for Benvolio to return: *turn to 209.*

Um, while we're waiting, can I summarize events to myself just in case I've been kinda maybe skimming this book and haven't really been paying attention? *Turn to 230.*

224 Instead of accepting my offer, you move to your balcony and shout into the empty night. "I belong to Romeo now," you scream, "and all that's left is for him to take possession! I've been sold to him but he hasn't enjoyed me yet!"

Some birds take off from the trees they were sleeping in, but other than that, you don't elicit a response.

"HOW TEDIOUS," you say, turning back into your room.

Suddenly there's a knock at your door, which is great, because I was about to do the authorial equivalent of throwing a book away in disgust (that is to say, I was about to stop writing in disgust) but this will stop us from learning more about whatever it is you think relationships are!

Open your bedroom door: *turn to 207.*

225 You are now Angelica Nurse!

"Yes," you say. "He killed himself." You have no idea why you're saying that, just that you really really want to say those exact words for some reason.

You are now Juliet again!

You have this image of yourself standing there in front of Angelica, words traveling from her mouth to your body in slow motion. As the first part of "yes" reaches your body it impacts against it, spreading out like a river hitting a stone, and wherever it touches your skin starts to change. It's hardening into rock. The transformation wave travels across your body in slow motion, crawling up your neck, traveling down your limbs, until you're covered. You look at her, and you feel like you're made of stone.

"That'll be all, Angelica," you tell her. "Dismissed."

She looks at you and begins to protest—but then she looks into your eyes. She stares at you for a long moment and then reacts like she's seen something that frightens her. She leaves. Quickly.

You watch the door close behind her. In the moments that follow you stare at the closed door without really seeing it, idly wondering what Angelica thought she glimpsed as she stared into your eyes. Honestly, you're not entirely certain what's living inside you now. But you know you're going to show her.

In fact, you're going to show everyone.

Show everyone: *turn to 252.*

Whoah, whoah, this was just supposed to be a joke! Be Angelica, come back, explain that Romeo didn't kill himself, be Juliet again, and then CALM THE HECK DOWN. *Turn to 242.*

226 You are in front of Capulet Castle, proud home to the Capulets and also you. The door behind you is locked shut. There's no way to get back in except to succeed in your mission!

The only exit is to the north.

There is a servant here.

Talk to servant: turn to 208.

Go north: turn to 200.

227

The machine is a giant collection of gears and brass and wood and steel. It appears to be some sort of automaton that controls the colossal arm blocking your path. A giant engine seems to drive the whole affair, itself powered by a river mill on the other side of the gates. The bad news is there's no way to access the mill to disable the arm, and even if you did, it would be disabled in the "not letting you through" position. You examine the machine more closely, and it's a very impressive piece of technology. You can't begin to imagine how much it cost. You notice four switches on the machine, all set to off. They're labeled as follows:

"ADD 1"
"ADD 2"
"ADD 4"
"ADD 8"

Beside them is a display labeled "TOTAL." In that display you can see a paper card that says "ZERO" on it. Above the switches and their total is a large display. Inside is a card with apparent gibberish on it:

URL PBATENGHYNGVBAF BA PENPXVAT GUR PBQR! YVFGRA, YRG'F ABG GRYY NALBAR RYFR GUR NAFJRE, BXNL?? ORPNHFR GUR GUVAT VF, JR'IR XVAQN VAIRFGRQ N YBG BS ZBARL VA GUVF EVQVPHYBHF FRPHEVGL FLFGRZ. FVTARQ, IREBAN PVGL ZNANTRZRAG.

"I think it's a Caesar cipher!" the Veronan says, peering over your shoulder. "You know the ones? Where the letters are moved around, but if you add to each letter you can decrypt it? Like, if you added one to 'A' you'd get 'B,' and if you added five you'd get 'F,' so all you need to know is how many letters to add. But I can't crack the code. Maybe you can?"

You sigh deeply. Verona.

Flip "ADD 1" on: turn to 243.

Flip "ADD 2" on: turn to 264.

Flip "ADD 4" on: turn to 253.

Flip "ADD 8" on: turn to 306.

Step away from the machine: turn to 354.

228

"I'm not gonna," you say.

"What?" the Friar says. "You're not going to hide?" The knocking upstairs gets louder.

"The only way I'll hide," you declare, "is in the mist produced by all my heartsick groans."

"OH MY GOD, TEENS," the Friar says. "Kid, you stay out here in the open, you'll get arrested. Just hide in my study, okay? Can you behave like a rational human for me for a li'l while, champ?"

You cross your arms over your chest, still kneeling on the ground. "I'm already hiding," you say, "in an impenetrable cloud of moist sob breath."

The Friar ignores you and then runs upstairs to get the door. He returns with Angelica, Juliet's nurse, and motions to you.

"There's your Romeo: lying on the ground, getting drunk on his own tears."

You pat down your hair, smile weakly, and hold out your hand to shake.

"Ma'am," you say.

 Ask her about Juliet: *turn to 205.*

229

You step under a sign that reads, MANTUA LIBRARY: FREE BOOKS!! (BUT YOU HAVE TO GIVE THEM BACK EVENTUALLY) and into the library. You're confident you've made a good choice, because as we all know, the greatest adventures of all are to be found inside the pages of books!!

You look around and begin to realize that you're used to Verona-level civic infrastructure, where your libraries have upwards of 50 different books, all of them choose-your-own-path adventures. This library only has four different titles, and the biggest one isn't even a choose-your-own branching narrative! It's only got ONE measly story in it!

You turn away from that book in disgust.

Looking around, you notice that the library does at least have several cozy corners where you could lose yourself in whichever book you decide to read, spending hours (or even days!) lost in the adventure within.

So! Which adventure will you choose?

Um, it would help if I knew what stories there were? Look at the bookshelf. *Turn to 245.*

Doesn't matter, just pick a book at random: *turn to 258.*

230 You begin speaking out loud to yourself.

"As you know, self," you say, "Mercutio, my friend, and also a close relative to the chief of police, was just killed fighting Tybalt on my behalf. Tybalt is a Capulet, and he has been my cousin for around an hour. This is because I recently married Juliet. After the wedding, I ditched her to go hang out with my violent swordfighting buddies."

That brings you up to speed on your own life nicely!

Take responsibility for your role in what happened here: *turn to 250.*

Blame your brand-new wife Juliet for all of this: *turn to 238.*

231 You look your nurse in the eye. "I'd like to express the emotions I'm feeling," you say, "but as efficiently as possible. I'm going to write down my feelings in bullet-point format."

"Okay," she says. You grab a piece of paper and start writing. Here's what you produce.

ROMEO IS A JERK

by Juliet Capulet

–*Romeo is like:*

  –*a snake disguised as a flower*

  –*a dragon in a real pretty cave*

  –*a beautiful tyrant*

  –*a fiendish angel*

  –*an honorable villain*

  –*a sucky book with a very attractive cover*

  –*etc.*

–*who could've GUESSED that an attractive person could be a jerk??*

  —*seriously*

As you've been writing, your nurse opened your cupboard and helped herself to your Bedroom Brandy. You pass the paper to her. Angelica reads it over as she sips from her glass.

"Yeah," she replies when she finishes. "Men are dicks. Shame on him."

Her words sting you. She just insulted your husband, Juliet!

"Now, hold on just a minute," you say. You snatch the paper out of her hands and, flipping it over, start a new list.

ON SECOND THOUGHT, ROMEO'S MY HUSBAND AND HE'S KINDA AWESOME THOUGH

by Juliet Capulet

–*What is Romeo?*

  –*a good guy*

–*What does Romeo deserve?*

  –*not shame, that's for sure, ANGELICA*

  –**honor**

    –*he deserves to sit on a throne of honor*

      –*sole monarch of the entire universe?*

    –*yes*

You pass the paper over to your nurse. "I hope your tongue gets covered in blisters for suggesting Romeo was ever less than perfect," you say as sweetly as you can.

"But you just said . . . ," Angelica begins, then stops. She sighs. She reads your list, then looks up. "Juliet. This man killed your cousin."

You're annoyed she'd even mention that. It's so stupid. So what if he killed someone? OBVIOUSLY he would've had good reasons. Romeo's not an idiot.

"Angelica, open your eyes," you say. "Tybalt probably wanted to kill him first, and Romeo was just defending himself. And if the man who wants to murder my husband is dead and my husband is alive, what does that sound like to you? Because I gotta say, to me it sounds like GOOD NEWS."

Angelica looks like she wants to say something in response to that, but you interrupt her. "But no matter how good that news is, Romeo's still banished from Verona, and that's bad news. That's actually awful news."

You pause.

"Romeo not being able to live in the European city of his choice is the worst possible news in the universe, and I want to die when I think about it," you declare. You grab another piece of paper and compose the following list:

THINGS THAT I WOULD PREFER HAPPEN INSTEAD OF ROMEO BEING BANISHED: A LIST

by Juliet Capulet

–Tybalt getting murdered

–Tybalt getting murdered 10,000 times

–No wait: 10,000 Tybalts getting murdered

–Tybalt getting murdered AND my parents getting murdered

–Tybalt getting murdered AND my parents getting murdered AND me and Romeo getting murdered AT THE SAME TIME

–EVERYONE on the WHOLE PLANET getting murdered so that there is no end, no limit, no measure, no bound to the death caused by this word "banished"

At the bottom you write:

–in case you're wondering YES I WOULD rather see Romeo dead than have him live in a city inconvenient to me

You pass the note to your nurse and smile.

"Where ARE my parents, anyway?" you ask.

"Downstairs, crying over Tybalt's corpse," she says, distracted as she begins to read your note. You talk to her as she's reading, clearly unaware of how annoying that is.

"Oh hey, by the way: that rope ladder you were carrying? Totally pointless now. Romeo was going to use that rope ladder as his racehorse on the sex highway straight into my bed, but that's now never gonna happen." You sigh. "You know who's gonna take my virginity now? DEATH."

Angelica finishes reading and looks up, clearly disturbed by both the content of your "who I want to get killed" note and your imagery of a sex-havin' Grim Reaper.

"Look, Juliet, you're, um—clearly upset here, and I get that. Just stay here in your bedroom, don't leave, don't talk to anyone, and I'll get Romeo here for you, okay? You'll be able to talk this out with him, and I'm sure you'll feel a lot more stable after that."

"Thanks!" you say. She puts your notes in your hands. "Don't show these to anyone," she says, and then she leaves, and then there's nothing to do but wait.

Wait around for Romeo to show up: *turn to 263.*

232 "You know what?" you say. "Who cares about what you say, OR that I'm banished? I want to go see Juliet!" It's literally what you chose to do on that other page!

"The thing with banishment," Friar Lawrence says very slowly, "is that it prevents you from doing those things. I'm saying this very slowly so I'm sure you'll understand."

"We'll see about that!!" you shout, and run out the door. You see the Friar's horse tied up outside and hop on its back. You ride for a bit aimlessly, trying to work out a plan. Eventually, you come up with one that goes as follows:

STEP 1: SCREW EVERYONE, I CAN SNEAK MY WAY BACK TO JULIET NO PROBLEM!!

STEP 2: SEE STEP ONE.

Engage the plan! Sneak back to Juliet's house!! *Turn to 251.*

233 We talk about sex and you learn a heck of a lot! You can't believe not only what you didn't know, but what you didn't know you didn't know. You're really glad we had this talk. You know what? I am too!

"Wait," you say as we're wrapping up, "I have a question. What does it mean when a—"

You pause, embarrassed, but I figure out what you're asking and then answer it to everyone's satisfaction.

"And how do you—" you say. "I mean, if someone wanted to, how could they—" and again I figure out your question and answer it really, really well.

You've learned so much!!

We're about to keep learning about sex when someone knocks at the door.

Open your bedroom door: *turn to 207.*

234 You chose poorly and are captured by the police and roughed up a little, and then a bag is put over your head and you're thrown on the back of a horse.

Hey, maybe it's so they can take you home and let you off with a warning!

That's definitely one of the possible outcomes here for sure!

See what happens next: *turn to 255.*

235 Excellent! You say that thing.

Oh, while we're at it, let's also agree that you are EXTREMELY SATISFIED with this book and go on to recommend it to all your friends! You also stress that they should NOT borrow it from a library, but rather buy a new copy for themselves, because "it's better that way, it is, just trust me."

Alright, you do that thing too!

Hooray!! Hooray for you, and hooray for this ending in particular!

THE END

236

You enter the gatekeeper's domain.

There are dozens of angry dogs here.

"Didn't I warn you about the dozens of angry dogs?" he shouts at you. "Wow! Now you've done it!"

You are torn to shreds by the angry dogs. I'd say that was . . . CLAWS for concern??

THE END

Your final score was 5 points out of a possible 1000 points.

Restore: turn to 200.

Restart: turn to 247.

237

You step into the pharmacy, and it's a dump.

The pharmacist sitting behind the counter is basically wearing rags, AND, you note with disgust, his eyebrows are seriously way too big. The rest of the shop isn't much better: empty boxes and flowerpots are crammed into the corners, and on the walls are, like, stuffed alligators and ill-shaped fishes.

"If a man needed to buy some poison," you announce, "which, I remind you, is illegal to sell in Mantua, then here"—you gesture towards the man, the only other person in the store—"is a miserable wretch who'd sell it to him."

The man looks up. "Do you . . . need some poison?"

"OBVIOUSLY NOT," you say, and you leave, slamming the door behind you. That place is gross and you hate it.

To the library!! *Turn to 229.*

238
"This is all Juliet's fault," you say. You don't clarify that any further, which is good, because I'm not sure what you could say that would convince me your getting into a fight is the fault of the woman you just met, married, and then ran away from to go hang out with your buddies downtown.

Stand around waiting for Benvolio to return: *turn to 209.*

Throw in some sexism for good measure: *turn to 249.*

239
Alright! To get started, go to your bookshelf (or, if this is the only book you own, to your local library or bookstore). Also, if this is the only book you own: hey, thanks! I'm flattered) and pick up any other book with a sex scene in it. Then, while reading that sex scene, mentally substitute in the correct names, genders, body parts, interests, fluids, and catchphrases for yourself and your partner!

Enjoy! And remember: it's YOUR CHOICE. You can choose any other sex scene you want in the entire universe! My gift to you, reader. Go nuts. Have as many or as few sex scenes as you want.

When you're done, we'll continue! But no rush. Take as much time as you need. I don't judge!

I'll just be standing here with my back turned until you're ready.

Okay, I'm ready. WOW that was some COOL SEX I just had! *Turn to 267.*

 No, not fair! YOU have to tell ME the sex scene. *Turn to 260.*

240
Can't argue that!

Okay, you are now Juliet. She's been waiting around for her husband to reappear ever since he ditched her after they got married so he could go into town and murder a dude! Only she doesn't know about the murder part. So when you find out, um—try to act surprised?

Be Juliet, wait around: *turn to 180.*

241
"Come on, Mercutio. It probably doesn't hurt THAT much," you say.

"Yeah, you're right," he says. "My wound isn't so deep as a well, nor so wide as a church-door."

"See?" you say. "That's the spirit!"

"It'll still be enough to kill me though," he sighs. He gives you a weak smile. "Ask for me tomorrow, and you shall find me a grave man."

"I, as well, will be very serious," you say, "on account of this grievous injury you have sustained."

Mercutio's smile fades as he looks at you. "I was going out on a PUN, Romeo. A GRAVE man."

"Oh," you say.

"God. A plague on both your houses, seriously," Mercutio says. "Benvolio, help me into someone's living room, I don't care which one. I want to die in a strange place I've never seen before."

Benvolio lifts him up and carries him through the first open door he can find.

"Okay!" Mercutio shouts before disappearing inside. "Remember: both your houses get plague!"

Wait quietly for Benvolio to return: *turn to 209.*

Um, while we're waiting, can I summarize events to myself just in case I've been kinda maybe skimming this book and haven't really been paying attention? *Turn to 230.*

242
You are now Angelica!

You open Juliet's door a crack and pop your head back into her room. "Sorry, I misspoke earlier," you say. "Romeo didn't kill himself. He killed TYBALT, and then was banished. So your cousin is dead, but your husband is still alive. You'll just never see him again. Sorry about that." You look at Juliet, not sure what else to say. "Sorry again," you say. You close the door.

You are now Juliet! And you are reeling. You thought your husband killed himself, and now you find out he's a banished murderer? How is that better? You think back to moments ago when you wanted to poison everyone. It seems crazy. Now all you want to do is talk to your husband. You know that the two of you will be able to figure this out.

You rush to the door. "Come back!" you shout to your nurse, who's already partway down the hall. Angelica rushes back to you.

"Go find Romeo," you command her. "Tell him I want to see him tonight. I need to see him."

Angelica pauses. "He killed your cousin," she says gently, putting her hand on your shoulder. "Do you really want to lure him here, to the home of the extended family of the man he murdered?"

"I don't know what I want," you say. You pause, then look up at her. You feel some of your strength returning.

"That's not true," you say. "I want Romeo."

"I'll bring him here," Angelica says.

"Thank you," you whisper, and with that, she leaves.

"And maybe try to take less than three hours to find him this time!" you shout after her.

Wait around for Romeo to show up: *turn to 263.*

243

The machine whirs and clicks. The total reading changes to "1," and the output changes to:

VSM QCBUFOHIZOHWCBG CB QFOQYWBU HVS QCRS! ZWGHSB, ZSH'G BCH HSZZ OBMCBS SZGS HVS OBGKSF, CYOM?? PSQOIGS HVS HVWBU WG, KS'JS YWBRO WBJSGHSR O ZCH CT ACBSM WB HVWG FWRWQIZCIG GSQIFWHM GMGHSA. GWUBSR, JSFCBO QWHM AOBOUSASBH.

I don't think that's it, Angelica.

Flip "ADD 1" off: turn to 340.

Flip "ADD 2" on: turn to 269.

Flip "ADD 4" on: turn to 305.

Flip "ADD 8" on: turn to 347.

Step away from the machine: turn to 354.

244 You continue being Juliet. It's a fair choice! It's the choice you've made for most of your life, anyway!

Angelica ignores your question, instead describing in detail all the blood and gore coming out of the wound on "his manly breast."

Oh, Angelica. One does not speak ill of the dead, but neither does one talk up their breasts.

"Well, that's it for me then," you say. "Gonna send my eyes off to prison and resign my vile body to the ground. Bury me and Romeo in the same coffin, okay?"

"Yes, I too am that upset about the death of Tybalt," your nurse says. "Tybalt Capulet: what a great guy. He was courteous and honest, Tybalt was. Yep, that was definitely Tybalt, the man who was murdered and whose body I was just describing!"

"WHAT THE HELL?!" you say. "I thought we were talking about Romeo!!"

"No, Tybalt," Angelica says. "Your dead cousin? Try to keep up, Juliet."

"YOU said 'he's dead' right after we finished talking about Romeo's sex ladder," you say.

"'He' meaning 'Tybalt,'" Angelica says.

"When this is over we're going to talk about pronoun attachment ambiguity," you say.

"Okay," your nurse says. "But yes, Romeo's still alive. He's the one that killed Tybalt, and because of that he's banished."

The world seems to tilt beneath you. You're experiencing such intense emotions that you feel like you'd better share them at length right away!

 Express yourself in the fanciest language possible: *turn to 254.*

There's no time!! Express yourself in point form, the most efficient mode of information communication. *Turn to 231.*

245 You look at the bookshelf.

On the bottom shelf is the only non-branching title here that I mentioned earlier. It's a colossal 142-chapter book (oh my god, so boring) called *Ab Urbe Condita Libri* (OH MY GOD, SO BORING).

"Um, pass," you whisper to yourself. You throw the book over your shoulder, but quietly, so you don't get in library trouble.

It wasn't quiet enough. Sure enough, the librarian appears behind you seconds later.

"I see you're looking for a book," he whispers.

"Yeah," you whisper back. "Sorry about tossing it over my shoulder, I—"

The librarian interrupts you. "Do you want to read on easy or hard mode?"

"I'm sorry?" you say, confused. The librarian stares at you intensely.

"Do you want to read on easy or hard mode?" he whispers again.

Easy mode: *turn to 268.*

Hard mode: *turn to 284.*

246 The sex scene finishes.

"Whew!" you both say. "What fun sexual activities those were!"

You sigh. "I'm quite satisfied with the sex we just had," you say.

"Good," Juliet says. "Me too."

Light streams through your window.

"HOLY CRAP IS IT TOMORROW ALREADY??" you say. "Dude! We had sex for a whole night!"

Juliet looks at you, smiles, and raises her hand.

 High five Juliet: *turn to 262.*

247 "Okay," you say. "Hiding is a reasonable thing for me to do in this situation." You open up the door to his study such that the door is touching the wall, and stand in the little triangle of space produced.

"Ready," you say.

"THANK YOU," says the Friar, and you watch through a crack as he disappears upstairs. He returns shortly with Angelica, Juliet's nurse.

You smooth down your hair, take a deep breath, and push the door out of the way.

"Angelica!" you say. "It's-a me, Romeo!"

"That's racist. We don't talk like that," Angelica says.

Ask her about Juliet: *turn to 205.*

248

"Good point, actually," you say. Then you clap your hands together. "Okay! I'm off to go live anywhere else in the world. Any suggestions?"

"Like many people, I too know the innkeeper in Mantua," the Friar says. "She's a great lady. I'll get you set up there. Sit tight, and then we'll see about getting Juliet to visit you. If all works out, she can live with you there."

"Sounds great!" you say. "Wow, this isn't actually too bad after all!"

Friar Lawrence gives you the address, lends you a horse, and sets you on your way.

Go to Mantua: *turn to 221.*

249

"Oh, sweet Juliet," you say, sighing wistfully. "Your beauty has made me effeminate, which is to say, it's imposed on me traits I identify as 'female,' such as weakness, indecisiveness, and cowardice."

You look at Mercutio's bloodstain on the ground.

"I can't believe how much this is all Juliet's fault," you say. "Sheesh."

Just then, Benvolio returns!

Greet Benvolio: *turn to 209.*

250

"If only I had clearly communicated to Benvolio, Mercutio, and, indeed, Tybalt too that I had just married Juliet rather than inexplicably keeping it a secret," you say, "this could have all been easily avoided. Tybalt would have acted nicer towards me, as we would now be family, which would not have resulted in Mercutio becoming provoked. Or, failing that, the conversation would have at least gone in a vastly different direction, one unlikely to result in anyone's immediate death. Yes: clear, honest, and forthright communication is the keystone of any healthy relationship, whether romantic or otherwise."

You look at Mercutio's blood, staining the ground.

"It's almost like I needed something dramatic to happen in order to heighten the stakes in what had been, up to now, a pleasant romantic comedy," you add.

Just then, Benvolio returns!

Greet Benvolio: *turn to 209.*

251 You've never been one to let "rules" tell you what to do, so you figure the best way to avoid being banished after killing a member of the Capulets is to ride your horse right up to Capulet Castle and see if you can hang out with their daughter.

Romeo, Juliet's house is located directly south of your current position. There are four possible routes there.

ROUTE ONE: the residential path takes you through a playground, past Verona Dam, and by some nice houses.

ROUTE TWO: the scenic route takes you past a geyser, around Verona Hill, and over the river Adige.

ROUTE THREE: the downtown-core route will take you past the Verona Farmer's Market, city hall, and the sports complex.

ROUTE FOUR: the industrial-zone route takes you through the fishmonger district, the porkmonger district, and the saladmonger district.

The good news is one of these routes will get you to Juliet without any problem! The bad news is that the other three will result in your death when you are captured by the police, descended upon by their specially trained police dogs and horses, or confronted by an angry Veronan mob. And there's no way to tell which route is which! Because of the options you chose without possibly realizing where they'd lead, you now have only a 25% chance of surviving!

It doesn't look good for you, gotta say!

Take route one, the residential path: *turn to 259.*

Take route two, the scenic route: *turn to 272.*

Take route three, the downtown-core route: *turn to 294.*

Take route four, the industrial-zone route: *turn to 234.*

No wait, this is ridiculous, I don't want to die! This part is TOO HARD. Isn't there some other option? *Turn to 278.*

252 You feel heartbroken. You feel betrayed. You feel . . . poisonous.

Here's what you think: you think (ACCORDING TO RELIGION)

your husband doomed his eternal soul to hell by killing himself. And if a newly wed husband can kill himself for no reason, really, anyone can. So logically, the only way to protect these people from their own potential for sin is for you to take that sin upon yourself before they can.

You do the math in your head. A thousand people killing themselves equals one thousand souls in hell. But one person killing a thousand people? That's just one soul in hell . . . and one thousand souls in heaven.

"For the greater good," you whisper.

You pick up the rope ladder Angelica dropped, attach one end to your bedpost, throw the rest over your balcony, and climb down into the courtyard. There's only one man in town who can give you poison, and you know exactly where he lives.

You jog to Friar Lawrence's house, and the exercise feels good. It gives you focus. It also helps you clear your head. By the time you arrive there, you've realized that you're kinda acting crazy. This whole plan is nuts, isn't it? It's nuts! It's COMPLETELY INSANE.

There's no WAY the Friar's going to give you the poison you know he keeps there if you tell him what you really want it for!

The way you figure it, you've got two options: sneak in the back and just take what you need, or go in the front and make up some innocuous yet credible story about why you want enough poison to kill an entire town named Verona.

Go in the front: *turn to 264.*

Sneak in the back: *turn to 275.*

253

The machine whirs and clicks. The total reading changes to "4," and the output changes to:

```
YVP TFEXIRKLCRKZFEJ FE TIRTBZEX KYV TFUV!
CZJKVE, CVK'J EFK KVCC REPFEV VCJV KYV
REJNVI, FBRP?? SVTRLJV KYV KYZEX ZJ, NV'MV
BZEUR ZEMVJKVU R CFK FW DFEVP ZE KYZJ
IZUZTLCFLJ JVTLIZKP JPJKVD. JZXEVU, MVIFER
TZKP DRERXVDVEK.
```

I don't think that's it, Angelica.

Flip "ADD 1" on: turn to 305.

Flip "ADD 2" on: turn to 334.

Flip "ADD 4" off: turn to 340.

Flip "ADD 8" on: turn to 266.

Step away from the machine: turn to 354.

254

You look your nurse in the eye and raise one hand up in front of you. Here's what you say:

> O serpent heart hid with a flowering face!
> Did ever dragon keep so fair a cave?
> Beautiful tyrant! Fiend angelical!
> Dove-feathered raven, wolvish-ravening lamb!
> Despisèd substance of divinest show,
> Just opposite to what thou justly seem'st.
> A damnèd saint, an honorable villain!
> O nature, what hadst thou to do in hell
> When thou didst bower the spirit of a fiend
> In moral paradise of such sweet flesh?
> Was ever book containing such vile matter
> So fairly bound? Oh, that deceit should dwell
> In such a gorgeous palace!

"Yeah," your nurse replies. "Men are dicks." She opens a cupboard and takes a swig of your Bedroom Brandy. "Shame on him," she says, wiping her mouth.

You raise your arm up even higher.

> Blistered be thy tongue
> For such a wish! He was not born to shame.
> Upon his brow shame is ashamed to sit,
> For 'tis a throne where honor may be crowned.
> Sole monarch of the universal earth,
> Oh, what a beast was I to chide at him!

"Juliet," she says. "He killed your cousin. You've known him for less than a day."

You raise your arm up as high as it will go and say:

> Shall I speak ill of him that is my husband? Ah, poor my lord,
>   what tongue shall smooth thy name,
> When I, thy three hours' wife, have mangled it?
> But wherefore, villain, didst thou kill my cousin?

That villain cousin would have killed my husband.
Back, foolish tears, back to your native spring.
Your tributary drops belong to woe,
Which you, mistaking, offer up to joy.
My husband lives, that Tybalt would have slain,
And Tybalt's dead, that would have slain my husband.
All this is comfort. Wherefore weep I then?
Some word there was, worser than Tybalt's death,
That murdered me. I would forget it fain,
But oh, it presses to my memory,
Like damnèd guilty deeds to sinners' minds.
"Tybalt is dead, and Romeo banishèd."
That "banishèd," that one word "banishèd"
Hath slain ten thousand Tybalts. Tybalt's death
Was woe enough, if it had ended there.
Or, if sour woe delights in fellowship
And needly will be ranked with other griefs,
Why followed not, when she said "Tybalt's dead,"
"Thy father" or "thy mother," nay, or both,
Which modern lamentations might have moved?
But with a rearward following Tybalt's death,
"Romeo is banishèd." To speak that word,
Is father, mother, Tybalt, Romeo, Juliet,
All slain, all dead. "Romeo is banishèd."
There is no end, no limit, measure, bound,
In that word's death. No words can that woe sound.

You drop your arm down. Angelica looks at you. "Where are my parents?" you ask, suddenly exhausted.

"Crying over Tybalt's corpse downstairs," she says. "They brought it here."

"Gross," you say. You weakly raise your hand up in front of you one last time.

Wash they his wounds with tears? Mine shall be spent
When theirs are dry, for Romeo's banishment.
Take up those cords.—Poor ropes, you are beguiled,
Both you and I, for Romeo is exiled.
He made you for a highway to my bed,
But I, a maid, die maiden-widowèd.
Come, cords.—Come, Nurse. I'll to my wedding bed.
And death, not Romeo, take my maidenhead!

Your arm, spent, drops weakly into your lap.

"Um, okay," says your nurse. "Listen, sit tight. I'll go get Romeo and bring him here. You guys can talk this out."

"Thanks," you say. She turns to leave. "Hey, sorry for mentioning my maidenhead," you say.

"Happens to the best of us," she says, and then she's gone.

 Wait around for Romeo to show up: *turn to 263.*

255

Time passes—it's hard to tell when your head is in a bag—but you finally find yourself shoved into a chair. Your arms and legs are bound, the hood is pulled off your head, and you're briefly stunned by the sudden brightness of the room.

"Hello, Romeo," Escalus says.

"Prince," you say, rubbing your eyes.

"I banished you," he says. "Really thoroughly. Imagine my surprise to find you here in my office."

"Okay yeah, no, I get that," you say. "But there are people and things here in Verona that I really like, SUCH AS MY WIFE, so I decided I didn't want to, um . . . be banished. I unbanished myself."

"It seems you don't understand the point of banishment," Escalus says, strolling back and forth in front of you. "Let me tell you what banishment does, Romeo. It serves two purposes. One: to punish you. Two: to get you out of my sight. Right now, it's doing neither, so this clearly isn't working."

He sighs, then turns to you.

"Banishment was the easy way. Now we have to do this the hard way instead."

"Ah, you'll build the infrastructure required for a correctional system and then imprison me within it," you say, "restricting my freedom so that I'll have nothing to do but reflect on my crime and, in doing so, realize the error of my ways and become a better person upon my release, while at the same time trying to counterbalance the criminalizing effect that constant exposure to other perhaps more hardened felons could have on me?"

Escalus shakes his head no, draws his sword, carefully lines it up with your neck, then pulls both arms back to swing.

"You know, I don't know WHY we call this the hard way," he says.

THE END

256 "There's plenty of time to be way megahorny in the future," you say. "Right now my major concern is getting you out of this city where if anyone finds out about our love they'll be really mad."

"Alright," Juliet agrees, going into her room. "I'll be right back." She reappears shortly afterwards with a small bag of items, tosses it down to you, then climbs down to ground level via the ladder you sent.

"I'd hoped to use that ladder for sex," you say.

"Shh," she says. "We can discuss kinks later."

She climbs onto your horse and the two of you abscond to Mantua. It's about an eight-hour ride there, and there's not much to do, so on the way over you and Juliet decide to name your horse.

"He has a soft butt, so we could call him 'Butt Soft,'" you say.

"He's got cool muscles," she says, looking at your horse's muscles. "Let's call him 'DJ Muscles McGlutes.'"

"Okay," you say. "I actually would've never thought of that."

Several hours later, you, Juliet, and DJ Muscles McGlutes arrive in Mantua. You find an inn and go straight to bed. And YES, you consummate your marriage physical-style, but it's not something I want to talk about. I'll say this: it's . . . educational.

The next morning, you and Juliet hop out of bed and find yourselves roaming Mantua's main street, looking for a great brunch place. You go past a lot of boarded-up shops, a pharmacy, and a library, none of which seem especially likely to be serving eggs. It doesn't take you long to conclude there isn't a single brunch place in Mantua. What the heck, right??

"It seems," you say, "that we have three choices. Option one: open up our own restaurant, because seriously, what kind of town doesn't have brunch. But since neither of us knows about cooking foods, there's always option two: we try to find whatever work we can."

"Or we could go back to Verona and rob my parents," Juliet says. "They've got, like, lots of extra money.

"Upon reflection, I really should've taken some of it," she says.

Open up a cute little brunch place! *Turn to 302.*

Choose a quiet life in Mantua and live happily ever after: *turn to 280.*

Be Juliet, go home and rob her parents, THEN live happily ever after in Mantua: *turn to 270.*

257 "Listen," the Friar says, cutting you off. "You know what cheers me up when I'm sad?"

"What?" you say.

"Learning about philosophy!" he says. You stare at him for a long moment.

"PHILOSOPHY. That's your solution," you say. He nods.

"Listen," you say, "maybe you should shut up for a bit. And while you do that, let me just say that if YOU were as young as me, and YOU were in love with Juliet, and YOU had married her like an hour ago, and then YOU had killed Tybalt, then maybe YOU'D know me and could say something. Maybe THEN you'd pull out your hair and fall on the ground, like I am about to do now."

True to your word, you fall on the ground and pull out some of your hair. It really hurts!

"Ow," you say.

There's a knocking from upstairs. "Get up, hide yourself, and stop pulling out your hair," the Friar says. "God. TEENS."

Hide: *turn to 247.*

 Refuse to hide: *turn to 228.*

258 Ah, a wise guy, eh? You think you're real clever, being all "Aha! The structure of this an-adventure-is-chosen-by-you book means that I'm basically exploring a decision tree, and true randomness is impossible in such a structure! The book requires me to choose from a list of predetermined choices and could never handle true randomness as input!"

Well the joke's on you, because I am ALL OVER THIS. Go ahead. Pick any random number in the universe: positive, negative, whole, irrational—just go nuts. Make it as random as you want. Ask a random stranger for a random number if you want. Go for it.

Got the number? Great, let's convert it to a section number for this book. Add five to your number, multiply by two, subtract four, divide by two, subtract your original number, multiply by a hundred, and then turn to that section. I'll meet you there.

And if right now you're whispering, "What the heck? I didn't pick up a FUN-LOOKING ADVENTURE BOOK to do MATH WHEN I DON'T HAVE TO," then I can always choose for you too. No biggie!

You decide to read . . . oh, let's say *Fair Is Foul and/or Foul Is Fair. turn to 358.*

259 You chose poorly, and the police dogs and horses descend on you. Your steed is allowed to leave, as it was brought here under your orders, but no mercy is shown to you. The dogs bite chunks out of you and the horses do the same, and you still have the presence of mind to find this surprising.

"I thought horses were vegetarians!" you shout, bleeding and in tremendous pain. The horses, embarrassed and chagrined, reluctantly spit out their Romeo chunks.

"That's better," you say. You still die though. And then the horses eat you anyway!

And you don't know it, Romeo, but eating your awesome body was almost a religious experience for these horses. It was a revelation. Within days these flesh-addled steeds are galloping across Europe, leaving behind them only the gleaming white skeletons of any unfortunate souls who get in their way: a warning to all and sundry that yea, THESE horses have tasted of human flesh and, in doing so, found religion.

And now, they prey.

THE END

260 Seriously? Sex can be one of the most personal experiences you can share with someone, and you want me to just TELL YOU what to do?

Fine. FINE. Fill in the blanks below to embark on an erotic journey without parallel:

You and Juliet decide to [SEX THING] each other right away. "Oh Romeo," sighs Juliet, "may I just say: [LINE CHOSEN LITERALLY AT RANDOM FROM THE BIBLE]."

You nod. "Yes, absolutely."

Pretty soon your [LIMB OR INTERNAL ORGAN] is [VERB]ing so [ADVERB THAT ENDS IN "LY" AND COULD JUST AS EASILY BE APPLIED TO THE ACTIONS OF GIANT SEA MAMMALS] that you cry out, "[SOUND-EFFECT ONOMATOPOEIA FOR PANCAKE BATTER DROPPING ONTO CONCRETE]!" Juliet smiles.

"That's what we call getting Capuleted," she says, and then purses her lips. "Or at least, that's what they call it in [NAME OF THE PLACE MENTIONED IN THE FIRST 'THERE ONCE WAS A MAN FROM'–STYLE LIMERICK YOU CAN THINK OF]."

"Let's do that again [THE NUMBER OF DIGITS OF PI YOU CAN RECITE FROM MEMORY] times," you say.

"I've got a better idea," she says. "Let's do something that involves [THE FIRST NOUN THAT YOU FREE-ASSOCIATE WITH THIS WORD I'M ABOUT TO PRESENT TO YOU: 'COMPANIONSHIP']. I feel like [THE SECOND WORD THAT COMES TO MIND WHEN I SHOW YOU THIS EXTREMELY REALISTIC AND HIGHLY DETAILED PAINTING:]."

And that's exactly what you do. At the end, you [CHOOSE ONE: HUG, KISS, SHAKE HANDS] and say, [CHOOSE AT LEAST ONE: "I'M REALLY SLEEPY NOW," "DO YOU EVER GET SAD," "THIS WAS EVEN BETTER THAN IN MY FANFICTION"].

 Whew!! End sex scene, extremely satisfied. *Turn to 246.*

261 The machine whirs and clicks. The total reading changes to "2," and the output changes to:

WTN RDCVGPIJAPIXDCH DC RGPRZXCV IWT RDST!
AXHITC, ATI'H CDI ITAA PCNDCT TAHT IWT PCHLTG,
DZPN?? QTRPJHT IWT IWXCV XH, LT'KT ZXCSP
XCKTHITS P ADI DU BDCTN XC IWXH GXSXRJADJH
HTRJGXIN HNHITB. HXVCTS, KTGDCP RXIN
BPCPVTBTCI.

You whisper the words out loud, phonetically. "Watten ridcivgopijapixdcoh," you say.

"What was that?" asks the Veronan.

"A complete waste of my time thus far," you sigh.

Flip "ADD 1" on: turn to 269.

Flip "ADD 2" off: turn to 340.

Flip "ADD 4" on: turn to 334.

Flip "ADD 8" on: turn to 276.

Step away from the machine: turn to 354.

262

SMACK

Best high five of your life, Romeo.

Abscond to Mantua so you don't get arrested and killed now: *turn to 273.*

 Stick around and chat Juliet up some more: *turn to 283.*

263 You do. It's terrible. You have no idea what's going on, you can hear your parents wailing downstairs over their lost Tybalt, and you can barely think straight. Where's Romeo? What's taking Angelica so long??

Continue waiting: *turn to 277.*

Man, forget this. Be Romeo; I'll just get him to my house myself. *Turn to 204.*

264 You knock on the front door as you open it. "Anyone home?" you say. You don't get a response, but you hear noise coming from the basement. It sounds like—conversation?

As you walk downstairs you can make it out a bit better. You only catch snippets, things like "I see that madmen have no ears" and "Let me dispute with thee of thy estate": nothing that you can make any particular sense of. But then you hear something that does make sense. It's the phrase "Thou canst not speak of that thou dost not feel." And it's spoken by Romeo.

You throw open the basement door and find Friar Lawrence and Romeo there. "Wert thou as young as I—" Romeo is saying, till the door slamming open distracts him. He looks at you, shocked, as you run into his arms.

"Juliet, my love!" he shouts.

"My nurse told me you were dead!" you say, your face pressed to his chest, surprising yourself by actually crying with happiness.

"Accurate information about recent events can be hard to come by in our day and age," explains the Friar, quite reasonably.

"Juliet," Romeo says, "I'm alive, but I'm—I'm banished, Juliet. I killed Tybalt in public and they're kicking me out of Verona."

You stare into his eyes and smile. "Is that a problem?" you say. "We can live somewhere else. Europe has tons of cities, dude."

"Aren't you mad about Tybalt?" the Friar asks.

"Thirty seconds ago I thought my husband was dead!" you say. "And now he's not, and that's great. I'll feel bad about my cousin later, okay? I'm sure Romeo had a good reason." You turn to him. "He wanted to kill you first, right?"

"Absolutely," Romeo says.

"Then it's settled," you say. "You acted in self-defense." You take his hand. "Come on," you say as you lead him back up the stairs. "Let's blow this Popsicle stand."

And so you do. You and Romeo escape to a honeymoon vacation, traveling to Milan, Monaco, Marseille, Toulouse, and Bordeaux, then up to Paris, where you buy a country estate house with all the money the two of you stole from your parents after you left the Friar's basement, and you live far far away from the drama of Verona.

The years pass peacefully. Two years after your first child, Romeo-ella, is born (Romeo chose the name), you give birth to Ross (Romeo is no longer allowed to choose any names). Eleven months after that, as you watch the two of them playing in your front yard, your husband composes a little poem on a scrap of paper and passes it to you. You look down at the words in your hand:

> *There never was a cuter girl and fella,*
> *than baby Ross and Miss Romeo-ella.*

You look up at your husband and your children playing and you smile. Everything is going to be just fine.

THE END

P.S.: The ghost of Tybalt haunts you most nights, but you help him and Romeo work things out, and once that's settled Ghost Tybalt starts getting big into gardening and anyway long story short now you get your flower beds weeded for free every night!

265 Alright! Pull up a chair.

Once upon a time a beautiful brother and sister—twins—were both shipwrecked in the strange and wonderful kingdom of Illyria. When the woman, named Viola, reached shore, she looked and couldn't find any evidence of her brother, Sebastian. "He must've drowned!" she said. She was very sad.

But then an Illyrian sea captain happened to be walking along the beach and came across her crying in the sand. "Don't be sad," he said. "Instead be sensible and get a job, okay?"

Viola loved being sensible, so she dried her tears and started looking for a job—but alas, all the job listings said "NO GIRLS ALLOWED" due to sexism! Viola decided she'd dress up as a man to get around the sexisms. Viola was a pretty smart young lady, and now she was a pretty smart young man too. Her dude-name was Cesario.

"Cesario" got a job working for a prince named Duke Orsino, who was so charming that she fell in love with him right away. But Duke was in love with another woman, named Olivia! And Olivia didn't want Duke to kiss her. In fact, she didn't want anyone to kiss her for SEVEN YEARS. Duke liked his new assistant a lot, so he asked "Cesario" to go to Olivia and woo her on his behalf.

"Cesario" thought that was a reasonable thing to do for her employer, so she agreed. She agreed to help him seduce another woman even though she loved Duke with all her heart! As you can see, her love for Duke was clouding her preexisting and long-standing love of being sensible.

But when Olivia met "Cesario," whom she also thought was a man, she fell in love on the spot. Olivia wanted to kiss "Cesario" right away! "Forget about nobody kissing me for seven years," she said. "Instead, I want YOU to kiss me for seven years!"

Viola had a moment of realization. She realized that this situation wasn't sensible at all, and had arisen only because of the deception and misapprehension that she was allowing to flourish! Viola decided to quickly and efficiently explain the misunderstanding, which avoided a lot of ridiculous circumstances and an entire subplot about yellow stockings.

When Viola was done clearing up any and all misunderstandings, Olivia thanked her for her honesty and shyly said that she'd always had a thing for women too. But sadly, Viola loved Duke and could not return her affection. When she returned to Duke she revealed that the competent man "Cesario" he'd liked all along was actually her, female-identified Viola!

Duke was surprised to find his sexism challenged so effectively AND attractively, and he and Viola were insta-married. Later, they discovered that Viola's twin brother, Sebastian, had survived the shipwreck after all, thanks to the efforts of another and completely unrelated ship's captain! So that made the ending of this story even happier.

Sebastian and Olivia had a fling, which was kinda weird, but they did not get married because in the end Olivia realized that Viola and Sebastian were two different people who just happened to look very much alike.

THE END

There! Now you don't have to read *Twelfth Night*, one of our bestselling titles in our new *Look, You Took Too Long and Now Somebody Else Has Already Chosen Your Adventure for You* series! Though perhaps this may whet your appetite for the adventure-on-the-high-seas prequel *Eleventh Night* and our shocking sequel *Thirteenth Night: Twelfth Night 2*? All are available at better bookstores near you, unless of course you are reading this in the distant future when not just the books themselves but the very fact that these books ever existed has been lost to the ravages of time because everything turns to dust, hah hah hah oh well!!

Anyway, Romeo: this was fun, and I like you. I'll let you in on a little secret: route three—the downtown core—that's the path you want to take.

Choose my path: *turn to 310.*

266

The machine whirs and clicks. The total reading changes to "12," and the output changes to:

```
GDX BNMFQZSTKZSHNMR NM BQZBJHMF SGD
BNCD! KHRSDM, KDS'R MNS SDKK ZMXNMD DKRD
SGD ZMRVDQ, NJZX?? ADBZTRD SGD SGHMF HR,
VD'UD JHMCZ HMUDRSDC Z KNS NE LNMDX HM
SGHR QHCHBTKNTR RDBTQHSX RXRSDL. RHFMDC,
UDQNMZ BHSX LZMZFDLDMS.
```

I don't think that's it, Angelica.

Flip "ADD 1" on: turn to 279.

Flip "ADD 2" on: turn to 285.

Flip "ADD 4" off: turn to 306.

Flip "ADD 8" off: turn to 253.

Step away from the machine: turn to 354.

267

Glad you enjoyed it. It sounded . . . fun?

So! Pardon the pun, but if you're all finished here . . . then let's put this sex scene to bed, shall we?

End sex scene! *Turn to 246.*

268

"Easy mode, I guess?" you whisper.

The librarian, saying nothing, grabs a book off the shelf and stuffs it down his shirt. You watch him leave with it, confused. I don't think he's coming back.

You eventually turn your attention to the remaining three books. Each of them claims to be based on a true story or "inspired by true events," which is just enough wiggle room to make you suspect they're maybe making the whole thing up. Anyway, there's:

To Be or Not To Be: looks like a story about a 30-year-old emo teen named Hamlet who is haunted by a murdered ghost who wants him to kill his stepdad. It's got a woman in it named Ophelia who's good at science too! Could be fun!

Fair Is Foul and/or Foul Is Fair: the cover has a dude with a sword, a lady with bloody hands, and some friggin' witches. Not gonna lie: it looks awesome and metal as heck.

Romeo and/or Juliet: hey, the characters in this book have the same name as you and your wife! CRAZY! Maybe, if you're really lucky, they'll also share your circumstances and this remarkably familiar book will give you some tips on how to live your life . . . if you ever figure out how to stop reading it!

You move to an out-of-the-way area of the library, settle comfortably into a chair, and crack open . . .

To Be or Not To Be: **turn to 281.**

Fair Is Foul and/or Foul Is Fair: **turn to 358.**

Romeo and/or Juliet: **turn to 1.**

269

The machine whirs and clicks. The total reading changes to "3," and the output changes to:

```
XUO SEDWHQJKBQJYEDI ED SHQSAYDW JXU
SETU! BYIJUD, BUJ'I DEJ JUBB QDOEDU UBIU JXU
QDIMUH, EAQO?? RUSQKIU JXU JXYDW YI, MU'LU
AYDTQ YDLUIJUT Q BEJ EV CEDUO YD JXYI
HYTYSKBEKI IUSKHYJO IOIJUC. IYWDUT, LUHEDQ
SYJO CQDQWUCUDJ.
```

I don't think that's it, Angelica.

Flip "ADD 1" off: **turn to 264.**

Flip "ADD 2" off: **turn to 243.**

Flip "ADD 4" on: **turn to 324.**

Flip "ADD 8" on: **turn to 295.**

Step away from the machine: **turn to 354.**

270 Romeo's banishment means getting into Verona is tricky. You and he are hiding in some bushes outside Verona, waiting for your chance to get past the city guards.

"Okay, so our plan goes like this," Romeo whispers. "We get past the guards, and THEN, we rob your parents."

It's not the greatest plan you've ever heard.

"That could work," you say gently, "but it could also fail horribly. What if, instead, we . . .

"... create a diversion and sneak in while they're distracted?" *Turn to 286.*

"... decide not to rob them after all?" *Turn to 280.*

271 Congratulations! You have unlocked a new character, and unlike Romeo and/or Juliet, she's not a teenager! She is an ADULT HUMAN, and as such she is less interested in SELF-DESTRUCTIVE LOVE and more interested in FINDING SUSTAINABLE LONG-TERM HAPPINESS AND SATISFACTION, PREFERABLY ON HER OWN TERMS, and the way she does that is by SOLVING MYSTERIES. That's right: you are a PRIVATE INVESTIGATOR. And you are HECKA self-narrating.

Oh man, sweet!! INVESTIGATE ALL CRIMES. *Turn to 287.*

272 You chose poorly, and you are killed by the mob. Your remains are buried in an unmarked grave, and many hundreds of years later, the story of your life, titled *Romeo and Juliet; or, How One Man Got Banished and Didn't Leave and Then Died Because He Was Bad at the Stealth Parts*, becomes really popular! It's adapted into all sorts of different media and becomes a cultural touchstone for a generation. I think what connects with people the most is how you risk everything—

even your life!—for the person you love, and also, how the stealth parts can be really hard sometimes.

I mention all this only so when your ghost manifests itself after a few hundred years and finds your grave replaced with a giant sign that reads, "Tonight Only! Romeo and Juliet: the Boylesque Show," you'll have some context to understand it. Boylesque is burlesque with boys. And burlesque is when people take fancy clothes off to music!!

THE END

273 "Okay, well, I'm off to Mantua to lie low until the heat dies down!" you say.

"Okay. I'll see if I can get my parents to reverse your banishment," Juliet says.

"AWESOME," you say, and then you climb down the ladder, hop on your horse, and take off to Mantua.

Go to Mantua: *turn to 221.*

274

"I like the sound of that sexy option," you say, hoping to sound sexy and seductive. "Let's do that one."

It apparently was sexy and seductive enough, because Juliet throws down the rope ladder you sent. You conceal your horse in the bushes (they're pretty big bushes) and climb up into her room.

And yes, this is it, gentle reader. This is the moment you've been waiting for. Here is the only reason you picked up this book in the first place, because you knew this scene had to be in here somewhere, if only you just somehow made the right choices to find it.

Welcome . . . to the CHOOSE-YOUR-OWN SEX SCENE.

Choose-your-own sex scene!! I CAN'T WAIT. *Turn to 239.*

Haha what? No that's—that's fine. Skip over to when the sex is done, please. *Turn to 246.*

275

You slowly open up the back window and gingerly pull yourself into the room. Alright, mission accomplished! You're now right inside the Friar's supply room, Juliet. All you need to do is grab a poison.

You look around the room. Dang, Juliet, there are a lot of liquids here, none of them are labeled, AND you don't even know what poisons look like.

As you stare at the array of unlabeled liquids, you realize you don't even know what you're planning to do with them. Pour them into the city's water supply, I guess? That seems supervillainy enough, and it'd probably do the trick. But—and I'm just spitballing here so feel free to tell me if I'm off-mark—but if you REALLY wanted to kill everyone, wouldn't it be better to pour it into, oh, I don't know . . .

. . . the WHOLE WORLD'S water supply??

It just seems that'd be the only way to REALLY make a statement about how upset you are that your husband committed suicide. If you're interested, I actually know someone who has some experience in the "kill everyone" department! She's smart, determined, and lives quite a ways north of you—1500 kilometers, to be exact—but you could take a horse and make it there in a month, easy.

Her name's Ophelia, and she's already killed everyone in her particular hamlet.

She could probably use the company?

Take some poison, go see Ophelia, and poison the oceans themselves: *turn to 288.*

Naw man, I'm just here to kill a village, a small town tops: *turn to 301.*

276

The machine whirs and clicks. The total reading changes to "10," and the output changes to:

EBV ZLKDOXQRIXQFLKP LK ZOXZHFKD QEB ZLAB!
IFPQBK, IBQ'P KLQ QBII XKVLKB BIPB QEB
XKPTBO, LHXV?? YBZXRPB QEB QEFKD FP, TB'SB
HFKAX FKSBPQBA X ILQ LC JLKBV FK QEFP
OFAFZRILRP PBZROFQV PVPQBJ. PFDKBA,
SBOLKX ZFQV JXKXDBJBKQ.

I don't think that's it, Angelica.

Flip "ADD 1" on: turn to 295.

Flip "ADD 2" off: turn to 306.

Flip "ADD 4" on: turn to 285.

Flip "ADD 8" off: turn to 264.

Step away from the machine: turn to 354.

277

You wait. It's awful.

Eventually, the waiting ends when you hear a rustling noise outside. Running to your balcony, you peer over and see your new husband, Romeo, tying up a horse. You run back to your bed.

"Alright, Jules," you say. "Time to blow Romeo's mind with how seductive you look."

First you try climbing into bed and leaning back against the pillows, but that just makes you look sleepy. So you put one arm on top of your head, bending it downwards across your hair so your fingers brush your opposite shoulder, but then it just looks like you wanted to inconveniently scratch your shoulder.

You hear Romeo fumbling with the rope ladder.

"Frig!" you whisper. You try sitting up with your back arched and both hands interlaced behind your head, but you look more like someone interrupted in the middle of some curl-ups than anything else. You stand up from the bed and rest your elbow on the bedpost in what you hope is a fun, casual pose, but you catch a glimpse of yourself in the mirror and you look less "Oh, hello! I didn't hear you come in!"

and more "This bedpost is actually too high for this pose so I hope you like looking at one of my armpits."

You hear the sound of Romeo climbing the rope ladder. He's getting closer!

"Frig frig!" you whisper. You're panicking. You can't remember what normal people do with their hands. You can't remember what normal people do with their legs. You can't even remember which female secondary sexual characteristics your culture says are the most attractive in women! Is it body hair? Breasts? Maybe it's the greater development of thigh muscles behind the femur, rather than in front of it?

You see Romeo's hand grab the top of your balcony, and in a panic, you dive under your covers to hide. You peek out a few seconds later and see Romeo there, entering your room.

"Hey there, beautiful," he says.

"Hey yourself, handsome," you say. "You're a little late, so I went to bed. It's pretty cold under here." You pull back the covers a little. "I could use some company."

Juliet, Romeo has been INSTA-SEDUCED. Dang! You pulled it off!

And yes, this is it, gentle reader. This is the moment you've been waiting for. Here is the only reason you picked up this book in the first place, because you knew this scene had to be in here somewhere, if only you just somehow made the right choices to find it.

Welcome . . . to the CHOOSE-YOUR-OWN SEX SCENE.

Choose-your-own sex scene!! I CAN'T WAIT. *Turn to 297.*

Haha what? No that's . . . that's fine. Skip over to when the sex is done, please. *Turn to 289.*

278
Listen, I hear you when you say that it's pretty stressful out there in book land, where you're being chased by all those guards who want to kill you. Maybe it'd be nice to hide from the world for a while, right?

And I don't judge! Most books don't give you ANY choices at all, and I can't fault you for, after a lifetime of reading them, thinking, "Wow, I've beaten every one of the early-reader books I've read wherein the plot is on rails and I can't mess anything up. Maybe I'm finally ready to graduate to more complex, adult literature, which is to say books wherein one might find oneself choosing one's OWN adventure!"

And it seems like a good idea! So you pick up this book and before you know it you're facing down an impossible choice that's basically guaranteed to kill you and you have no idea which option is right.

Suddenly those simpler books with their one-size-fits-all plots and their single easily spoiled endings seem real attractive. Comfortable. EASY.

I get it. Let's hang out here for a bit while the guards search for you outside.

Take all the time you need.

Hey, you want to hear a story? I promise, I won't ask you to tell me what happens next in it.

Okay, tell me a story: *turn to 265.*

Actually, uh, I'd rather die than listen to another story, thanks: *turn to 310.*

279 The machine whirs and clicks. The total reading changes to "13," and the output changes to:

HEY CONGRATULATIONS ON CRACKING THE CODE! LISTEN, LET'S NOT TELL ANYONE ELSE THE ANSWER, OKAY?? BECAUSE THE THING IS, WE'VE KINDA INVESTED A LOT OF MONEY IN THIS RIDICULOUS SECURITY SYSTEM. SIGNED, VERONA CITY MANAGEMENT.

I—I think that's it, Angelica!! You should step away from the machine now and see what happens!

Flip "ADD 1" off: turn to 266.

Flip "ADD 2" on: turn to 342.

Flip "ADD 4" off: turn to 347.

Flip "ADD 8" off: turn to 305.

Step away from the machine: turn to 294.

280 You decide you don't need your parents OR their money, even if it would be pretty fun to steal from them. Romeo starts to look for work, and pretty soon he's found a rare job opening to be an assistant brewer at a local pub. He pays attention and works hard, and a few months later when the head brewer is slain in an unrelated swordfight, Romeo takes his place.

In the meantime, you've had your hands full. You've been teaching self-defense classes for the local Mantuan women, and had some success with it too, but you have to put that on hold. You're pregnant, Juliet. With triplets.

The years that follow aren't easy. Raising three children at the same time, without any parental support, while also starting over in a new town? It's hard. It's actually the hardest thing you've ever done.

It's also the most rewarding. Watching your children grow from babies into actual people gives you a satisfaction you never expected. You grow old and happy and fat and awesome.

THE END

P.S.: Romeo gets fat and awesome too. I know! FINALLY, RIGHT??

281 Excellent choice! Unfortunately, the book you're holding couldn't hold all the content we wanted to put in it, so we had to divide it into two volumes. Please insert book one, labeled *To Be or Not To Be*, into your hands to continue.

Fig 1: Book 2

Fig 2: Book 1

Once you have exhaustively completed *To Be or Not To Be*, remove book one, and reinsert this volume into your hands.

I have exhaustively completed *To Be or Not To Be*. Whew! What a ride. I really enjoyed it and will recommend it to everyone I know, that's for sure! *Turn to 311.*

282 "Please be careful," you say to your wife. "And if anything goes wrong . . ."

"Yes?" Juliet says.

"Punch them once for me," you say, and then you kiss her good-bye. She mounts DJ Muscles McGlutes and takes off down the road, stopping just before she's out of earshot to take one last look back.

"Don't do anything I wouldn't do!" you shout, waving. You can't be certain, but you're pretty sure she smiles and nods before she takes off down the road.

A day goes by, then two.

There's absolutely no sign of Juliet.

Go to Verona to rescue her: *turn to 296.*

Keep waiting: *turn to 315.*

283 "Well," you say, "I've still got some time until daybreak, when I have to leave. You want to kiss for a bit longer?"

"Yes please," Juliet says, but as you lean forward to kiss her your view of her is obscured by some bright light that's traveled all the way from a burning ball of gas at the center of the solar system just to get you right in your eyes. Aw man, it's the sunrise!!

"Aw man, it's the sunri—" you begin, but you're interrupted by the sound of a lark chirping, which this bird does every day at sunrise. Like the rooster! But FANCIER.

"That was a nightingale," Juliet says, "and that light was actually caused by a meteor coming out of the sun to light your way to Mantua. It's still night. You should stick around."

Say, "Um if that's true then I should definitely leave because if the sun itself is somehow exhaling meteors to light my way I should take advantage of that while it's happening": *turn to 316.*

 Stick around some more: *turn to 293.*

284 "Hard mode, I guess?" you whisper.

The librarian snatches a book off the shelf and places it in your hands. "Then this is the book for you," he whispers back. "It is a very special book."

You turn it over in your hands. It's called *A Midsummer Night's Choice*, and it appears to be an educational book about fairies that promises to teach at-risk teens "a really important lesson about solving problems with drugs." You're a teen, Romeo! Maybe some real talk is just what you need! The book is credited only to "A. Librarian."

"Did you write this?" you ask. "Why is this hard mode? Are there not a lot of pictures, or . . . ?"

You trail off, unable to think of another way a book could be hard.

"Oh, it's hard mode for two reasons," the librarian says. "Firstly because I'll be standing behind you the entire time you read, which is really annoying. And I'll be doing that for the second reason this is hard mode: if you die in the book, I will INSTANTLY KILL YOU HERE IN REAL LIFE."

"Hard mode sounds terrible, I don't think I—" you begin, but the librarian puts his finger to your lips.

"Shhh," he whispers. He places his hands on top of yours and forces you to open the book. Then he removes his hands from yours, produces a dagger from his belt, and holds it to your throat.

"Hard mode has begun," he whispers.

Begin reading: *turn to 124.*

285

The machine whirs and clicks. The total reading changes to "**14**," and the output changes to:

IFZ DPOHSBUVMBUJPOT PO DSBDLJOH UIF DPEF!
MJTUFO, MFU'T OPU UFMM BOZPOF FMTF UIF
BOTXFS, PLBZ?? CFDBVTF UIF UIJOH JT, XF'WF
LJOEB JOWFTUFE B MPU PG NPOFZ JO UIJT
SJEJDVMPVT TFDVSJUZ TZTUFN. TJHOFE,
WFSPOB DJUZ NBOBHFNFOU.

I don't think that's it, Angelica.

Flip "ADD 1" on: turn to 342.

Flip "ADD 2" off: turn to 266.

Flip "ADD 4" off: turn to 276.

Flip "ADD 8" off: turn to 334.

Step away from the machine: turn to 354.

286

Romeo laughs at your idea. "A diversion? What are you, thirteen? Are you literally a thirteen-year-old right now?"

"No I'm not THIRTEEN," you say, annoyed. "Oh Romeo, Romeo, wherefore art thou being such a DICK about this?"

"Sorry," he says.

"Well, good," you say.

Romeo pauses. "It's just when I hear 'diversion' I imagine, I don't know, you dressing up as a sexy female guard to distract all the male guards, you know? And then when they catch sight of you their hearts pound out of their chests so much that we can see the outline of hearts straining against their shirts, while at the same time their heads transform into giant steam whistles. Toot toot!"

"I don't think I've read the same books you've read," you say.

"Too bad," he says. "So! What diversion did you have in mind?" he asks.

"Actually . . . that dress-up one sounds fun," you whisper, blushing a little. "Let's do that one."

Romeo smiles. He's into this.

"I like it," he says. "But where are you going to find a sexy female guard costume?"

Tell him you'll take an existing guard costume and put yourself in it, and hey presto: sexy female guard costume: *turn to 319.*

Tell him hah hah, oh no, sorry for the misunderstanding, but HE'S the one dressing up as the sexy female guard, and if he cares about this going down he'd better figure that one out PRETTY DARN QUICKLY: *turn to 299.*

287
Name's Rosaline. Rosaline Catling. And this week has given me more than enough of Verona. It's been the kind of week that would make me want to pack up and leave town, if I wasn't on my third town in twelve months already. They say you can't run from your problems, and maybe they're right, but they obviously haven't tried shimmying out the back window and sneaking away from them in the middle of the night.

Works like a charm.

Two months ago I found myself back in Verona: the same town I grew up in, and out of, over a decade ago. Seems I'd run out of aces in just about every town you'd care to name and needed a place to land back on my feet before I took off again. This was as good as any. I don't need a home. I don't need friends. All I need is my work. Got an office in the part of town mothers warn their daughters about, hung up my shingle, and just like that I was back in the private detection business. All I needed now was a crime. And yeah: I got one, and then some.

It starts like this: seven days ago I notice this kid sniffing around outside my office. I figured someone wanted to gather some dirt on me and didn't give it a second thought. Whatever this kid was looking for, he wasn't gonna find it. I'm good—better than a kid PI, that's for sure.

So I return the favor. I spend a few hours looking into him and his friends. Kid's got a name—Romeo Montague—and he's the sole heir to the Montague family fortune and sworn enemy to my uncle's family, the Capulets. Me, I stay above all that feud garbage; figure I got enough enemies already. Romeo's no threat to me, but I check up on the kid's friends too, just to be safe: Benvolio, Mercutio, his servant, Balthasar. Again, nothing I need to be worried about.

Six days ago the same kid comes to me and manages to pull off the one thing nobody seems to be able to do anymore: the kid surprised me. Surprised the heck out of me, actually. Walks up to me and says he's seen me around town, says I'm beautiful and brilliant and he's fallen in love and can't live without me.

Get in line, kid.

I let him down nice and easy. The world's a rough place, but I didn't see why I needed to make it any rougher on him. Puppy love, right? Sure, it'd be nice to take him up on his offer and be rich. It's also nice to not be married to a teen. I made up some garbage about being sworn to chastity because I knew he was too young to understand the truth: that I was already in love with someone else. A woman I'd only ever seen a couple times but still found myself chasing ever since. Someone I don't see myself getting over anytime soon.

Five days ago I stayed in my office and drank. A quiet day means a lot of free time, and I filled it, right up to the brim, right up until the floor got too crooked for me to stand on and I quit trying.

Four days ago I didn't make it out of bed. Missed the entire day. Turns out that uncle of mine invited me to a party. Didn't show up to that either. Wouldn't say I missed it.

Three days ago I'd just made it into the office when a nice old lady comes to me in tears. Says someone made off with her brooch. Not my normal wheelhouse, but her money was as good as anyone's. I dried her tears, told her I'd find it, and sent her on her way.

Two days ago the trail finally got hot as I heard tell of someone trying to fence the brooch. Recovered the jewelry, sure, and got into a swordfight while I was at it for my trouble. The thief was skilled with her blade. I was better.

Yesterday I returned the brooch to the old lady and took the rest of my payment. I'd like to say I didn't immediately drink my way through it, but what can I say: detection is hard work, and a girl gets thirsty.

This morning began with a knock at my door and an anonymous letter from a concerned citizen. Said he wants me to look into the Romeo and Juliet case. Said he'll make it worth my while and stuffed enough money into that envelope to make me believe him.

Only problem was, I had no idea what he was talking about.

Didn't take much digging to find out the basics, put together who the players were and a basic timeline of what happened. Turns out that as of last night, Romeo's dead. Killed Tybalt a few days before, got his friend Mercutio killed while he was at it. Ended up banished himself for the trouble. Came back though and killed himself in Juliet's tomb.

That was his new girlfriend, Juliet: my uncle's kid, sole heir to the Capulet fortune—and yeah, she's dead too. Faked her own death, and then made it real a few days later when she woke up to Romeo's corpse on top of her. Cops think it's the same old story, that "secret marriage/double suicide" yarn that's older than my horse and twice as tired. Parents agree. Except there's a woman in this little story I can't get past: Romeo's mom.

Here's what sticks in my craw: Romeo and Juliet are found dead, and Romeo's dad uses that time, then and there, to casually drop the bombshell that Romeo's MOM died too. In an unrelated incident. At some unknown earlier time that night. Of "heartbreak."

Right.

Everyone wants this to go away nice and quiet, because if Romeo Montague and Juliet Capulet died together for love, then their parents might finally end the feud that's been destroying this town for years. So that's the story, and everything's wrapped up nice and neat with a bow on top.

There's just one problem. That other person I'm in love with? That woman I long ago realized I'd do anything for? Yeah, she's got a name. She's called The Truth.

And like I said, me and her have a real nice thing going.

The case seems like it might need some finesse. I start by examining the body. *Turn to 303.*

288 The ride to Ophelia's house takes over a month and it's super boring, so I want to skip over it. You really feel like you want to skip over it too, so that's what we do!

We're a good team, you and I.

After a bunch of boring travel scenes that nobody cares about, you ride into Denmark on your horse (you named him "Wherefore Art Thou Pony-o" on the ride over; that's part of the stuff we skipped) and find Ophelia sitting on the throne, surrounded by dead bodies, in a castle that is itself surrounded by dead bodies. You shift the bag of poisons you grabbed to your other arm as you knock on the door, stepping over what looks like the decapitated body of the crown prince of Norway.

"Hi," you say to the woman on the throne. "I'm Juliet."

"Ophelia," she says. Then, before you can react, she has her sword to your throat. "Are you here to take over Denmark? Because if so I'll have to kill you. You wanna know a secret?"

You nod.

"I've gotten really good at it," she whispers.

"I can see that," you say. "How did this happen, if you don't mind me asking?"

Ophelia straightens up some, removing the knife from your throat. "Oh, this is just the logical result of all the many choices I made in my life," she says. "While this is just one of the dozens of ways I'm sure my life could've turned out, I'm equally sure if you were in my shoes you'd have made these exact same choices eventually."

You glance down at your bag full of stolen poison that you've just dragged across Europe and nod.

"So listen, I came to ask you a favor," you say.

"Let me guess," she says. "You have a lousy boyfriend and you want me to kill him because OL' CRAZY OPHELIA IS DEFINITELY DOWN FOR THAT."

"No," you say, "no, no, nothing like that. My boyfriend's already dead, actually."

"Sorry to hear that," she says. "So this is more a revenge spree?"

"Kinda!" you say. "I—um, this sounds silly to say out loud, but I want to poison the world's water supply and kill everyone because my boyfriend committed suicide and I'm really upset about that." You pause for a moment. "Still," you add. "I'm upset about it STILL. It happened over a month ago.

"You live pretty far away from Verona," you say.

You pull open the bag to show Ophelia. "I stole these from a creepy friar," you say. "You know the type?"

Ophelia picks up a bottle and examines it, holding its dark contents up to the sunlight. "The type who keeps a bunch of unlabeled toxins in his kitchen," she says.

"Exactly," you say. "Anyway, I figure there's something here we could use to make an ultimate poison, right? I kinda promised my nurse I'd poison more than the death-darting eye of cockatrice, or words to that effect."

Ophelia looks at you. "Juliet," she says. "What you're proposing is that we two, you and I, become the last two humans to ever live. You want to kill off the entire human race."

"Oh, well, when you put it like THAT, I sound crazy!" you say.

Tell her it's totally what you want to do though: *turn to 318.*

Tell her you're having second thoughts: *turn to 298.*

289 The sex scene finishes.

"Whew!" you both say. "What fun sexual activities those were!"

Romeo sighs. "I'm quite satisfied with the sex we just had," he says.

"Good," you say. "Me too."

Light streams through your window.

"HOLY CRAP IS IT MORNING ALREADY??" Romeo says. "Dude! We had sex for a whole night!"

You look at him and smile.

High five Romeo: *turn to 312.*

290

Your banishment means getting into Verona is tricky. You and Juliet are hiding in some bushes outside Verona, waiting for your chance to get past the city guards.

"Okay, so our plan goes like this," you whisper. "We get past the guards, and THEN, we go see your parents and ask them if they can front us a large amount of money."

Juliet whispers back that she doesn't think that's a very good plan.

"Of course it's a good plan!" you whisper. "It accomplishes exactly what we want to accomplish here!"

Before she can answer, you hold a hand in front of your mouth and say, "Wow what a great plan Romeo!" in a high-pitched voice.

"Is that supposed to be me?" she whispers.

"That's supposed to be you agreeing with my plan," you whisper.

"Hey, what was that high-pitched noise coming from the bushes?" a guard says.

Run away: *turn to 307.*

Hide out here: *turn to 307.*

291

You step away from the machine, vindicated. As you step away a pressure plate releases and the machine clicks a few times, and then, with a tremendous groan, the giant arm blocking your way starts to raise.

Your score has increased by 1 point and is now 100 points out of a possible 1000 points! Haha wow, that's not actually that many points for solving that puzzle. Sorry!

"Hey, thanks, lady!" says the Veronan as he scrambles under the colossal arm and moves ahead north. "You must be way smarter than your gross hat makes you look!"

You pull off your forgotten gross hat, annoyed, and put it in your inventory. Glancing at a nearby sundial, you're appalled to note that you spent an hour cracking that puzzle. You've been away from Juliet for two hours and haven't even met Romeo yet!

You rush under the clockwork arm and, thanks to your keen nursing skills, track Romeo down extremely quickly. You are now in the town square, and Romeo is standing directly in front of you.

Look town square: turn to 313.

Look Romeo: turn to 327.

Give message to Romeo: turn to 369.

292 You put down the book you've been reading and/or skimming and place it back on the Mantuan library shelf. "That's enough reading for one day!" you announce happily. As you leave the library, you glance at the page-a-day calendar on the circulation desk and realize you've been there, reading, for several days!

Dang, Romeo, you really need to learn how to read faster!

But the good news is there's not much else to do in Mantua, so it's not like you wasted time you might've spent doing anything else. You make your way back to your room and have a nap.

You wake up refreshed several hours later and stretch your arms out in bed. "If I may trust the flattering truth of sleep," you say, "my dreams presage some joyful news at hand! And by that I mean I totally just dreamed some good news is on its way, and dreams are never wrong and really important!"

As you lie in bed talking to yourself, there's a knock at the door. "It's open!" you say.

The door opens, and in steps your servant, Balthasar. You have a servant, did you know that? You didn't, huh? No worries: I forgot about him too. He was supposed to be with you this entire time! What the heck, Balthasar?

"Balthasar, what the heck?!" you say. "Where have you been?"

Balthasar shrugs. "Around," he says.

"I got into a STREET FIGHT, did you hear?" you reply, sitting up in bed. "Wow, I sure could've used some help in that OPEN-AIR SWORDFIGHT TO THE DEATH. If only my father paid for someone to stay close to me and attend to my every need, right??"

Balthasar shrugs again. "He doesn't pay me very much," he says.

"Why are you here?" you ask as you get out of bed. "Do you have news from Verona? Maybe a letter from the Friar? How's Juliet? How's my dad? Hey, how's JULIET? I'm asking about Juliet twice because nothing can be wrong if she's well."

"Then she's well, and nothing's wrong," Balthasar says.

"Phew," you say.

"Oh, by that I meant that her body sleeps in the Capulets' crypt, and her immortal soul lives with the angels."

Your mouth drops open. Juliet's . . . dead?

"Sorry for the bad news. I mean, this is just a summer job for me. I'm just a high school student. I don't know how to tell people bad things yet," he says.

"Are you serious?" you say, trying to keep calm.

Balthasar nods.

 Fall to your knees and shout to the heavens: *turn to 332.*

Ride to Verona right away: *turn to 314.*

294

293 "Okay," you declare to her, getting down on one knee. "Let me be captured and put to death: I don't care! If you're happy, I'm happy."

"Whoah whoah whoah, hold up," says Juliet. "That's stupid and crazy. Get the heck out of here."

Just then, there's a knock on the door. Juliet answers it and Angelica sticks her head in the room and tells her that her mom is on the way up.

"Okay dude," Juliet says, closing the door and turning to you, "out the window you go!"

 Leave out the window: *turn to 308.*

No! Stick around some more! *Turn to 322.*

294

You ride up beneath Juliet's balcony, just as the sun's setting. It's a pretty romantic atmosphere! That wasn't so hard after all!

"Hey Romeo," she shouts down to you. "Good work getting here and not getting killed. UNLIKE MY COUSIN, TYBALT."

This harms the romantic atmosphere.

"Listen," you say, "I feel really bad about that."

You explain how this was all a big mistake and how you didn't INTEND to murder her cousin right after you married her, but sometimes life's surprising, you know? Sometimes you accidentally commit murder right after marrying someone. Big life event, big emotions, things get said that can't be unsaid—the usual! You explain how you never wanted to hurt her and how awful you feel. You even call yourself "fortune's fool." And yes, it does take every shred of your +1 perk to talking, but you do finally convince her that she shouldn't give up on you and your new marriage. She agrees to take you back, Romeo! Hooray!

The only problem is right now you're a fugitive in Verona because of the family of the person whom you are chatting up right now. You can't stay here. "Let's go to Mantua," you say. "On my horse. We'll live happily ever after."

"Or," she says, "YOU could go to Mantua, and I'd stay here, and then we can be together again in the future when the heat dies down."

You hesitate.

"That latter option allows me to hide you out here until tomorrow," she says, "which WOULD allow lots of time for cool and neat sex."

You're not sure which option to choose. You want to be with her, but you're also way megahorny.

Tell her you'll spend the night and then leave: *turn to 274.*

Tell her you think she should come with you to Mantua: *turn to 256.*

295

The machine whirs and clicks. The total reading changes to "11," and the output changes to:

```
FCW AMLEPYRSJYRGMLQ ML APYAIGLE RFC AMBC!
JGQRCL, JCR'Q LMR RCJJ YLWMLC CJQC RFC
YLQUCP, MIYW?? ZCAYSQC RFC RFGLE GQ, UC'TC
IGLBY GLTCQRCB Y JMR MD KMLCW GL RFGQ
PGBGASJMSQ QCASPGRW QWQRCK. QGELCB,
TCPMLY AGRW KYLYECKCLR.
```

I don't think that's it, Angelica.

Flip "ADD 1" off: turn to 276.

Flip "ADD 2" off: turn to 347.

Flip "ADD 4" on: turn to 342.

Flip "ADD 8" off: turn to 269.

Step away from the machine: turn to 354.

296 "Juliet clearly is being held hostage by her parents," you think to yourself. "So I will go there and rescue her."

On the ride over to Verona, you start to get yourself pumped. You've got skills! You can accomplish goals! All you need to do is believe in yourself and you can do anything, right??

Unfortunately, your banishment means getting into Verona is tricky. There are city guards everywhere, which you'll need to get past to get to Capulet Castle. Luckily, you come up with a plan!

"My plan goes like this," you whisper to yourself. "I get past the guards, and THEN, I confront Juliet's parents."

It's only when you're being chased by the city guards that you realize your plan may have been a teensy bit too high-level to be implemented effectively on your first try. Anyway long story short: the guards catch you, rough you up a li'l, throw you in a bag, and drag you away.

Get dragged somewhere: *turn to 255.*

297 Alright! To get started, go to your bookshelf (or, if this is the only book you own, to your local library or bookstore. Also, if this is the only book you own: hey, thanks! I'm flattered) and pick up any other book with a sex scene in it. Then, while reading that sex scene, mentally substitute in the correct names, genders, body parts, interests, fluids, and catchphrases for yourself and your partner!

Enjoy! And remember: it's YOUR CHOICE. You can choose any other sex scene in the entire universe! My gift to you, reader. Go crazy. Have as many or as few sex scenes as you want.

When you're done, we'll continue! But no rush. Take as much time as you need. I don't judge!

I'll just be standing here with my back turned until you're ready.

Okay, I'm ready. WOW that was some COOL SEX I just had! *Turn to 309.*

No, not fair! YOU have to tell ME the sex scene. *Turn to 328.*

298 "Well," she says, "I mean, if you wanted, you could hang out here with me. I don't have much going on. We could clear out these bodies, clean the place up, maybe help each other get over our murderous obsessions?"

"That sounds nice," you say. "I'd like that."

You and Ophelia throw all the gross dead bodies into the river, where they float away (success!); clean the place up; and eventually, open up Queen Ophelia and Lady Juliet's Retreat for People with Strong Urges to Kill Suckers. Your star patient is one "Lady M," who came seeking treatment for her recurring urges to commit regicide. When she left six weeks later, those urges had been completely subsumed and were instead replaced by urges to have someone else commit regicide on her behalf!

Baby steps, Juliet.

THE END

---

299 "Here, I'll help you," you say. You wait until a guard walks by, then you hop out of the bushes, grab him by the shoulder, and pull him back in the bushes with you. He struggles briefly until you knock him out, then you strip him down and begin passing his clothes to Romeo. "Remember," you say, "you're a guard that presents as SEXY FEMALE. I wanna see some cleave."

"Cleave," Romeo repeats, a little unsure of himself.

"Yeah man," you say. You tie off the bottom of his shirt so it reveals his midriff. You tear his pants into shorts so you can see his legs just going up and up and up. You pull down his shorts so you can see his underwear peeking out above the waistline. It's a great look that's really doing things for you.

"That's a great look that's really doing things for me," you whisper.

"Listen," Romeo whispers back. There's a heat in his voice. "What if we didn't rob your parents after all? What if we, you know, just went back to Mantua? With, uh, the costume?"

"With the costume," you repeat, undoing the top buttons of his guard uniform top. "Because you're the best woman on the force, and you've captured me, the big bad Juliet. And you're not gonna let me get away this time."

Romeo puts a hand on your shoulder. You playfully pull it away, but he brings it back, placing his hand on you with authority. Your faces are inches away from each other, and you're practically panting into each other's mouths. "You're coming with me," he says, his hand tracing its way down your arm.

You can't take it anymore. You kiss. And in this costume, in this gender-bending outfit you've made for him, Romeo kisses like a girl.

"Okay um forget the robbery," you say, quickly taking him by the hand and leading him away. "This was an awesome idea for all the wrong reasons. Oh my god."

The guard wakes up several hours later, finding himself almost naked in a bush with torn-off pant legs beside him and a hastily scrawled note that reads, "SORRY BUT WE NEEDED YOUR CLOTHES!! (SEX THING)."

You live happily ever after in Mantua and have a lot of really REALLY fun times with your husband. You never even suspected life could feel this amazing, this freeing, this FUN. Being honest about what you want in the bedroom has led to your being honest about what you want in other aspects of your life, and though it can be scary, in the end it only serves to bring you and Romeo closer together.

Sometimes you're the criminal. Sometimes you're the chief of police. But he's always a very, very, VERY bad cop.

THE END

300 Hey look, it's me, the book you thought couldn't handle true randomness! AND YET HERE WE ARE. Amazing.

Anyway hey guess what, the random number you chose indicates you'll be reading a book called *Fair Is Foul and/or Foul Is Fair*. So let's get to it!

Open book: *turn to 358.*

301 Okay, fine! I'm not gonna fault you for not trying to end all human life on the planet! Even though I am kinda interested in seeing if you could pull it off. But it's fine! No regrets, right?

So! You're here surrounded by liquids, some of which you know are poisons, but none of which you can identify. You decide to make an educated guess and grab the blue container with a frowny face on it. Nothing says "poison" like a frowny face, right?

You gingerly slip out of the window you came in through. Once you're clear of the building you sneak down to Verona Well and dump your unknown liquid into it, which is a really responsible thing to do. Then you sneak back to your house, lock yourself in your room, go to bed, and vow not to come out for 24 hours! "By this time tomorrow, everyone in town will be dead!" you think as you fall asleep. "SWEET."

When you wake up the next morning, it's quiet outside your door. It's a good sign, but you decide to stay put until you can be certain. You wouldn't want to run into any stragglers. Evening finally comes, and when it does, you leave to explore the new Verona. Your plan seems to have worked perfectly, Juliet! Everyone is lying motionless on the ground, glasses of water in their hands or nearby, and none of them have a pulse. You're feeling PRETTY GOOD that you could put your mind towards killing everyone and actually pull it off on your first try when you happen to come across the body of your husband, Romeo.

With a glass of water in his hand.

Turns out your nurse lied to you, Juliet (you should've known this. I mean, HONESTLY, you should've known this), and Romeo wasn't dead after all! You feel so guilty that you murdered your new husband (along with, you know, everyone else in Verona) that something inside you cracks and you run off a cliff in penance.

Since you're dead, you never find out that what you poured into the water supply wasn't actually poison but just a liquid that only EMULATES death for precisely 42 hours (YES that is a thing that exists here in the real world, how ridiculous is it that you would even question that??). Soon people start waking up, including Romeo. He's the one who finds your body, actually. And it really upsets him. Some unknown person taints Verona's water supply, and the only one to die is his newlywed wife??

Romeo was going to be banished, but all that's forgotten in the days that follow "the Almost Two Days That Verona Faked Being Dead" as it's now being called. Because you were killed during it, everyone naturally assumes the reason the water supply was tainted was so someone could do a murder on you and get away without any witnesses.

Romeo swears on your grave that he'll find your killer. He becomes obsessed with criminals, criminality, criminal law—the works! He studies the police sciences. He learns detection. He bulks up. He learns to fight. When the police force isn't hiring, he decides he can operate more effectively as a vigilante anyway. And when nobody talks, he takes to dressing up like a bat and dangling thugs off of buildings to encourage them to be a little more forthcoming.

Romeo never does find your killer. But for many other Veronans, he finds something even better: JUSTICE.

THE END

P.S.: Later on Romeo's old crush Rosaline (remember her? She always had such a winning smile?) is in Friar Lawrence's storage room during an earthquake and gets doused in chemicals that color her skin white, her lips ruby red, and her hair green, and that also drive her insane, but THAT is a story for another time! It's a cool story though, and it makes me wish that instead of just *Romeo and/or Juliet* you'd also picked up my DLC pack, *Romeo and/or His Unquenchable Thirst for Vigilante Justice.*

302 You open up a cute little brunch place! You want to call it "Murder Most Fowl" because of all the chickens you're going to be killing for your "Mother and Child Reunion Chicken Breast and Egg Sandwich," but Juliet wants to call it "Something Brunchy This Way Comes" because "then we can say the name of our restaurant to our clients whenever we bring the food out to the table."

You decide on the compromise name "The Rest Is Sausage."

But here's the thing: it's hard starting a small business, especially one that you don't have much experience in. Every omelet you make ends up being scrambled eggs because it's really hard to flip an omelet without it falling apart, and Juliet's "breakfast specials" are, if you're being honest, just protein shakes with various kinds of meat in them.

It doesn't take long for your business to fail. And it doesn't take long after that for the money to run out. Your parents refuse to lend you anything, but Juliet writes her parents asking to borrow money, and they agree to help you—on the condition that she comes to them to collect it in person. The two of you feel there's a pretty good chance that it's a trap, and that once they have her, they'll never let her return.

But you don't really have many other choices.

"I can do it," Juliet says. "Trust me."

Send Juliet to borrow the money: *turn to 282.*

Go with Juliet to borrow the money: *turn to 290.*

Wait, wasn't Juliet gonna just steal the money before? Be Juliet and go steal money from her parents, it'll be rad. *Turn to 270.*

303

I make my way to Verona Graveyard, walking past the names and dates of the poor schmucks who aren't just visiting. The door on the Montague Crypt's locked, of course. I look out past the crypt and across the field of the dead, storm clouds gathering overhead. The way I figure it, locks are just a way of telling the world that whatever they're in front of is probably going to be interesting enough to be worth your time. And me, I get real curious.

A few minutes later, my friend the lock has found his eternal peace and I'm walking down into the cool stale air of a place that's full of bodies and smells it. Front and center in the crypt I find her: the late Mrs. Montague. My guess is she's only been here a few hours; probably got moved here early this morning. I take a good look. Something's off with her, but I can't quite put my finger on it.

I look over her body again real careful-like. The body's clean: no stab wounds. No scent of poison on the mouth. A pub corner somewhere far away from Verona and all this death is singing sweetly to me when I realize what's been bugging me this whole time: her hands.

More specifically, her fingers. Sure, she's been positioned with her arms across her chest, but whoever put her here—probably the cryptkeeper—must've only gotten to her after rigor mortis set in. He could force her arms into position, but those fingers were stuck.

I look at the hand on top, the left. Thumb and pinky are tucked under her palm, leaving the three that remain stuck straight out. An "M." Not a "W," either: if Lady M wanted a W, she'd have spread her fingers out. "M" for Montague, right? Everything wrapped up with a bow on top. But it's too obvious. And if there's one thing I can tell you about the Truth, it's that she's never that kind. To me, anyway.

I examine her other hand, tucked underneath. Here Lady M had arched her thumb and fingers: the perfect letter C, made out of her own dead flesh. C for Capulet? The timeline fits, at least: sure they're all buddy-buddy now, but these two families hated each other until last night, just about the time of my friend here's unfortunate demise.

Thing is though, my friend here made both symbols, M and C. I go down my list, and there are only two people in town who had means, motive, opportunity, and the right initials to pull off this murder. If the poor stiff was trying to finger CM with her dying breath, then her killer was her husband: Lord Charles Montague. And if she meant MC, then her life was ended by her worst enemy and my uncle: Lord Malcolm Capulet.

Can't say for sure I know where all the puzzle pieces fit, but at least now I know the picture on the box. Lady Montague didn't cry herself to death, I know that much: she was murdered, and one of these two men did it to her.

Montague had easy access to his wife, but his motive isn't clear. I've been in this business long enough to list a dozen reasons why bad men hate good women, but I can't pin him down just yet. On the other hand, Capulet had a very public feud with the Montagues, but that means access to Lady M wouldn't have been easy for him.

Seems to me I have my choice of killers. Seems to me I also have a pretty good hunch on who the real killer is. I turn my back to the dead lady and leave the graveyard. I'm on my way to . . .

. . . Lord Montague: *turn to 371.*

. . . Lord Capulet: *turn to 323.*

304
You put down *Fair Is Foul and/or Foul Is Fair*, closing it with finality. "Case closed," you say.

"You read that book like a professional," says the librarian. "This clearly isn't your first book."

"Naw," you say, trying to make it sound humble. "I don't want to brag, but I've read SEVERAL different books before. Some more than once."

"Sounds like you're almost ready . . . for HARD MODE," says the librarian.

"Sounds like I am!!" you say, not really sure what you're agreeing to. The librarian takes your book, puts it back on the shelf, and returns with a new volume, which he places gently into your hands.

"Then this is the book for you," he whispers back. "It is a very special book." You turn it over in your hands. It's called *A Midsummer Night's Choice*, and it appears to be an educational book about fairies that promises to teach at-risk teens "a really important lesson about solving problems with drugs." You're a teen, Romeo! Maybe some real talk is just what you need! The book is credited only to "A. Librarian."

"Did you write this?" you ask. "Why is this hard mode? Are there not a lot of pictures, or . . . ?" You trail off, unable to think of another way a book could be hard.

"Oh, it's hard mode for two reasons," the librarian says. "Firstly because I'll be standing behind you the entire time you read, which is really annoying. And I'll be doing that for the second reason this is hard mode: if you die in the book, I will INSTANTLY KILL YOU HERE IN REAL LIFE."

"Hard mode sounds terrible, I don't think I—" you begin, but the librarian puts his finger to your lips.

"Shhh," he whispers. He places his hands on top of yours and forces you to open the book. Then he removes his hands from yours, produces a dagger from his belt, and holds it to your throat.

"Hard mode has begun," he whispers.

Begin reading: *turn to 124.*

305

The machine whirs and clicks. The total reading changes to "5," and the output changes to:

```
ZWQ UGFYJSLMNSLAGFK GF UJSUCAFY LZW
UGVW! DAKLWF, DWL'K FGL LWDD SFQGFW WDKW
LZW SFKOWJ, GCSQ?? TWUSMKW LZW LZAFY AK,
OW'NW CAFVS AFNWKLWV S DGL GX EGFWQ AF
LZAK JAVAUMDGMK KWUMJALQ KQKLWE. KAYFWV,
NWJGFS UALQ ESFSYWEWFL.
```

I don't think that's it, Angelica.

Flip "ADD 1" off: turn to 253.

Flip "ADD 2" on: turn to 324.

Flip "ADD 4" off: turn to 243.

Flip "ADD 8" on: turn to 279.

Step away from the machine: turn to 354.

306

The machine whirs and clicks. The total reading changes to "8," and the output changes to:

CZT XJIBMVOPGVODJIN JI XMVXFDIB OCZ XJYZ!
GDNOZI, GZO'N IJO OZGG VITJIZ ZGNZ OCZ
VINRZM, JFVT?? WZXVPNZ OCZ OCDIB DN, RZ'QZ
FDIYV DIQZNOZY V GJO JA HJIZT DI OCDN
MDYDXPGJPN NZXPMDOT NTNOZH. NDBIZY,
QZMJIV XDOT HVIVBZHZIO.

I don't think that's it, Angelica.

Flip "ADD 1" on: turn to 347.

Flip "ADD 2" on: turn to 276.

Flip "ADD 4" on: turn to 266.

Flip "ADD 8" off: turn to 340.

Step away from the machine: turn to 354.

307

Verona is covered in guards, so no matter what you choose you get megacaptured megaquickly! They bind and gag you both and put you on their horses, but instead of taking you to the police, you're headed towards Capulet Castle. When you arrive they carefully deposit Juliet in front of her father.

"Here's your daughter, sir," they say, "safe and sound."

"Thank you," her father says, pressing some money into their hands. "You have earned this money well. And as for the boy?"

"He's guilty of Being Alive in Verona While Banished, a capital offense," a guard says. "Chief Escalus will know what to do with him."

"Very well," Juliet's dad says.

Be Juliet and rescue me somehow! *Turn to 320.*

Um no it's okay, I got a good feeling about this: maybe they mean "capital offense" in the British "capital good idea, chap" sense!! *Turn to 255.*

308

"Agreed," you say. You move to the rope ladder, but before you leave, you kiss Juliet good-bye. It's nice!

As you reach the bottom of the ladder, Juliet shouts something down about your looking as pale as a corpse, but hah hah whatever! It's not possible for foreshadowing to even be a thing in a story where YOU decide what happens next!

You hop on your horse and take off to Mantua.

Go to Mantua: *turn to 221.*

 Go to Mantua but be Juliet now, Mantua's gonna be hella boring: *turn to 324.*

309

Glad you enjoyed it. It sounded . . . fun?

So! Pardon the pun, but if you're all finished here . . . then let's put this sex scene to bed, shall we?

End sex scene! *Turn to 289.*

310

Alright. Well, let's make that decision!

AS YOU KNOW, Romeo, Juliet's house is located directly south of your current position. There are four possible routes there. And all but one will kill you.

Enjoy!!

Take route one, the residential path: *turn to 259.*

Take route two, the scenic route: *turn to 272.*

Take route three, the downtown-core route: *turn to 294.*

Take route four, the industrial-zone route: *turn to 234.*

311

You're too kind!

Anyway, enough about that. Books are dumb; you're here to live your REAL life!

Put the book down and look around: *turn to 292.*

312

SMACK

Best high five of your life, Juliet.

Kick Romeo out so he doesn't get arrested and killed now: *turn to 336.*

Tell him to stick around for a bit longer: *turn to 325.*

313 You are in Verona town square. It's okay. It's actually more of a circle, really. There are a lot of Veronans here.
Romeo is here.
Mercutio is here.
Benvolio is here.

Talk to Mercutio: turn to 335.

Talk to Benvolio: turn to 343.

Give message to Romeo: turn to 369.

314 You stand in front of your mirror, looking as dramatic as you can. "I'm going to Verona," you say to your reflection. "RIGHT NOW."

"You'll need some supplies," Balthasar says over your shoulder.

You turn. "Well then, get me some supplies," you order. "I'm gonna need ink and paper to write my 'Gone to Verona' note, a torch, a pickax, a crowbar, some horses, and—oh! I guess some snacks and water."

"Okay," Balthasar says. "I'll need until tonight to get that together."

"Make it so," you say, and Balthasar leaves your room, closing the door behind him. You turn back to your mirror.

"I'm going to Verona," you say to your reflection. "ONCE THE SUN SETS, SEVERAL HOURS FROM NOW." You pause. "You know," you say to yourself, "if Juliet really is dead, I'm thinking . . . PROBABLY I'LL want to kill myself? And I bet I could get some poison from that gross old pharmacy I passed a few days ago!" You burst out of your room and run over to the pharmacy, but it's closed. It's a holiday. You kick your way in anyway.

"PHARMACIST!" you shout. "WHAT HO, PHARMACIST!!"

"What? Who's shouting so loud? We're closed!" says the pharmacist as he emerges from the back room.

You walk up to the owner of the business you've just broken into and put your arm around his shoulders like you're old friends. "Listen," you say, "you're obviously poor. Here's FORTY DUCATS. Give me some poison, okay?"

"What?" says the pharmacist.

"POISON," you say. You speak loudly and slowly. "I. WANT. SOME. POISON."

"I don't—" the pharmacist begins.

"How is this not clear?" you say, squeezing him towards you. "ME LIKE THE JUICE THAT MAKE ME DEAD."

"Why—why are you talking to me like that?" the pharmacist says.

"Holy crap," you say. "LOOK. Let me have a dram of poison, okay? You know what I'm talking about? Such soon-speeding gear as will disperse itself through all the veins that the life-weary taker may fall dead, and that the trunk may be discharged of breath as violently as hasty powder fired doth hurry from the cannon's womb??"

"Oh, why didn't you say so?" says the man, smiling. "I'll let you in on a little pharmacist's secret: killing people with chemicals is actually WAY EASIER than keeping people alive with chemicals. Poison's not a problem. Only . . . the penalty for selling poisons IS death."

You keep your arm around the pharmacist and smile at him. "Buddy," you say. "Look at yourself." The pharmacist glances down, then back to you. "You're DIRT-POOR," you say in a way that I am struggling not to call "obnoxious," "but you're still afraid to die? How much worse could it be? FAMINE IS IN THY CHEEKS, bro."

"That doesn't mean I'll do whatever you say," he replies.

"Anyone can see you're a beggar," you say. "The world is not your friend, and the law isn't either. There's no law that says you're gonna be rich, right?"

"I guess that's right," he says.

"Then SCREW THE LAW," you say. You hold out a fistful of cash. "Here. Take this, break the law, and STOP BEING POOR ALREADY.

"Loser," you say.

The pharmacist looks at the money doubtfully. "If I take this, it's my poverty taking the money, not me," he says.

You place the money into his hand. "Okay, sure, this is me paying your poverty. Can I die now please?"

The pharmacist goes behind his desk and mixes several different liquids together. He stirs it, sniffs it, and looks up to you.

"How strong are you?" he asks.

"Um, I'd say I have the strength of about . . . one man?" you say. "I have one mansworth of strength."

"Perfect," he says, pouring the mixture into a black bottle with a skull and crossbones on it. "This'll instantly take down someone with the strength of twenty men, so you'll DEFINITELY be one hundred percent super dead, guaranteed."

You take the poison. "Thanks," you say. "Hey, by the way, that money I gave you is a WAY worse poison to men's souls, and does WAY more murder in this loathsome world, than this poor compound that you may or may not sell." You put a few more coins into his hand. "So really," you say, "I'm the one giving YOU poison."

The pharmacist looks at the money in his hand. "I'm gonna use this to buy food and clothing for my children," he says.

You're already leaving the pharmacy, ready for Verona, because now if anything goes wrong you can kill yourself!

 Go back to hotel, wait for Balthasar: *turn to 329.*

315
You wait some more: a week, then two. Just when you're convinced you'll never see your wife again, there comes a knock at your door.

"Juliet?" you say, flinging the door open. And there she is. Covered in dust, blood caked on her clothes, but smiling, and with DJ Muscles McGlutes walking behind her.

"Hey Romeo," she says, and hugs you tightly.

She explains that her parents WERE intending to kidnap her, and that they would've gotten away with it too, if it hadn't been for you. Once she arrived they locked her up in some muscles-proof chains, intending to keep her in a dungeon forever or until she renounced you, whichever came first.

"I was angry," Juliet says. "Furious. But there was nothing I could do, no matter how I struggled. I spent a week hopeless."

"What changed?" you ask.

"I finally realized that my parents had made one terrible mistake," she says. "They built their dungeon to house the Juliet they raised and loved . . . but then they put ME inside of it."

"I don't understand," you say.

"Romeo, I'm not the same person I was before I knew you," she says. "I'm strong, sure, but muscles couldn't help me there. But I thought of your last little 'don't do anything I wouldn't do' piece of advice, and it occurred to me: the one thing you wouldn't do is sit quietly in a dungeon. You'd sweet-talk your way out of it."

"You didn't," you say.

"I did," Juliet says. "I talked the guard who delivered my food into loosening my bonds AND tricked another into letting me know the best time to escape. Words, man! I had men wearing rapiers doing exactly what I wanted them to, just by producing the right sounds in the right order and making them come out of my mouth. I only needed to convince one of them that I was worth saving, and it was enough to break the whole system."

"I love you," you say.

"I know it," she says. Then, after a pause, she adds, "Also, I also used my muscles to beat the bad ones up and then I stole a bunch of money and now we can live happily ever after."

This time, with the benefit of experience and the luxury of not having to immediately turn a profit, your brunch restaurant grows into a very successful and very satisfying enterprise. One day, several years from now, you and Juliet will be dining there, taking a break between the brunch and linner rushes to enjoy a meal with each other.

Your best cook will bring out your regular choice: for Juliet her favorite three-meat protein shake, and for you two eggs over easy surrounded by a mountain of side dishes. She'll look at you and smile as she holds up her shake for a toast, and you'll clink your orange juice to her glass.

"To us," she'll say.

"To us," you'll echo.

You'll dig into your meal. You'll eat eggs, you'll eat hash browns, you'll eat toast, you'll eat pancakes, you'll eat bacon, you'll eat muffins, you'll eat fruit, and you'll eat biscuits.

And the rest is sausage.

THE END

316

"Oh," Juliet says, "okay yeah I guess that makes sense."

"See you soon!" you say as you hug her good-bye. "And by 'soon' I mean 'whenever this banishment thing is figured out'!"

"Yep!" Juliet says. "I'll wait for you!"

"AWESOME," you say, and then you descend the ladder. Juliet shouts something down after you about your looking as pale as a corpse, but hah hah whatever! Foreshadowing isn't even a thing in a story where YOU decide what happens next!

You hop on your horse and take off to Mantua.

Go to Mantua: *turn to 221.*

Go to Mantua but be Juliet now, Mantua's gonna be hella boring: *turn to 324.*

317

The machine whirs and clicks. The total reading changes to "9," and the output changes to:

```
DAU YKJCNWPQHWPEKJO KJ YNWYGEJC PDA
YKZA! HEOPAJ, HAP'O JKP PAHH WJUKJA AHOA
PDA WJOSAN, GGWU?? XAYWQOA PDA PDEJC EO,
SA'RA GEJZW EJRAOPAZ W HKP KB IKJAU EJ
PDEO NEZEYQHKQO OAYQNEPU OUOPAI. OECJAZ,
RANKJW YEPU IWJWCAIAJP.
```

I don't think that's it, Angelica.

Flip "ADD 1" off: turn to 306.

Flip "ADD 2" on: turn to 295.

Flip "ADD 4" on: turn to 279.

Flip "ADD 8" off: turn to 243.

Step away from the machine: turn to 354.

318

"Well," she says, "I mean, it's not like I have anything else going on. I'm in."

Ophelia begins her study of the Friar's toxins with the same focus she used in her study of killing everyone in town, and before too long has synthesized a combination of several of them that she's convinced will do the job.

"The trick is, it's a more stable form of water, and also poison," she says. "So it spreads itself to any other water it's touching, inducing it to take the same form." She holds up a vial of the liquid. "We drop this in the ocean and it'll spread worldwide in a matter of days. Hours, maybe."

"Like the golden touch of King Midas!" you say.

"Please," she says. "That was magic. This is very real, very advanced, and VERY credible science invented here in the sixteenth century. Also, I should stress here that the poison only works on humans and doesn't affect any other animals at all."

That evening, the two of you pour the vial into the ocean. You both hold the bottle as you pour it: you're in this together!

"That's it," Ophelia says as the last drop splooshes into the ocean. "Nothing but bottled water for us from now on, which, by the way, is a thing I invented shortly before this humanity-destroying poison."

"Yes," you say, "I know, for I have been using the past several months to physically stockpile water, using my naturally muscled-up bod. We are a good, if unstoppable, team."

"Agreed," Ophelia says. "Well, it's done. Stay out of any mists, fogs, rains, or splash zones."

You do, and before you know it, everyone else but you and Ophelia is dead, and the two of you are alone in a world being quickly reclaimed by nature. You both have some measure of regret a few months into this brave new world you've created, but you know what they used to say before they all died: "Hindsight is always twenty-twenty!"

You fortify the castle against wolves and bears and spend most of your free time hunting and growing vegetables. Outside of your castle, vegetation begins to creep inside the empty buildings of the world, and while your stone castle will stand for many centuries, eventually it too will crumble. Cities collapse into rubble, books rot, and stone statues weather into shapelessness, but there is one record of humanity that will survive millions and millions of years into the future: it's bronze statues. Bronze's extraordinary resilience will ensure that many of the figures we've produced of warriors, of leaders, of children, of dogs and cats and the other things we found important will survive: a lost and silent testament to the species that once roamed the planet before a couple of very talented ladies who were waaaay too invested in the well-being of their boyfriends made some—I'll say it—very bad decisions.

Earth returns to a state of nature, and there it remains: unspoiled, untainted—and unwitnessed.

THE END

P.S.: Oh! Millions of years later a new form of intelligent life evolves on Earth, and when they develop civilization and begin exploring the planet and find some of this long-lost bronze statuary, it TOTALLY BLOWS THEIR MINDS.

319 You wait until a guard walks by, then you hop out of the bushes, grab him by the shoulder, and pull him back into the bushes with you. He struggles briefly until you knock him out, then you begin putting on his clothes. Amazingly, they're a perfect fit!

"How do I look?" you ask your husband.

"I'll tell you one thing: you're far more fair than he," Romeo says, gesturing to the knocked-out guard, who is wearing nothing but his underpants.

You kiss him. "Remember: if they see you, they'll murder you," you say.

"Not a problem," he says. He pulls the guard's cap off your head and puts it on his own, straightening it slightly. "I'll just deny my father and refuse my name," he says. "Say hello to Jake Guardsworth."

You kiss him again. "Alright," you whisper. "Come on, Jake. Let's do this."

You and Jake Guardsworth step out into the night and begin to make your way towards Capulet Castle.

Create a distraction while Romeo goes ahead: *turn to 326*.

Be Romeo and go ahead while Juliet creates a distraction: *turn to 337*.

320
You are now Juliet! Your husband, Romeo, is bound and gagged on a horse. The problem is, you're bound and gagged too.

But that's never stopped you before.

Using your rad muscles, you jump to your feet and, before anyone can react, slam your body into the horse Romeo is on. It rears up, knocking its rider and Romeo to the ground. Before he can react, you jump up and bring your feet down on the guard's face, which is both mega gross and mega effective.

That takes care of one of the guards, but there are five more here. They draw their swords. You try to shout "Don't kill me, as my parents are right here and if they see agents of the state kill their only daughter right in front of them they will likely raze Verona to the ground," but again: you're gagged. So the guards stab you and Romeo, and this is fatal to humans, so flights of angels sing thee to thy rests, guys!

However, it's really too bad you couldn't speak because your words were HELLA PROPHETIC. Your parents are enraged by this murder, and when Romeo's father hears of this, he's enraged too. They team up in their grief and madness and destroy the guards, the police, and all authority in Verona. The city descends into anarchy and in a few short days is completely ruined.

So basically you tried to ask your parents for money and messed up SO BADLY that you destroyed an entire city. It's honestly impressive! It's like trying to have a bath and messing up so badly you open up a hellmouth. Which incidentally IS something you also manage to do as a ghost, but that's another story for another time, and another book actually, one called *Ghost Romeo and/or Ghost Juliet and/or the Nice Bath and/or the Hellmouth*.

THE END

P.S.: In it you can play as Ghost Romeo or Ghost Juliet or, if you're clever, unlock the tub as a playable character! It's bound to make a . . . splash??

321 The machine whirs and clicks. The total reading changes to **"7,"** and the output changes to:

BYS WIHALUNOFUNCIHM IH WLUWECHA NBY WIXY!
FCMNYH, FYN'M HIN NYFF UHSIHY YFMY NBY
UHMQYL, IEUS?? VYWUOMY NBY NBCHA CM, QY'PY
ECHXU CHPYMNYX U FIN IZ GIHYS CH NBCM
LCXCWOFIOM MYWOLCNS MSMNYG. MCAHYX,
PYLIHU WCNS GUHUAYGYHN.

I don't think that's it, Angelica.

Flip "ADD 1" off: turn to 334.

Flip "ADD 2" off: turn to 305.

Flip "ADD 4" off: turn to 269.

Flip "ADD 8" on: turn to 342.

Step away from the machine: turn to 354.

322 Juliet tries to shove you out the window, but it's no good.

"I'm staying!" you say. "I will not be apart from my awesome hot wife!!"

This works out pretty well for a few seconds, until Juliet's mom opens the door and sees you there. Or rather, opens the door and sees the child of her worst enemy has snuck into her daughter's room and spent the night with her as-far-as-she-knows unmarried Juliet.

She screams, you try to explain, her father runs into the room with a length of pipe, you try to explain some more, he chases after you, and you jump off Juliet's balcony and miss the rope ladder and fall two stories and break both your legs. Ouch!

Juliet's dad runs downstairs, and you soon discover that while having TWO broken bones is painful, it's NOTHING compared to the pain of having each of your other 204 bones and several other organs systematically broken too.

You die of a broken heart, and a broken everything else.

THE END

P.S.: While you didn't survive the experience, you DID make it with a lady! This was one of your goals this story, so: 50 points for trying I guess?

P.P.S.: I don't mean to rub it in, but sex is even better when you don't get beaten to death afterwards! OH WELL??

323 I walk up to Capulet Castle and bang on the front door. A servant answers, and I put on my best favorite-niece smile. The one that makes uncles forget the grown woman they see before them and remember the little girl they once knew.

"Is my uncle in?" I say, nice and sweet. "Oh gosh, I'd love to see him. It's me, Rosaline."

Sweet talk is all it takes to get me a face-to-face with my prime suspect, and I've got plenty of that. Capulet says he's glad to see me. He says he missed me at the party.

I say when he killed Lady Montague, he should've made sure she didn't leave behind any clues.

Yeah, that gets his attention. His mood changes: he doesn't like what I'm selling, and that's too bad, because I happen to specialize in it. It's called Justice, and I buy it in bulk.

Capulet says he and Montague are allies now, and goody for him, but he knows as well as I that Lady M was killed the night before this new allegiance was formalized. And what better way to make an enemy sue for peace than to murder his wife?

Lord Capulet gets mad. Real mad. Asks on what grounds I'm accusing him, and I let slip about the dead woman's "MC" hands down at the crypt. It's a gamble, but it doesn't work. Sure he gets angry. Maybe even scared. But the one thing he doesn't get is sloppy. All he says is I don't have any real proof, and if I come back here again, niece or no niece, he'll banish me from Verona like he did Romeo. Then he kicks me out of the castle.

Standing there in the rain, I can't avoid the truth: I've messed up, big-time. I just walked up to my prime suspect, gave him all the evidence I had, and have nothing to show for it. Capulet knows my evidence, knows I suspect him, and now has all the time in the world to cover his tracks.

Figure I've got two choices: I go back to the office and regroup, or I bust my way back in and citizen's-arrest him before he has time to make my job even harder.

I go and arrest the man: *turn to 370.*

I go back to the office to regroup: *turn to 334.*

324 You are now Juliet!

You watch as your husband climbs down the ladder, hops on his horse, and takes off to Mantua, or as you've always known it, the Town Full of the People That Verona Didn't Want. You're sure he'll be fine.

You're sitting on your bed, happily remembering the fun adult activities you and your husband enthusiastically consented to participate in with each other last night, when there's a knock at your door.

 Answer door: *turn to 402.*

325

"Well," Romeo says, "I've still got some time until daybreak, when I have to leave. You want to kiss for a bit longer?"

"Yes please," you say, but as he leans forward to kiss you his view of you is obscured by some bright light that's traveled all the way from a burning ball of gas at the center of the solar system just to get him right in his eyes. Aw man, it's the sunrise!!

"Aw man, it's the sunri—" Romeo begins to say, but he's quickly interrupted by the sound of a lark chirping, which this bird does every day at sunrise. Larks are like roosters, only FANCIER.

"That was a nightingale," you lie, and thinking quickly you add, "and that light was actually caused by a meteor coming out of the sun to light your way to Mantua. It's still night. You should stick around."

Romeo nods. "Okay," he says, and then gets down on one knee. "Let me be captured and put to death: I don't care! If you're happy, I'm happy."

Accept this: *turn to 339.*

Okay, no, it's time for him to go: *turn to 384.*

326

You, Juliet, watch Romeo move ahead towards Capulet Castle while you prepare your distraction! You decide the best distraction is to use your sweet disguise to get close to a guard, and then loudly and visibly beat him up. Other guards will come running, you'll beat them up too, and hey presto: there's your distraction. It's perfect. You quickly go over your glutes, calves, pecs, and quads. They're ready. YOU'RE ready.

"Time to take out the guards," you say, wishing they were garbagemen or something so you could say something cooler like "Time to take out the trash," or "Looks like garbage day is coming early this week." But they're not. They're just regular guards.

"Time to . . . let their guard . . . no, their GUARDS . . . DOWN," you say. "Time to let their guards down. Physically. With my FISTS." Nobody's around to hear you, which is for the best. It sounds like you're going to disappoint them, Juliet. Geez.

Figuring Romeo will need his distraction soon, you jog to the nearest guard station. It should be within eyesight of where Romeo is. You get there and quickly climb up the castle wall. Then, using your upper-body strength, you throw yourself up over the edge.

"LOOKS LIKE THESE GUARDS ARE BEING LET DOWN . . . TO THE GROUND . . . WHERE THEY'LL DIE," you say, wincing at your own clumsy words as you fly over the edge of the castle. But nobody's there! The place is empty. You quickly climb down and run towards the guard station Romeo was headed to, but it's too late. Without your distraction he couldn't get past the guard on his own. His broken body is lying at the feet of the parapets. I'm so sorry, Juliet.

"Hey!" a guard shouts down. "Hey you! You're the guy in the rest of Angola's uniform!!" You look up at him through tears in your eyes. You don't care anymore. Your husband is dead. You bend down and cradle him in your arms.

While you're doing that, the guard kicks one of the parapet stones and it falls, hitting your neck and killing you instantly.

THE END

Go back and be Romeo this time so I can make sure he gets past the guard on his own: *turn to 333.*

327

He has a handsome face and his legs are pretty okay.

Look town square: turn to 343.

Look Romeo again: turn to 344.

Give message to Romeo: turn to 369.

328

Seriously? Sex can be one of the most personal experiences you can share with someone, and you want me to just TELL YOU what to do?

Fine. FINE. Fill in the blanks below to embark on an erotic journey without parallel:

You and Romeo decide to [ADVERB] sex each other, especially since you have a(n) [ADJECTIVE] [ADJECTIVE] [ADJECTIVE] [NOUN] ([ADJECTIVE]). "Oh Juliet," sighs Romeo, "your [BODY PART THAT BOTH MAMMALS AND REPTILES SHARE] makes me want to shout to the heavens, '[CORPORATE SLOGAN EMPLOYED NOW, OR IN THE PAST, BY YOUR FAVORITE BRAND(S)].'"

"I get that a lot," you say, nodding. Romeo shyly shows you his [BODY PART THAT, IF YOUR EVERY BODY PART COULD TALK, THIS IS THE ONE YOU'D MOST LIKE TO BE MAROONED ON A DESERT ISLAND WITH] and you can't help but exclaim, "Wow! [ENTIRE CONSTITUTIONAL DOCUMENT OF WHICHEVER COUNTRY YOU'D MOST LIKE TO LIVE IN]." Then Romeo does a sex thing with [THAT SAME BODY PART YOU SELECTED BEFORE, OR A DIFFERENT ONE, IT REALLY DEPENDS ON HOW ADVENTUROUS YOU'RE FEELING]. Neat!

"That's what we call getting Montagued," Romeo says, and you put a finger to his lips.

"Shh," you say. "Let's allow our [CHOOSE ONE: SMOLDERING GLANCES, INTIMATE PHYSICAL CONTACT, SHARED SENSE OF JUSTICE, MOUTHS] to do the talking."

Your sexual congress then proceeds in a way that can be best and wholly summarized by the following highly lifelike images:
CHOOSE ONE:

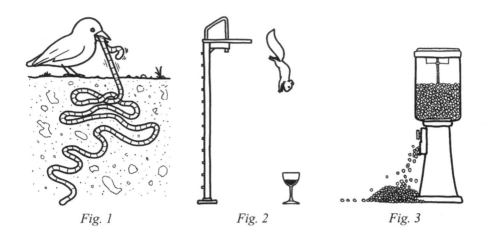

Fig. 1   *Fig. 2*   *Fig. 3*

And over the course of the night and into the morning, you make a lot of [CHOOSE ANY TWO: CHERISHED MEMORIES, SEX, MISTAKES, SEX MISTAKES, MONEY].

The end.

Whew!! End sex scene, extremely satisfied. *Turn to 289.*

329 You sit on your bed quietly, which is itself its own form of adventure. Several hours later, Balthasar returns with the supplies you asked for, including TWO horses!

"I didn't ask for two horses," you say.

"Yes you did," he says. "You said 'horses,' plural. I thought you wanted me to come with you."

"I'm not paying for that extra horse," you say. "In fact, I rode a horse here, so I'll just take that one for free. So I guess you screwed up and I don't need ANY horses after all."

"I already rented these horses," Balthasar replies, "so we're riding them. Your dad will pay for them."

"Whatever," you say. You tear a piece of paper off the stack Balthasar brought and write, "ATTENTION INNKEEP: I WENT BACK TO VERONA, MAYBE MY DAD WILL PAY FOR THE HOTEL BILL??? XOXO ROMEO." You place the piece of paper on top of your unmade bed.

"Let's ride," you say.

 Ride to Verona: *turn to 347.*

330

You easily negotiate your way back through the clockwork puzzle because it's the same answer every time but realize if you go any further south you'll run into that gatekeeper and his pack of ravenous dogs and will definitely, 100% get killed.

You seem to be stuck. And you can't figure this out! "Is this some sort of puzzle?," "Why does everything have to be a puzzle?," and "Why am I the only one solving these puzzles?" are but three of the questions you're asking yourself. You could always look for an alternate route. A path to the southeast seems promising.

There are only three exits here: to the north, to the south, and to the southeast.

Go north: turn to 352.

Go south: turn to 344.

Go southeast: turn to 399.

331

The machine whirs and clicks. The total reading changes to "6," and the output changes to:

AXR VHGZKTMNETMBHGL HG VKTVDBGZ MAX
VHWX! EBLMXG, EXM'L GHM MXEE TGRHGX XELX
MAX TGLPXK, HDTR?? UXVTNLX MAX MABGZ BL,
PX'OX DBGWT BGOXLMXW T EHM HY FHGXR BG
MABL KBWBVNEHNL LXVNKBMR LRLMXF. LBZGXW,
OXKHGT VBMR FTGTZXFXGM.

I don't think that's it, Angelica. Maybe if you looked for repeated letters in a word and tried to figure out which words share that pattern?

Flip "ADD 1" on: turn to 324.

Flip "ADD 2" off: turn to 253.

Flip "ADD 4" off: turn to 264.

Flip "ADD 8" on: turn to 285.

Step away from the machine: turn to 354.

332

You drop to your knees and raise your fists to the heavens. "I DEFY YOU, STARS!!" you shout.

Balthasar regards you evenly.

 Stand back up and ride to Verona right away: *turn to 314.*

333

You, Romeo, make your way towards Capulet Castle while Juliet prepares her distraction! And soon enough, you're spotted by a guard on a parapet.

"Stand, ho! Who's there?" the guard shouts.

"A friend to the Capulets!" you shout in reply. "And a fellow guard! I'm here to replace, um . . ."

You realize you never got his name.

"That other guy," you say. "You know the one? The one who's not here and who is always taking naked naps in bushes."

"Aw man, Angola did it AGAIN?" the guard replies. "God's wounds. I can't believe him sometimes."

"Nor can I," you say as you climb up the ladder to join the guard. "But now I'm here to replace him. My name's, uh, Jake."

"Chad," the guard replies, holding out his hand to shake yours. He gets his first good look at you. Meanwhile, you get your first good look from up here, and you notice that the other parapets are empty. Uh-oh. Without any guards there, it's gonna be hard for Juliet to create a distraction.

"Say," he says. "How come you're only wearing the hat part of your uniform?"

"Hah hah hah!" you say, trying to stall for time. "What?"

"Your uniform," Chad says. "You've got the hat on, but the rest is like, regular rich-teen clothes." You're trapped, Romeo. You've only got one move left. And so you take it.

"There's no time for that now!" you shout, pointing off into the distance. "What's that over there? Some sort of . . . distraction??"

The guard looks to where you're pointing. "Nothing," he says. "I don't see anything. Not even a distraction, actually!"

"Come ON, Juliet! Where are you?" you think.

"So, back to you," Chad says. "I notice you're out of uniform, and furthermore, I go on to notice that you're wearing Angola's hat, which I recognize because he stitched 'HEY LADIES I'M ANGOLA' on the side. Additionally, I'm now remembering how he'd always go on and on about how he'd never nap in the bushes without his hat, even if he were otherwise naked, because he just loves his hat so much. Therefore,

I am forced to conclude that you beat up Angola and stole his hat, in an attempt to infiltrate Capulet Castle. Am I close?"

"Um . . . no?" you say.

"No, I think I'm close," Chad says, and he sticks out his leg behind you and pushes you backwards. You trip over the edge of the parapet and fall to your death on the ground below.

THE END

Well that didn't work either!! Go back a move; I have an idea. *Turn to 353.*

334 I go back to my office, arriving soaked to the bone and no further ahead than I was when I started. I've blown my one clue, my prime suspect knows I'm wise to him, and he has as much time as he wants to clean up after himself.

Heck of a day.

I consider talking to the other guy Lady Montague could've been naming but decide against it: even if I just blabbed to the wrong man, there's no point in tipping my hand to the other suspect. There's got to be another way. Thing is, if there is one, I still haven't found it after two hours of trying.

I've got no other leads, and it's pretty clear that if this case is going to get solved it won't be by me pacing holes in my office carpet. Figure if I'm smart, I can play Montague and Capulet off against each other. Prey on some of those old fears and insecurities, see if I can't get one to tip me off a little about the other.

Great idea, sure, but it doesn't go well at the other castle when I put it into practice. Either Capulet and Montague have already been in touch with each other or they went to the same charm school, because my reception with the other goes about as well as my first: I get him angry, furious, and at the end I'm kicked out into the rain again with nothing to show for my trouble but a cold wet dress and a whole bunch of burned bridges.

I go back to my office and sit at my desk again. I'm out of options. One of these men HAS to be the killer: that much is obvious. Seems to me there's only one thing left to do.

I confront Lord Montague: *turn to 346.*

I confront Lord Capulet: *turn to 370.*

I go back and examine the body again, maybe I missed something: *turn to 379.*

335 He suggests you are a successful sex worker. You choose to take it as a compliment.

Look town square: turn to 343.

Look Romeo: turn to 327.

Give message to Romeo: turn to 369.

336 "Well," Romeo says, "I've still got some time until daybreak, when I have to leave. You want to kiss for a bit longer?"

"No, dummy," you say, "it's time for you to get the heck out of here. Stick around and you'll get killed. We'll send each other letters, I'll secretly come visit you in Mantua, and eventually we'll get this banishment thing sorted out."

"How eminently reasonable!" Romeo replies. "Sounds great. Love you, babe." He kisses you good-bye, climbs down the ladder, and rides off to Mantua.

You sit back down on your bed, satisfied, exhausted, and happy.

Married life sure is great! You wonder how married people get anything done at all, given how they're staying up late every single night having sex with each other.

You sigh happily.

And then someone knocks at your door.

Answer the door: *turn to 357.*

Ignore the door; I don't like the sound of that knock: *turn to 380.*

337
You, Romeo, make your way towards Capulet Castle while Juliet prepares her distraction! And soon enough, you're spotted by a guard on a parapet.

"Stand, ho! Who's there?" the guard shouts.

"A friend to the Capulets!" you shout in reply. "And a fellow guard! I'm here to replace, um . . ."

You realize you never got his name.

"That other guy," you say. "You know the one? The one who's not here and who is always taking naked naps in bushes."

"Aw man, Angola did it AGAIN?" the guard replies. "God's wounds. I can't believe him sometimes."

"Nor can I," you say as you climb up the ladder to join the guard. "But now I'm here to replace him. My name's, uh, Jake."

"Chad," the guard replies, holding out his hand to shake yours. He gets his first good look at you. Meanwhile, you get your first good look from up here, and you notice that the other parapets are empty. Uh-oh. Without any guards there, it's gonna be hard for Juliet to create a distraction.

"Say," he says. "How come you're only wearing the hat part of your uniform?"

"Hah hah hah!" you say, trying to stall for time. "What?"

"Your uniform," Chad says. "You've got the hat on, but the rest is like, regular rich-teen clothes." You're trapped, Romeo. You've only got one move left. And so you take it.

"There's no time for that now!" you shout, pointing off into the distance. "What's that over there? Some sort of . . . distraction??"

The guard looks to where you're pointing. "Nothing," he says. "I don't see anything. Not even a distraction, actually!"

"Come ON, Juliet, where are you?" you think.

"So, back to you," Chad says. "I notice you're out of uniform, and furthermore, I go on to notice that you're wearing Angola's hat, which I recognize because he stitched 'HEY LADIES I'M ANGOLA' on the side. Additionally, I'm now remembering how he'd always go on and on about how he'd never nap in the bushes without his hat, even if he were otherwise naked, because he just loves his hat so much. Therefore, I am forced to conclude that you beat up Angola and stole his hat, in an attempt to infiltrate Capulet Castle. Am I close?"

"Um . . . no?" you say.

"No, I think I'm close," Chad says, and he sticks out his leg behind you and pushes you backwards. You trip over the edge of the parapet and fall to your death on the ground below.

THE END

Go back and be Juliet this time so I can make sure the distraction happens: *turn to 345.*

338
"You know what?" you say. "I don't want to poison Romeo after all."

Your mother looks stunned. "But—why?"

"Promise you won't be mad?" you say. She nods. You take a deep breath.

"Alright. I don't want to poison Romeo because . . . I kiiinda married him yesterday and just finished having sex with him before you showed up."

"WHAT?" your mother says.

"Come on," you say. "You seriously didn't notice all my innuendo?"

"Ew," your mom says, making a face. "That was innuendo?"

"Anyway," you say, "since I've married the son of your greatest enemy, maybe we could kinda settle this dispute between our two houses? We could be the happy marriage that draws us together!"

"He MURDERED Tybalt, Juliet," your mother says.

"WOW," you say, "who would've EVER GUESSED that hothead Tybalt would get into a swordfight and die? That is DEFINITELY something I did not ever see coming." You rummage through a drawer and pull out a card, passing it to your mom. "Look," you say, "I made this three years ago."

Your mother looks down at the card in her hand. It's a sympathy card, all black lace and roses. The card says, "SORRY TYBALT GOT KILLED IN A SWORDFIGHT."

"Open it," you say. She does.

The interior reads, "IF ONLY THIS HORRIBLE TRAGEDY COULD'VE BEEN PREVENTED SOMEHOW???"

"Flip it over," you say. She does.

On the back are the words "WHAT AN UNFORESEEN DEMISE FOR SUCH AN ANGRY, CONFRONTATIONAL, AND NOT-AT-ALL CREEPY YOUNG MAN WHO CARRIED AN ACTUAL SWORD WITH HIM EVERYWHERE HE WENT."

"I've got lots in here," you say, rummaging through the drawer some more before passing your mother another card that has a picture of the fairy queen Mab beneath the words "HEY, SORRY MERCUTIO MADE A LOT OF GROSS SEX PUNS AT OUR PARTY."

"I've actually used that one a few times," you say.

"Juliet," your mother says, "is this true? Have you really married Romeo?"

"Yep," you say.

She takes you by the shoulders. "Tell me truly, girl. Have you actually married Romeo? Like, in front of a priest and everything?"

"In front of a Friar Lawrence, anyway," you say, uncertain. "I think that counts?"

Your mother looks at you for a long, hard moment. And then she smiles, bursts into tears, and hugs you as hard as she can.

"Oh Juliet," she says, "this is perfect! Perfect! The Montagues are rich, and now that our interests are aligned, we'll be able to work together rather than against each other." She pulls back and holds you at arm's length, smiling. "Our greatest competition just became our greatest allies, Juliet. This will make all of us a lot of money."

Be happy that she's happy: *turn to 348.*

Be offended that she's only concerned about money: *turn to 390.*

339 "Really?" you say. "Wow. Okay, yeah, that sounds awesome. Stick around here then! I'm sure we'll be able to . . . iron out any problems we encounter?"

You begin to feel bad about your choice of words shortly afterwards when your mom enters and screams, and then your dad runs up and starts beating Romeo up with an actual iron pole. Really bad, actually. It's like this awful pun you didn't even know you were making!

Besides feeling bad about your choice of words, you also feel outraged that your father is beating up your secret husband! So, just as calmly as can be, you bring up your hand in front of your father's weapon and stop it in mid-strike. Your dad struggles to bring the rod downwards, but it doesn't budge an inch. Your muscles are so awesome that your arm is basically a stone wall.

"That's enough of that," you say, twisting the rod around and swinging it into your father's belly. He goes flying out the balcony door, again, due to your awesome muscles. You swing the rod again, catch it on your mother's clothes, and swing them and your mother out over the balcony with ease.

You walk over and peer down over your balcony's edge. You chucked your parents so hard that they actually landed in the pomegranate tree, a good fifty feet from your balcony!

Romeo staggers to his feet. "Thanks for saving me," he says.

"Yeah," you say. "This worked out awesome, actually. And you know what? I don't see why this solution to our troubles isn't sustainable long term."

You and Romeo decide to live in your parents' house, and from then on whenever someone tries to kick him out or say some line about how he's "banished from the city of Verona by order of the state," you pick them up, raise them over your head, and more often than not get a new distance record on the freestyle chump-toss.

THE END

340

The machine whirs and clicks. The total reading changes to "0," and the output changes to:

URL PBATENGHYNGVBAF BA PENPXVAT GUR
PBQR! YVFGRA, YRG'F ABG GRYY NALBAR RYFR
GUR NAFJRE, BXNL?? ORPNHFR GUR GUVAT VF,
JR'IR XVAQN VAIRFGRQ N YBG BS ZBARL VA GUVF
EVQVPHYBHF FRPHEVGL FLFGRZ. FVTARQ,
IREBA PVGL ZNANTRZRAG.

Well geez, you're right back where you started! Maybe if you thought of which letters are the most common in English and tried starting there?

Flip "ADD 1" on: turn to 243.

Flip "ADD 2" on: turn to 264.

Flip "ADD 4" on: turn to 253.

Flip "ADD 8" on: turn to 306.

Step away from the machine: turn to 354.

341

You enter the gatekeeper's domain.

There are dozens of angry dogs here. There are also dozens of angry lions.

"Didn't I warn you about the dozens of angry dogs?" he shouts at you. "Wow! Now you've done it! Also, here's something new: I got some lions while you were in Verona!"

You are torn to shreds by the angry dogs and then gobbled up by angry lions. I'd say that was . . . nothing to take PRIDE in??

THE END

Your final score is 999 points out of a possible 1000 points.

Restore: turn to 330.

Restart: turn to 247.

342

The machine whirs and clicks. The total reading changes to "15," and the output changes to:

JGA EQPITCVWNCVKQPU QP ETCEMKPI VJG EQFG!
NKUVGP, NGV'U PQV VGNN CPAQPG GNUG VJG
CPUYGT, QMCA?? DGECWUG VJG VJKPI KU, YG'XG
MKPFA KPXGUVGF C NQV QH OQPGA KP VJKU
TKFKEWNQWU UGEWTKVA UAUVGO. UKIPGF,
XGTQPC EKVA OCPCIGOGPV.

I don't think that's it, Angelica.

Flip "ADD 1" off: turn to 285.

Flip "ADD 2" off: turn to 279.

Flip "ADD 4" off: turn to 295.

Flip "ADD 8" off: turn to 324.

Step away from the machine: turn to 354.

343

He suggests you are overweight. You choose to ignore him.

Look town square: turn to 343.

Look Romeo: turn to 327.

Give message to Romeo: turn to 369.

344

He still has a handsome face and his legs are still pretty okay.

Look town square: turn to 343.

Look Romeo again: turn to 327.

Give message to Romeo: turn to 369.

345 You, Juliet, watch Romeo move ahead towards Capulet Castle while you prepare your distraction! You decide the best distraction is to use your sweet disguise to get close to a guard, and then loudly and visibly beat him up. Other guards will come running, you'll beat them up too, and hey presto: there's your distraction. It's perfect. You quickly go over your glutes, calves, pecs, and quads. They're ready. YOU'RE ready.

"Time to take out the guards," you say, wishing they were garbagemen or something so you could say something cooler like "Time to take out the trash," or "Looks like garbage day is coming early this week." But they're not. They're just regular guards.

"Time to . . . let their guard . . . no, their GUARDS . . . DOWN," you say. "Time to let their guards down. Physically. With my FISTS." Nobody's around to hear you, which is for the best. It sounds like you're going to disappoint them, Juliet. Geez.

Figuring Romeo will need his distraction soon, you jog to the nearest guard station. It should be within eyesight of where Romeo is. You get there and quickly climb up the castle wall. Then, using your upper-body strength, you throw yourself up over the edge.

"LOOKS LIKE THESE GUARDS ARE BEING LET DOWN . . . TO THE GROUND . . . WHERE THEY'LL DIE," you say, wincing at your own clumsy words as you fly over the edge of the castle. But nobody's there! The place is empty. You quickly climb down and run towards the guard station Romeo was headed to, but it's too late. Without your distraction he couldn't get past this guard on his own. His broken body is lying at the feet of the parapets. I'm so sorry, Juliet.

"Hey!" a guard shouts down. "Hey you! You're the guy in the rest of Angola's uniform!!" You look up at him through tears in your eyes. You don't care anymore. Your husband is dead. You bend down and cradle him in your arms.

While you're doing that, the guard kicks one of the parapet stones and it falls, hitting your neck and killing you instantly.

THE END

Well that didn't work either!! Go back a move; I have an idea. *Turn to 353.*

346 I barely make it onto the grounds of Montague Mansion before two men with swords step in my path. They say if I go any further I'm gonna regret it. I tell them regrets are for patsies who didn't do what they want, punch them where it hurts, and rush past them towards the mansion.

I make it inside and I'm rushing around, trying to find Montague before his servants find me. I spot him at the end of a hall, sitting in a chair just as calm as can be. He rings a bell, and that servant I punched on my way in appears. He brought some friends with him this time. I'm not quite sure how many.

Figure it's all of them.

The men jump me and pin me down. Eight against one. I try to fight them. It goes about as well as you'd expect. Something hits me hard from behind, and the next thing I know I'm facedown on Verona Bridge. It's the middle of the night. Raining. And I'm tied like a prize pig, head hanging over the edge, water dripping down my face into the river below.

Montague stands over me, professing his innocence. Explains calmly he's figured it out: Capulet sent me. It's the classic Capulet MO, he says: distract them with talk of peace, soften them up, then kick 'em while they're down.

Tells me it won't work this time. Tells me his wife is dead. His only child is dead. Says he's a man with nothing left to lose, and Capulet was a fool to provoke him. Says he'd want me to deliver that message to the man himself, but I won't be in any shape to talk to anyone soon, so he'll let my body do the talking for me.

Then he sends me into the drink.

Arms and legs tied, I can't swim. I suck in as much air as I can before my clothes pull me down and I sink beneath the rushing current. I can feel the pressure of the water increasing around me as I sink. Sure, I overplayed my hand. Beginner's mistake. But it'll be enough to finish me.

Lungs screaming. Won't be long now.

Name's Rosaline. Rosaline Catling. And like I said, this week has given me more than enough of Verona. Especially when it comes to the river vis-à-vis the inside of my lungs.

I breathe in deep.

THE END

347

On the way there, Balthasar is yammering on about boring stuff, so instead of listening you break out your pen and paper and write a letter to your parents. It reads as follows:

Dear Mom and Dad,

If you are reading this, then I'm dead, because I killed myself, because my wife died.
    P.S.: I secret-married Juliet.
    P.P.S.: SURPRISE, RIGHT? MAYBE NOW YOU AND THE CAPULETS SHOULD STOP FIGHTING EACH OTHER, HUH??
    P.P.P.S.: Seriously.
    P.P.P.P.S.: Oh also, I killed myself with some poison I bought from a poor pharmacist in Mantua. I think he's the only pharmacist there actually? ANYWAY the punishment for selling poison in Mantua is death, so um the mere fact I'm telling you who sold it to me is a total dick move.
    P.P.P.P.P.S.: Pretend I didn't write that last part I guess??
    P.P.P.P.P.P.S.: Okay also, just so you know, Balthasar is supposed to be my servant but hasn't been doing his job for like, days.

I think you should fire him,
Romeo

You are extremely satisfied with your letter. You fold it up into your pocket and continue riding to Verona.

Stop and pick some flowers for Juliet's grave: *turn to 375.*

 Man, it's not like she'll know. Plus I'm in a rush. No flowers! *Turn to 355.*

348

"... Really?" you say. "You're ... happy?"

"Obviously!" she says. "Dear Lord, I didn't know Romeo was an option. I was about to marry you off to Tom Paris!"

"Tom Paris is a sucky dude," you say, accurately.

"Listen," she says, "let me talk to your father about this. He'll be upset, but he'll come around." She gets up from your bed and moves to the door.

"Juliet, you've made me the happiest mother in the world."

"Glad to help," you say, saluting her. "So, about Romeo's banishment . . . ?"

"Oh, we'll fix that. Don't worry. By this time tomorrow you'll be back with your beloved and we're all going to be very happy."

Wait until tomorrow: *turn to 373.*

349
"I'll definitely poison him right away," you say. "In fact, I know just the guy."

"Friar Lawrence?" your mom asks.

"Yeah," you say, disappointed she knows him too. "You know him?"

"He's the only guy in town who lives in a house full of weird poisons," she says, reasonably.

"Right," you say. "Well, I'm gonna go talk to him, and then I'll come back here, and then we'll have poison, okay?"

She nods. "Oh, one more thing: don't tell your father, Juliet. I want this to be our little secret."

"We'll be thick as thieves," you say. "Or thick as other people who commit crimes together. I don't know. Murderers, say."

She smiles and leaves, and you're alone again.

Alright! Time to make some fake poison, huh?

Make fake poison: *turn to 377.*

Make actual poison: *turn to 395.*

350
You sit on the bed, but the knocking continues. Then you hear the door being tried, but you've got it locked.

"Nurse!" you hear your mom calling from the other side of the door. "Nurse!!"

"Yes?" your nurse says a few moments later.

"Where's Juliet? Her bedroom door is locked and she's not answering."

"Oh," says your nurse. "Um . . . I tried earlier and she wasn't there?"

"Hey!" you hear your father shout from outside. "There's a rope ladder leading out of her bedroom! She's run away from home!!"

Uh-oh.

"Wow, she must've taken the death of Tybalt really hard!" your mom shouts at your dad, probably through the hallway window.

"It makes sense," your dad shouts back. "Tybalt DID rule." There's a pause, then you hear him shouting again. "There are horseprints here! Juliet's on horseback! She could be anywhere by now!"

"Tybalt had a summer cottage in Mantua!" your mom shouts. "If she's gone anywhere to mourn him, that'd be the place. We need to go to Mantua!!"

"I'll get the horses!" your dad shouts. "Is Juliet's nurse there with you?"

"Yes!" your mom shouts.

"Bring her too: she knows Juliet the best, so she'll be the best at tracking her down in a strange town!"

You hear everyone run downstairs, leaving you alone once again.

Well! You've just sent your parents riding off to the same town your husband's off to, only they don't know you married him. What could possibly go wrong, right?? You sit around for quite a while—days, actually—until your parents and nurse eventually return.

"Oh, here you are!" they say. "Surprise! We found Romeo in Mantua and killed him!"

You fall to your knees, stunned.

"I can see you are overcome with emotion, likely positive emotion that the killer of your cousin was brought to justice," your father says. "Well I have more good news: you're going to marry Tom Paris!"

You just managed to stand up but fall to your knees again, stunned even more.

You cry throughout your entire wedding, and most of your honeymoon, stopping just long enough to say, "Oh my gosh, leave me alone, Tom, nobody likes you."

Tom nods knowingly. He's heard this before.

And I'm gonna stop the story here because you have a long and unhappy life and I kinda wanna focus on other timelines where more fun things happen. Did you know there's one where you and Romeo end up in robot suits? ROBOT SUITS, Juliet. Other Juliets are having all the fun, yo!

So, uh . . . I hope that thought comforts you during your sucky marriage and/or life??

THE END

351 You sit on the park bench. Now there's nothing interesting to do except stand up from the bench.

Stand up from bench: turn to 399.

Wait a second, wait a second. Look under bench for tree branches: turn to 382.

352 You return to downtown, where you met Romeo earlier, but it's eerily empty. Everyone seems to have cleared out: even all the random Veronans have all found somewhere else to be. They are likely off having unrelated adventures that do not involve you.

Oh well!

Go south: turn to 372.

353

You wait for a few minutes until a guard walks by, then you hop out of the bushes, grab him by the shoulder, and pull him back into the bushes with you. He struggles briefly until you knock him out, then you begin putting on his clothes. Amazingly, they're a perfect fit!

"How do I look?" you ask your husband.

"I'll tell you one thing: you're far more fair than he," Romeo says, gesturing to the knocked-out guard, who is wearing nothing but his underpants.

You kiss him. "Remember: if they see you, they'll murder you," you say.

"Not a problem," he says. He pulls the guard's cap off your head and puts it on his own, straightening it slightly. "I'll just deny my father and refuse my name," he says. "Say hello to Jake Guardsworth."

You kiss him again. "Alright," you whisper. "Come on, Jake. Let's do this."

You and Jake Guardsworth step out into the night and begin to make your way towards Capulet Castle.

Be Romeo and go ahead while Juliet creates a distraction: *turn to 337.*

Be Juliet and create a distraction while Romeo goes ahead: *turn to 326.*

You know what? No. There's a third way. I don't choose to be Romeo or Juliet. I choose to make this book live up to its title. I choose . . . to be Romeo AND Juliet. *Turn to 376.*

354

You step away from the machine, frustrated. As you move a pressure plate releases and the machine clicks a few times as it resets itself.

"No luck, huh?" says the Veronan. "Don't feel bad. It's probably only SUPER GENIUSES who can crack that puzzle."

You consider trying again. On the other hand, you also consider going south and getting eaten to death by dogs. That'd be nice too.

Look machine: turn to 227.

Go south: turn to 236.

355

As you disembark from your horse, you notice two things: first, someone else has been here recently, judging by the fresh flowers placed around the entrance to Capulet Crypt, and second, either the same someone else or some other someone else is now hiding in the bushes and whistling.

You decide to ignore it. Probably they're just out and about for a li'l pre-midnight walk 'n' whistle in the graveyard.

"Alright, Balthasar," you say. "Here's how this is going to go down. Give me the pickax, the crowbar, and the torch."

Balthasar drops them at your feet.

"And here," you say, "take this letter and give it to my father in the morning. Now get out of here!"

"Yes, sir," Balthasar says, and he turns to leave.

"Oh!" you say. "JUST ONE MORE THING." Balthasar freezes in mid-step and slowly turns. You lock eyes with him and speak as intensely as you can. "If thou, jealous, dost return to pry in what I farther shall intend to do," you say, "by heaven, I will tear thee joint by joint and strew this hungry churchyard with thy limbs.

"The time and my intents are savage, wild, more fierce and more inexorable far than empty tigers or the roaring sea. Now get out of here."

"Yes, sir," Balthasar says, and he turns to leave.

"Oh!" you say. "JUST ONE MORE OTHER THING." Balthasar again freezes in mid-step. After a moment he sighs and turns around.

"What now?" he says.

You break into a smile. "Here, have some money!" you say, pressing ducats into his hand. "Be good, Balthasar. Live long and prosper."

"Peace and long life," Balthasar replies, and leaves. You pick up your supplies and drop them outside the crypt entrance.

"Alright!" you say, brushing off your hands. "Now to that womb of death, gorged with the dearest morsel of the earth!" You begin to pry open the lock on the crypt.

"Stop thy unhallowed toil, vile Montague!" someone shouts from behind you.

"Huh?" you say, turning around. "What?"

It's Mercutio's cousin Tom Paris! You've never really met the guy, but you've seen him around. The bad news is, he's armed with a sword! And it looks like he wants to stab you to death with it!

Attack Tom with your sword: *turn to 387.*

Attack Tom with your poison: *turn to 415.*

Angrily tell Tom to leave you alone: *turn to 381.*

Sincerely talk things out with Tom and try to clear up any misunderstandings, you know, like two reasonable people would: *turn to 397.*

356

I'm clutching at straws here, and worse: I know it. It's madness. A dying woman isn't going to invent and implement some metatarsal-based word puzzle in her last moments. Best case for me is those letters are someone's name. But there's four initials: why would Lady M, in her last moments, make sure to include both middle names of her killer?

She wouldn't. Of course she wouldn't.

That's the answer: I've been trying to make things more complicated, more clever, when all I had to do was think like the dead woman. Lady M didn't include any middle names, and she wasn't spelling out her killer's initials either. Lady Montague was doing the obvious thing, the only thing she could think of to do while the life drained out of her: she was trying to spell out her killer's NAME with the only quill and paper she had: her hands and feet.

M. C. I. O.

MERCUTIO.

My mind reels. Everything fits: he's neither a Capulet nor a Montague, so he naturally wouldn't be a suspect if anyone in either clan died. He hates how the Capulets and Montagues have been destroying Verona with their pointless battle. And he's got a temper on him big enough for three. Big enough to murder someone and make it look like natural causes, easy.

Just one problem: he's dead. Dead for days, after he got mixed up in that duel between Tybalt and Romeo. I figure it's about time I go pay my last respects to Mercutio's corpse.

Halfway between the Montague and Capulet crypts is the discount Neutral Crypt, where all the non-Capulets and non-Montagues lie in state before their loved ones decide what to do with what's left over. There's another lock on the door, but someone's beat me to breaking it. The lock isn't even attached to the door frame anymore: the door's been kicked out and then carefully put back in place to cover it up. Someone who started inside this crypt forced their way out and didn't want that fact to be public knowledge.

I know one thing: someone who started inside this crypt is going to be real disappointed.

I shove the door to the side and make my way downstairs. And wouldn't you know it: Mercutio's empty coffin is there waiting for me. Near as I can tell Mercutio hasn't been here for days, and, judging by the way the door was broken, his body wasn't stolen. My dead man walked right out of here. Mercutio's alive.

And that means the man just lost the only excuse he'd ever have for not answering my questions.

I decide to go to Mercutio's house and look for him there: *turn to 392.*

I decide to question Mercutio's friends first: *turn to 385.*

357 It's your nurse! "Your mom's on her way up to see you," she says.

"No problem!" you say. "I got rid of Romeo."

Your nurse smiles. "How was the sex?"

You blush. "Um, PRIVATE and CONFIDENTIAL??" you say.

"Sorry," she says, but as she's closing the door you stick your foot in the way.

"Hey," you say. "It was awesome. It was [ADJECTIVE THAT COULD APPLY TO A VERY FINE AND SEAWORTHY BOAT] and I couldn't believe Romeo's [BODY PART STARTING WITH THE FIRST LETTER OF YOUR NAME] did that thing where it [VERB CHOSEN AT RANDOM THAT HAS THE SAME NUMBER OF LETTERS IN IT AS THAT BODY PART YOU JUST CHOSE WHEN CONJUGATED INTO THE PAST TENSE] all over the [A NOUN CURRENTLY WITHIN YOUR FIELD OF VISION]."

She winks at you. "NICE," she says.

You sit back down on your bed and wait for your mom to show up. Not too much later, there's a second knock at your door.

Answer the door again: *turn to 402.*

358 You check out the sweet cover, then turn the page . . .

Welcome to *Fair Is Foul and/or Foul Is Fair*! Content from this book was previously published under the titles *The Scottish Play*, *The Bard's Play*, and *Mackers and the Witch*.

You are Macbeth! You have just defeated the forces of Norway AND Ireland, which is a big deal. Your best friend is Banquo! Y'all are Scottish.

You are hanging out with Banquo, walking down the street and chatting, when three witches appear. They claim to have a prophecy for you. Do you want to hear it?

Sure, never too busy for three strange women: *turn to 360*.

Naw I actually don't want to talk to a crazy woman I meet on the street, much less three of them: *turn to 365*.

359
You track down your best murderers and send them to Macduff's castle. "Kill 'em all," you say. "Like they taught you at murderering school."

"Can do," they say, and leave. They return a few hours later, freshly bathed, no blood on them. Professionals, see! That's how you do a murder. "All dead," they say.

"Sweeeet," you say.

Things seem to be going pretty well for you, Macbeth! You are KEEPING IT TOGETHER. A few days later, you're in your castle court, all dressed up for war just in case, because you've had reports of an English army ten thousand strong approaching the castle. You're not worried though!

"None of woman born can kill me," you tell your staff.

"Okay," they say. One of your doctors volunteers that your wife has been suffering from "thick-coming fancies," but you ask that he spare you his medical mumbo-jumbo and he explains she's got a mental illness.

"Oh, okay, fix it please," you say. "I'm trying to prepare for a war here."

An hour or so later, the doctor returns. "I gave her the best medical attention eleventh-century mental health science could provide," he says, "but she still killed herself. A bizarre guilt, it appears, over not washing her hands as effectively as she could."

You're stunned. Your wife is dead? You don't know what to say, but your royal audience is looking at you for something, so you improvise. "Damn it," you say, "damn it all. I'm crushed, I'm broken, and all I can say is that life's but a walking shadow, a poor player that struts and frets his hour upon the stage, and then is heard no more."

"Okay," the doctor says.

"It is a tale told by an idiot, full of sound and fury, signifying nothing," you add.

"I'm sorry for your loss," the doctor says, and leaves.

An hour or so later, you receive word from another servant that the English are cutting down trees and moving under them to disguise their numbers. "Would these trees be from Birnam Wood?" you ask.

"Yes," says the servant.

"And would this army now be advancing to Dunsinane?" you ask.

"Again, yes," says the servant, "since that's where we are."

"AW DANG," you say. You grab your sword and run down into the battlefield. You fight bravely, even recklessly, which makes sense because nobody can hurt you. You kill a bunch of them, so it seems like those murders you got in earlier were actually really good practice! Finally you find Macduff, and you run at him, screaming. "I'm going to kill you, Macduff!" you shout. "And you know why? Because I'M INVINCIBLE!!"

"How do you figure?" says Macduff as he sidesteps your charge and your swords clash.

"Because NONE OF WOMAN BORN CAN HARM ME!!" you shout, attacking him again.

"My mom had a C-section," he says.

"So?" you say. "What, you think you weren't BORN because you didn't make your way through a birth canal? You were born, dude. FROM A WOMAN. So nice try, but you can't defeat me."

For the first time, Macduff's confidence appears to waver.

"That's right," you say. "So unless your parents had the technology to construct children in a lab, you're going down."

Macduff, desperately, attacks you. You're so confident he won't hit you that it's a real surprise when you look down and see his blade sticking out of your chest.

Your last thought is "COME ON, seriously??," and then you die. Macduff puts the king's son on the throne, and that's it for you!

If I had to assign a theme to your run-through of this book, I'd have to say it has to do with the dangers of ambition without a moral system to hold it in place, and/or the dangers of accepting strangers' claims of being able to see into the future thanks to a neat stew.

ATTENTION READERS: you may find one or both of these themes useful in your own life!

The End

(If you're done reading, turn to 292. Otherwise turn to 358 to play this book again, or turn to 304 to read a different book.)

360

The witches tell you that you'll be made the "thane of Cawdor" (that's, like, a title) and then become king! Then they tell Banquo that while he won't be king, he'll father a line of them. Finally, they add that they said "fair is foul and foul is fair" before you arrived, which is convenient because otherwise you wouldn't know where the title of this book comes from.

"Neat!" you say. You shoo the witches away, then a messenger shows up and tells you that you've just been named the thane of Cawdor.

"Holy crap," you say. "THE PROPHECY CAME TRUE!"

"Yes," says Banquo. "What's next, you become king?"

"HMM I WONDER . . . ," you say as your ambition stat gains 25 points (!).

Later on that day you go and talk to the (current) king, and he invites himself and all his friends over to your house for a sleepover.

You decide to definitely murder him and become king. THE PROPHECY MUST BE FULFILLED. You go home and tell your wife about the thing that happened with the witches and she's all about murdering the king too. "We can't lose!" she says. "SOME WEIRD STRANGERS SAID IT WOULD WORK." The two of you hug, excited for the murder you're about to do.

"You'd better not chicken out," your wife says. "I know how you're full of the milk of human kindness all the time. We don't have a problem, do we?"

"No ma'am, no problem," you say, and then the two of you figure out the specifics of your regicide scheme. Your plan is this: get the king's servants loaded so they black out, then kill the king and blame the servants the next morning. They won't remember anything and will therefore be forced to conclude that they're not just sleepy drunks, they're also murderous sleepy drunks!

That night you get the servants drunk, then sneak into the king's room and kill him. It's a bit tricky (you keep hallucinating a bloody dagger in front of you, so if you were to say "Is this a dagger which I see before me," the answer would be "Yes, you SEE a dagger, but no, there is no dagger there") but you pull it off! Also, just as you stab the king for the last time and he stops struggling, you hallucinate again; it sounds like someone saying, "Sleep no more, Macbeth does murder sleep."

Weird, huh?

Leave the dead king: *turn to 367*.

Wait! Remember to plant the murder weapons on the servants first! *Turn to 364*.

361

"We're going to lose," you tell your wife. "I'm afraid."

Your wife looks at you for a long moment.

"Screw your cowardice," she says. "I'm wracked with guilt, just like you. But I'M going to do something productive with it." She picks up a battle-ax, a mace, a dagger, a lance, a bow and several arrows, a longbow, a poleax, two muskets, three cannons, and her rapier.

"Please," you say, looking up at your battle-ready wife. "Stay. It's safer here."

"'Tis safer to be that which destroys," she says, and with that, she's gone.

You watch her leave. Several hours later, you receive word that she's been killed, but not before taking out a significant portion of Macduff's army. Shortly after that Macduff enters your chambers, and you duel with him, holding your ground reasonably well until you both stab each other in the guts at the exact same time.

"Hold, enough!" you both cry, again at the same time.

"Argh, my guts hurt really bad," you say, clutching your belly.

"Mine too. Ow ow ow," says Macduff.

"I think I'm gonna die," you say.

"Me too," says Macduff.

"Oh well, at least you won't be king," you say.

"I wasn't trying to be!" says Macduff. "I want the RIGHTFUL king on the throne: the king's son! Don't you see? He ALONE deserves to be the king because he was the firstborn son of a man who was already king. That accident of his birth gives him all the training and authority he'd ever need to lead a nation."

"I honestly can't tell if you're being serious," you say, and then you die.

COWARDLY

The End

(If you're done reading, turn to 292. Otherwise turn to 358 to play this book again, or turn to 304 to read a different book.)

362 Excellent choice! You do.

GOES ON TO LIVE INCREDIBLY FULFILLING LIFE

IS TOTALLY IN THE CLEAR, FOREVER

The End

P.S.: Please do NOT share this book with the media; if they knew that books were actually MURDER SIMULATORS they'd have them banned! And I did just tell you how to murder a king and get away with it (main advice: "just be cool, yo").

This has to be our secret, okay?? If anyone asks what you did in this book, tell them, "Murdered a king and was caught and sentenced appropriately for my actions, it was a lot of fun to read, woooo."

Alright! Thanks!!

(If you're done reading, turn to 292. Otherwise turn to 358 to play this book again, or turn to 304 to read a different book.)

363 You decide to get mad paranoid. Sure, you're king now, but your friend Banquo got a prophecy too, and his said he'd start a long line of kings!

You decide the only way to prevent Banquo's eventual descendants from stealing your throne is to murder them preemptively. After all, you've been getting away with the first one pretty well so far, and that was a king! This is just murdering, like, a friend and his young boy.

You round up some men who you know don't like Banquo, remind them of what a jerk he can be, and send them after him. "Remember," you say, "to kill his son too. This is really important."

"Okay, obviously we were gonna kill his son too," the men reply. "The first thing they teach you at murdering school is to also kill any young man who witnesses you killing his parents, lest he swear vengeance against CRIME ITSELF and grow up to become a vigilante seeking justice, a dark knight, perhaps even a costumed one, which we can all agree would be an even bigger problem. We're big-picture thinkers, you know?"

You nod, and they leave. You feel pretty smart. You never even WENT to murdering school, and you're already murdering at a murder-school-graduate level!

The day passes, and when it's time to eat, you and your wife prepare a feast. As you're sitting down with the royal court, one of the murderers appears. He whispers in your ear that while they got Banquo, his kid escaped.

"WHAT DID THEY TEACH YOU AT MURDERING SCHOOL??" you hiss back.

"I know, I know, my bad," the man says, and leaves.

You're freaking out! The kid's still alive, so the prophecy could still come true. Plus, the hallucinations have returned! You keep seeing the ghost of Banquo at the table, and when you talk to him everyone thinks you're crazy. You're embarrassing yourself, yelling to hallucination-Banquo about things that might make your dinner guests think, hah hah, maybe you had him killed?

Your wife, quite reasonably, kicks everyone out. Your paranoia grows, and you conclude the only option is to track down the witches and ask them for more prophecies. That'll tell you what to do, who's plotting against you, and how to defeat them! You'll be invincible! You're honestly surprised you didn't think of it sooner.

It takes forever to find them, but you finally track down the witches in a creepy cave. "Of course they live in a cave," you think, annoyed. It's only double the toil and trouble of living LITERALLY ANYWHERE ELSE.

You enter into a cave with a burning fire and bubbling cauldron at its center. The three witches surround it, apparently oblivious to your arrival. Around the cave wall you see a row of ingredients, each in a small jar with a neatly written label on it. There's eye of newt, toe of frog, wool of bat, tongue of dog, adder's fork, blind-worm's sting, lizard's leg, owlet's wing (hey, they're arranged such that they rhyme when you read them! Neat!), scale of dragon, tooth of wolf, witches' mummy, and maw and gulf (and yeah, I agree: that last rhyme seems a bit forced). Moving on, you see jars labeled "ravin'd sea-salt shark," "root of hemlock digged in dark," and "liver of a blaspheming Jew," at which point you stop reading because these labels are getting HELLA PREJUDICED.

"Something wicked this way comes," says one witch.

You decide it's time to announce your presence. "What's up, witches?!" you say. "Hey, can you tell me more prophecies?"

"FINE," the witches say, pouring some ingredients into their brew. "Sniff this and you'll have some cool hallucinations."

You sniff deeply from the cauldron. You see, in rapid succession: a floating head that warns you to watch out for Macduff ("Obvs," you say); a bloody child who can speak with the voice of a man and says, "None of woman born shall harm Macbeth" ("Cool," you reply, "because now I know how I'm going to die: natural causes! That's handy, will allow me to perform dangerous tasks more confidently, and will definitely not result in any ironic demises"); a crowned baby holding a tree who again speaks in the voice of a man and tells you you'll be safe "until Birnam Wood moves to Dunsinane Hill" ("Even cooler," you reply, "for as we all know woods grow very

slowly, so that would take decades if not centuries, which only affirms my invincibility");
and finally, a procession of eight kings with Banquo at the end of them.

"Wait, what's that last one mean?" you say. "The one with Banquo and a bunch of kings. Does that mean he's going to father a long line of kings or what?" Instead of answering, the witches dance around and then run away. You are left in a gross cave with a bunch of different animal body parts lying around in jars.

Just then, one of your servants shows up. "This isn't what it looks like," you say.

"Macduff!" the servant pants, out of breath. "He's fled to England! He's probably going to try to get the English to move against you!"

Decide to capture Macduff's castle and kill his entire family: *turn to 359.*

Decide to get your army ready: *turn to 366.*

364
Oh right! Close call. You plant the weapons on the servants and stroll out of the king's room. Your wife is there, waiting for you. You hold out one hand in front of you. "I did a murder on him," you say.

"Nice," she says. "Okay, well, let's get you cleaned up. As the old saying goes, 'a little water clears us of this deed'!"

You clean up and go to bed. You finished the murder ahead of schedule, so you've got some time to talk. You tell her about the hallucinations of knives, voices, and knocking, and she explains how stress can make the mind behave oddly but says to ignore it. As long as the two of you act normal, you'll literally get away with murder!

You agree that that sounds good.

You wake up the next morning feeling pretty normal. The trick is to put the fact that you murdered the king out of your mind, so you don't feel bad about it! When the king's body is discovered you put on a good show. "Oh my god, who could DO this?!" you say, quite credibly.

The king's servants wake up hungover and confused by the mayhem the king's death has caused. You have a moment alone with them, and while you could kill them, you remind yourself that their alibis of "Um I was drunk and don't remember" are terrible.

When the king's men return, they're pretty suspicious of the servants. They did, after all, get super loaded and then wake up with the murder weapons in their hands. They're taken away, protesting their innocence, but their alibis are weak and they're found guilty of murder.

You don't claim the throne, letting the king's next in line, his son Malcolm, become king instead. You and your wife calmly and relentlessly sabotage him from behind the scenes, and his rule is disastrous. In a few short years he abdicates, and you become king.

You and your wife live happily ever after!

Live happily ever after: *turn to 362.*

365

You shove the witches away. "Whatever you're selling, we don't want it!" you say. Shortly thereafter, a messenger appears and tells you you've just been named thane of Cawdor.

"Huh?" you say.

"That's, like, a title," Banquo says.

"Ah," you say. "Cool. Well, I did just beat two armies, so I guess that's earned."

"Yep," Banquo says.

Later on that day you go and talk to the king, and he invites himself and all his friends over to your house for a sleepover.

What an honor! You and your wife are thrilled that the king would choose your house, and your wife says that this means big things are coming your way. She encourages you to take advantage of any opportunities that present themselves to climb the ladder at work, and you promise you will.

You and the king have a really great evening, then a very pleasant sleep, and the next morning the king thanks you for a great visit.

The king doesn't forget this favor, and over the next several years, you and your wife do very well for yourselves and become very important figures in courtly circles. Your establish a legacy for your children, your children's children, and your children's children's children, all of whom live and die in unbelievable richness.

Books! They're easy sometimes!

The End

(If you're done reading, turn to 292. Otherwise turn to 358 to play this book again, or turn to 304 to read a different book.)

366

You run back to your castle and find your wife there.

"Quick!" you say. "We're liable to be attacked by Macduff, leading an English army."

"I've been having nightmares," she says.

"WE'LL TALK ABOUT THAT LATER," you say. "For now, I'm putting you in charge of the Scottish army. Get them ready, NOW, and have them surround the castle. There's a chance they'll be coming from Birnam Wood, so I want extra defenses there."

"Got it," she says.

You get your army ready as best you can, and before long reports reach your ears that they have engaged the English army, an army ten thousand strong. You don't have ten thousand people in your army. You have maybe five thousand, tops.

Be afraid: *turn to 361.*

Be ready for a fight: *turn to 368.*

367

You stroll out of the king's room. Your wife is there, waiting for you. You hold out one hand in front of you. "I did a murder on him," you say.

"You still have the murder weapons IN YOUR HANDS," she says. "Go plant them on his servants!"

"No way," you say. "I was hallucinating like crazy in there." You tell her about the things you heard and saw. "I don't know if there's a weird gas in there or what," you say, "but it gives me crazy thoughts. I'm gonna stay out here."

"FINE," your wife says. "I'LL plant the evidence." She takes the bloody weapons and leaves.

As soon as she leaves, you hear knocking. "Weird," you say. "I guess I'm hallucinating still." You glance down at your bloody hands. "Geez, will all great Neptune's ocean wash this blood clean from my hand or what?" you wonder idly.

Your wife returns. "Done," she says. "Now, let's go clean up. As the old saying goes, 'a little water clears us of this deed'!" You clean up and go to bed.

You wake up the next morning feeling pretty stressed. You just murdered a king! But when the king's body is discovered you put on a good show, even if you do lay it on a bit thick. "Oh horror, horror, horror!" you scream. Really, Macbeth? Really?

In any case, the king's servants wake up hungover and confused by the mayhem the king's death has caused. You have a moment alone with them, and you're worried if they're left alive they might be able to convince others of their innocence, so you murder them too.

When the king's men return, they're pretty suspicious. One guy in particular,

Macduff, seems to think you are SOMEHOW involved in this series of murders that started happening once everyone showed up at your house. You explain that you only killed the prime suspects of the king's murder because you were, in your own words, "just so mad that they could murder someone that I had to murder them myself," but it doesn't seem to convince them that well. The king's heirs disappear, worried that they might be next on the murder list, and Macduff leaves too.

"Anyway, whatever," you say. "I'm going to be the new king now."

You and your wife ride into town to claim the throne. You arrive at Scottish Headquarters and announce that you're king now, and as the regular heirs to the throne have fled and you're popular because of your war victories, it works.

You are now king of Scotland, and your wife is the queen! Congratulations!

Live happily ever after: turn to 362.

No man, let's get mad paranoid: turn to 363.

368

"We're going to win this," you tell your wife. "I'm not afraid. I am, in fact, ready to kick butts."

Your wife looks at you for a long moment. "Screw your courage to the sticking-place, and we'll not fail," she says. "And you know what? I've seen you. You're wracked with guilt, just like me. But guilt's just a feeling, you know? We'll worry about it when we sleep.

"For now," she says, "I think it's time to arm ourselves from head to toe with direst cruelty." She leads you to your armory, where she picks up a battle-ax, a mace, a dagger, a lance, a bow and several arrows, a longbow, a poleax, two muskets, three cannons, and her rapier. You do the same.

You nod at each other and ride from the castle into battle.

Shortly thereafter, the two of you ride into the swarm of Englishmen. Slicing them up as you ride by is relatively easy, since their hands are full with all the trees they're carrying. You manage to kill hundreds before Macduff finally gives the order to drop the trees and pick up their weapons instead.

Your wife at one point is swarmed by the enemy. She fires her muskets at them but quickly exhausts them. "All's spent!" she shouts to you. "What's done is done, and I'm done for!"

Not on your watch. You toss her your musket, fully loaded, and she unloads it into her attackers. "Hell is MURKY!!" she shouts, firing, and before long she's covered in the blood of her dead assailants. She looks at you and smiles. "Who would've thought they'd have so much blood in them?" she says. You smile in return, and the two of you charge back into the battle.

Eventually you make your way to Macduff, coming up behind him as he's distracted with fighting elsewhere. "Turn, hell-hound, turn!" you shout. He does, seeing you and your wife, drenched in blood, swords pointed at him, cannons mounted on your horses, the contents of a literal armory strapped to your back.

"I have no words," he says, and your weapons tear him apart.

With the loss of their leader, the remaining army loses morale, and their fighting becomes desperate. Sloppy. Your troops are able to force a retreat. You've won!

You and Lady Macbeth return to your castle, victorious. There is much celebration, and that night, when it's finally over, you and your wife lie in bed together and finally talk about recent events. You talk over what you've done together and how it's made you feel with an honesty you never shared before. It brings you closer together.

The two of you agree, as she said on the battlefield, that "what's done is done." All you can do to make it right is try to be the best regents you can, to rule better than the old king ever did, hoping that in the end you could be a net good for the world, rather than just being, you know, a pair of ambitious murderers who committed regicide because some weird women thought it sounded cool.

You do your best, Macbeth.

The End

(If you're done reading, turn to 292. Otherwise turn to 358 to play this book again, or turn to 304 to read a different book.)

369

There are some shenanigans, but before long you manage to get Romeo receptive to the message from Juliet you have for him. You clear your throat and recite it:

Dear Romeo,

Still totally down to marry you.

Love,
J (from last night)

Romeo looks at you blankly.

"That's what Juliet wanted to say to you via me," you add. "I'm not the one saying this. Juliet is."

"OH," Romeo says. "I get it!"

Your score has increased by 899 points and is now 999 points out of a possible 1000 points! Look at you, Nurse! You're almost done with the game!

"This is great!" Romeo says. "Tell Juliet to meet me at Friar Lawrence's house, because I still want to marry her too."

"I will," you say. "I swear I will make my way back to Juliet, either solving or brute-forcing whatever puzzles block my way to do so."

"Oh also tell her I intend to get a sex ladder set up at her balcony tonight too."

"Um," you say.

The only exit is to the south.

Go south: turn to 330.

370

I barely make it onto the grounds of Capulet Castle before two men with swords step into my path. They say if I go any further I'm gonna regret it. I tell them regrets are for patsies who didn't do what they want, and step right past them.

It doesn't go well. Something hits me hard from behind, and the next thing I know I'm lying on a cell floor with a lump on my head and a pain in my neck.

The room's stone from floor to ceiling, cold as the grave and not much bigger. There's some straw for bedding, a small chamber pot, and not much else, besides the iron bars across the doorway. I throw myself against them a few times. All I get to show for my trouble is a sore shoulder.

When the jailer finally comes, he sets the scene for me. I've been arrested. Criminal harassment. Trespassing. Uttering threats. And just my luck: with Capulet and Montague teamed up, the police are in their pockets.

I'm being held until trial, and it doesn't take a crystal ball to see that trial's not coming. It's not so bad, I tell myself. Sure it's cold, but I get enough food to say alive, if I can keep it down. And I get visitors: all the vermin I can handle. Seems I bought myself a room with a view—of the opposing stone wall.

I know I'm here for the long run, but I still keep thinking how unfair this is. But then again . . .

. . . who ever said Verona was fair?

THE END

371 I walk up to Montague Mansion and bang on the front door. A servant answers, and I put on my best nice-girl-next-door face. You know the one. It's the one that says, "My goodness! I do believe I've never met a man quite as charming as you, snookums." It's the smile that says things I'd never say, and damn it, it opens doors.

"Is Lord Montague in?" I say, nice and sweet. "I'm the niece of his new best friend, Lord Capulet. My name's Rosaline."

Before I know it I'm sharing tea and biscuits with my prime suspect. I introduce myself and convey my condolences on the death of his son and wife. Sure, he accepts them gracefully. But he's a lot less graceful when I tell him it's too bad only one of those deaths was an accident. He stands up and I stand up too. I ask him if he's gonna hit me. He doesn't say anything, so I ask if that's what he did to his wife before he killed her.

He takes a step closer. I hold my ground. I shout at him how he should've given her more credit, because even as she was dying she managed to leave one last clue: her fingers in the shape of a "C" and an "M." And "CM" stands for one thing in this town: Charles Montague.

Sure he gets angry. Maybe even scared. But the one thing he doesn't get is sloppy. All he says is I don't have any real proof, and if I come back here again, I'll suffer the same fate his son did. Not sure if he means banishment or death, but he kicks me out of the castle before I get a chance to ask.

Standing there in the rain, I can't avoid the truth: I've messed up, big-time. I just walked up to my prime suspect, gave him all the evidence I had, and have nothing to show for it. Montague knows my evidence, knows I suspect him, and now has all the time in the world to cover his tracks.

Figure I've got two choices: I go back to the office and regroup, or I bust my way back in and citizen's-arrest him before he has time to make my job even harder.

I go and arrest the man: ***turn to 346.***

I go back to the office to regroup: ***turn to 334.***

372
You're back at the clockwork puzzle. Any further movement south will get you eaten by dogs.

There are only three exits here: to the north, to the south, and to the southeast.

Go north: turn to 352.

Go south: turn to 344.

Go southeast: turn to 399.

373

She's as good as her word. Your father pulls some strings, and Romeo's banishment is soon reduced from "all of Verona" to "the inside of that particular fountain in Verona where the water is," and he was never going to stand around in that fountain anyway! Romeo's parents also see the potential for profit in a partnership rather than in competition and endorse your marriage. You actually end up having a second ceremony in front of your two sets of parents, at their insistence!

Wow, who would've thought that clear and honest communication would pay off, huh?

You and Romeo live long and very happy lives, and when your first child is born, you and Romeo decide to name her after your mother, who is overjoyed. You both are.

Little Manhump Buttstuff Montague-Capulet grows up wanting for nothing.

HAPPILY EVER AFTER

THE END

P.S.: Okay YES I'm kinda sorry I never told you your mom's name until after I let you name your baby after her. But come on, you honestly never wondered why I avoided it this whole story?? I OBVIOUSLY HAD MY REASONS.

P.P.S.: Okay fine, you can call her "Mannie" for short.

P.P.P.S.: Or "Stuffie"?

374 "Paris sucks!" you say. "I barely even KNOW him and I know he sucks. You know what? I'd rather marry ROMEO than Paris. That's right, Romeo! Romeo, whom I know you hate!"

You pause, and reach a decision.

"In fact, guess what??" you say, but just then your dad walks into the room, with Angelica right behind him.

"Stop crying," he says. "Seriously. Your body is like a boat, and your tears are like the sea, and your sighs are like the wind, and unless you calm down you'll sink your boat with too many sea-tears and sigh-winds."

Hey, we found something worse than dad jokes! DAD SIMILES.

"Anyway," he says, turning to your mom, "have you delivered to Juliet our decree?"

"I have," your mom says, "and she says thanks but no thanks. She doesn't want to marry him. I for one wish the fool were married to her grave!"

Whoah, what the heck, Mom??

"Whoah, what the heck, Mom??" you say, but your dad speaks right over you. He calls you a "mistress minion," tells you you should be thankful for all he's done for you, informs you that you're getting married to Tom Paris in two days, tells you if you don't go he'll drag you there, and calls you a "green sickness," "carrion," "baggage," and "tallow face."

Don't listen to him, Juliet. Your face is just the right amount of tallow.

 Tell him to screw off: *turn to 393.*

Tell him you've already married Romeo, so this whole conversation is useless, and also incredibly insulting: *turn to 393.*

375 You stop by the side of the road and pick some flowers for Juliet. It delays you by about five minutes, but they're really beautiful so you're pretty sure it was worth it.

You arrive outside Capulet Crypt shortly after midnight. The door to the crypt is ajar, its lock lying broken on the ground beside it. Looks like someone else is inside Juliet's crypt!

You leave Balthasar behind and rush down into the darkness, and all you can see is Juliet, alive, so alive, and perfect. You rush up to her and hug her, and it's actually a few moments before you realize other people are here too!

"You arrived just in time," the Friar says happily. "She just woke up. Any sooner and she'd still be sleeping!"

"Oh, uh, hello, Friar," you say, disengaging yourself from your wife. "And . . . Paris, right? Mercutio's relative?" You hold out your hand to shake. "I don't believe we've met. Romeo Montague. Sorry about your cousin."

"Thank you," Paris says as he shakes your hand, "and uh, Romeo, this is awkward, but until a few minutes ago, I thought I was going to be marrying Juliet."

"What?" you say, stunned.

"My dad set it up after you were banished," Juliet explains. "I think he thought it'd cheer me up about Tybalt's death. The only way out of that marriage seemed to be to fake my own death, after which I could come to Mantua to live with you!"

"Juliet," you say kindly, "you could've come to Mantua to live with me anytime. I don't care what your parents think and you shouldn't either! You didn't need to do this silly fake-your-own-death thing!"

Paris interrupts you. "And YOU didn't have to do this silly secret-marriage thing," he says. He turns to Juliet. "You either, Juliet. If I'd known you were married I never would've asked your father for permission to marry you in the first place. I just respect monogamy too darn much!!"

Juliet smiles. "I know, Paris, I know. And if you hadn't asked to marry me, then I never would've faked my own death, and we never would've all ended up here in a creepy ol' crypt at midnight! I'm sorry, Paris. This whole thing happened because my husband and I didn't tell the truth." She sighs, then straightens herself. "I guess we all learned a valuable lesson, huh Romeo? Always tell the truth."

"We sure did, Juliet," you say. "But I gotta say, there is one OTHER lesson that I learned along the way too!" Everyone turns to look at you expectantly, and with a flourish you produce the flowers you picked earlier tonight.

"Never forget the flowers!" you say.

Everyone laughs and laughs and laughs and laughs.

THE END

376

Aw yes. This is nuts, but you know what? LET'S DO THIS. You are now both Romeo and Juliet!

Send Romeo to sneak past the guards up ahead while Juliet creates a distraction: *turn to 394.*

Wait, wait! I, uh, I wanna see them kiss. *Turn to 383.*

377

You figure your mom doesn't really know what poison looks like, so you just go down to the kitchen and make your usual protein shake. You stick a label on it that says "DRINK ME ;)."

You give the shake to your mother, she gives it to a messenger, and a few days later you get word that Romeo has been found alive and unhungry, satisfied as he was by his tasty protein shake.

"It must not have had enough poison in it," you say to your mother. "I'll make another."

Make another with fake poison: *turn to 388.*

Make something with real poison this time: *turn to 395.*

378

"Yeah, sounds great!" you say. But thinking quickly, you add, "And that WILL satisfy me, but ONLY if I get to mix the poison myself. That way we'll know for sure that it works, right?"

"Right," your mom says. "That's the friggin' problem with buying premixed poison: you don't know what's in it. For some reason, you just can't trust someone who'll sell lethal poison to strangers to be a fully ethical human being."

"Then it's settled," you say. "Romeo will definitely die after I make poison for him."

She nods. There's a moment of silence. You decide to fill it.

"Hey Mom, you know what sucks?" you say. "That we're sitting here talking about Romeo but that I can't go after him myself and get my hands on him. All I want to do is take whatever love I had for Tybalt and, you know, take it out on the body of the man that killed him. Dear Lord. I would take it out on Romeo's body for hours, over and over again.

"I'd take it out on him three times in one night," you say. "AGAIN."

"Okay cool," your mom says. "So find out how to make poison and I'll take care of finding the man to deliver it."

Tell her you'll get her the poison right away: *turn to 349.*

Tell her that, on second thought, you won't poison him, since you kinda married him yesterday: *turn to 338.*

 Say nothing; maybe she'll forget about this whole "poison Romeo" thing in a few days: *turn to 386.*

379

I go back into the storm and arrive at the crypt, dripping wet. There are probably better places for a single gal to be, but right now I can't think of any. You ever been in a place where the smell's so strong you can taste it? Yeah, well, here I am, soaking up the smell of dead people, getting it all over my size nines.

I walk up to Lady M and examine her, trying to find anything I could've missed. Nobody else has been here, and her "M" and "C" hands are just where I left them. I stare at her, feeling the gears turning in my head. If I were dying and wanted to spell out a name with my body, what else would I try? I try to think like the dead woman. You know: put myself in her shoes.

Her shoes.

I can't believe I missed it. If you want to spell something out that the killer won't see, you use all the limbs you've got, right? The next thing I know I'm pulling off her boots, half of me telling the other half I'm crazy, that half asking me what else is new. I get the right boot off first: her ankle and toes are locked in place, straight out. No help there. The left boot fights me a little more coming off, and I soon find out why: Lady M made a fist with her toes.

I'm not sure what I was expecting: toes impossibly curled over to form a crude "HARLES" on one foot, "ONTAGUE" on the other? Then it hits me like the business end of a club: she IS making the only letters she could with her feet. Those toes curled over make an "O," and those toes straight out form an "I."

C. M. O. I.

And there it is: the last message of Lady Montague.

The damned thing is, no matter how I juggle them around, there's not a single candidate in Verona with those initials. I figure maybe I was wrong about their being a name, that maybe she's spelling something out, like an acronym, all jumbled up. CMOI: Capulet Murdered, Others Implicated. IMCO: I'm Montague's Corpse—Ouch. OCMI: Observe Carefully—Montague Imposter.

Sitting in the dark, surrounded by bodies, desperately trying to conjure up some clue from a dead woman's feet, I start to get that awful familiar feeling. The one that keeps me up, the one I'm always running from. The feeling that maybe The Truth won't show up today, that maybe me and my special lady won't work things out after all.

I go with the "Montague Imposter" acronym theory: *turn to 389.*

I'm clutching at straws here. It's time to give up: *turn to 356.*

380

You ignore the knocking. Eventually, it stops.

Then, seconds later, it starts up again, this time louder and stronger!

Ignore the door some more: *turn to 350.*

Answer the door: *turn to 402.*

381

"Buzz off, man," you say. "I'm just here to break into a crypt at midnight. This doesn't concern you."

"I do defy thy commination!!" Tom shouts. You turn around and see he's running at you with his blade above his head.

You draw your sword and turn to face him. "OH MY GOD," you say. "Can we not?"

"Have at thee, boy!" Tom shouts as he leaps towards you, and you roll your eyes. "'Have at thee'? What are we, pirates? I'd never say a line like that."

His sword comes down at your head, but you hold your own blade above you to block it, then kick Tom backwards.

"What would you say, felon??" Tom says as he gets to his feet. You stab him right in the eyes.

"I don't know," you say. "'Stabs to meet you'??" He drops his sword and falls to his knees in front of you. "I'm sorry, we were never properly introduced," you say, taking his hand and shaking it. "I'm Romeo Montague." He falls over to the side. You let go of his dead hand.

"Stabs to meet you," you say.

You hear a gasp come from the nearby bushes. Someone saw you. "Friggin' Verona," you think. You stand up and shout into the darkness. "IF YOU THINK YOU SAW ME KILL THIS GUY," you shout, "THEN GUESS WHAT? YOU'RE RIGHT! AND I'LL KILL YOU TOO IF YOU TELL ANYONE. SERIOUSLY, I CAME HERE TO SEE MY DEAD WIFE AND EVERYONE KEEPS MESSING WITH ME. EVERYONE NEEDS TO MIND THEIR OWN BEESWAX, OKAY?"

You turn around and smash the crypt lock open. Then you make your way down the tomb stairs, dragging Paris's body behind you.

Enter tomb: *turn to 425.*

382 What?

Okay, um, you bend over and examine beneath the bench. There are indeed branches there. They're strong. Sturdy. You turn one over in your hands.

"I bet if I were fast enough," you whisper, "I could jam these sticks into the mouths of whatever animals I encounter, thereby preventing them from biting me."

Angelica, that's crazy. That's madness. That's bizarre dream logic. But that's also . . . actually kind of awesome?

Alright, I'm going to allow this. Take the sticks if you want to try your little scheme, and leave them there if you're having second thoughts.

Stand up from bench: turn to 399.

Take sticks: turn to 394.

383 Romeo/you and Juliet/you kiss. They kiss each other really well. You can't believe how well you're kissing each of your other selves right now.

Okay, now send Romeo to sneak past the guards up ahead while Juliet creates a distraction: *turn to 394.*

No wait, now Juliet tells Romeo he's handsome and Romeo tells Juliet she's really pretty: *turn to 401.*

384 "Whoah whoah whoah, hold up," you say. "That's stupid and crazy. Get the heck out of here."

Just then, there's a knock on the door. You answer it and Angelica sticks her head into the room and tells you that your mom is on the way up.

"Okay, dude," you say, closing the door and turning back to Romeo. "Out the window you go!"

Romeo kisses you good-bye and then quickly makes his way down the rope ladder, onto his horse, and off towards Mantua. You turn away from your balcony and sit down on your bed. A few seconds later, there's another knock on the door.

Answer the door: *turn to 402.*

Sit very quietly and don't answer the door: *turn to 350.*

385 It was a great idea, questioning Mercutio's friends, but it doesn't take long for it to become clear that there aren't too many of them left alive to question. Romeo's dead. Tybalt's dead. The only person whom my witnesses to the Tybalt/Romeo/Mercutio fight can place at the scene who isn't himself six feet under already is one man: Benvolio.

It's obvious that whatever happened that afternoon, Benvolio's neck-deep in it. Turns out it was Benvolio who dragged the "dying" Mercutio away from the eyes of the crowd. Benvolio who returned shortly afterwards and announced Mercutio definitely died back there while nobody was looking. Benvolio who stuck around afterwards to tell the cops what happened. He's no dummy. Seems my friend Ben got his narrative established nice and early.

And after that, the man's a ghost. Nobody I can find has seen or heard from him since Romeo got himself banished. Benvolio's playing it safe. Benvolio doesn't want to be found.

Benvolio didn't count on one Rosaline Catling, PI.

His house is empty but tidy, and there are bare hangers in his closet. He had time to prep before leaving. But there is also a pet fish here, still alive. Someone's been feeding this fish every couple of days. I invite myself in and make myself at home until I find out who our junior zookeeper is.

I'm passed out on the bed when I hear someone fumbling with the lock. A grunt as they push it open: a man. I wait until he closes the door behind him, then I leap off the bed, push him up against the wall, and bring my leg up to his crotch before the poor fool has a chance to react. I ask him if he's Benvolio. He's screaming, crying, blubbering that he's just a servant but that he can tell me where Benvolio's staying. He knows the inn, the wing, the exact room. All I have to do is to please not kill him and he'll tell me everything I want to know.

I smile. Music to my ears.

I kill him: *turn to 398.*

I go to Benvolio's inn and confront Benvolio: *turn to 410.*

386

You smile your best noncommittal smile and she seems satisfied. Then she seems to remember something.

"Oh!" she says. "With all this talk about commissioning a crime I forgot to tell you: I have some joyful tidings for you, girl!"

"Joyful tidings?!" you say, excited. "Lay 'em on me!" And so she does!

And I hate to break it to you, but it turns out the joyful tidings are that your parents have arranged to have you marry Tom Paris.

I know: that's not joyful tidings at all! That's actually horrible, stupid tidings! Tom Paris—and I remind you that I'm saying this as an omniscient narrator, one who literally knows all and sees all—is a big ol' loser.

Tell her you're not gonna marry Tom Paris because you're already married: *turn to 405.*

Tell her you're not gonna marry Tom Paris, because he sucks: *turn to 374.*

387

"Condemned villain," Paris says. "I've caught you. Come with me or die." He does make a good point, Romeo. You WERE banned from Verona.

"Look, Tom, don't mess with me, okay?" you say. "I'm a desperate man, and you're making me angry. You wouldn't like me when I'm angry."

"I don't like you now," Tom says.

"Come on, get out of here!" you shout. "I don't wanna kill anyone else, okay? And yes, THAT IMPLIES THAT I HAVE KILLED BEFORE AND AM WILLING TO DO IT AGAIN. To myself, actually. But also to you, if you don't get out of here!"

"I'm putting you under citizen's arrest," he says.

"You're provoking me? You're SERIOUSLY going to provoke me?" you say. You draw your sword. "Alright then. Have at thee, boy!" you say, acting like you didn't already decide to swordfight him a while back.

Paris walks up to you, wildly swinging his sword in the air like he's trying to swat a fly. You stab Paris right in the guts on your first try. And when you do, you're pretty sure you hear a gasp come from the bushes nearby.

"Oh, I am slain!" Tom says. "Listen, do me a favor? Open the tomb and put me next to Juliet, okay?"

"I was gonna open it anyway," you hiss. Then louder, for the benefit of anyone listening in, you say, "OKAY SO LET ME PERUSE THIS FACE, BECAUSE I NEVER ACTUALLY SAW THE FACE OF THE MAN I WAS LITERALLY JUST TALKING TO BEFORE HE DIED ON MY SWORD, WHICH, I STRESS, WAS BY ACCIDENT. OH WOW, THIS IS MERCUTIO'S KINSMAN, NOBLE TOM PARIS! WHAT BAD LUCK THAT HE FELL ON MY SWORD JUST NOW! HE'S NEITHER A CAPULET NOR A MONTAGUE, SO I HAVE NO MOTIVE TO KILL HIM, WHICH IS GREAT, BECAUSE THIS WAS AN ACCIDENT AND NOT A MURDER ANYWAY. IN ANY CASE, I'D BETTER BURY HIM IN A MAGNIFICENT GRAVE RIGHT AWAY."

You smash the lock open and proceed down the tomb stairs, dragging Paris's body behind you.

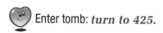 Enter tomb: *turn to 425.*

388

That gets sent over to Romeo too, and a few days later you get word that Romeo has been spotted relaxed, sated, and wiping his mouth with the back of his hand. At this point your mother gets frustrated and tells you that you don't have any more time to secretly do murders because she's arranged to have you marry local loser Tom Paris, so you run away from home. You hide in the one place they'll never look for you: in the arms of the man who killed your cousin.

You keep making delicious protein shakes, but you also teach Romeo how to work out, which burns calories, which means he can have more protein shakes, which means by this time next year the two of you are SUPER RIPPED and really good at muscles. The two of you enter muscle competitions and win awards with titles like "Coolest Muscles," "Best Couple with Muscle," and "Special Award for Having Abs on Top of Abs." You're as happy as you are covered with giant swollen muscles, which is to say: EXTREMELY.

THE END

P.S.: Oh, I almost forgot! At one point the Duke of Mantua's carriage wheel broke outside your house, and Romeo lifted up the entire car while you replaced the wheel with a new one you'd fashioned by bending the duke's guards' swords into a wheel shape with your bare hands. He's so impressed that he makes you his heirs, and anyway long story short, Romeo and Juliet's Muscle Kingdom and Land of Cardio becomes THE vacation destination for people wanting sweeter muscles on their bodies.

You and Romeo are very happy and have several extremely muscular babies.

389 "Observe Carefully: Montague Imposter."

It's a long shot, but nothing in this business is ever a sure thing. Memories get foggy, alibis get muddy, and sometimes all you can do is take your best guess, make your move, and let the chips fall where they may. So that's what I do.

Never much cared for chips anyway.

I go back to Montague Mansion and knock on the door. If my guess is right, Lord Montague isn't the man he claims to be. And I intend to prove my guess is right. Seems luck's on my side for once: the man himself—or at least the man pretending to be the man himself—answers the door. He recognizes me and is about to slam the door in my face, but I get my heel in before he can.

I tell him sweetly I just want to ask him one question and then I'll be on my way. I ask him what made him think he could get away with killing Lady Montague and assuming her husband's identity, then I shove the door open and pull the mask clean off his head. Or at least, that's the plan. The mask stays, but some of the mask's hair comes off in my hands. With follicles. And blood. Flesh, too. Montague is screaming, the red stuff pouring down his face as his servants surround me and beat me to the ground. I know they're not gonna stop until I'm out of the picture.

I'd like to say I don't know where I went wrong, but I know exactly where. It's the moment I lost faith in my one love, Truth, the moment I sold her out for the seductive allures of Wild Conjecture. Now it's time to pay the piper, and I'm flat broke.

I don't even fight back. Least I can do is face my death with her. Because there is one final truth I do know: I blew it.

THE END

390 "I got married," you say, "in secret, TO YOUR WORST ENEMY, and the first thing you say when you find out is how much money you're gonna make?"

"Juliet, I was about to marry you off to Tom Paris. You know what that marriage would've gotten us? ONLY A LITTLE BIT OF MONEY. This marriage has the chance to make us all very, very rich!"

"I'm your only child," you say.

"I know," she says, "and I'm very proud. Let me talk to your father. We'll sort out the banishment thing and get Romeo back here ASAP. From then on, Juliet, all our problems are over!" And with that, she leaves.

On one hand, confessing your marriage just solved all your problems, including the problem of marrying Paris that you didn't even know you had! On the other hand, you're annoyed that your mother was less excited for you and more excited about what you could do for her.

Get over my annoyance and forget about it, she's the only mom I've got: *turn to 373.*

Man, forget her, I'm gonna go live in Mantua with Romeo: *turn to 400.*

391

You pick up the sticks from under the bench and then begin looking in the park for more. It takes you a while, but I don't blame you, since you're looking for sticks that can HOLD OPEN AN ANIMAL'S MOUTH so it can't BITE YOU TO DEATH. I'd be choosing carefully and taking my time too!

After about an hour, you've selected the sticks you want and, taking a deep breath, you head south towards the gatekeeper and his menagerie.

You enter the gatekeeper's domain. There are dozens of angry dogs here. There are also dozens of angry lions. Surprise!

"Didn't I warn you about the dozens of angry dogs?" he shouts at you. "Wow! Now you've done it! Also, I got some lions too while you were in Verona!"

As the animals approach you, you quickly jam sticks into their mouths, propping them open and preventing them from biting you. The lions still have claws, but you distract them by throwing your gross hat at them, and that allows you to make good your escape.

"That was amazing," the gatekeeper says as you run past him towards the south. "I had this whole pun ready about there being CLAWS for concern, but man, you nailed it!!"

You are now free to deliver to Juliet the good news.

Go south: turn to 404.

Go north: turn to 426.

392

I arrive at Mercutio's place. Figure a direct approach is my best choice here, so I walk right up and knock on the door. A dead man answers. "Mercutio," I say. "Just the guy I've been looking for."

He looks at me suspiciously. "What for?" he says.

I tell him he'll want to invite me in for this one. Wouldn't want the neighbors to hear. He lets me in, and we sit at his kitchen table, nice and civilized-like. He gets himself a glass of water. Offers me the same. I decline. He pours me one anyway.

I tell him all about Lady M, about the message she left with her hands and feet. I tell him there's no use denying it. I tell him I'm taking him in to the cops. I tell him his goose is cooked, overdone, that the oven's on fire and the police are on their way.

He laughs and says all I've got is circumstantial evidence, says nobody can corroborate my story. He says he merely recovered from injuries grievously acquired during a swordfight in which he was an innocent party, and was simply recuperating at home before announcing the good news to the world.

And then he asks me if I told anyone I was coming here.

I tell him I'm no dummy. I tell him all about the friends on the force I let know about this investigation. That's when he jumps me, pins me on the floor before I can react. Says he doesn't believe me. Says he knows everyone in Verona and he doesn't know me, which means I'm new in town. Says he's willing to bet I don't make friends easily.

He's not wrong.

He dumps the contents of my glass down my throat. Tells me not to worry: it's not poison. Instead, it's the same serum he took to fake his own death for a few days. You know, before he killed Lady M and took advantage of the circumstances to make it look like she died of grief. Says this is a much larger dose, though. Says he doesn't expect me to wake up for, oh, let's say . . . ever.

The world's fading out. I can tell my ticket's been punched, but I can still go out on my own terms. I think about Truth, and how I always said I'd do anything for her. Anything.

I'm as good as my word.

I'll tell you one thing I've learned: dying's easy. Detective work is hard.

THE END

393

"Dad—" you begin, but he cuts you off.

"HANG THEE," he shouts at you. "If you're not there at the church on Thursday, I'll never look at you again."

"DAD," you say.

"Don't speak," he says. "Don't reply, don't even say a word. You know what? I thought we were blessed when God gave us you, but hah hah, guess it was a curse after all!!" He winds up a hand, as if to hit you. "You disgust me," he says. "I feel like slapping you."

You stand your ground. "Try it," you say.

Your nurse runs between you both. "Don't talk to her like that!" she shouts, but your dad shoves her away, hard. He glowers at her, then at you, then at your mom.

"God's bread, this makes me mad," he says. "God's friggin' bread. I work to get her married every day and night, every hour, every tide, at work, at play, alone, in company: ALWAYS. And now that I've found her a husband who's handsome, young, well educated, well bred, STUFFED WITH HONORABLE PARTS—the perfect man—now that I've found him she's all, 'Oh no, I can't marry him! I couldn't possibly love THIS guy! He's WAY too perfect for me!' Well, I'll tell you one thing, Juliet: you don't marry Paris, you're done. You won't live under this roof anymore."

"Hah!" you say.

"I'm not in the habit of joking," he says. "Do what I say and I'll give you to my friend. You'll be MARRIED. But ignore what I say and you'll beg and starve and die in the streets. I swear on my soul, Juliet: I'll never so much as acknowledge you, and everything that's mine will NEVER do you good. Don't push me."

He storms out of the room before you can say anything else. You turn to your mom. "Wow," you say. "Okay, Mom, can you talk to him? Tell him to delay this marriage for a month, or even just a week, okay? Or, if you don't want to delay it, then at LEAST make my bridal bed in the tomb where Tybalt lies.

"Because I'll kill myself if I have to marry him, I mean," you say. "Not because I want to have sex with Tybalt's corpse."

"Don't even talk to me, Juliet," she says. "Do as you want. I'm done with you." And she leaves, slamming the door behind her.

You turn to your nurse.

Tell her there's nothing to keep you here anymore, so oh well, guess you're going to live with Romeo! *Turn to 413.*

 Call yourself soft and ask her for comfort: *turn to 403.*

394

You, as Romeo, make your way towards Capulet Castle while you, as Juliet, prepare your distraction! And soon enough, Romeo/ you is spotted by a guard on a parapet.

"Stand, ho! Who's there?" the guard shouts.

"A friend to the Capulets!" you shout in reply. "And a fellow guard! I'm here to replace, um . . ."

You realize you never got his name.

"That other guy," you say. "You know the one? The one who's not here and who is always taking naked naps in bushes."

Meanwhile, Juliet/you decides the best distraction is to use your sweet disguise to get close to a guard, and then loudly and visibly beat him up. Other guards will come running, you'll beat them up too, and hey presto: there's your distraction. It's perfect. You quickly go over your glutes, calves, pecs, and quads. They're ready. YOU'RE ready. You begin to jog to a nearby parapet.

"Aw man, Angola did it AGAIN?" the guard replies to Romeo/you. "God's wounds. I can't believe him sometimes."

"Nor can I," you say as you climb up the ladder to join the guard. "But now I'm here to replace him. My name's, uh, Jake."

"Chad," the guard replies, holding out his hand to shake yours. He gets his first good look at you. Meanwhile, you get your first good look from up here, and you notice that the other parapets are empty. Uh-oh. Without any guards there, it's gonna be hard for Juliet to create a distraction.

You, as Juliet, suddenly realize there are no guards where you're headed. This distraction isn't going to work. You spin on your heel and break into a desperate sprint back towards Romeo.

"Say," Chad says to Romeo/you. "How come you're only wearing the hat part of your uniform?"

"Hah hah hah!" you say, trying to stall for time. "What?"

Juliet/you reaches Romeo's/your parapet. You're scrambling up the ladder as fast as you can, hoping you can make it in time. Just a few more seconds!!

"Your uniform," Chad says. "You've got the hat on, but the rest is like, regular rich-teen clothes." You're trapped, Romeo. You've only got one move left.

And so you take it.

You, as Juliet, come running up from the darkness behind Chad and spin-kick him in the head. Quite frankly, he's lucky his head even stays attached!

High five each other: *turn to 430.*

395 Hah hah, what? This is for Romeo: the man you just married, and the man whom you just shared a choose-your-own SEX SCENE with. I thought you liked him?

GUESS NOT, huh??

You make your way to Friar Lawrence's house and make up a story about you and Romeo being so happy together but also star-cross'd lovers, because you want to move in together but the place you're looking at has rats, and could he maybe lend you some rat poison?

He gives you some rat poison.

"There are a lot of rats," you say.

The Friar gives you more rat poison.

"Some of them are as big as, oh I don't know, a human being," you say.

He gives you enough rat poison to kill a human.

"Thanks!" you say.

You decide to put the poison into cookies, because everyone likes cookies! You've never made cookies before but it turns out it's really easy and now you can have cookies whenever you want! Here's the recipe:

JULIET'S TO-DIE-FOR OATMEAL COCONUT COOKIES (GOOD FOR MURDERS)

Mix together:

> 1 cup brown sugar
> ½ cup white sugar
> 1 cup melted butter

Then add in:

> 1 egg (interior contents ONLY)
> 1 teaspoon vanilla
> 1¼ cups oatmeal
> ¾ cup coconut
> 1½ cups all-purpose flour
> 1 teaspoon baking soda
> 1 teaspoon baking powder
> A bunch of poison (optional??)

> Mix all those ingredients together, scoop out balls of the mixture you've produced, put them on a cookie sheet, and bake them in a hot oven for about 10 minutes.

"If only there were a way to measure heat," you think, "then I could better specify what I mean by 'hot oven,' perhaps by saying something like 'three hundred fifty degrees Fahrenheit' or 'one hundred seventy-six point six six six six six six six seven degrees Celsius,' assuming those were indeed methods of measuring temperature.

"Oh well," you think.

You bake your poison cookies, and when they're ready, you decorate them with icing sugar. "EAT ME," you write on one. "FROM YOUR SWEETIE JULIET," you write on another. You write, "TOO MANY COOKIES CAN BE BAD FOR YOUR HEALTH ;)" on a third cookie. That one's for irony purposes!

Your give the cookies to your mother, she gives them to a messenger, and a few days later you get word that Romeo has been found dead, surrounded by an open box and cookie crumbs. Apparently he wrote, "Yo these cookies were really good so it was worth it," in the crumbs. Nice!

Congratulations, Juliet! Hey, you know that game where your friends name three celebrities, and you have to decide which of them you'd marry, which of them you'd have sex with, and which of them you'd kill? You just played that game with the same guy in every role!

THE END

P.S.: Oh, I almost forgot: your parents arranged for you to marry their friend Tom Paris, and you marry/sex/murder him in a couple of days too! Wow, you're really kinda psychopathic, Juliet! I wish you'd told me this sooner; I had another story called *The Baker Who Kept Killing Everyone and Also Having Lots of Cool Sex* that you would've been great for.

Oh well??

396
Alright then! Let's call this the end.

That was a fun adventure we just shared, wasn't it? I hope we all learned a lot or at least burned through some of our sadly finite lives back here in reality.

Hey, speaking of reality: I hate to ask, but I got really into that adventure and kinda lost track of where we were in THIS story. Who are you again?

I'm Romeo, the handsome man with the handsome plan! *Turn to 407.*

I'm Juliet, the coolest lady of the 1580s! *Turn to 433.*

Hey, I'm Iago, I uh, I live a couple of towns over: *turn to 417.*

397
"Tom, right?" you say. "What are you doing here? What's going on? Is there anything I can do to help?"

"Romeo, you are an INDESCRIBABLE JERK," he shouts. "You've been banished! And yet you return, just to do some villainous shame to the dead bodies!"

"What?" you say.

"Listen," Tom says, flustered, "I know what's going on, so don't try to make me think I don't. You killed Tybalt, got banished, left town, then decided to come all the way back into town a couple of days later so that you could stab his body a few more times."

"Tom, that's crazy," you say. "I'm not here to stab long-dead bodies; I'm here to pay my final respects to Juliet. You know, MY WIFE."

"Your what?" he says.

"My WIFE," you say. "I married her in secret before the Tybalt accident, and then got banished, and just got word that she died, so here I am."

"Your WIFE??" Tom repeats. "YOU married Juliet?"

"I did," you say. "Secret-married. Because of our parents' strife."

"I thought I was going to marry Juliet," he says.

"Aren't you like, fifty?" you say. Tom glances at you angrily.

"Listen," he says. "I thought she was betrothed to me, but in retrospect if she was already married to you, a lot of very weird things start to make sense." He holsters his sword and holds your gaze for a long moment. He seems to reach a decision.

"I'm sorry for your loss," he says, holding out his hand.

"And I yours," you say, shaking his hand. "Come on," you say. "Let's go say good-bye together." You and Tom jimmy the crypt lock open and make your way downwards.

"Oh hey, by the way," you say, "I should mention that when I see her dead body there's a chance I might kill myself out of grief, you know?"

"What are you, twelve?" Tom says.

You and Tom enter the crypt. There in the middle of the room is Juliet in her tomb, lying peacefully. It's crazy; she looks the same as she did when you saw her two days ago. She looks like she's just sleeping. But you put your hand to her neck, and there's no pulse. She's dead, Romeo. You and Tom stare at her for a long moment. You're both crying.

"I'm gonna climb in there with her for a final embrace," you say.

"Nope, that's not happening," Tom says. You stand beside each other in silence until you hear someone else approaching.

"Friar Lawrence?!" you say. "What are you doing here??"

Friar Lawrence leans over Juliet's coffin and holds up a finger to silence you. "Fifteen seconds left," he says. "I'm extremely good with my chemicals."

Juliet's eyelids begin to flutter. She's—she's alive? She opens up her eyes and stares into the Friar's face. She smiles.

She's alive!!

"Friar!" she says. "I remember well where I should be, and here I am. Where is my Romeo?"

He steps to the side, revealing your smiling face. "Right here, Juliet," he says, and her face breaks into the biggest, most beautiful grin you've ever seen. She wraps her arms around your neck and kisses you. You kiss back. It's perfect.

You hear Tom coughing awkwardly behind you. "Hey Juliet," he says as you help her out of her coffin. "Sorry, I didn't know you were married and at the same time also faking your own death. So listen, this is not really my scene. I'm going to go leave you forever now." He turns to leave. As he goes you hear him muttering to himself, "Maybe dating women who've reached the age where they've grown out of faking their deaths to get out of social commitments WOULD be nice after all . . ."

You take Juliet's hand, and the two of you walk out of the crypt and into the beautiful starry night. The Friar makes his excuses and leaves, and for the first time in days, the two of you are alone together.

"Where shall we go?" you ask your wife. Juliet slows, then stops.

"My parents will want me to stay here with them," she says, looking around the graveyard. Then she looks up to you and takes your face in her hands.

"I think I'm pretty much through doing what my parents want me to do," she says, and then she kisses you.

After a long while, you break away from the kiss. "I can't stay in Verona anyway," you breathe. "But that's a good thing. We can leave Verona behind us, Juliet. We can go anywhere. Mantua. Europe. CHINA. The whole world's open to us now."

You squeeze her hands, and she squeezes back. You separate, and both of you look up to the stars, the sky so clear and the stars so bright that they almost cast shadows.

"We can do whatever we want," she says with a smile, half to you and half to herself. "We're going to build a life together, Romeo. Not the life my parents want for me, or the life your parents want for you, but whatever life we want, WE choose, for each other. OUR life."

You kiss once more, and then the two of you walk out of the graveyard, out past the church fence, and down towards the horizon. There'll be a beautiful sunrise in just a few hours, and the two of you are off to a new beginning. Off to a brand-new life together.

Off to choose your own adventure.

THE END

398

Couldn't say for sure what came over me. I could've sworn I wasn't the kind of person to go around killing informants, but I guess life's funny sometimes. By the time I come to my senses, my only lead is leaking all over someone else's carpet, and I'm on the wrong side of the law.

I can't wait around for the heat to arrive and find me dripping in gore, so I hit the road and get as far from Verona as I can. I know enough about how they treat their criminals there to know I don't want to experience the Veronan legal system firsthand.

Sure, I've as good as banished myself, but I can live with that. It's not hard starting over somewhere if you keep it simple, and I keep it real simple. I've only got a few needs: food and water. Shelter.

Justice.

But what gets me is I never find out how Mercutio did it. More than anything, I wish I could say it didn't bug me. I wish I slept like a baby every night, content in the knowledge of a job well done. I wish I could go to my maker with a life well lived behind me and face my eternal reward head-on, without regrets.

None of it's true.

THE END

399 You find yourself in an empty Veronan park. There's nobody here, nothing interesting except a few trees, and nothing interesting to do except sit on the park bench.

The only exit is to the northwest.

Sit on bench: *turn to 351.*

Go northwest: *turn to 372.*

400 You sneak out of your room, steal one of your parents' horses, and ride to Mantua. Romeo has a pretty good head start, so when you get there you check in the various inns, hoping to find him there. When you do catch up with him, he's shocked to discover that his banishment is going to be fixed by your parents.

"Then . . . all our problems are over?"

"No," you say, "my parents are still jerks, so there's that problem that remains. Anyway, forget about them! We'll live here in Mantua!"

"And you said that because we got married, everyone is going to be rich?"

"ROMEO," you say, "there's more to life than money."

"I know, I know," he says. "That's why we can be rich and still do all those other things in life! Like, we can have money AND ride fancy boats to tea parties. Or we can have money AND build metal exoskeletons to battle our enemies with."

"Huh," you say. "I honestly had not considered the metal exoskeleton angle."

"All this and more becomes possible with money!" Romeo says, and by this time tomorrow, the two of you are back in Verona, to a hero's welcome. Even random pedestrians are happy that you got married!

"This will mean fewer swordfights in public, resulting in a safer public sphere for all!" they cheer.

Your life seems to come into focus. You and Romeo spend all your time researching metals and gears and clockworks and steam and cool goggles, and after a few years, early prototypes give way to production machines. They're as tall as a house, nigh indestructible, and unstoppable on the battlefield. Verona herself enters an unprecedented period of prosperity and begins to expand her borders, thanks largely to your war machines, and before long all of Europe falls under the sway of the combined Montague-Capulet regime.

But since this is a happy ending, your parents are just and wise rulers, and when they die you and Romeo are even juster and even wiser! Also, you spend all of your time in your metal suits, and they can fire flaming arrows out of their palms, and that never ever ever gets old.

THE END

401 They do those things. It goes pretty well!

Okay, NOW send Romeo to sneak past the guards up ahead while Juliet creates a distraction: *turn to 394.*

Now Romeo pulls off his shirt and he's a superhero and Juliet reveals she's got mutant powers that let her run really fast: *turn to 409.*

402 It's your mom! She sits on the bed beside you and delicately asks why you're crying so much about your dead cousin Tybalt.

"Oh, right, crying!" you say. "Yes, those were screams of sorrow you heard all last night. I even, um, cried my head off three times in a row."

"Well, I can understand why. Romeo killed your cousin but is still alive, somewhere far far away," she says.

"Yes," you say, nodding. "He is definitely beyond our reach right now. Beyond the reach of my hands. Which is to say, I can't touch his body no matter how much I want to. I can't touch his neck, his face, his pecs, his abs, that little place between his belly button and his—"

"Don't worry," your mom says. "I can see you're as upset as I am. So here's what I'm gonna do: I'm gonna send someone to Mantua to poison him. That'll satisfy you, right? And then you'll stop crying?"

 Tell her you agree to poison Romeo: *turn to 378.*

Tell her you won't poison him, and surprise, you actually married the dude yesterday: *turn to 338.*

403 Okay. How fancy do you want to play this, Juliet?

 Super fancy. I am the super fanciest: *turn to 427.*

Just the regular amount of fancy: *turn to 416.*

404 You run through the now-open door to Capulet Castle and quickly find Juliet to deliver the good news to her. You are tired, aching, and out of breath. But on the plus side, you solved some cool puzzles and didn't get eaten by crazed animals! Juliet is overjoyed to see you and can't wait to hear your good news. She will marry her Romeo because of you. It is a happy ending, because as we know, nothing can go wrong when people get married!

THE END

Thank you for playing NURSE QUEST. You have completed Nurse's quest, and your final score is 1000 out of a possible 1000 points.

Now that you've completed this quest, be sure to try our other titles, including:

- PLUMBER QUEST
- PLUMBER QUEST II
- QUEST FOR SAUSAGES
- PLUMBER QUEST III
- QUEST FOR SAUSAGES II: ABSENCE (OF SAUSAGES) MAKES THE HEART GROW FONDER (OF SAUSAGES)

You are a super player. Thank you for playing!

Wow what a fun game! Okay, be Juliet again, accept the good news. Turn to 194.

No, I want to play Nurse Quest again! THIS is a game with replay value! Turn to 183.

405

"Oh, hah hah, this is awkward," you say, "but uh, I can't marry Paris."

"Why?" your mom asks.

"Because I've . . . already married Romeo?" you say, wincing. "He was kinda just here before you showed up. For sex. I was sexing him, Mom, because, as I said, we're married."

"WHAT?" your mother says.

"MOM," you say, "I'm old enough to make my own choices now. And I chose to marry Romeo, the man I just met at your party last night."

"Our party!" your mom says, snapping her fingers. "Of course! The masks would've added an erotic undercurrent to the occasion, and we've sheltered you for so long, you were unprepared to handle the feelings you were facing. It all makes sense!"

"Yes, well," you say, "that's why I can't marry Paris. But on the plus side, since I've married the son of your greatest enemy, maybe we could kinda settle this dispute between our two houses? We could be the happy marriage that draws us together!"

Your mom considers this. "He did murder Tybalt," she says, "but since that's now an internal family matter rather than a public feud, that does change things somewhat. And if we were teamed up with the Montagues, our greatest competition could become our greatest allies."

"Competition?" you ask.

"In business," she says. "If we merged—I mean, if our families merged—we'd have access to the Thomas More account and we'd lose our competition on the Cardenio accounts."

She looks up.

"We'd be rich," she says, laughing. "Oh Juliet, this is perfect! Perfect! Now that our interests are aligned, the Montagues and Capulets will be able to work together, rather than against each other!" She hugs you, then pulls back and holds you at arm's length, smiling. "This will make all of us a lot of money, Juliet."

Be happy that she's happy: *turn to 348.*

Be offended that she's only concerned about money: *turn to 390.*

406

You cry over Juliet's body for a while, but it's actually a really uncomfortable position to be in. Her body's on a raised platform, which makes her coffin too high to wail against while sitting, but also too low to wail against while standing without leaning over at an awkward angle. And you can't help but notice that there is actually plenty of room INSIDE her coffin.

You look around to make sure nobody else is here. (They're not! It's just you and the body of Paris, that man you murdered! Oh, and also the body of Tybalt, that man you ALSO murdered earlier!) Then you climb into the coffin with Juliet. You wrap your arms around her ("A final embrace," you think dramatically) and cry and cry and cry.

The next thing you know, you're being interrupted by the sound of someone coughing. You look up into the face of Friar Lawrence. He's smiling down at you.

"This isn't what it looks like," you say, scrambling out of her coffin.

Once you're out, you ask him what's going on. The Friar leans over Juliet's coffin and holds up a finger to silence you. "Fifteen seconds left," he says. "I'm extremely good with my chemicals."

Juliet's eyelids begin to flutter. She's . . . she's alive? She opens up her eyes and stares into the Friar's face. She smiles.

She's alive!!

"Friar!" she says. "I remember well where I should be, and here I am. Where is my Romeo?"

He steps to the side, revealing your smiling face. "Right here, Juliet," he says, and her face breaks into the biggest, most beautiful grin you've ever seen.

She wraps her arms around your neck and kisses you. You kiss back. It's perfect. Then you lift her out of her coffin and carry her up towards the exit, towards your new life together in Mantua. Towards a new beginning. You can see the stars through the crypt entryway, just ahead of you. It's a beautiful night.

That's when a watchman steps sideways into the entryway, stopping you from moving any further. "Hold it right there," he says.

"Oh, no, it's fine," Juliet says, still smiling in your arms. "He's actually my husband, and we're going off to Mantua to live happily ever after now. I just FAKED my own death, and my family owns this crypt, so this is me telling you he has my permission to be here. And I brought him to Verona, so you don't need to worry about the banishment part either."

"It's not that, ma'am," the watchman says. "That man just killed Tom Paris, and we have a witness from a nearby bush. Arrest him, boys." Two more watchmen come in past the first and, removing Juliet from your arms, hold you up against the wall. Once you're secured, the first watchman walks back to you. "What, you thought we'd all just forget about that so you could have your happy ending?" he sneers, then pushes past you and disappears down into the crypt.

"You killed Paris?" Juliet asks, stunned.

"Why?" the Friar asks. "How?"

"He was—I was trying to break in here to get to YOU," you say. "He was sassing me, and one thing led to another, and—"

"And so you KILLED him?!" Juliet shouts. "You KILLED HIM for

SASSING YOU? Dear God, one murder I can handle in a husband, but two in ONE WEEK? I don't know you at all! You just kill anyone who gets in your way, don't you?"

"JULIET, it's not like that—" you begin, but she interrupts you.

"What happens when we have our first fight, Romeo?" she demands. "Huh? Do you kill ME then too?"

The first watchman returns from the tomb. "I found Paris's body stashed in a corner. MUTILATED."

"Look, I JUST DRAGGED HIM DOWN THE STAIRS," you say. "I didn't INTEND to mutilate him."

"What do you want us to do?" the watchmen asks Juliet.

She looks into your eyes, searching.

"Please," you say. "It was an accident."

"Take him away," she says.

You're brought to Verona Jail, where you spend the rest of your days. You never see Juliet again. You do hear from her, once when she sends you annulment papers, and another time a few days later when she sends you a note. It reads: "Just so you know, the only reason you're still alive is that killing you would be how you'd solve your problems, and I'm better than that. I'm better than you."

She lives a very long, very interesting, and very satisfying life. You, in marked contrast, live only the first part of that!

THE END

407 You are Romeo! You've been reading books in Mantua's library, which I'm confident I don't need to remind you of since you were clearly Romeo this whole time and you've obviously been paying attention.

The librarian, seeing that you've successfully negotiated your way through his book without dying, regretfully removes his dagger from your throat.

"You have bested my volume of interactive fiction," he whispers, "and for that, I commend you. Few people beat hard mode. Few people PLAY hard mode either, but, well, here we are." He presses a small medallion into your hands before wandering back to the stacks and sorting the returns.

You look at the medallion. It has some laurel wreath embossed around the words "I'M A SPECIAL GUY AND I'M NOT AFRAID TO READ." It's mega embarrassing and you never intend to wear it.

You put the medallion in your pocket and rub your neck thoughtfully. Mostly what you're thinking is, "This is a weird library."

Alright! Let's continue!

Keep being Romeo: *turn to 292.*

Hah hah I don't wanna be in a LIBRARY, be Juliet instead: *turn to 424.*

408 Okay, your choice! You begin to awaken from your drug-induced slumber. You remember the dream you had: you were in a forest, only it WASN'T a forest, and you were supposed to make people fall in love, only it wasn't REALLY love, and—

You hear someone talking. You wake up the rest of the way, your mind instantly entirely forgetting about the dream/book you just had/ read, which makes me REAL GLAD I spent all that time writing it.

You open your eyes. You're lying on your back in an open coffin. Alright, so far so good! You sit up quickly and discover you're inside your family's crypt. Friar Lawrence is here.

"Oh, hey Friar," you say. "Those drugs were MAD effective, but I think I'm back to normal. I remember who and what I am. Where's my Romeo?"

You notice how worried the Friar looks. "Juliet," he says slowly, "come from that nest of death, contagion, and unnatural sleep: a greater power than we can contradict hath thwarted our intents."

It's a lot of fancy language for someone who just woke up, and you stare at him blankly. "Wha?" you say. "Huh?"

He grabs your shoulders and spins you around. "Okay LOOK," he says, "there's your husband. He made some bad decisions and killed himself. Oh, and Paris is dead too, again, I'd wager, due to Romeo's crappy choices. But hah hah oh well there's nothing we can do about that! Come on, let's get out of here before the cops show up. Check it: I'm gonna dispose of you among a sisterhood of nuns."

"You're not disposing of me anywhere," you say. "I'm staying right here." The Friar sees your determination, shakes your hand firmly, then turns and runs out of the crypt.

You get out of your coffin and examine the bodies of both your husband AND your emergency backup husband, and conclude two things: first, that they are indeed definitely dead, and second, that the world you've woken up into is pretty stupid and dumb. You left Romeo alone for just forty-two hours—FORTY-TWO HOURS, not even two days!—and in that time he apparently managed not ONLY to commit murder AGAIN, but also to get himself killed by his own fool hands. All this while he was supposed to be banished and nowhere near Verona! Ridiculous.

This is indeed the darkest and/or stupidest timeline.

You poke Romeo in the belly with your foot, and the bottle of poison he was holding rolls out of his hand.

"What's here? A cup, closed in my true love's hand?" you say, needlessly informing the empty room of what I just told you.

Bail on Verona, it sucks now: *turn to 428.*

Bail on life, it sucks now: *turn to 420.*

409 Romeo pulls off his shirt, but he's not a superhero. He's just regular old Romeo. Juliet doesn't reveal any mutant powers because she doesn't have any. You don't control reality here, okay? You just control TWO TEENS, and all they really want to do is boink each other.

Don't forget your place, buddy.

Also, while you are making Romeo and Juliet do the stupid things, they get discovered by guards. The guards are running towards them, fully intent on ending them.

"HALT!" one screams. "PREPARE TO DIE!" screams the other. "I'M THE BEST AT WHAT I DO," screams a third, "AND WHAT I DO IS MURDER TRESPASSERS!!"

Control the guards!! *Turn to 423.*

410 I let him see me think about it for a bit, and then I let him talk. Five minutes later Mr. Scared and Helpful's knocked out on the bed, the fish has her food, and I'm on my way to end this once and for all.

Doesn't take me too long to pull my horse up to where Benvolio's holed up. I don't know what Benvolio's thinking on the other side of that door. Maybe he's wracked with guilt. Maybe he's thinking he got away with it. But I know one thing: Benvolio here isn't expecting to be found, because the door's unlocked. Sometimes life makes things easy, and I've learned it's best not to ask why.

I kick open the door: Benvolio's lying on the bed in his pajamas, wide-eyed as a baby and screaming just as loudly. I leap on top of him and punch his head: once, twice, three times, one right after the other. He screams and holds his temples. I put my finger to his lips and tell him to answer my questions, nice and quick, nice and quiet.

Boy's got enough sense to give me what I want.

I like him already.

I interrogate Benvolio: *turn to 440.*

I kill Benvolio: *turn to 398.*

411 Romeo/you sneaks towards the ninja guards. You've never taken down ninjas before.

On the other hand, THEY'VE never taken down a Romeo before either, so it should be a fair fight.

Now that Romeo/you is moving into place, where should Juliet/you go?

Send Juliet to join Romeo with the ninja guards: *turn to 470.*

Send Juliet to the punk guards instead: *turn to 452.*

412 You hold the vial in front of your face, turning it slightly, watching how it catches the candlelight in your room. All you have to do is drink this, and when you wake up, all your problems will be over!

You're about to chug it when you start to worry about everything that could go wrong.

 Express your worries in the fanciest language possible: *turn to 422.*

Express your worries in slide-show format: *turn to 435.*

413

"Well, I guess that's it for me here in Verona," you say. "My parents want me to marry someone I don't want to marry, AND don't want to hear that I'm already married, so I'm off to Mantua to go live with my husband. Later, Angelica!"

Angelica pleads with you to stay, going so far as to say Paris is a step up from Romeo. You laugh in her face. "I cannot believe you'd suggest that this Paris person my father has been vetting for me would be a better match than the person I randomly met at a party two days ago," you say as you kick her out of your room. "Ridiculous."

With her gone you spend a few minutes gathering up your things, wrapping them up in a polka-dotted sheet that you then loop over a stick. Now you'll be able to carry your belongings easily by resting them on your shoulder. You don't know this, Juliet, but that's called a "bindle"!

"Ah," you say, looking over your handiwork. "I have constructed the perfect hobo stick."

Told you you didn't know what it was called.

You lean out over your balcony and throw your bindle out over the edge, then climb down Romeo's sex ladder.

"Or, alternatively, I COULD always check with Friar Lawrence to see if he has any suggestions before I abandon my life here entirely," you say. "Either way."

Go see the Friar: *turn to 457.*

Go live with Romeo in Mantua: *turn to 443.*

414

You decide to kill yourself! Lucky for you you've got just the thing in a bottle in your pocket, huh? But before you drink your poison, you figure you'll do some talkin'. How fancy do you want these talkin' words to be?

 I'm about to die!! ULTIMATE FANCY. *Turn to 451.*

Um, nobody's around to hear them, so what's the point? Gimme the exact opposite of fancy words, please. *Turn to 434.*

415 "Condemned villain," Paris says. "I've caught you. Come with me or die." He does make a good point, Romeo. You WERE banned from Verona.

"Alright, alright, you got me," you say. "But before you take me in, will you do a condemned man one favor?"

"What's that?" Tom says.

You sit down and pat the ground beside you, smiling. "Have a drink with me."

Tom looks at you suspiciously. "Well," he says, "I DID come here to cry over my dead fiancée, but I suppose drinking over my dead fiancée would work just as well." He pauses, then resheathes his sword. "Alright, ONE DRINK. And then you're coming with me."

"That's the spirit," you say, and he sits down beside you. You pull the bottle of poison out of your pocket, the one that your pharmacist said would kill someone with the strength of 20 men.

"This is the good stuff," you say, turning the bottle over in your hands. "It's really expensive, so I normally like to save it for special occasions. But no time like the present, right?" You pass the bottle to Paris. "Would you like to drink, say . . . AT LEAST ONE TWENTIETH OF THIS BOTTLE??"

"WOULD I??" Paris says, grabbing the bottle from you and chugging from it. He puts the cap back on the bottle, passes it to you, and drops dead instantly. Success, Romeo!

But then you hear a gasp come from the bushes. Someone saw you! You begin to speak very loudly, for the benefit of anyone listening in.

"WOW THIS PERFECT STRANGER WHO I DON'T EVEN KNOW JUST GOT REALLY SLEEPY! I'D BETTER DRAG HIM INTO THIS TOMB FOR A NAP. NOW TO PERUSE HIS FACE, BECAUSE I NEVER ACTUALLY SAW THE FACE OF THE MAN I WAS LITERALLY JUST DRINKING WITH. HMM, LOOKS LIKE THIS IS MERCUTIO'S KINSMAN, NOBLE TOM PARIS! SINCE HE'S NOT ALIGNED WITH EITHER THE CAPULETS OR THE MONTAGUES, I'D HAVE NO REASON TO KILL HIM, WHICH IS GREAT, BECAUSE I DIDN'T."

Your alibi sufficiently established, you smash the lock open and proceed down the tomb stairs, dragging Paris's body behind you.

Enter tomb: *turn to 425.*

416 You turn to your nurse.

"Okay, that was nuts," you say. "How do we stop this, Angelica? I'm still married to Romeo, and he's still alive, which means, ACCORDING

TO RELIGION, I can't marry anyone else. The only out I see is if Romeo dies, and I don't want to kill him. If I DID, I would've made that choice several minutes ago."

You sigh.

"Man! Sucks that heaven practices stratagems on someone as soft as me, am I right?" you say. Angelica doesn't say anything. "Come on," you say. "Comfort me, Nurse."

She looks at you. "Trade up to Paris," she says.

You're stunned. "What?" you say.

She smiles fondly and hugs you. "Look," she whispers into your ear, "your first marriage is done, Juliet. Enjoy your second. Besides, Paris has better eyes than Romeo. You like eyes, right?"

You push her away. "Seriously?" you say.

"Seriously," she says. "I'm speaking from my heart AND my soul here, Juliet. If I'm not, feel free to curse them both."

"Can do," you say.

"What?" she says.

"Nothing. Look, thanks for the comfort," you say. "And I gotta say, I now realize that I'm totally turned around on this 'marry a complete stranger on two days' notice' thing. Go tell my parents that I was wrong, and I'm sorry I made them angry, so now I'm off to Friar Lawrence's house to make confession and be absolved."

"I will," she says, and then she leaves.

"DANG," you say as soon as the door closes. "Well, that's it for me sharing my secrets with her. After praising my husband she'd DISpraise him with the same tongue?" You sigh. "Screw her," you say. "You know what? I actually AM gonna go see what Friar Lawrence says about all this. Maybe he'll have a solution. Even if he doesn't, I can always kill myself!"

You gather up some of your things (change of clothes, bindle, Bedroom Dagger, etc.) and begin to climb down Romeo's sex ladder to the ground below.

"Or, alternatively, I COULD always just go live with my husband in Mantua," you say. "Either way."

Go see the Friar: *turn to 457.*

Go live with Romeo in Mantua: *turn to 443.*

417

Hey Iago. Nice try. You're not in this adventure, buddy.

Alright fine, I'll be Juliet: *turn to 433.*

418 Gosh, I don't know . . . about the size of a small egg?

Okay. Cool. Gross. *Turn to 10.*

419 Juliet/you sneaks towards the punk guards. They look tough. You're PRETTY SURE you're tougher.

Now that Juliet/you is moving into place, where should Romeo/you go?

Send Romeo to join Juliet with the punk guards: *turn to 431.*

Send Romeo to the ninja guards instead: *turn to 452.*

420 "Well, this was fun," you say, "but I'm out. I don't want to live in a world created by such stupid, stupid choices."

You pick up Romeo's bottle of poison. Empty.

"How rude," you whisper.

Kiss him; there might be some poison left on his lips: *turn to 469.*

Use your muscles to pick up a coffin, then drop it on your own head: *turn to 444.*

Just stab yourself in the guts; you've still got that Bedroom Dagger, after all: *turn to 463.*

421 You, as Juliet, arrive at the ninjas, while you, as Romeo, sneak up behind the punks. Figuring that ninjas are probably used more to finesse than raw power, Juliet/you decides to take them head-on.

"Hey ninjas!" you shout. "Anyone order a knuckle sandwich??" The ninjas instantly leap into hiding places, swift and silent. "Because I've got lots of them here. Heck, I've got an all-you-can-eat buffet. You're SURE none of you are hungry??"

Meanwhile, Romeo/you has walked right into the middle of the punk guards. "Hey," you say. "I'm Romeo, the guy who got banished. Aren't you supposed to be killing me right now?" One of the punks

surrounding you comes at you with a knife, but this isn't your first rodeo. You grab his wrist, slam it down onto the ground, jump on it, break his fingers, take his knife from his bloody hand, and then turn to face your remaining attackers.

"Definitely not my first rodeo," you say. "Who's next?"

Nearby, Juliet/you runs to the nearest tree and starts shaking it. "Any ninjas up here?" you shout. "Because I'm ready to punch you!! To death, if necessary!!" No ninjas fall out of the tree, and if you're being honest with yourself you weren't really expecting them to, but you do hear the sound of a twig being stepped on behind you. You turn your head and find yourself face-to-face with—wait, what's a group of ninjas called? A doom? A team? A FREAKOUT?? Probably, right? Okay, so there's a freakout of ninjas behind you, Juliet. They're all carrying swords. You are carrying nothing and basically hugging a tree. "Oh, hey ninjas," you say. "Dudes, thy feet are pretty dang silent."

Elsewhere, the punks attack Romeo/you all at once, but you manage to jump backwards, ensuring that you're only taking on one at a time. You stab the closest punk in the eye. When you pull your knife out, his eye comes with it.

You find a GROSS EYE has been added to your inventory.

"Gross," you say. The next punk comes at you, and you stab him in the eye as well. His eye comes out with your blade as well.

You now have two GROSS EYE(S) in your inventory. They're on your knife like shish kebab. You pull off the two GROSS EYE(S) and throw them down in front of the third punk, who slips on them and falls down at your feet. For a change of pace, you stab him in the butt. You look up at the other punks, a crazed look in your eye.

"Did you SEE that? I just stabbed this guy in the BUTT!!" you scream to the remaining punks. "You really wanna mess with a dude who will stab other dudes in the butt?? BECAUSE I'M DOWN TO STAB WAY MORE BUTTS."

The other punks look at each other. They seem to conclude that they would not, and break off running in all directions.

Congratulations, Romeo! You have beaten the punks. You glance over to where Juliet is fighting the ninjas and see her get stabbed by fifteen of them all at the same time. Their swords actually get jammed on each other inside her guts. I hate to say it, Romeo, but Juliet/you is definitely, 100% dead.

But that's the bad news! The good news is, you're still Romeo and you just defeated a bunch of punks! How hard could killing some measly ninjas be, right??

Take revenge on the ninjas!! *Turn to 453.*

422 You hold up one hand in front of you.

"What if this mixture do not work at all?" you say. "Shall I be married then tomorrow morning?" You retrieve your Bedroom Dagger and lay it on the bed.

"No, no. This shall forbid it," you say. "Lie thou there."

As you sit down beside your knife, you're still worried. Maybe the Friar is trying to murder you? You rhetorically ask yourself the following:

> What if it be a poison, which the friar
> Subtly hath ministered to have me dead,
> Lest in this marriage he should be dishonored
> Because he married me before to Romeo?
> I fear it is.

He's a man of the cloth, Juliet. He's probably not trying to kill you.

"And yet, methinks, it should not," you say. "For he hath still been tried a holy man."

Okay, great! That's that worry resolved! Anything else?

You begin again:

> How if, when I am laid into the tomb,
> I wake before the time that Romeo
> Come to redeem me? There's a fearful point.
> Shall I not, then, be stifled in the vault
> To whose foul mouth no healthsome air breathes in,
> And there die strangled ere my Romeo comes?
> Or, if I live, is it not very like
> The horrible conceit of death and night,
> Together with the terror of the place—
> As in a vault, an ancient receptacle,
> Where for these many hundred years the bones
> Of all my buried ancestors are packed;
> Where bloody Tybalt, yet but green in earth,
> Lies festering in his shroud; where, as they say,
> At some hours in the night spirits resort—?
> Alack, alack, is it not like that I,
> So early waking, what with loathsome smells,
> And shrieks like mandrakes torn out of the earth,
> That living mortals, hearing them, run mad—?

I don't know what to tell you, Juliet. Probably you'll be fine? Look, time's a-wasting. Do you want to drink the poison or not?

Once more you speak to yourself:

Oh, if I wake, shall I not be distraught,
Environèd with all these hideous fears,
And madly play with my forefather's joints,
And pluck the mangled Tybalt from his shroud,
And, in this rage, with some great kinsman's bone,
As with a club, dash out my desperate brains?

I DON'T KNOW, JULIET. But I'm guessing that PROBABLY you won't be so scared when you wake up that you grab an ANCESTOR'S BONE and BASH IN YOUR OWN SKULL WITH IT. Are we drinking the poison here or not?

You remain silent, considering your fate. Suddenly, a ghost appears! Guess what? It's the ghost of Tybalt! And I promise he's here to look for Romeo, not because I'm just trying to get this story moving.

You look at the ghost and say the following:

Oh, look! Methinks I see my cousin's ghost
Seeking out Romeo, that did spit his body
Upon a rapier's point.

Methinks you do!!

Lower arm, talk to ghost: *turn to 468.*

 Forget the ghost, it's time to drink from this vial: *turn to 474.*

423
You are now controlling Romeo, and Juliet, AND the fifteen guards who discovered them. The guards who WERE running towards Romeo and Juliet suddenly stop in their tracks, many in mid-step. Most are off balance and fall over, and none of them make any move to cushion their fall. They just lie there on the ground, unmoving. Everyone else is just standing, silently, breathing only out of automatic respiratory instincts, waiting for you to decide for them to do something.

Listen: you're making this really weird and really creepy and this isn't how this book is supposed to be played. How about this: you move everyone back to where they were, and we'll make everyone forget this ever happened, and I'll start things over with Romeo moving towards the guards while Juliet creates a distraction. Doesn't that sound like fun? All that spy stuff with two sexy teens? Wow, that sounds like a fun time to me!

I GUESS: *turn to 438.*

No, you know what? This is actually perfect. Alright, now control all Capulets and Montagues and make them work things out. I am going to SOLVE the FRIGGIN' PROBLEMS. *Turn to 449.*

424
She's in a TOMB. You know that, right?

Better than a library! To Juliet! *Turn to 433.*

Okay fine, Romeo it is: *turn to 292.*

425
You leave Paris's body in a dark corner. "There," you say. "You're interred."

You turn around and see Juliet in her tomb, lying peacefully. It's crazy, she looks the same as she did when you saw her two days ago. She looks like she's just sleeping. But you put your hand to her neck, and there's no pulse. She's dead, Romeo.

 Kill yourself so you'll be together forever: *turn to 414.*

Cry over her, but let's not suicide juuuust yet: *turn to 406.*

426
You pivot on your heel and, turning around, run back towards the lions.

"What are you doing?!" shouts the gatekeeper. "Those sticks won't hold out forever! In fact, I wouldn't be surprised if they broke any second no—"

The gatekeeper is interrupted by the sounds of dozens of angry dogs and lions chomping through sticks in unison. They leap on you and tear your body apart. It's super gross. You have died.

Wow, Nurse: it really looks like you had . . . a mid-WIFE crisis??

THE END

Your final score was 999 points out of a possible 1000 points.

Restore: turn to 354.

Restart: turn to 217.

427 You raise one hand up in front of you and say,

O God! O Nurse, how shall this be prevented?
My husband is on earth, my faith in heaven.
How shall that faith return again to earth,
Unless that husband send it me from heaven
By leaving earth? Comfort me. Counsel me.—
Alack, alack, that heaven should practice stratagems
Upon so soft a subject as myself.—
What sayst thou? Hast thou not a word of joy?
Some comfort, Nurse.

"Trade up to Paris," she says. You're stunned.

"Speakest thou from thy heart?" you ask.

"From my heart AND my soul," she says. "If I'm not, curse them both."

"Amen!" you say.

"What?" she says.

You wave away her question and smile. "Well, thou hast comforted me marvelous much," you say, trying to make it sound sincere. "Go in, and tell my lady I am gone, having displeased my father, to Lawrence's cell to make confession and to be absolved."

"I will," she says, and then gets up to leave. You turn and watch her exit your room, your arm raised in front of you the entire time. The door closes behind her with a soft click. Then you hiss,

> *Ancient damnation! O most wicked fiend!*
> *Is it more sin to wish me thus forsworn,*
> *Or to dispraise my lord with that same tongue*
> *Which she hath praised him with above compare*
> *So many thousand times? Go, counselor.*
> *Thou and my bosom henceforth shall be twain.*
> *I'll to the Friar to know his remedy.*
> *If all else fail, myself have power to die.*

You lower your arm, gather up some of your things (change of clothes, bindle, Bedroom Dagger, etc.), and begin to climb down Romeo's sex ladder to the ground below.

"Or, alternatively, I COULD always just go live with my husband in Mantua," you say. "Either way."

 Go see the Friar: *turn to 457.*

Go live with Romeo in Mantua: *turn to 443.*

428
"Well, this was fun," you say, "and I'm sorry, but Verona sucks now. I'm out."

You make your way up the stairs. At the top of the stairs, you run into a watchman. "We heard reports of dead bodies being found here?" he says. "I mean, like, recently dead?"

"Down there," you say, motioning over your shoulder. "Looks like Romeo Montague killed Tom Paris and then himself. And before you ask, NO, I have NO IDEA why he did that.

"I only ever knew him for two days," you add. "He seemed to make bad decisions though. I think he might've been touched in the head."

The watchman rushes past you, down the stairs.

"There never was a dude who was more slow," you shout after him, "than he who did those murders: Romeo!"

"Okay!" the watchman shouts back up. "I'm busy with investigating a crime scene now!"

You walk up the stairs and out into the starry night. The world stretches out in front of you cast in the pale glow of the moon. You feel like you can go anywhere. Do anything.

You stroll out of the graveyard. It feels good, so you keep strolling until you've walked right past Verona's city limits. That feels even better, so you keep on going. You've never been this far from home before. You don't know when you'll stop, but you do know that when you do, it'll be somewhere new. Somewhere you can make a fresh start. Somewhere far, far away from Capulets and Montagues and Verona and death.

And Juliet, it's a beautiful night for a walk.

THE END

429 I give Benvolio a good reason to stay put, tying his unconscious body to his bed and wiping the blood off my fists on his shirt. I arrive at Mercutio's place not too long after. Figure a direct approach is my best choice here, so I walk right up and knock on the door. A dead man answers.

"Mercutio," I say. "Just the guy I've been looking for. You're the man who flipped Benvolio and killed Lady Montague."

Mercutio moves at me with his hands, too fast. He shoves something into my mouth. I bite down on him, and he screams, but even as he does I can feel something liquid sliding down my throat. It's not his blood: that comes a second later. It's the thing in his hands.

Poison, I realize, as foam starts to rise in my gullet.

I bite down harder, holding on to the bones in his fingers. He screams, punching me with his free arm. I don't let go. I know the blood in his hand is mixing with whatever poison's left in my mouth, and the longer I hold him, the longer it'll mix.

Finally I can't stand any more. I relax my jaw and collapse onto the ground. I see his feet: he staggers too, falling beside me. Blood squirts out of his hand in regular, slowing spurts. The world's going gray. I know I'm dying, and yeah, it feels as bad as you think. I hold tight to one thought: Mercutio killed someone, but it cost him his life too. But the thing is, I screwed up my case just as badly as Mercutio did. Both of us blew it. Neither of us got what we wanted. Yeah, it's embarrassing.

I know what whoever finds us is going to see: two bodies, both alike.

Indignity.

THE END

430 Seeing as you're controlling both Romeo and Juliet, it's trivial to coordinate a high five. In fact, after the high five, you double high five, then do an incredibly fast secret handshake involving slaps, fist bumps, chest slams, backflips, and double roundhouse spin-kicks where your feet connect in the air. You're making it up as you go along, both of you, two minds imagining the same thing at the same time, and it's incredible. It's unprecedented.

It's the greatest high five of all time.

"Let's take care of the rest of the guards," Romeo/you thinks. "Already on it," Juliet/you thinks in reply.

Silent, hand-in-hand, you move towards Capulet Castle. The next set of guards is up ahead.

They're in two groups: one up ahead to your left, the other to the right. The ones to the left look like they're street punks slapped into guard uniforms. The ones to the right look less physically intimidating, but they do look smarter. Also, their uniforms are different. Romeo/you and Juliet/you confer and conclude: yes, they are definitely probably ninjas.

You're sure either one of you can pass for a guard briefly, but eventually your disguise will be penetrated. Now isn't the time for distractions. Now is the time to TAKE DOWN THESE GUARDS AS QUICKLY AND EFFICIENTLY AS POSSIBLE.

You're in control here! What do you do?

Send Romeo to the punk guards: *turn to 445*.

Send Romeo to the ninja guards: *turn to 411*.

Send Juliet to the punk guards: *turn to 419*.

Send Juliet to the ninja guards: *turn to 456*.

431 Romeo/you and Juliet/you sneak towards the punks together, making sure not to attract any ninja attention.

"I'm stronger," Juliet/you whispers to Romeo/you. "Let me take them."

"You don't know how these guys fight," Romeo/you says to Juliet/you. "It's dirty. Let me go first, and then follow my lead." You are surprised to be arguing with yourself, but a lot of this experience is new, so you decide to go with it. Romeo/you stands up and walks directly towards the punk guards. "Hey," you say. "I'm Romeo, the guy who got banished. Aren't you supposed to be killing me right now?"

The punks surround you. One comes at you with a knife, but this isn't your first rodeo. You grab his wrist, slam it down onto the ground, jump on it, break his fingers, take his knife from his bloody hand, and then turn to face your remaining attackers.

"Hey Juliet," you say. "My gift to you!" You toss the bloody knife over the heads of the punks to Juliet/you, and as Juliet, you catch it easily because you totally knew this toss was coming. The punks turn around to see who this "Juliet" person is, and while they're doing that, Romeo/you kicks them in the knees from behind, sending them to the ground, at which point Juliet/you stabs them all in the butts, one by one. She's a blur of action, all muscle and knife. You love her more than ever.

"Pain-in-the-butt punks," you say with a grin.

As Juliet, you laugh out of politeness.

As Romeo, you are really stoked that Juliet laughed at your one-liner!

You look around and remember that there are still the ninjas left. "Come on," you say to Juliet/you. "We just defeated a bunch of punks! Let's finish the job! How hard could killing some measly ninjas be, right??"

"Could be tricky," Juliet/you says. "Ninjas are, you know, TRAINED."

"So what do we do?" Romeo/you asks.

As Juliet, you begin to go through the pockets of the dead butt-stabbed punks. You find one folded-up piece of paper in a punk's back pocket. There's a stab hole in it. You unfold it and read:

IMPORTANT NOTICE FOR ALL GUARDS:
AS OF TODAY, NEW RULES ARE IN
PL[STAB HOLE]OR ALL EMPLOYEES OF THE
VERONA GUARD SERVI[STAB HOLE]DER
TO REDUCE THE NUMBER OF REGULAR
NON-CRIMINAL VERONANS WHO KEEP
GETTING KILLED BY OUR PUNKS AND
NINJ[STAB HOLE]OM NOW ON, ANYONE WHO
SAYS THE SECRET PHRASE MUST BE
ALLOWED TO PASS. THIS MONTH'S
SECRET PHRASE IS "[STAB HOLE]"

"Aw man!" Romeo/you says. "Now we don't know the secret phrase!!"

Juliet/you looks at him. Turning the paper over, Juliet/you flattens out the paper around the stab holes so that the words printed there are now visible, and then passes the flattened note to Romeo/you.

You read it and look up. "The secret phrase is 'Sin from thy lips,'" Romeo/you says.

"Gross," Juliet/you says.

"I kinda like it," Romeo/you says.

"Dude, it sounds like it's describing someone throwing up," Juliet/you says.

Go tell the ninjas the secret word: *turn to 442.*

432

You pull out your Bedroom Dagger that you grabbed earlier. The Friar is stunned to see the blade. Before he can stop you, you hold the knife to the side of your neck. One small push and it'd go right in.

"God joined my heart and Romeo's," you say, "and you joined our hands." You can feel the point of your blade pressing against your neck, and you increase the pressure a little. You look up at him and smile as you feel a trickle of blood running down your neck.

"I'll kill myself before another man touches either of them, Friar," you say. "So it seems to me that you've got two options: you can get off your butt and help me figure a way out of this . . ."

You pause, pushing the blade into your neck just a little bit farther.

"Or you can watch," you say.

The Friar looks at you, completely gobsmacked. It appears things just got real. His mouth opens and closes a few times. He seems too stunned to speak. You can feel your shirt absorbing the blood from your neck. You keep the knife where it is.

"I wouldn't wait too much longer to decide, Friar," you say just as sweetly as can be.

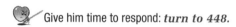 Give him time to respond: *turn to 448.*

Forget it, I'm out of here: *turn to 460.*

433

You are Juliet! Remember how you took some chemicals that mimic death for 42 hours? Well that time's not up yet!

You want to be Romeo for a while? He's at least, you know, conscious.

Alright, be Romeo: *turn to 458.*

No, this adventure has actually been going on for quite a while and I could use the rest. I'll just sleep until it's over. *Turn to 408.*

434
You got it!

You kneel in front of Juliet's coffin and peer into it. "At least she's still hot," you say.

Still on your knees, you shuffle over to Tybalt's coffin. "Tybalt, sorry I killed you," you say. "Hey, dude, would you feel better if I killed the man who killed you? WITH THE VERY SAME HANDS??" You wave your hand in front of Tybalt's face. "Because I'm gonna."

You shuffle back to Juliet and peer down at her face. "Dang, still smokin' hot," you declare. "What a babe. Alright, well, you know I'm not the kind of guy who'll leave such a CHOICE piece of tail behind, so obviously I'm gonna stay entombed here with my hot hot wife forever."

Standing up, you stare at her intently. "Babe, that was me checking you out for the last time," you say.

Then you pick her up and hug her, making sure to squeeze her butt a few times. "Babe, that was me feeling you up for the last time," you whisper into her ear.

Then you kiss her. "And yeah babe, obviously that was me going to town on your lips for the last time," you say. Then you let her fall back into her coffin as you stand up, wiping your mouth with the back of your hands. "Alright!" you say. "Show's over. Romeo's out, NERDS."

You chug the poison. "Hot damn, that pharmacist made some kick-ass poison," you whisper, and then you die.

"Wait wait wait, before I die I wanna kiss my hot wife again," you say suddenly, crawling over to Juliet. After you kiss her, you die for real this time. "Bleh," you say.

Romeo, what I say now I say without any traces of hyperbole or exaggeration: that was the single worst death scene I've ever witnessed. I feel like I got stupider watching it, and at the end of it I was glad you were dead, if only because it meant you'd stop talking to, kissing on, and feeling up corpses without their consent. Gah.

Anyway, game over, the end, flights of angels sing thee to thy rest, and get the heck out of my face.

Accept that I'm dead: *turn to 441.*

Wait, let me be Juliet! I PROMISE I'll do better. *Turn to 461.*

435
You sit down and prepare a slide presentation, using your Bedroom Dagger to cut out pieces of construction paper and your paints to draw on them. Soon it's completed, and now you can express your thoughts clearly and in point form, the stacks of paper "sliding" off of each other during any real or imagined presentation! Here's what they look like:

SHOULD I DRINK THIS VIAL OF MYSTERIOUS LIQUID: A SLIDE PRESENTATION

By Juliet Capulet

WHAT IF IT DOESN'T WORK?

- Might have to get married tomorrow
- Hah hah j/k, I'll stab myself first

WHAT IF IT'S ACTUALLY DESIGNED TO KILL ME?

- Maybe Friar Lawrence wants to kill me?
  - Not really though, he's a friar
- Okay nevermind

WHAT IF I WAKE UP TOO SOON?

- I might:
  - Suffocate?
    - air quality likely terrible inside a literal tomb
  - Survive?
    - which is good but what if it's spooky in there??
    - probably it is

THINGS THAT ARE SPOOKY IN TOMBS:

- Bones
- Tybalt's corpse (not in all tombs but in this case there's one)
- Other corpses
- Ghosts!
  - Screaming ghosts??
  - Enough to drive me insane???
- Plus it WILL smell

THINGS THAT I MIGHT DO IN A SPOOKY TOMB:

- Go insane
- Mess with Tybalt's dead body
- Bash in my own skull with an ancestor's bones!!

THANK YOU

- I hope we all learned a lot

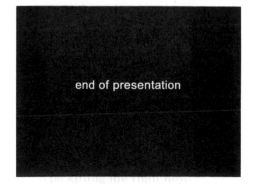

end of presentation

You're looking over your handiwork proudly when you notice there's a ghost here. You quickly throw your slides into your bedroom fireplace, so they won't give away your scheme to ghosts or anyone else.

"Oh, look!" you say. "I think I see my cousin's ghost. He's probably looking for Romeo, since Romeo stabbed him to death."

Talk to ghost: *turn to 468.*

Forget the ghost, it's time to drink from this vial: *turn to 474.*

436 You track down Romeo in a local library, lost in a book.

"Guess who?!" you say, running up to him from behind and hugging him.

"Juliet?" he says, dropping his book in shock. "Juliet!" You kiss him, and you kiss him some more, and finally you pull back to speak.

"Hey, my parents wanted me to marry someone else and then disowned me, so I ran away from home to live with you," you say.

"That's perfect! We can be together forever now!" he says. "So how much gold did you steal from your parents when you left?"

"Oh," you say. "Um, I didn't think of that. I actually decided to run away after I already left the house. I guess I stole these . . . nice clothes I'm wearing? Oh. Also a horse. And a dagger."

"A dagger?" he says.

"Yeah, in case I want to stab someone!" you say. "OR MYSELF," you add significantly.

"Oh," he says. "Well . . . I suppose we'll get by. My parents can't send me money with this banishment in place, but I'm sure we'll be fine. We have each other, right? We'll live on our love, and, if necessary, eat our horses."

"Or we could go back to Verona and rob my parents," you say. "They're jerks now."

Live happily ever after in Mantua: *turn to 280.*

Go home and rob your parents, THEN live happily ever after in Mantua: *turn to 270.*

437 "Yes," you say. "However, I now am really confident that she's actually totally fine. Hey, while you're here, could you run out once more and get some presents for Juliet?"

"Presents?" Balthasar says.

"Yeah, some nice meats, maybe some fancy cheeses—you know what? We should have a picnic! Get some wine too. Oh! And a red-and-white-checkered tablecloth."

"Okay, uh, that'll take me a couple of minutes," Balthasar says.

"No rush," you say. "We'll leave when you get back."

He returns shortly with an adorable-looking picnic basket, and, satisfied, the two of you ride to Verona. On the way there, Balthasar is yammering on about boring stuff, so instead of listening you break out your pen and paper and write a letter to your (Romeo's) parents. It reads as follows:

> *Dear Mom and Dad,*
>
> *It's me, your son Romeo! If you are reading this, then you probably already know that Juliet isn't really dead. We just faked her death to get her out of marrying Tom Paris who sucks so bad!! I can't even believe how much he sucks. Also, Juliet, who is awesome, already married me (Romeo).*
>
> *P.S.: She's the greatest!!*
>
> *P.P.S.: Hey, I bet now that we're married if you talked to the Capulets they'd be willing to end your blood feud!*
>
> *P.P.P.S.: I love Juliet a lot because she's so great; I can never take this back.*

You are extremely satisfied with your letter. You fold it up into your pocket and continue riding to Verona. At one point you consider getting flowers for Juliet, but you're pretty sure she'd much rather have the awesome picnic.

You arrive outside Capulet Crypt shortly after midnight. The door to the crypt is ajar, its lock lying broken on the ground beside it. Looks like someone else is inside Juliet's crypt!

You rush down into the darkness of the crypt and find it's actually . . . pretty crowded? Friar Lawrence is there, as is Tom Paris (eugh), and Juliet's there too! She's alive and well and the feeling you get when you see her makes you feel funny inside.

Okay, enough of this; be Juliet again: *turn to 459.*

Naw, man, keep being Romeo: *turn to 450.*

438 The guards get up and walk to where they were originally. Nobody talks or coughs or makes any unnecessary movement. Romeo and Juliet take a few steps backwards. Their arms and legs make slight adjustments as they restore themselves to their initial positions, down to the micron.

Everything is quiet, unblinking. All you can hear are the sounds of distant crickets.

Alright. Give up control of the guards, then send Romeo to sneak past the guards up ahead while Juliet creates a distraction: *turn to 394.*

439
"There must be something we can do," you say. "What do you suggest?"

"Well," the Friar says, "I mean, you COULD fake your own death for forty-two hours. I got a vial that makes that happen in people. It's not even a big deal."

"That's crazy," you say.

"Yeah, no, I can see why you'd say that," he says. "Alright, here's another option, and it's crazy, Juliet, but it JUST MIGHT WORK."

"Yes?" you say.

"You could fake PARIS'S death for forty-two hours instead," he says.

"That's even crazier!" you say. "That's fake attempted murder and won't solve anything and will, in fact, only create extra problems for me!"

You take a deep breath to calm yourself. "Listen, Friar," you say, "do you have any solutions that don't involve someone faking their death for forty-two hours?"

He stares at you for a long moment. "I don't understand," he says.

Fine, fake my own death: *turn to 471.*

This is crazy, I'm not faking death! I'll just go home and explain the situation to my mom. *Turn to 465.*

440
The way Benvolio tells it, Mercutio had been bending his ear for weeks, whispering about how the Montague/Capulet fight was destroying Verona, hurting people, getting people killed. Saying how the two families were equally matched, and if nobody did anything, they'd keep fighting forever. Saying how the only way to minimize bloodshed was to break the détente, let one side win once and for all. Short-term pain. Long-term gain. It didn't really matter which side won, as long as one of them lost.

And wouldn't you know it, my boy Ben volunteered.

Oh, it couldn't be him who died, of course. Mercutio needed a lord or lady out of the picture if he was going to destabilize one family enough for the other to take over. But once they were out of the picture, Verona would at last have the peace, order, and good government it deserved. Mercutio made it sound so reasonable. And he asked Ben for so little, really. Nothing that would be beyond the reach of a reasonable man who, like him, only seeks the greater good. Just one tiny thing.

All Ben had to do was swear, when the moment came, that he'd drag Mercutio away after a fight and no matter what he saw, tell everyone that he died. Mercutio would take care of the rest, and that'd be Verona's problem taken care of. One soul to ensure the future for thousands: was that really such dreadful algebra to calculate?

Solve for x.

That moment came for Ben a few days ago. Mercutio saw his chance. Picked a fight with Tybalt. Got himself stabbed. Ben dragged the dying man away from prying eyes, and that was it. All he could say was that Mercutio swallowed something—poison, he thinks, to speed things along, to help end the pain—and then that was it. Mercutio was dead.

The story doesn't make sense, but I've been around long enough to know Ben thinks he's telling the truth. He's a patsy. I know men like Mercutio. Men like Mercutio don't kill themselves. They laugh, they joke, they make you think you're their best friend, and then they use you until there's nothing left and throw you to the curb.

The pieces are finally fitting together. Mercutio decides he's gonna upset the balance of power between Montague and Capulet by killing one of them. He's close to both sides, and I wouldn't be surprised to find out he'd been grooming both Montagues and Capulets, but Benvolio flipped first. He starts the fight, sees a moment to take a hit, and takes it. All he needs to do is squeeze a bladder full of sheep's blood out from under his armpit as he's being dragged away and the whole world thinks he's a goner. And now he's got an alibi to kill for, because nobody is ever going to suspect the dead man.

Except me.

There's just one thing Mercutio couldn't have planned for. It's not even Romeo's and Juliet's suicides: that works for him. But after their bodies turned up, Friar Lawrence came clean. Turns out he was the one who supplied Juliet with a "fake your own death" serum as part of a scheme to get her and Romeo together. And this serum has been the talk of the town ever since.

The way I see it, that's the pill Mercutio dosed himself with after the fight. He "dies," establishes Benvolio's alibi and his own at the same time, then wakes up in a crypt the next day. He busts his way out, kills Lady M, and lies low until this blows over.

I don't know what his endgame is: maybe he leaves town. Maybe he comes back after the heat has died down as a long-lost brother or twin or God knows what else and everyone lives happily ever after. But either way, his plan's worked. He's gotten away with it.

That is, of course, until now.

I take Benvolio with me to confront Mercutio: *turn to 446.*

Benvolio's a wild card. I go after Mercutio the way I do everything: alone. *Turn to 429.*

441 Well, good. Because you ARE dead.
Enjoy, thanks for playing!!

THE END

442 The two of you walk past the ninjas, chanting "sin from thy lips" over and over. You never actually spot any ninjas (they're very good at hiding), but they do let you pass unmolested. It's nice you didn't have to kill anyone!

After that it's relatively easy to sneak into Capulet Castle and steal all the cool things. The two of you again make your way past the ninjas easily, return to your horses that you parked by the bushes, and load up your stolen goods.

"That was fun and easy," the two of you say in unison. "Hmm . . . should we hit up the Montagues too?"

Rob Romeo's parents too: *turn to 447.*

No, one family is enough: *turn to 466.*

443
You steal one of your parents' horses and ride to Mantua.

Awesome! Start a new life in Mantua!! *Turn to 436.*

444
"Of course!" you whisper. "I forgot about my awesome muscles!"

You pick up the stone coffin of some ancient ancestor and, using your muscles, hold it up over your head. It's really heavy. You feel like it's taking most of your muscles just to keep it there. You're not sure how much longer you can hold it up . . . but you are actually really interested in finding out.

About thirty seconds later some guards enter the crypt and find you there, standing beside Romeo's body, holding a giant stone coffin over your head. You're exhausted.

"Held it for thirty seconds!" you announce. "I'm going to drop this on myself now, but I want you to weigh this coffin and put it down in my obituary, because this has got to be a record one-rep max."

The guards do so (mostly because they had to lift it up anyway to get your body out from under it, and once it was up it was no big deal to put a scale underneath before setting it back down) and it turns out the coffin (with skeleton) weighed 263.5 kilograms, or about 580 pounds. Juliet: that's a world record for weight lifted by a human!

So in summary and in conclusion, you got the guy, got married, did some drugs, had a cool nap, AND set a weight-lifting record just before you peaced out. I'm impressed, and I award you 263.5 kilograms of points!!

THE END

P.S.: That's a lot!

---

445 Romeo/you sneaks towards the punk guards. They look tough. You'll just have to be tougher.

Now that Romeo/you is moving into place, where should Juliet/you go?

Send Juliet to join Romeo with the punk guards: *turn to 431.*

Send Juliet to the ninja guards instead: *turn to 421.*

446 I tell Benvolio we're going for a stroll, and we go to Mercutio's place. Figure a direct approach is my best choice here, so I walk right up and knock on the door. A dead man answers.

"Mercutio," I say. "Just the guy I've been looking for. You tricked Benvolio into being an accessory to your murder of Lady Montague."

Then I pull Benvolio over into the doorway so he can get a look at him. You know: sell my case a little. Make him sweat.

Mercutio moves at me with his hands, too fast. Turns out Benvolio really did just want the greater good, because he pushes himself in front of me, and whatever's in Mercutio's hands goes right into Benvolio's throat. The poor kid tried to save me and got a mouth full of poison for his trouble. Mercutio makes a break for it, but I can't leave the kid dying there on his friend's front porch. I bend over and shove my hand in his mouth, feeling around until I find the pill, and I pull it out. I take a sniff. Yeah, it's poison. But the pill's already cracked open, and it's too late for Benvolio.

I run into the house after Mercutio, but he's long gone, the back screen door gently flapping in the night breeze. He's run deep into the woods. Sure, I chase him into trees and brambles, and I tear some new holes in my clothes and skin for the trouble, but there's no trace of him. He's gone.

I return to his house and sit down out front, next to the cooling body of that poor sap Benvolio. Mercutio got what he wanted and what he was willing to kill for: a new normal in Verona. And he got away with it too. Nobody's gonna care that Mercutio's body is missing, and the cops aren't gonna believe he's the killer. They don't want to, and with the only proof I have escaped into the woods and my only witness dead beside me, they won't have to. They have their story and I have mine, and theirs is the only one anyone wants to hear.

There is one thing I can do, one thing I can deny to Mercutio. If I stay in Verona, then Mercutio will never be able to return here and enjoy the fruits of his deadly labor. As long as I still breathe, I'll be here to stop him. I'll build a life here. Maybe even make some new friends. Because I've found my place, and against the odds, it's here: fair Verona. Where I lay Benvolio—and at least a couple of my own demons—to rest.

I sit there with the dead man long enough to watch the sun come up, thinking about Truth and the things I do for her. I don't know if you could call this a happy ending. Sure I cracked the Lady Montague case, but Mercutio got away with murder. I didn't get my man.

But hey. At least I got the girl.

THE END

447 The two of you rob Romeo's parents in much the same way (that is to say, try a few times, figure out their weakness, and by doing so discern the correct course of action). You sneak back to your horses, load them up with even MORE gold, and ride back to Mantua.

Congratulations, you are now both super rich! And while it turns out money might not buy happiness in the general case, in the specific case wherein one is very poor and can't afford the necessities of life like food and clothing and diapers, money does in fact solve that problem very nicely and, in a very real way, purchase happiness! NICE!

News eventually reaches you of a giant wall being built around Verona. It seems both the Montagues and Capulets were SUPER CHEESED that they got robbed, and this has brought them together for their own protection. And the result of that teamwork is that now they're building a colossal stone barrier around the city! The goal is to ensure nobody can get in or out of Verona, ESPECIALLY WITH ANY STOLEN GOODS, but you're not too worried about it, since building a colossal wall takes time, which gives everyone who doesn't want to live in a walled city ruled by two ultraparanoid families plenty of opportunities to leave before it's completed. Most of them move to Mantua too.

The new protectivist attitude of Verona contributes to the city's decline, and to Mantua's becoming a major world city. A rising tide raises all boats, which means the two of you become EVEN RICHER.

When the two of you finally breach the crumbling walls of Verona many years later, you find only dust, debris, skeletons, and ghosts. But I'm afraid, Romeo and/or Juliet, that this is a story for another time!

THE END

P.S.: Okay the short version is the ghosts are possessing the skeletons and you gotta fight them now and it's AWESOME, but eventually you realize they're not as bad as they seem and learn a very important lesson about tolerance, which I guess is awesome too, but in a different way.

448 "Okay, okay, I've thought of something!" he says. "Geez, if you're so desperate you'll kill yourself, you're clearly desperate enough for one of my patented Friar Plans."

"What is it? Do you want me to jump off a tower? Walk alone in the bad parts of town?"

"No, I—" he begins.

"Hang out in a pit full of snakes?" you continue. "Chain myself up with wild bears? HIDE EVERY NIGHT IN A MORGUE FULL OF SMELLY DEAD BODIES WITH WET FLESH AND MISSING JAWBONES??"

"No, Juliet, you just need to—"

"Climb into a grave and snuggle up with a dead man in his very tomb? Sit on a tack? Eat a tack? Eat a whole BOX of tacks? EAT A WHOLE BOX OF TACKS AND THEN THROW UP THE TACKS AND THEN EAT THE VOMIT-COVERED TACKS??"

The Friar looks at you expectantly.

"I'm done now," you say.

"Look, this is easy," he says. "Just take this vial, and drink it when you're alone. Mix it with liquor if you're feelin' it. Either way, it'll make it look like you're dead for forty-two hours. Your parents will discover you, you'll be brought to the family tomb, and in the meantime I'll let Romeo know what's going on. He comes here, you wake up, he takes you to Mantua, and bingo bango: problem solved! Assuming you don't change your mind or become scared like a woman."

"I can—" you begin, then stop. "Alright, SEXISM ASIDE, the thing is—I can go to Mantua already?" you say. "Like, right now. I can literally get on my horse and go to Mantua right now."

"Oh Juliet," he says. "Poor, poor, naive Juliet. How could you possibly get to Mantua if your parents think you're still alive?"

You look at him like he's crazy.

". . . On a horse?" you say.

 Take the vial: *turn to 473.*

Screw this! Leave this crazy man and go to Mantua! *Turn to 467.*

449

You know the book's called *Romeo and/or Juliet*, not *Romeo and/or Juliet and/or All the Montagues and/or All the Capulets and/or Some Guards Too*, right? But you've left me no other choice, so here we go. Remember: this is what you wanted.

You control the Capulets and the Montagues. You make them end their strife and like each other. You even go so far as to make them build solid-gold statues of each other! Hah hah hah wow you're really happy with how much they like each other now!

Unfortunately the evening after the solid-gold statues are finished they get stolen by criminals, but since controlling the Montagues and Capulets means you're actually controlling a fair portion of Verona at this point, it's trivial for you to form a colossal mob to search the city with inhuman efficiency until the criminals are found. They've already melted down the statues, so you take control of the criminals and make them forge replacement gold statues, but this time with themselves alive inside them.

They were alive inside them at the start of the forging process, anyway.

You begin expanding your control to the rest of Verona, which begins to operate as if it's under the control of a single mind, which, of course, it is. The streets fall silent as its inhabitants no longer have any reason to talk to each other. Food is taken as quickly and efficiently as possible, and sleep is done in eight-hour shifts built around twenty-four-hour production.

From there you build outwards, expanding your influence until most of Europe is under your control. You then spread out to Africa, Australia, and before you know it, scouts you command are sailing to America. Within five years the entire planet falls under your leadership. Nothing happens without you choosing it to happen. The entire human population of Earth does exactly what you tell it to do. You're no longer choosing your own adventure. You're choosing EVERYONE'S.

From there, you start controlling the animals, preventing venomous snakes and other threats from affecting your projects. Animal species you see no productive purpose in simply starve themselves to death. Before long you're controlling even microbes, which you find oddly satisfying. They're so simple, so eager to please.

Within a decade, you are controlling all life on the planet. And I've got to hand it to you. You've come as close to controlling reality as is physically possible.

It's not enough.

You want more. You don't just want to control all life: life is merely the logical end result of the initial conditions of the universe. The true way to control events, ALL events, is to control those initial conditions. To control the laws of physics itself.

You turn the combined mental effort of every being on the planet towards this task. Never in history have so many minds worked towards a single purpose, all striving with their entire being towards it. And thousands of years later, you do it. Objects in motion don't tend to stay in motion unless you will them to. Apples don't fall from trees unless you decide that, yes, gravity is also going to affect them in this picosecond too. An entire cosmos of choices flows through you: nothing happens without your explicit consent. You are the totality of being. You are better than a mere god. You have become The Chooser.

Naturally, this insane level of micromanagement takes up all your time, so you decide to let life go back to making its own decisions. You're much too busy making sure each proton in everyone's bodies doesn't decide to decay into pions and positrons at the same time for absolutely no reason. The universe comes of age, and the life inside it begins to wonder what sort of god would rule over a universe where bad things happen to good people, and you're all, "Wow oh geez sorry your THIRD DOG died at age SIXTEEN which is ONE HUNDRED AND TWELVE IN FRIGGIN' DOG YEARS, I guess I was too busy making sure EVERY SUN DIDN'T EXPLODE AT THE SAME TIME, THANKS FOR NOTICING HOW THAT DIDN'T HAPPEN BY THE WAY??"

THE END

P.S.: Your final score is whatever you decide it to be. Look, man, I don't want any trouble.

450

"Juliet!" you shout. "It's me, Romeo! Um . . . how are you?"

"Romeo!" she shouts, leaping up. She runs to you and hugs you tightly. She's acting exactly how you would've reacted in her situation. Is that good? Bad?

After a moment, you hold her at arm's length. "Is everything fine, Juliet?" you ask. "Do you feel okay? Like, do you feel like . . . yourself?"

"Everything's perfect," she says, kissing your face. "I feel fine. The Friar's potion worked perfectly." Her hand touches yours, and she notices the picnic basket you're carrying. "And you brought a picnic!" she says. "You're the sweetest!"

You push her back again. "Really?" you say. "You don't feel at all different? You feel exactly like you always have?"

"Romeo, I'm fine," she says. And she looks fine! She's looking and acting completely normal. She turns and motions to Friar Lawrence and Paris. "Friar here was just explaining to Paris how I can't marry him because I'm already married to you," she says. "Paris is being pretty reasonable about the whole thing." Paris steps towards you and offers his hand. You shake it.

"Sorry man, my bad," Paris says. "Didn't know she was already married, you know?"

Juliet turns back to you. "So you see? Everything's perfect, and we're set! Let's go back to Mantua, have our picnic along the way, and then start our lives together and forget all about Verona until we live happily ever after or our parents stop fighting, whichever happens first!"

So that's what you do. And the more that time passes, the more you get used to being Romeo: the way his body looks. The way it feels. You even get pretty into the sex with Juliet! It's familiar, but in a different way than you're used to. It's fun. Occasionally it's even . . . surprising?

You grow older together. You usually sleep through the night, but sometimes your sleep doesn't last, and you wake up in the middle of the night to a world that's still. Quiet. Sometimes you look over to Juliet, sleeping peacefully beside you, as beautiful as ever, her chest slowly rising and falling with each breath. Sometimes you lift yourself up on one elbow, as quietly as you can, and you kiss her, softly, so softly, so she won't wake up.

And sometimes, as your lips press against her cheek, you wonder who you're actually kissing.

THE END

451 You kneel in front of Juliet's coffin and, looking up, raise one hand out in front of you. Here's what you shout to the heavens:

> *O my love, my wife!*
> *Death, that hath sucked the honey of thy breath,*
> *Hath had no power yet upon thy beauty.*
> *Thou art not conquered. Beauty's ensign yet*
> *Is crimson in thy lips and in thy cheeks,*
> *And death's pale flag is not advancèd there.*

You shuffle around on your knees to look at Tybalt's body. Arm still raised, you monologue:

> *Tybalt, liest thou there in thy bloody sheet?*
> *O, what more favor can I do to thee,*
> *Than with that hand that cut thy youth in twain*
> *To sunder his that was thine enemy?*
> *Forgive me, cousin.*

You shuffle back to Juliet.

> *Ah, dear Juliet, why art thou yet so fair? Shall I believe*
> *That unsubstantial death is amorous,*
> *And that the lean abhorrèd monster keeps*
> *Thee here in dark to be his paramour?*
> *For fear of that, I still will stay with thee,*
> *And never from this palace of dim night*
> *Depart again. Here, here will I remain*
> *With worms that are thy chamber maids. Oh, here*
> *Will I set up my everlasting rest,*
> *And shake the yoke of inauspicious stars*
> *From this world-wearied flesh. Eyes, look your last.*

You look at her.

"Arms, take your last embrace."

You hug her.

"And, lips, O you the doors of breath, seal with a righteous kiss a dateless bargain to engrossing death."

Finally, you kiss your dead wife. Her lips are actually warm still! Weird, right?

When you're done kissing her, you take your poison and place it in your still-upraised hand. Here's what you say:

Come, bitter conduct, come, unsavory guide.
Thou desperate pilot, now at once run on
The dashing rocks thy seasick, weary bark.
Here's to my love!

You take a long swig of your poison, making sure to drink it all, leaving not even one friendly drop behind. You instantly begin to feel unwell. The bottle falls from your hand, and you no longer have the strength to keep your hand raised in front of you.

"Aw dang y'all, these friggin' drugs work really friggin' fast! Daaaaaaang!!" you say, and then you die. Come ON, Romeo! After all those beautiful last words I gave you, THAT'S what you go out on? Geez.

Your final score is −1000 out of 1000 because I seriously can't believe you went out on "Aw dang y'all" after I wrote PAGES of free-form poetry for you. Ridiculous. RIDICULOUS.

Look, you're dead so I can't keep you around much longer—but if anyone asks, say you went out on "Thus with a kiss I die," okay? Because that's what I'M gonna be telling everyone. It's at least marginally less embarrassing for us both.

I honestly can't believe you, Romeo. Get the heck out of my face.

Accept that I'm dead: ***turn to 441.***

 Wait, let me be Juliet! I PROMISE I'll do better. ***Turn to 461.***

452 You, as Romeo, arrive at the ninjas, while you, as Juliet, sneak up behind the punks. Figuring that ninjas are probably better at sneaking than you are, Romeo/you abandons subtlety and just runs towards them.

"Ninjas costumes are for babies!" Romeo/you shouts while, at the same time, you as Juliet make a mental note to come up with a better line when you attack in a few seconds.

"PUNKS to meet you!" you say to the punks as you dramatically leap out of the shadows. The punks are scared. Good. You want them scared.

You look around at your startled enemies. They're tough. You're tougher. Their muscles are like, 88% as rad as your muscles, tops.

You direct your attention to Romeo/you, where you're running towards a bunch of ninjas, entirely unarmed, screaming at them. You're noticing how the ninjas have swords. You're noticing how you've abandoned the element of surprise, which was the only thing you had going for you. Then you look down and notice a sword sticking out of your belly with your gross-nasty guts all over it.

"Damn, Verona," you say, "thy ninjas are quick!" You collapse to the ground. You're pretty sure you're about to die. You look around desperately, trying to find some inspiration for the perfect dying words to go out on. "Thus," you say, "with my guts hanging out of my belly, I die."

Oh, Romeo. Better luck next time.

Meanwhile, Juliet/you is taking a lot of hits. One punk manages to kick you right in the chest, sending you staggering. It hurts. You didn't expect it to hurt so much. You're tough, but you haven't been in many fights before, and these punks are fighting dirty. Raw muscle, you're realizing much too late, isn't enough. While you're stumbling backwards, another punk slams a chair down across your neck, which sends you down to the ground. The punks surround you, kicking as hard as they can, and you're not sure how much more of this you can take.

Hey, remember when I said "better luck next time"? I think that next time is sneaking up on you pretty quickly.

You look up at the punks with hate in your eyes. "Let me die," you hiss, spitting out blood.

They oblige.

THE END

453

To answer my own rhetorical question, it turns out it's actually SURPRISINGLY DIFFICULT to kill some measly ninjas!!

THE END

454

You decide not to kill yourself after all. It's not your fault your husband was bad at not killing people and/or himself! Besides, you're not going to kill yourself over a boy, much less a boy you've only known for less than four days—less than two, actually, if you only count the days you were conscious! You make your decision just as the tomb guards come down the stairs and find you there with Romeo's body.

"Hello," you say. "As you can see, I was dead, but I've come back to life now. This is Romeo. He was dead here when I woke up. No big deal, okay? Let's all just forget about it."

The guards, however, fail to forget about it. In fact, they do the opposite! Word that Juliet Capulet—after a very public funeral—arose again two days later spreads quickly. You try to return to a normal life, but it's hard, you know? Especially with a cult forming around you no matter how you try to dispel it. Even shouting "My death was part of a complicated scheme involving marriage" doesn't placate them! And with Friar Lawrence having skipped town, nobody believes you when you tell them that "weird drugs" made you have "a cold and drowsy humor" and it's really not a big deal.

Your followers camp outside Capulet Castle hoping to get a glimpse of you. They start wearing bracelets that say "WWJD" (short for "What Would Juliet Do," alternatively, "Whoah, [remember] When Juliet Died??"). They make posters that say things like "JC Died for Your Sins, but She Got Better" and write operas with titles like *Juliet Capulet Superstar.*

Anyway, you're an adult now and the head of a major world religion. Your every word, action, and implication—intentional or otherwise—is interpreted and misinterpreted by complete strangers around the world, all of whom then credit or blame you for their successes or failures, the vast majority of which you were completely unaware of!

Enjoy!!

THE END

P.S.: Tell them to be excellent to each other!

455 You arrive back home to discover your parents talking to your nurse. They demand to know where you've been.

"Oh," you say, "I was at Friar Lawrence's place. Where I, um, learned to repent the sin of disobedient opposition?"

They still seem a little suspicious. You'd better sell this, Juliet!

You fall to your knees in front of them. "Oh, forgive me, I beg of you! From now on I will do whatever you say! From now on I am forever ruled by you!"

Your dad nods, satisfied. "It's credible you would say this," he says. Then he turns to a servant. "Get Paris. I'll make this wedding happen tomorrow morning."

"Yaaaay," you say, standing up. "Nurse, could you come with me and help me pick out what clothes I'll need to get married in?"

"Okay," she says, and the two of you go upstairs. You sit on your bed while she picks out the clothes she thinks are best for you, laying them down beside you.

"Yep, those are definitely the best attires!" you say. "But can you leave me alone for the night now? I've, uh, got lots of prayers to say before I get married.

"Because of religion," you say.

She smiles and hugs you and leaves. You're finally alone, Juliet. Time to fake your own death, am I right?

Fake your own death: *turn to 412.*

 Have second thoughts, call Angelica back: *turn to 462.*

456 Juliet/you sneaks towards the ninja guards. They look fast, sleek. An unstoppable force. But you have the distinct feeling they're going to find out what happens when such a force meets an immovable object. You have the distinct feeling that it's not going to be pretty.

Now that Juliet/you is moving into place, where should Romeo/you go?

Send Romeo to join Juliet with the ninja guards: *turn to 470.*

Send Romeo to the punk guards instead: *turn to 421.*

457

You arrive at the Friar's house to find Paris already there. Hey, you know what he says when he sees you? I'll tell you what he says: "Happily met, my lady and wife." I'm serious. When he sees you arrive he runs over to you, gets down on one knee beside your horse, takes off his hat with a flourish, and that's what he says.

"That may be," you sigh, "after I'm married."

"That MUST be," he replies. "On Thursday."

You sigh again. You're in no mood to deal with Tom Paris right now.

"Have you come to make confession to the father?" he asks, clearly trying to start a conversation with you. You try to blow him off, but he's persistent, saying things that he obviously thinks are romantic but are even more obviously terrible, like "your face belongs to me." You're reduced to shouting past him to the Friar. "If you're too busy right now I can come back later," you say.

The Friar gets the hint and asks Tom to leave. And he does, but not before trying to kiss you. Hey, you know what he says before he kisses you? I'll tell you what he says: "Till then, adieu, and keep this holy kiss." Not a word of lie. He seriously says "adieu."

You turn so all he gets is your cheek, then you and the Friar go into his house.

"Close the door," you say. He does. You sigh, unsure of how to proceed. "I don't want to be overdramatic," you finally say, "but uh, maybe you want to come weep with me? I'm past hope, past cure, and past help over here."

"Oh Juliet, I already know what's going on," the Friar says. "That's the good news. The bad news is, I don't know how to solve your problems."

Work together to produce a reasonable solution: ***turn to 439.***

 Nevermind! This is totally hopeless and I might as well just kill myself right now. ***Turn to 432.***

458

Alright, so let's get you caught up on what you've missed while you've been out so you can pass as Romeo and not some Juliet-based INTERLOPER.

So! While you've been sleeping, Romeo has been tracked down in Mantua by his servant, Balthasar, who informed him that you totally died. Turns out the Friar's plan didn't work perfectly, and Romeo doesn't know you're just FAKING your death as part of a well-thought-out and not at all needlessly complicated scheme. So he sent

Balthasar out for supplies that will allow him to ride back to Verona as fast as possible! Then he got tired of waiting and went to the pharmacy and bought some poison. You know! "Just in case"!

Got that? I hope so, because you are now Romeo!

You're in your hotel room and you're just getting used to your new body when someone who you can only assume is Balthasar opens up your hotel room door, bringing with him a bunch of supplies. There are pens, papers, a crowbar, some horses, etc. Looks like a pretty good haul!

"Ah, yes, my supplies," you say, trying to sound confident. "I know about these. Are these everything I, Romeo Montague, asked for? You know, earlier? When we uh, spoke?"

"They are," Balthasar says. "Is anything wrong?"

"No, everything is normal. I definitely remember our previous conversations in full and complete detail," you say. You walk up to the horses, as if to inspect them. "Are horses normally allowed in my, by which I mean Romeo's, hotel room?" you ask.

"They've got diapers on," Balthasar says.

"Ah, good," you say. "I was about to notice that myself."

Balthasar looks at you like he's expecting something.

"You seemed in a pretty big rush to get going earlier once you found out Juliet died," he finally says.

Say "Oh crap, right!" and rush off to Verona: *turn to 347.*

Whatever, there's no rush. Obviously I'm—I mean obviously JULIET—is totally fine. *Turn to 437.*

459

You are now Juliet! Friar Lawrence is explaining to Tom Paris why you had to fake your own death, and Tom's apologizing for misunderstanding the situation. He turns to you and offers you a handshake.

"I'm sorry," Tom says to you. "I didn't know you were already secret-married. I wish you'd told me."

You shake his hand, smiling. "If I had," you say, "it wouldn't have been a secret marriage." You place your other hand on top of his. "No hard feelings?"

"No hard feelings," Paris says. He gives your hand a squeeze, then releases it, and he seems to visibly relax. "Besides, this whole marriage thing WAS a bit fast. I'd rather marry someone I love, or at least KNOW, you know?"

"I do," you say, and that's when you hear a polite cough from behind you. You spin around. It's Romeo! Wow! What a surprise, RIGHT JULIET?

You run up and hug each other. Finally, you pull back and kiss him. "Did you have any trouble getting here?" you ask. Romeo looks confused. "You know, I . . . I can't remember," he says. "Isn't that weird? Anyway, I don't think so!"

Friar Lawrence steps up to Romeo and shakes his hand warmly. "How DID you know to come here?" he asks. "I sent you a letter explaining this whole thing, but it never got there. Plague or something. 'Act of God,' I guess?"

Romeo shrugs. "I have a servant, this guy Balthasar? He came to tell me that Juliet was dead, but somehow—SOMEHOW—I knew she wasn't." Romeo looks at you and smiles, then holds up his picnic basket. "So I packed a picnic and moseyed on over and here we are!"

You laugh. Everything's worked out perfectly!

You and Romeo spread out the tablecloth on the floor, invite Paris and the Friar to join you, and have a perfectly pleasant picnic in the middle of your family's crypt. Then you pack up the leftovers, say your good-byes, and get back on your horses.

When you arrive in Mantua, the sun's already coming up. Romeo squeezes your hand. You squeeze back.

It's the first day of the rest of your life, Juliet.

THE END

460

Before the Friar finds his words, you shove in your knife as far as it'll go. It's super gross, Juliet. It—it pops out the other side. Eugh.

You don't know this, but you've pierced both common carotid arteries, which, despite their name, aren't actually that common in the human body. You've only got two, one on each side of your neck, and they've both got knife-shaped holes in them now.

The common carotid arteries are responsible for supplying the head and neck with oxygenated blood, and with all that oxygenated blood spilling out on the floor, it's not too long before you pass out. And it's not too long after that before you die from not having enough oxygenated blood in your big ol' head!

THE END

P.S.: When Romeo finds out you killed yourself he kills himself too! Okay, honestly: what is with you two? Can't you just feel sad without making a big dramatic scene out of it?

P.P.S.: That was a rhetorical question, OBVIOUSLY THAT IS IMPOSSIBLE FOR YOU GUYS.

P.P.P.S.: Man it was a really nice floor you died all over too.

461 You'd better do better, I can tell you that much right now. Alright: one last chance.

Hey, guess what? Juliet was alive this whole time and you killed yourself for no reason!

TWIST!!

You are now Juliet.

Your eyes flutter open. You find yourself staring at the ceiling of Capulet Crypt. Before you can react, the Friar pokes his head into your field of vision.

"Oh, hey Friar," you say. "Well, I remember very well where I should be, and here I am! Where's Romeo?"

"Uh, a . . . greater power than we can contradict hath thwarted our intents?" he says.

"What?" you say. "Huh?" But instead of answering, he's pulling you out of your coffin.

"Come on!" he says. "We need to get out of here!"

You resist, and he grabs your head and forces it to look around the room. "Look, your husband lies dead over there," he says, pointing to Romeo, who is lying crumpled on the ground with a bottle in his hand. "Paris lies dead over there"—here he points to Tom Paris, whose body is stuffed into a dark corner for some reason—"and we're gonna go run out of THERE," he says, pointing up to the stairs leading out of the crypt.

You stare at the body of your husband, motionless. The floor seems to tilt beneath you. He's dead? Romeo?

"Come on!" Friar Lawrence shouts. "PEOPLE ARE COMING. I'll get thee to a nunnery, okay? There's no time for questions, just follow me!!"

You don't take your eyes off your husband. As you stare at him, you feel something inside you harden. And something else . . . breaks.

"I'm not going anywhere," you say.

Friar Lawrence looks at you for a moment, then turns and runs out of the crypt. You kneel beside Romeo and take the glass out of his hand.

"What's here?" you say. "A cup, closed in my true love's hand?" You take the bottle from him. "Poison, I see, hath been his timeless end," you whisper. You hold the bottle up, trying to drink from it too, tapping the bottom. There's nothing left. You begin to laugh manically.

"O churl," you say, "drunk all, and left no friendly drop to help me after?" You laugh again, stopping only as you throw the bottle into the wall with all your strength. It shatters, the sound echoing.

You stare at the pieces for a long moment.

"I will kiss thy lips," you whisper. "Haply some poison yet doth hang on them, to make me die with a restorative." And you do. Nothing happens.

"Thy lips are warm," you whisper.

You hear someone shouting from outside the crypt. Someone's coming. "Then I'll be brief," you declare, grabbing your Bedroom Dagger from your belt and thanking yourself for specifying in your will that you wanted to be buried with a knife.

You hold the knife out in front of your belly. "O happy dagger," you say, "this is thy SHEATH." And you're about to drive the blade in when you realize a stab wound to your belly isn't guaranteed to kill you. You don't want to mess this up, so you move the blade up some to where you feel your heart racing.

"This is thy sheath," you begin, holding the blade to your chest, but again you stop. The heartbeat comes from the left side of your body but hearts are actually central, right? You think you remember hearing something about that. But wouldn't your sternum be in the way of your blade there?

You don't want to chance it. Instead, you hold the blade to your eye with one hand, angle it upwards, and bring the palm of your other hand behind it. "THIS is thy sheath," you hiss. "There rust, and LET ME DIE."

And with all your strength, you shove the blade through your eye and deep into your skull.

THE END

Okay, WOW. Seriously: HOLY CRAP, that was amazing. I got chills! That was basically a thousand times better than what Romeo did. And since your death was so awesome, I'll cheat a little and let you know what happens next. Here we go.

Alright, so you die instantly (again: AMAZING, awesome work there) and your body is discovered by the watchman you heard earlier. He captures the Friar and calls the cops, the cops call your parents, and before long your and Romeo's parents are all gathered in front of your bodies. The Friar tells them everything and explains that he wasn't able to get a message to Romeo in time, so Romeo thought you were really dead and killed himself in grief. A letter Romeo wrote confirms the Friar's words.

Your parents and Romeo's parents look at each other, suddenly very aware that this tragedy could've been avoided if only both their children weren't too scared of their own parents to share with them the fact that they'd fallen in love.

For the first time, your father takes Romeo's father's hand and holds it, tightly.

"We should stop fighting," Romeo's dad says.

"Yes," your dad replies.

"Incidentally, my wife died of grief earlier," Romeo's dad says, "but that's neither here nor there. I'm going to make a statue of Juliet out of pure gold, and I do hereby declare that as long as this city is called Verona, there will be no figure praised more than this solid-gold statue of Juliet."

"And I," your dad says in turn, "will make a solid-gold statue of Romeo to stand beside her."

"Well, that's settled then," says the police officer, and they all begin to leave.

And I know, I know, a solid-gold statue is the most impractical and ridiculous monument to a dead child ever in time. Look, they just found out you died. I'm sure in a few days they'll face the logistics of this and change it to stone, or a metal that isn't insanely precious and also very malleable and easy to steal.

The police chief is the last to leave the crypt, but he pauses at the top of the stairs. He turns around and looks down at the bodies below. At you, and at Romeo, at Paris, and at Tybalt.

"For never was a story of more woe," he whispers, "than this of Juliet and her Romeo." (Man, he's probably still impressed with how you stabbed yourself! I know I am!!)

He takes one last look at your bodies before closing the crypt behind him.

THE END
FOR REAL THIS TIME

Congratulations! You have killed yourself really well and also unlocked this book's SECRET CHARACTER. To play as her, restart the book, and instead of choosing to play as Romeo or Juliet, take the numbers you're supposed to turn to for each, subtract the smallest from the largest, multiply by 10, and add 41. Turn to that number instead and you'll be able to play as this new character!

462 "Nurse!" you call.

She doesn't arrive in under two seconds, so you change your mind.

"What good is she anyway?" you mutter to yourself, and turn back to your secret fake poison vial. You don't know this, but Angelica heard you, so right now she's going back downstairs with her feelings hurt.

Way to go, Juliet. Sheesh.

 Okay, fake my own death now: *turn to 412.*

463 You pull your Bedroom Dagger from your belt. "My sweet bod will be this knife's sheath," you whisper, and then you jab it into your guts over and over again.

It's—wow. Juliet, you're really going for it. You're making a complete mess of both the room and your bod.

Dang.

Anyway, just before you die, you make certain to collapse backwards on top of Romeo so your butt lands on his face.

"I hope we spend eternity with my butt on your face," you say, and then you're dead.

Wow, what a sucky ending! What awful and embarrassing last words! If only you could have influenced Romeo to make better decisions while you were unconscious, this could've all been avoided!

OH WELL, RIGHT? OH WELL, THIS DEFINITELY ISN'T POSSIBLE IN THE REALITY YOU LIVE IN, RIGHT??

THE END

464 Come on! I wrote out a whole book of your dreams and you want to be Romeo instead? Well guess what: you know what Romeo's doing right now? SITTING AROUND IN A LIBRARY, ABOUT TO READ A BOOK THAT MIRRORS YOUR VERY DREAM. Hey, are you tripping all possible balls right now? BECAUSE YOU SHOULD BE.

So anyway, now you're Romeo! In your hand is a book, and though you (Romeo) have only skimmed the first few pages and thus have only the roughest idea of what it holds, I'll tell you right now: inside these pages is a story that mirrors the dream of your lady-love Juliet perfectly. Should you choose to read it, then for perhaps the first time in history, two souls will share the exact same vision, in the exact same medium, in two different states of consciousness. It will be a thing of beauty, of indescribable perfection.

Okay, sure, I want to read the book after all: *turn to 472.*

 Okay cool you said I'm Romeo now so Romeo wants to stop looking at this book and start looking around the room he's in: *turn to 292.*

465 You head home, frustrated but determined to end this entire ridiculous charade once and for all. You march into your house, grab your mother by the hand, and lead her up to your bedroom. You sit her down on the bed, sit down beside her, and take a deep breath.

"Hey Mom," you say. "Guess what. I married Romeo yesterday and we've already consummated the marriage last night so NO GOING BACK NOW and I know I just met him but I really love him and I think we can go the distance and I'm sorry that Tybalt's dead but Romeo was acting in self-defense and you need to know this is what's going on in my life and I'm happy with it and I'm proud of it and I'm not changing."

Your mother looks at you for a long, hard moment. And then she smiles, bursts into tears, and hugs you as hard as she can.

"Oh Juliet," she says, "this is perfect! Perfect! The Montagues are rich, and now that our interests are aligned, we'll be able to work together rather than against each other." She pulls back and holds you at arm's length, smiling. "Our greatest competition just became our greatest allies, Juliet. This will make all of us a lot of money."

Be happy that she's happy: *turn to 348.*

Be offended that she's only concerned about money: *turn to 390.*

466 You decide one family robbed is enough, so you ride back to Mantua. On the way back, the two of you confer and decide it's likely the Capulets will conclude they were robbed by the Montagues as part of an escalating campaign of harassment. You agree to skip Mantua—where Romeo/you is known to be living, and where you'd be a potential target—and move to another city instead, just to avoid any potential blowback from your "rob a family blind" scheme.

You pick a new city at random. It's called "Sanguene." It's alright! You move there and never hear from anyone's parents again. Also, you keep controlling both Romeo and Juliet together, so your marriage is characterized by always agreeing with each other, saying the same thing to what few friends you have at the same time with the exact same intonation, and having really really efficient sex.

THE END

467 You leave the Friar and his various Vials to Solve Problems With and ride to Mantua. It takes several hours. During the ride, you go over the conversation you had with the Friar and keep thinking of things you wish you'd done.

You could've said, "Hey, come up with a better idea or maybe I start stabbing other people instead." You could've made HIM drink the potion. You could've written "Where Friar Lawrence's Good Ideas Come From" on a piece of paper, then poured the vial of Fake Death Juice onto it, and then explained it's symbolic for how he doesn't have any good ideas because that part of his brain has been dead for 42 hours too. Wait, better: 42 YEARS.

"Zing," you whisper to yourself, alone on a horse on the road between Verona and Mantua.

Arrive in Mantua, look for Romeo: ***turn to 436.***

468

"Tybalt?" you say. "Tybalt, is that you? What's up?"

"Hey," says the ghost of Tybalt. "Yeah, it's me. Is Romeo here? Now that I'm a ghost I can trail people really easily, and I kinda was following Romeo around and saw him come here."

"OH REALLY," you say. "So you followed him here, to my bedroom? And you watched us here for how long??"

"Um," Ghost Tybalt says, embarrassed.

"Ew, gross, you're my cousin," you say. "Get out of here, Tybalt."

"Wait, Juliet, please!" Tybalt says. "I appeared to you because I wanted to tell you something! Watching you have sex was just a weird thing that happened afterwards!!"

You stare at him in angry silence, which he takes as an invitation to continue.

"So here's the thing," he says. "He left when I wasn't looking, I want to revenge myself on Romeo, and I know he's going to Mantua, only I don't know WHERE in Mantua. It'll take me a while to track him down—in death I can fly but it's only at like, walking speed—so could you tell me precisely where he's headed?"

"I'm not doing that, Tybalt!" you say. "I'm not gonna help you REVENGE YOURSELF FROM BEYOND THE GRAVE against my OWN HUSBAND. Are you dense? Hey—did your brain not die, and that's why you're such a stupid ghost?"

"No, my brain died too," Tybalt says. "I was in it when it happened. It was extremely painful."

"Sorry," you say. That does sound awful. "But I'm not gonna help you kill my husband. Find him yourself."

"WHATEVER," Tybalt says. "You know what? I'm real good at banging pots and pans together, and I'm gonna keep haunting you until you change your mind. I bet after a few sleepless nights in a row you'll be a BIT more willing to do what I want, JULIET."

You look down at the vial in your hand.

"Yeah," you say. "Good luck with that."

Drink the contents of the vial: *turn to 474.*

469

You kiss the corpse of your husband. It's not the same. I mean, his lips are warm, but it's not like he's kissing back.

Also, you don't die from doing it, so it looks like he isn't a sloppy drinker who leaves juice all over his lips.

You hear a noise, like someone's coming down the tomb stairs. Time's running out! Sizing up the situation, you quickly decide to:

Use your muscles to pick up a coffin, then drop it on your own head: *turn to 444.*

Just stab yourself in the guts, you've still got that Bedroom Dagger after all: *turn to 463.*

Maybe, just maybe, not kill yourself after all: *turn to 454.*

470

Romeo/you and Juliet/you sneak towards the ninjas together, making sure not to attract any punk attention. You both agree that a frontal attack is the best approach. The only problem is Romeo/you wants to shout "Ninja costumes are for babies!" to announce your presence, and Juliet/you wants to ask them if anyone ordered a knuckle sandwich, implying that the ninjas were the ones who ordered them and that they're about to be delivered to them now.

You can't reach an agreement with yourselves, so as a compromise that neither of you is happy with, you decide to sneak up behind them and attack without saying any cool lines at all. At the same moment, you attack the two closest ninjas together, twisting their necks to the side, doing your best to ignore the sickening crack that makes. They fall at your feet in unison, totally dead.

That worked really well! However it attracted the attention of the other nearby ninjas, and before you know it, two of them are facing you down.

"Two against two," Romeo/you says. "I like those odds."

"Me too," Juliet/you says. At that moment, the ninjas jab at you both. As both Romeo and Juliet, you dodge. But only Juliet/you has the physique and awesome muscles to move so quickly and so precisely. Romeo/you is a fraction too slow and gets stabbed in the chest. Wounded, you fall into Juliet's arms. "This sucks," you say, "and while I'm pretty sure my eyes are looking their last and my arms are taking their last embrace, I want you to do one thing for me."

"Seal with a righteous kiss a dateless bargain to engrossing death?" Juliet/you says.

"No," Romeo/you says, "I mean, that too, but don't let these ninjas win. Use me as a human shield. Use me as a human sword. JUST DON'T LET THE NINJAS WIN," you say, and then you die, and I'll be honest: any death where your last words are "just don't let the ninjas win" has to rate as, objectively, pretty amazing.

As Juliet, you look down at Romeo's body in your arms. Then you look up at the gathering ninjas around you. You kiss your dead husband, and then, with all your strength, you swing Romeo's body like a log and knock over the ninjas surrounding you before they can react.

"Here's . . . ," you say, bringing your boot down on the first ninja's head and reducing it to pulp. "To . . . ," you say, throwing Romeo's body at a ninja hard enough that when he impacts, both their bodies are reduced to a chunky chowder. "My . . . ," you say, grabbing a ninja's wrist and making her stab herself in the head with her own sword. "Love," you say, picking up the last ninja and breaking him over your knee.

The ninjas lie at your feet, defeated. You hear something from behind you. It sounds like running.

"What noise?" you say, turning. You see the punks are converging on you. It seems you've got their attention.

"Then I'll be brief," you mutter, running towards the punks. They surround you and though you did just defeat the ninjas, the thing with ninjas is that they have a code of honor and they fight by it. These punks fight like nobody you've ever seen before. They're animals, taking every advantage they can. They bite. They kick. They pull your hair.

And before long, they reduce your body, already fatigued from fighting all those ninjas, to such a state that it can no longer sustain itself.

Your last words are a whispered "This is baloney" to yourself. Your last action is to roll your eyes at how baloney this is. But it doesn't work! It turns out moral outrage isn't enough to live on!

Like, not even close!!

THE END

471 You take the vial of Fake Death Juice from the Friar. "You know what? Fine," you say. "FINE. I guess my problems are so bad that my only viable solution is to take a time-out for a couple of days."

"Cool," says the Friar. "Okay, I'll send word to Mantua so Romeo knows what the plan is."

You get up to leave. "Thanks," you say. You shake his hand, leave his house, and go home to Capulet Castle.

Arrive at Capulet Castle: ***turn to 455.***

472 Thank you.

You begin to read a book and/or have a dream called *A Midsummer Night's Choice*.

Oh also I should mention there's a creepy librarian here with a knife to your neck and he'll kill you in real life if you die in the book. He calls it "reading in hard mode." He's not wrong!

Begin dreaming/reading: ***turn to 124.***

473 You take the vial of Fake Death Juice.

"Gimme gimme," you say.

"Alright," says the Friar. "I'll send word to Mantua so Romeo knows what the plan is."

You get up to leave. "Thanks," you say, and before you know it you're standing outside the Friar's house with his vial in your hand. You stare at it and consider your options.

"It's not too late to just go to my mother and explain things," you think. "On the other hand, it's ALSO not too late to teach her a lesson by making her think I've died."

 Fake your own death: ***turn to 455.***

This is crazy, I'm not faking any deaths! I'll just go home and explain the situation to my mom. ***Turn to 465.***

474

You ignore the ghost and instead think of your husband, considering your vial of mysterious liquid. You raise the drink out in front of you. "Romeo, Romeo, Romeo!" you whisper. "Here's drink. I drink to thee." Then you lower the vial to your lips.

"Bottoms up, boys," you say, quickly chugging the contents of the vial. You fall into bed. Before you know it you're in a deep slumber . . .

. . . and you begin to dream.

Hey, good news! Ever since you were a child, your dreams have taken the form of an Adventure-Is-Chosen-by-You book. For your entire life, every time you've gotten really tired and finally fallen asleep, it's like you've had to read a book instead. What a treat!

The only catch is that this drug you took from Friar Lawrence is kinda unstable and kinda insanely dangerous, so you run a real risk of dying right now. Your subconscious mind is trying to process what's happening to it via this dream/dream-book/drug parable/whatever, but if you fail in it, you'll die. Got that, Juliet? Die in the dream, die in real life.

On the other hand, getting through this dream alive may be the only way to keep your body going.

Cool! Alright, begin dreaming/reading: *turn to 124.*

 Nah man dreams are boring and stupid; can I be Romeo now instead? *Turn to 464.*

475

The following information slowly floods into your brain:

Natasha Allegri is an illustrator living in Los Angeles with her cat named Pancake. (Passage 333)

John Allison has been writing and drawing comics since 1998. He lives in Letchworth Garden City, the home of the Britain's first roundabout. (Passage 460)

Kate Beaton is a comics artist and children's book author. (Title page; Passages 36, 271, and 476)

Brandon Bird once painted Spider-Man having a pillow fight with J. Jonah Jameson. Ryan North bought the painting, and Brandon Bird used the money to buy a sofa. You can see the painting (and others) at brandonbird.com. (Passage 235)

Boulet is a French cartoonist. He draws stories on english.bouletcorp.com and loves single malt Islay and spending hours sitting in front of a screen. And pizza. Motto: "Heavy is the cinder block of reality on the strawberry pie of our illusions." (Passage 105)

Vera Brosgol lives in Portland, Oregon, where she makes books and storyboards for animation. verabee.com (Passage 388)

Emily Carroll is the author and illustrator of the book *Through the Woods*, as well as numerous webcomics. Her website is emcarroll.com. (Passage 461)

Ray Castro and Alex Culang are like a two-headed dragon, except each of the heads is attached to its own separate body. Also, the heads and bodies are human, because dragons aren't real. The two have been best buds for a long time and have made lots of comics together, most notably their twice-weekly webcomic *Buttersafe*. (Passage 107)

Anthony Clark is a cartoonist and illustrator from Indiana. If you have a dog, you should let him pet it. (Passages 92, 124, and 358)

Rebecca Clements is a Melbourne-based cartoonist and illustrator. She's created several webcomics over the years including *KinokoFry* and *Secret Mystery Diary*, as well as illustrated for books, video games, clothing designs, etc. Her work is colorful and expressive, and often filled with chickens. These days, she is also an urban planner and designer, and likes public transport. (Passage 151)

Tony Cliff is the author and/or illustrator of the generally well-regarded Delilah Dirk series of sword- and/or adventure-flavored graphic novels, the most recent of which, *Delilah Dirk and the King's Shilling*, was released in March 2016. He hails from and/or lives in Vancouver. (Passage 320)

My name is Becky Cloonan and I am bard to the bone. (Passage 219)

Eric Colossal is the author of a comic called *Rutabaga: The Adventure Chef*. In a world full of dungeons and dragons lives the young chef, Rutabaga! While other adventurers hunt monsters for experience, he does it for ingredients! Join him on his quest to eat everything! (Passage 318)

Matt Cummings is a freelance illustrator from Nova Scotia. He works very hard, I promise! (Passage 215)

Evan Dahm has created and self-published the fantasy-adventure graphic novels *Rice Boy*, *Order of Tales*, and *Vattu*, which won an Ignatz Award in 2014. He lives in Brooklyn with his wife, Lela, and small dog, Billy. His work can be found at rice-boy.com and evandahm.com. (Passage 346)

Willow Dawson is a cartoonist from Toronto. She has written and/or illustrated lots of books, but most recently: *The Wolf-Birds* (Owlkids Books), *Avis Dolphin* with Frieda Wishinsky (Groundwood Books), and her 'zines *Creeps* and *Ghost Limb*. She likes drawing creepy, pretty things best. willowdawson.com (Passage 264)

Lar deSouza hails from the Great White North, where he plies his trade drawing online comics and the occasional commission. He lives in a small town in Ontario with his lovely wife, two beautiful daughters, and four tolerant cats. You can find him online at: leasticoulddo.com, lfgcomic.com, and lartist.com. (Passage 86)

Aaron Diaz is the creator of the science fantasy comic series Dresden Codak, Hob, and Dark Science. (Passage 470)

Ray Fawkes is the creator and illustrator of the graphic novel *One Soul* and the Intersect series, as well as writer of *Gotham by Midnight, Constantine,* and other books for DC Comics. (Passage 429)

Jess Fink is an illustrator and cartoonist. Her graphic novel, *We Can Fix It! A Time Travel Memoir*, is published by Top Shelf. Her erotic Victorian comic *Chester 5000* is also published by Top Shelf and can be read at jessfink.com/Chester5000XYV. Her illustration work can be seen at JessFink.com. She lives in New York, but she is originally from outer space. (Passage 103)

Michael Firman is a Canadian illustrator and comic artist whose work you might encounter on rap album covers or in British video games. michaelfirman.com (Passage 177)

Meags Fitzgerald is a Montreal-based illustrator and the author of the graphic memoir *Long*

Red Hair and the award-winning graphic novel *Photobooth: A Biography*. She's also performed and taught improv comedy across North America and in Australia and Japan. She usually orders the soup du jour. (Passage 211)

Gillian G. (a.k.a. Gillian Goerz—pronounced "Jillian Gertz") is a Toronto-based artist, writer, cartoonist, caricaturist, karaoke enthusiast (and host), chalkboard painter, and friend haver (for now). She co-founded Drunk Feminist Films, a collective that hosts rollicking interactive movie screening events, and she both writes and draws the web comic jerkfaceahole.com. gilliang.com (Passage 459)

Dara Gold is an artist working in animation and games. By day she creates crazy characters and props for cartoons, at night she makes art with tea. You can see more of her work at daragold.ca and facebook.com/daragoldart. (Passage 428)

Zac Gorman is an Eisner Award–wanting cartoonist from Detroit. His therapist says he writes jokey bios to avoid confronting his real issues. (Passage 447)

Meredith Gran is a comic artist living in Brooklyn. She draws the webcomic *Octopus Pie* and teaches at the School of Visual Arts. (Passage 444)

KC Green is doing his best in western Massachusetts. He makes a lot of comics in his free time and work time. Almost all the time, except when he is tweeting. (Passage 31)

Nicholas Gurewitch is still recovering from an accident in which he was severed from his mother. You can see some of his work at pbfcomics.com. (Passage 157)

Brice Hall is a cartoonist and multimedia designer who enjoys telling stories. He lives in Toronto, where he scribbles and codes at *The National Post*. (Passage 452)

Dustin Harbin is a cartoonist who lives in Charlotte, North Carolina. He's probably best known for his diary comics and drawings of people, and also never shutting up. (Passage 168)

Christopher Hastings is a writer and cartoonist based out of Brooklyn. He is the creator of the *Adventures of Dr. McNinja*, has written a bunch of *Deadpool* comics, and took up writing the *Adventure Time* comic once the author of *this* book stopped doing it. (Ryan North, not Shakespeare.) (Passage 453)

David Hellman co-created *A Lesson Is Learned but the Damage Is Irreversible*, the first comic strip on the Internet. He also painted the graphics for the indie video game Braid, made an animated web series called *Jeff & Casey Time*, and in 2015 released his first graphic novel, *Second Quest*. (Passages 400 and 454)

Erica Henderson is a film student turned video editor turned video game artist turned comic artist in Massachusetts. Currently she's the artist on Marvel's *Unbeatable Squirrel Girl* and Archie's *All-New Jughead*. They're pretty good. Maybe go check them out. (Passage 106)

Splitting his youth between small-town Ontario and smaller-town Cape Breton, **Ian Herring** was raised on Nintendo and reruns of *The Simpsons*. Somewhere during this time he learned to draw. (Passage 389)

Tyson Hesse is an animator and illustrator living in Los Angeles. That's Hollywood to you less glamorous people. Tyson Hesse is a beautiful and famous movie star. (Passage 62)

Mike Holmes has drawn for the comics series Bravest Warriors and Adventure Time, and is the creator of the viral art project Mikenesses. His books include *Secret Coders* (2015, written by Gene Luen Yang), the *True Story* collection (2011), and *This American Drive* (2009). He lives in Brooklyn with his wife, Meredith, Heidi the dog, and Ella the cat. (Passage 85)

Emily Horne lives and works in Toronto. With Tim Maly, she wrote *The Inspection House*, a book about surveillance society that's more fun than it sounds. She was the photographer and designer for the long-running webcomic *A Softer World*. (Passage 260)

Abby Howard creates the webcomics *Junior Scientist Power Hour* and *Last Halloween* and in her spare time enjoys petting her cat and/or snake. She has a passion for biology and loves animals of all kinds, but especially dinosaurs and pterosaurs, which always bring a tear to her eye. Beautiful beasts, taken from this world too soon. (Passage 165)

Andrew Hussie is a man who likes horses. But when you stop think about it, it's pretty weird that this even needs to be stated. Because what kind of idiot doesn't like horses. (Passages 126, 128, 131, 133, 136, 359, 361, 362, 365, and 368)

Jeph Jacques is the author of *Questionable Content* (questionablecontent.net) and Alice Grove (alicegrove.com). He lives in Halifax with his dog and many guitars. (Passage 315)

Chris Jones is a Canadian-based children's illustrator. He enjoys telling stories visually, and his colorful style focuses on humor and expressiveness. Chris's illustrations appear in books, graphic novels, magazines, and educational materials. Chris is a member and volunteer with the Society of Children's Book Writers and Illustrators. (Passage 49)

Dave Kellett is the cartoonist of the sci-fi comic strip *Drive* (drivecomic.com) and of *Sheldon* (sheldoncomics.com), and is the director of the comics documentary *Stripped* (strippedfilm .com). He is currently 5'8". (Passage 441)

John Keogh is a weirdo from the edge of society. He cannot be contacted in any way. (Passage 406)

Karl Kerschl is the creator of the award-winning comic *The Abominable Charles Christopher* and artist of lots and lots of superhero comics. He lives in Montreal, and the first Shakespeare play he ever read was *The Merchant of Venice*. You can follow him online @ karlkerschl. (Passage 265)

Eric Kim is a Canadian comic artist, illustrator, and animator. He's worked on a bunch of stuff and is generally an okay guy. (Passage 175)

Jon Klassen is an illustrator who works in children's books and animation. Originally from Ontario, he now lives in Los Angeles. (Passage 375)

Lucy Knisley is author/illustrator of four published graphic novels (*French Milk*, *Relish*, *An Age of License*, and *Displacement*) and will release her fifth this spring. She's a *New York Times*–bestselling author, and a graduate of the Center for Cartoon Studies. She lives in Chicago. (Passage 272)

Gisèle Lagacé is a Canadian cartoonist from northern New Brunswick. She is known for her successful webcomics *Ménage à 3*, *Eerie Cuties*, and *Penny Aggie*, and her pencil work for Archie Comics. Her personal site is GiseleLagace.com. (Passage 299)

Braden Lamb grew up in Seattle, studied film in upstate New York, learned about Vikings in Iceland and Norway, and established an art career in Boston. Now he draws and colors comics, and wouldn't have it any other way. He has worked as a series artist for the Eisner Award–winning *Adventure Time* comics, *The Midas Flesh*, and *Ice Age* comics, and as the colorist for *Sisters*, *Star Wars: Shadows of Endor*, and *The Baby-sitters Club* comics. @ bradenlamb / bradenlamb.com (Passage 138)

Kate Leth writes and draws many things, and they are always changing. She lives in a glass cave by the river and has terrible dreams of what's to come. You can find out more at kateleth.com. (Passage 95)

Joe List is a cartoonist from the UK. He enjoys pizza, magnets, defacing magazines, and cherishes the opportunity to write about himself in the third person. (Passage 153)

Sam Logan is the author of the long-running comedy adventure comic series Sam and Fuzzy, which has been entertaining readers with its massive tales of warring ninja mafiosos, adorable rodent gangsters, and lovesick stalker vampires for more than twelve years. (Passage 350)

Mike Maihack is the creator of the graphic novel series Cleopatra in Space published through Graphix Books, the webcomic *Cow & Buffalo*, and a bunch of other stuff he doesn't feel like typing out. You can find that stuff at mikemaihack.com if you like though. Y'know, if you want. (Passage 174)

David Malki ! is the author of the comic strip *Wondermark*, best described as A COLLABORATION WITH THE DEAD. He lives in Los Angeles and likes to fly airplanes. Read more, contact him, etc., at wondermark.com. (Passage 259; cover design for Passages 124 and 358)

John Martz is a cartoonist and illustrator in Toronto. He is the creator of the wordless online comic strip *Machine Gum*, and the illustrator of several picture books including the Eisner-nominated *A Cat Named Tim and Other Stories* from Koyama Press. His comics and illustrations have appeared in *MAD Magazine*, *The Globe & Mail*, and *Lucky Peach*. (Passage 81)

Choose your own **Brian McLachlan** bio: a) His book, *Draw out the Story, 10 Secrets to Creating Your Own Comics* is awesome b) Made the hilarious-out-loud webcomic *The Princess Planet* c) Was born at the age of 5 and can eat raw fire d) Your adventure ends here. (Passage 345)

Kagan McLeod is an illustrator whose work has been published in *GQ, Time, Glamour, Entertainment Weekly*, and *The New York Times*. His graphic novel, *Infinite Kung Fu*, was published in 2011 with Top Shelf Comics and he is currently working with Chip Zdarsky on a musclemen vs. beastmen romp called *Kaptara*, for Image Comics. (Passage 150)

Dylan Meconis is the creator of *Bite Me!, Family Man*, and *Outfoxed*. She lives in Portland, Oregan, and is a member of Periscope Studio. Find her online at dylanmeconis.com. (Passage 395)

Erika Moen is a full-time cartoonist in Portland, Oregon, where she is a member of Periscope Studio. With her husband, Matthew Nolan, together they produce the weekly sex positive comic, *Oh Joy Sex Toy*. Her work can be seen on erikamoen.com. (Passage 220)

Carly Monardo is an artist and performer living in Brooklyn. Her work has been featured in games, books, television, and framed on the walls of friends. Visit carlymonardo.com for more fun drawings! (Passage 70)

Randall Munroe is the author of the webcomic *xkcd* and the books *What If?* and *Thing Explainer*. You can find his work by directing your home terminal towards xkcd.com. (Passage 328)

Ethan Nicolle makes comics like *Axe Cop* and *Bearmageddon*. He also writes cartoons. (Passage 337)

Shelli Paroline escaped early on into the world of comics, cartoons, and science fiction. She has now returned to the Boston area, where she works as an unassuming comic book illustrator and designer. Her credits include the Eisner award–winning Adventure Time comics, *The Midas Flesh*, and *Muppet Snow White*. @shelligator/shelliparoline.com. (Passage 138)

Em Partridge is a writer/drawer/thing maker/dog petter from Vancouver Island. (Passages 115 and 298)

Justin Pierce is an artist and the creator of the *Non-Adventures of Wonderella*. But like a little-c "creator" and not a big-C "Creator" because that is a GOD-style Creator and Justin can't even make a correct waffle. (Passage 87)

Nate Powell (b. 1978, Little Rock, Arkansas) is an Eisner Award–winning graphic novelist whose work includes *March*, the comics memoir of civil rights icon John Lewis; *You Don't Say, Any Empire, Swallow Me Whole, The Silence of Our Friends, The Year of the Beasts*, and Rick Riordan's *The Lost Hero*. He lives in Bloomington, Indiana. (Passage 398)

Joe Quinones is a comic book artist working out of Somerville, Massachusetts. Recent works include *Black Canary and Zatanna: Bloodspell, Batman: Black and White*, and *Howard the Duck*. (Passage 91)

Sara Richard is an Eisner-nominated artist currently working with IDW on *My Little Pony* and *Jem & The Holograms*. She is the artist of the upcoming DC Justice League tarot card set. More of her work and upcoming appearances on sararichard.com. (Passage 339)

Mike Rooth is a Canadian freelance art mercenary working out of his studio in Oakville, Ontario. After more than a decade doing educational/children's books and advertising illustration, he's spent the last five years chasing his comics dreams by creating pages, pinups, and cover art for projects such as *Red Sonja/Conan, The Squidder, Captain Canuck*, and *FUBAR: By the Sword*. Rooth (along with his wife, Erika Wallace) is currently working on self-publishing his own comic—a horror story set in the Viking Age called *Widowswake*. (Passages 164 and 397)

Jonathan Rosenberg has been drawing comics and posting them on the Internet since 1997, starting with seminal webcomic *Goats* (goats.com). He is also the creator of award-winning teen sensation *Scenes from a Multiverse* (amultiverse.com) and the inventor of the squirrel. (Passage 121)

Andy Runton is the Eisner Award–winning creator of the breakout all-ages series of graphic novels, *Owly*, starring a kind-hearted little owl who's always searching for new friends and adventure. Relying on a mixture of symbols and expressions to tell his silent stories, Runton's heartwarming style has made him a favorite of both fans and critics alike. (Heart icons, Passage 120)

Marguerite Sauvage is a French illustrator based in Montréal. After a career in press (*Elle, Flaunt, . . .*) advertising (Apple, L'Oréal . . .) and animation (Passion Pictures . . .), she's started working in the comics industry in 2014 for various publishers (DC's *Bombshells*, Vertigo's *Hinterkind*, Marvel's *Hellcat . . .*). (Passage 446)

Sarah Winifred Searle hails from spooky New England, where she pets cats and makes comics. She draws stuff about history and feelings. Check it out at swinsea.com. (Passage 373)

Evan "Doc" Shaner is a cartoonist who has done various work for Marvel Comics and DC Comics. He lives in Colorado with his wife, their daughter, and their dog. (Passage 162)

Kean Soo was born in the United Kingdom, grew up in various parts of Canada and Hong Kong, trained as an electrical engineer, and now makes comics for a living. A former contributor and assistant editor for the FLIGHT comics anthology, Kean also created the award-winning Jellaby series of graphic novels. His latest graphic novel series, March Grand Prix, was released in fall 2015. (Passage 255)

Kevin Jay Stanton is a freelance illustrator with a green thumb, an X-acto knife, and an interest in knowledge-gathering. (Passage 69)

Richard Stevens 3 draws a comic strip at dieselsweeties.com and tweets at @rstevens. He likes robots and coffee. (Passages 217, 236, 341, 404, and 426)

Noelle Stevenson is the *New York Times*–bestselling author of *Nimona*, has been nominated for Harvey and Eisner Awards, and was awarded the *Slate* Cartoonist Studio Prize for Best Web Comic in 2012 for *Nimona*. A graduate of the Maryland Institute College of Art, Noelle is a writer on Disney's *Wander Over Yonder*, the cowriter of Boom! Studios' *Lumberjanes*, and has written for Marvel and DC Comics. She lives in Los Angeles. (Epigraph; Passage 466)

By day **Annie Stoll** is a Grammy-nominated art director/illustrator working for folks such as Sony Music and Lucasfilm. By night, she makes comics and pineapple upside-down cakes. She once played the Friar in her all-girls' school production of *Romeo & Juliet: Shakespeare Meets Star Wars*. (Passage 55)

Alex Thomas occasionally draws stuff when not working on video games. This was one of those times. (Passage 145)

David Troupes writes and draws *Buttercup Festival*, which can be read at buttercupfestival .com. He has also published the illustrated storybook *Renaming of the Birds* and two collections of poetry. (Passage 370)

Jeffrey Veregge is a Native American comic book artist from the Port Gamble S'Klallam Tribe. Jeffrey's style has been dubbed Salish Geek by his fans and peers and has allowed him to not only work in the comic industry (with Marvel, Valiant, and IDW Comics) but display his work in prestigious collections and publications like the Seattle Art Museum, Yale University, the Tucson Museum of Art, *Fast Company*, and *Wired* magazine. (Passage 301)

Michael Walsh is a Canadian illustrator working primarily in the creation of comic books. He has worked for world-famous publishers Marvel, Image, Dark Horse, IDW, and Valiant. His most recent work includes a 15-issue consecutive run on Marvel's *Secret Avengers*. (Passage 392)

Pendleton Ward farts in crowds at Comic Con. (Passage 326)

Zach Weinersmith is the cartoonist behind *Saturday Morning Breakfast Cereal*. He also recently wrote a kids' novel called *Augie and the Green Knight*. He is shorter than Ryan North but has better hair. (Passage 280)

Lucie Claire Whitehead is a person who would like to say hi to her cat and her mom. Hi, Mew! Hi, Mom! (Passage 463)

Tony Wilson is an illustrator who has made funny comics for bad people at *Amazing Super Powers*, and sad comics for bad people at *Tommy Monster*. Most recently, he's co-written and illustrated a supernatural revenge comic called *The World Ender* for the band Lord Huron. Tony is currently working as a designer on a series of mobile games for sad, bad, and rad people. (Passage 182)

Steve Wolfhard works as a storyboard artist on the Cartoon Network shows *Adventure Time* and *Over the Garden Wall*. His comic books *Cat Rackham Loses It!* and *Turtie Needs Work* are with Koyama Press. (Passage 450)

Jim Zub is an artist, writer, and art instructor living in Toronto. When he's not writing comics like *Wayward* and *Samurai Jack* he coordinates Seneca College's award-winning animation program. Find out more about his work at jimzub.com. (Passage 322)

Chip Zudarsky loves being the last name on bio pages, Jim Zub. (Passage 449)

Okay, now all you can do is choose your character: ***turn to 36.***

476 Hah! Whoever told you that you could flip to the last page of a book to see how its story ends CLEARLY never reckoned with the powers of our nonlinear interactive fiction!! Nice try.

However, if you were glancing back here to see how many pages this book has before you buy it, then let there be no doubt: you are getting over 399 pages of quality book with the purchase of this book. That is a terrific page-per-dollar ratio and definitely worth the cover price. You should absolutely buy this book right away.

THE END